drowning
to
breathe

A
Bleeding Stars
Novel

A.L. JACKSON

Drowning to Breathe
Copyright © 2015 A.L. Jackson Books Inc.

First Edition

All rights reserved. Except as permitted under the U.S. Copyright Act of 1976, no part of this publication may be reproduced, distributed, transmitted in any form or by any means, or stored in a database or retrieval system, without prior permission of the publisher.

A.L. Jackson
www.aljacksonauthor.com

Cover Design by Mae I Design
Editing by Making Manuscripts
Formatting by Champagne Formats

The characters and events in this book are fictitious. Names, characters, places, and plots are a product of the author's imagination. Any similarity to real persons, living or dead, is coincidental and not intended by the author.

Print ISBN: 978-1-938404-95-5

More from A.L. Jackson

Bleeding Stars
A Stone in the Sea

The Regret Series
Lost to You
Take This Regret
If Forever Comes

The Closer to You Series
Come to Me Quietly
Come to Me Softly
Come to Me Recklessly

Stand-Alone Novels
Pulled
When We Collide

More Bleeding Stars Novels Coming Soon
Where Lightning Strikes
Through the Storm
Embers and Ash
Whispers in Winter

Also Coming Soon from A.L. Jackson
Hollywood Chronicles, a collaboration with
USA Today Bestselling Author, Rebecca Shea

drowning
to
breathe

prologue
Shea

I WEPT TOWARD THE sky.

Hemorrhaging.

Crumbling.

Breaking.

"No…Kallie…Kallie!"

Sebastian's arms tightened around me as the rain began to pour from above.

A torrent of pain splintered through my chest. As if it were cracking my ribs open wide, every hope I'd allowed myself to have spilling free.

Wind whipped through, like a deranged madness that swept along the ground, chasing after the taillights that blinked out at the end of the street.

Agony.

Agony.

Agony.

"No…please…how could I allow this to happen? Please… Kallie. My baby. My baby. He can't have her. I won't let him have her."

"Shh…" I felt his breath in my hair, the soft kiss at the top of my head. "We will get her back…I promise you, if it's the last thing I do, we will get her back."

"She's gone," I whimpered.

As the sick realization leached into my bones, I slumped into his hold.

She's gone.

This…this was my penance. The payment for my sins.

Punishment for every naive choice I had made.

For every deceit I had blindly swallowed.

For every lie that had fallen from my lips.

But every one of them I'd told for her.

To keep her safe.

To allow us a life he would never let us live.

But we can run as hard and as fast as we want, and until we put our pasts to rest, they will always catch up to us.

Now mine had us in its grip.

one
Sebastian

LIGHTNING FLASHED, AND THE heavens wept their torment from above. A furious fall of rain hammered into my body as harsh gusts blew through the downpour.

A frenzy of earth and wind and sky.

My entire being strained against it. I clenched my jaw as fat rivulets of water gathered in my hair and streamed down my bare chest and back to soak my jeans.

Two feet ahead, Shea stood in front of me. Facing away. Her head drooped between her shaking shoulders. My girl, bent in half, and broken in two. All that blonde drenched, like a swilling river overflowing with pain.

Around us, chaos howled like a demon.

A hurricane.

A fucking devastating storm.

Dark.

Dark.

Dark.

For once, I saw none of her light.

Rage blistered across the surface of my skin. The pain and fear I had for Kallie ate me alive. That rage headed south and twisted through my stomach, inciting the anger of betrayal throbbing from within.

"Who the fuck are you?" It scraped from my throat, low and bitter and confused.

It felt like an eternity passed before she slowly turned around. That face. That fucking gorgeous face I couldn't erase from my mind looked back on me with misery, and my chest felt like it just might cave.

"I'm just Shea," she choked out and hugged herself tighter, going back to the same thing she'd told me on the beach two days ago. *I'm just Shea.* Three little words that should mean nothin'. But they'd sent a ripple of warning through me then, my gut telling me whatever had brought on her discomfort was caused by whoever the fuck had fathered Kallie.

Of course, at that time, I'd been under the very misguided impression he was dead—whoever the piece of shit she'd chosen to keep a secret happened to be.

Now I could only wish he was.

Martin Jennings.

My skin crawled and my teeth ground with the accusation. "You lied to me."

A sob tore through her. The tortured sound ripped through my insides. "Yes."

I opened my mouth to make more accusations when I felt the figure approaching from behind.

"Shea," she whimpered over the driving rain. April, Shea's best friend, slowly edged down the first porch step, hanging on to the wooden rail as if she might fall to her knees.

More torment made a pass through Shea's expression. "He took her."

Every fear Shea'd ever had was wound up in the statement. I heard it. Fucking *felt* it.

"He took her," she said again, only this time she was begging, looking to April as if she might have the power to wipe it away.

Holy shit.

April knew.

Of course she did.

I felt like I'd been sucker punched.

Because that's exactly what I was.

A sucker.

A fool because I'd just let myself go…let go of all my control and gave it to this girl.

The girl I'd trusted with my fucking life because I'd wanted to give her that, too.

I felt like the brunt of a cruel, sick joke. An outsider looking in on Shea's dirty little secret. A secret kept from me when I was the one supposed to hold all her truths.

But this girl had just given me lies.

"We'll…we're going to get her back," April whispered almost maniacally, her dark brown eyes wide and scared.

"He took her." This time the words on Shea's tongue sounded foreign. Faraway. I saw the moment the reality crashed down on her and her knees went weak.

I rushed forward and scooped her into my arms just before she hit the ground. There was nothing I could do but pull her to me. Hold her. Couldn't stop the way my nose went into her hair or the way my mouth pressed to her temple. "I've got you."

I've got you.

Did I?

She buried her face in my chest, her arms clinging to my neck as if I could be her rock. "He took her, Sebastian. He *took* her."

Her breath seeped all over me. Plea after plea. Like she was asking me to make it better.

Asking me to be a part of it now.

I felt torn in a million directions. Shredded. My love for this girl, the devotion that pumped through me with every violent beat of my heart, at all-out war with the voice that kept whispering I didn't know her at all.

In what seemed like shock, I carried Shea up the walk and started to climb the porch steps. I twisted sideways to get by April who still clung to the railing. She seemed to be frozen in her own shock.

Wood creaked beneath my bare feet as I walked across the porch. I didn't stop when I hit the polished hardwood floors inside. I headed for the staircase.

I gulped over visions of the nightmare that had just transpired here—The little girl standing at the top of the landing whispering for her mommy, having no clue how her world was about to be crushed.

As soon as I crossed the exact spot where Kallie had stood, Shea yelped as if she were in physical pain.

"Kallie." Her gasped name hit the air like grief.

I gritted my teeth and pulled her a little closer. "I know, baby, I know."

Shea's room was just as dark as it'd been ten minutes before, the covers still rumpled, and the room smelling like sex. As if we were still back in that moment when I was confessing things I didn't think I'd ever get to feel.

Love for a woman I never thought I'd deserve.

Love for a child who'd caught me up in a whirlwind of tinkling laughter, unending smiles, and a precious, perfect world filled with butterflies.

Fuck. I wanted it.

I wanted it so bad but now I didn't know up from down. Didn't know who was who or where I belonged.

Carefully, I set a drenched, shivering Shea on the edge of her bed. Hunched over, she wrapped her arms across her chest as if looking for a way to hold herself together.

"Don't move." I went into the adjoining bathroom and grabbed a couple dry towels from the cabinet. Striding right back out, I wrapped one around her shoulders then began to work the other through the length of her hair.

Slowly, carefully, I looked down at her as she looked up at me. Her face was wet from the rain, but there was no mistaking the ceaseless tears streaming down her cheeks.

Caramel eyes latched onto mine, a molten stir of remorse and shame and outright fear. She reached up and wrapped her delicate hand around my wrist. An electric current streaked down my spine. A rush of light and heat and agony. The threads of that unfound tether that tied her to me pulled softly and steadily and somehow urgently.

I stilled my movements, strung up by her silent charge.

Didn't matter I didn't have the first clue who she really was. She still had the power to command all my senses.

Her bottom lip trembled. "I didn't want you to find out this way."

I took two steps back and let the towel drop to the floor.

The words wavered between severe and hurt. "Or you didn't want me to find out at all."

Wasn't really a question. Just another accusation that made me sound like a first-class dick, because there was no question in my mind she was hurting.

But shit...who could blame me?

I gave a harsh shake of my head, pissed at myself.

How many times had I wanted to go rooting around in her dark? Fucking drawn to it like it might be my saving breath.

Now here I was, drowning in it.

As if she accepted my anger, expected it, she dropped her gaze to her fingers twisting like blanched bows on her lap. "I didn't want you to find out this way," she murmured like an oath. "This is what I was trying to tell you when the social worker rang the doorbell."

I swallowed hard, feeling my eyes narrowing as I pinned her to the spot with the heat of my glare, with the demand. Because even though I already knew it was the truth, I needed to hear her admit it aloud. "Martin Jennings is Kallie's father."

Shea flinched like she'd been struck, lines of horror striking bold across her face.

Terror.

Hurt.

Regret.

All those emotions made my head spin almost as dramatically as it felt like my heart ached.

Sorrow squeezed my chest.

Fuck, I hated him. Had hated him since the second I saw him coming off the tour bus the night I'd gone in to find Austin sprawled face down on the floor. OD'ing on whatever the bastard had fed him.

Left him there to die.

Wasn't like I'd thought all that highly of him before then. Asshole had screamed nothing but seedy pretention and greedy arrogance. Like the snake he was, every strategic move he'd made had been to bring him one step closer to whatever devious goal he'd set his sight on.

Money.

Power.

Insatiable gluttony.

But that night was the first time the name Martin Jennings became synonymous with destruction. With the highest kind of threat.

Rocking, she hugged herself tightly. She breathed the admission toward her lap. "Biologically, yes, but in every other way, no."

Rapidly I blinked and began to pace, raking my hands through my sopping wet hair as I tried to process the fuckery that had spun my life out of control. One disaster after another.

Trouble.

Knew it the first time I saw her. There was just something about her that wouldn't let me go. Something deep and unfathomable. Funny, I'd still felt like I needed to protect her from the depravity that seemed to make up the definition of who *I* was.

And here she was, pouring on another layer.

Guess I was right. That shit found me anywhere I went.

Swinging back toward her, I stared her down, unable to contain some of the anger pushing its way free. "You lied to me? After all this time…after everything we've been through, you let me go on believing Kallie didn't have a father?"

"She *doesn't* have a father. He has *never* been her father."

My laughter was bitter, and I began to storm around the room, my feet eating up the floor while vile images of that sick bastard Jennings touching my girl ran through my brain on an unbearable loop.

I flew back around, my head bent down and cocked to the side as I approached her. Like maybe if I looked close enough, I could see everything she'd been hiding. "I thought we were finished with all the bullshit and lies. I thought I *knew* you."

My face suddenly pinched up with the hurt she'd inflicted. Because it was the truth. She'd gutted me. I'd trusted her, and here I was, uncertain if I'd been the pawn in some twisted game.

Everyone wanted a piece of Sebastian Stone.

Now I couldn't help but wonder if I'd been played.

My eyes locked on her. Soft and frail and glimpses of that light fighting for a comeback.

God, how could I even think for a second this wasn't *real?*

I fisted my hand at my chest, giving her raw honesty. "I gave you my fucking heart, Shea. All of it. Wanted to claim Kallie as my own. Wanted everything with you, and now it turns out I know *nothing*."

Tears distorted her voice, and her own truth bled free. "Do you really think you don't know me, Sebastian? Do you really think you don't know every single thing that counts? This room…this house…me being a mother to Kallie…*loving* you." She emphasized the last, and it struck me deep.

Tonight was the first time I'd truly accepted she could love me. Accepted maybe I deserved to love her back.

Creases deepened at the corners of her eyes. "Those are the only things in my life that count."

Fear welled up as frustration, and I fisted my hands at my sides. "You think it doesn't count that prick Jennings had the power to just roll in here and steal Kallie away from us?"

I took a step forward and lowered my voice. "You think that doesn't matter? And you want to know the sick part, Shea? The only fucking thing I want right now is to comfort you. Make it better. *Fix it*. And I don't even know what the fuck I'm fixin'. You lied to me…for months. I'm not sure I even know who you are."

"You know me," she pled. More tears fell, and she sniffled and inhaled. She brought those eyes up to mine. Something fierce billowed out from within them.

Her voice was a whisper, but there was no mistaking the strength behind it. "Yes, I lied to you. But it's a lie I've told everyone, including myself. It's the only way I knew how to survive. It was the only way Kallie and I could live a normal life. You don't know what that man is capable of, and if lying about his existence kept my daughter safe, then I would do it a million times over."

I swallowed hard. I'd be nothing but a hypocrite if I said I didn't understand. How many secrets had I kept locked up tight, refusing to show them to protect my family? My brother? The band?

I mean, fuck, Shea's and my entire relationship had been built on a foundation of lies. I was the one who'd kept my identity hidden in the first place. Now I knew what that shit felt like.

But her being Delaney Rhoads and wanting to leave behind a life she didn't want was one thing. Martin Jennings being Kallie's father was a whole different story.

Did she have any clue how tangled I was in Jennings's life-sucking web?

My words were strained. "That's where you're wrong. I know exactly what that asshole is capable of. That's what scares me most."

Another rush of chills trembled through her, and she nodded as if she were attempting to make sense of her own questions. "I can't believe you know him."

Biting laughter escaped me before I could stop it as I was struck with another rush of doubt. "But didn't you already know that, Shea?"

God, I was so back and forth. Swinging from sympathy and care to wondering if she was some kind of mole planted in my life with the sole purpose of ripping it apart.

Her chin quivered. "I would *never* have kept this from you as long as I did if I'd known."

"Then how?"

Helpless, she lifted a shoulder. "I don't know. Why were you in Savannah, Sebastian? You're the one who came into my life. I had no idea Martin was a part of yours." She squeezed her eyes closed, like maybe she didn't want to ask the question, before she opened to me. "I need to know how you know him."

More bitter laughter, and I paced again, wiping the back of a hand over my mouth like I could wipe away the sour taste.

I cut my attention to her. "Told you I might still be going to jail, Shea. Told you I wasn't any good for you because every time I turn around I'm doing something to threaten my freedom. And my freedom is threatened because of him...because he fed my baby brother pills, then walked away and left him for dead."

A shocked sob wracked through her and she covered her mouth with her hand. "Oh my God. No."

She blinked what seemed a million times, seeming to withdraw, like she wanted to shrink back into her bed and disappear.

Awareness slammed me hard and fast, and I reached for her, framing her face in my hands as my own terror barreled through me. I saw it, Shea's truth. "What did he do to you?"

She squeezed her eyes closed, withdrawing further.

I tightened my grip, and the demand scraped up my throat. "Tell me."

She shook her head against my hold. "I can't."

"You can't, or you won't?"

"Can't."

It felt like she burned me.

She gasped when I suddenly released her. Eyes narrowed with regret, I studied her. She looked so small sitting at the edge of her bed. Fucking broken, still the most beautiful thing I'd ever seen. All her colors striking bold. All that black and white, the deepest red and the darkest dark, trust and light. An outright fear distorted it all.

Like maybe she was begging me to see inside at the same time as she was shutting me out.

My phone rang from my jeans pocket, and my attention went back to what was most important—the tiny girl who'd been ripped from her home.

"It's Anthony," I said when I saw his name lighting the screen.

Hope swept her features.

I put the phone to my ear. "Anthony, tell me you have news."

His heavy sigh traveled across the line. Foreboding. I sucked in a breath.

"I do. I'm just sorry it isn't the kind of news you want to hear,

Baz. I got word Martin Jennings made a public statement an hour ago. He's playing the concerned father card. He says he knew he had to step in when he discovered you and Shea were dating. He's using the assault against him and your past possession and theft convictions as his ammo. He's claiming you're only with Shea to get back at him and using his daughter as a pawn."

The bastard was saying I was dangerous.

Which when it came to Martin Jennings, I was. A fucking loose cannon. I knew in my gut that asshole's involvement with Mark and my baby brother went far deeper than any of us fathomed.

And now it involved Shea and Kallie.

I turned away from the terror blanketing Shea's expression when she saw mine drop, unable to look at her as Anthony confirmed what I'd worried about most.

The shit going down in my life would be responsible for taking Shea down.

Knew it the second I saw him step from that car—Jennings was here because of me.

You were warned you'd regret fucking with me.

Point-blank, that's what he'd said with a devious smirk on his face. Same thing he'd warned at that doomed mediation.

Running a hand down the tense muscles at the back of my neck, I studied my feet as I paced the floor.

All along I'd known I was bad for her. *All. Along.* There wasn't anything right in my life, so how could I be *right* for her? But I'd pretended for so long I could possibly be that guy, I'd begun to believe it. Believed it when Shea had accepted me back after she'd found out who I was, because she recognized the man hidden underneath. Reached in far enough to touch him. To bring him to life through her beauty and light.

The one who wanted something more. To be something better.

I wanted it so fucking bad I'd gone and forgotten all the garbage still eating at my heels.

Forgot about the fact I was either going back to jail or back on the road. Instead, I carried on with Shea like I was always gonna be here, wanting her and Kallie as my own when the shit in *my life* owned me.

Now with Kallie and Shea being tied to Jennings?

I had no idea how to make any of this *right*.

He cleared his throat. "I know you're already well aware of this, but there is no question he's out for blood, and you've become his target. I won't pretend to know Shea or her little girl, but the fact he's willing to use his own child as bait shows how ruthless he is."

"She's not his child." I spat it out faster than I could think better of it, like I had the fucking right to claim it.

"No? That's not what the paperwork says." Exasperation laced his words, before they slowed with caution. "I've always been on your side, Baz, and I'm always going to be. You deserve happiness, more than just about anyone I know. But you're going to have to ask yourself if this is worth getting your hands dirtier than they already are."

Worth it?

Anthony had no clue Shea and Kallie were worth *everything*.

I'd give up anything and everything to protect them.

Even if it meant what I was giving up was them.

I didn't give him a straight answer. Instead, I gritted my teeth and forced out the words. "All I want you to worry about is getting that little girl back where she belongs."

Anthony pushed out a heavy breath. "Okay. I'm taking a red-eye. I leave in two hours. You and I will talk when I get there. But whatever you decide, I'm going to be at your side through all of this."

Of course he was. Never once had he let me down.

His voice took on the tone he reserved for business. "I got in touch with Kenny. He was able to contact a family attorney in Savannah. He's supposed to be good. Really good. He has a meeting set up for Shea first thing in the morning. I'll have the details with me when I get there."

"Thank you," I muttered roughly.

I hated the callus way he'd just laid everything out, not having a clue just how *deep* I'd gotten. Yet I couldn't find it in me to be pissed at my friend.

He didn't know how important Shea had become. What she meant.

Or what loving her might cost.

Guess I hadn't, either.

I ended the call, reluctant to look back on her.

She was shaking when I finally did. Her hands were clasped in front of her like she was sending up a prayer. "What did he say?"

"What I knew all along. Me bein' in your life is only gonna hurt you. Hurt Kallie. And there isn't a chance in this godforsaken world I'll be the one to stand in the way of you getting your daughter back."

I snagged my shirt from where it'd been discarded on the floor and yanked it over my head. The fabric stuck to my damp flesh. I shoved my feet in my boots. The whole time Shea watched me as if she couldn't comprehend what was happening any more than I could.

Then she rushed to stand. The towel dropped from her shoulders as she took an anguished step forward. "Don't you dare leave me, Sebastian Stone."

Her pink pajamas were still wet, the cut of those long, toned legs set firm in their defiance, shirt clinging to her soft, soft skin.

So perfect.

So gorgeous.

The girl everything I never knew I wanted.

"I'm sorry," I barely breathed. It was the truth. I was fucking sorry. Sorry I wasn't different. Sorry I wasn't better. Sorry she hadn't been more honest. Sorry our worlds had collided in a way they never should.

"The two of us?" I shook my head. "Maybe we're no good for each other, after all."

We were nothing but volatile, kindling and gas and the strike of a match.

I took a step toward the door. It hurt so bad my voice went flat. "I will do everything I can to help you get Kallie back. My attorney contacted someone who can help you. I don't care what it costs. I'll pay anything. Won't stop until it's done."

I turned and strode across the landing, focused ahead.

Shea clamored behind me. Her breaths came harsh and hard. "Sebastian...don't."

I made it down three stairs.

"Look at me," she begged.

My feet faltered. I couldn't resist. I looked back. Looked back on beauty. Both her hands were fisted between her breasts, right over her heart I was sure I could hear above the roar in my ears. That sweet, innocent spirit calling out for me above the slow seeping pain that groaned from within.

My chest ached like a bitch.

Slowly, she began to shake her head. "Don't you dare, Sebastian. I don't know what he said to you during that call, but it doesn't change anything."

"No, you're right, Shea. It doesn't change anything."

It was just a brutal reminder.

The danger in pretending is it becoming real.

"It was always this way," I said, my jaw clenching with a flash of pain. "Always knew I was never gonna be good enough for you. Warned you I was going to break you. Still, there was nothing I could do to keep myself from chasing you. *I did this.*"

Her storm gathered strength. I could feel it. The stir of energy that swelled in the room.

Dark.

Light.

Heavy.

Soft.

I wanted to sink into it and disappear.

This time forever, because I didn't want to forget, and I didn't ever want to come up for air, but I wasn't going to be the one who stood between her and Kallie.

Funny how I hadn't given a shit how badly Jennings could hurt me. The threat of jail time. The loss of money. Even the loss of my life. None of it mattered, just as long as it meant I was protecting my brother. My family.

Now the bastard had changed all the rules.

Frantic, she edged forward. "No. You know this wasn't just about you. It was the perfect storm."

I bit back a biting laugh.

Storm.

Maybe it was hers, the force of that hurricane inciting a war. Urging it forward. Bringing two enemies face to face.

But every battle has casualties, and I refused that to be Kallie.

Shea stumbled over her words. All of them tumbled out with a confession I didn't know could hurt so fucking bad.

"I haven't seen him since the day Kallie was born…but he made sure I wouldn't forget that one day he'd be coming for me. Never let me forget I owed him and he would be back to collect."

Hate raged through me. Every muscle in my body tightened with the need for revenge. With the need to track him down, find him, and kill the fucker for putting that look on her face.

Never had I felt so trapped, because not one solution I could find gave me the outcome I wanted.

The one I wanted most—the one every part of me demanded—was staying here with Shea. Even if a part of me felt betrayed, I knew I *knew* her. Knew her somewhere deep in a place only she could see. Knew without a doubt she needed to be loved the way I wanted to love her.

Supported and encouraged and maintained.

But that would mean Jennings would continue to use me against her.

I could give into the violence. The base desire to end Martin Jennings, which would be the end of me.

Or I could just walk away. Do what I could from a distance. Sink all my money into destroying Jennings, make him disappear… legally. Yeah, I'd be fucked, dredging up evidence that would only condemn my entire family.

But I knew without a doubt I would do it for her.

Because somewhere along the way she'd become *my family*.

Shea took a pleading step forward. Just as pleading as the words pouring from that sweet, sweet mouth. "The whole time he's been keeping tabs. Waiting for the moment to come in and make our lives hell. Even while I spent years pretending he was dead, I still *knew* it."

I took one more step down, and Shea took a stumbling one forward. An explanation tumbled from her like a petition. "The day Kallie was born…he…he showed up at the hospital. He forced me to add him to the birth certificate. He said if I didn't, he would fight me for custody. Nothing in the world seemed worse than that monster taking my baby away, so I caved. I was eighteen, Sebastian. *Eighteen* and terrified of the man who had tried to rule my life."

Terrified.

Monster.

Those words spun around me like a poisoned vortex.

Anger bristled beneath the surface of my flesh, arrows staking me deep.

No, I had no clue what she'd been through. But the expression clouding her face promised it was worse than I could ever imagine.

My hands curled into fists.

Shea continued to fumble through the confession. "At the time, I thought it was the best option. The *only* option. He didn't even look at her. He just turned and walked out. But not before he stopped at the door and told me I'd never get so far that I'd be out of his reach."

Just like he'd promised me.

Pride.

Pride.

Pride.

How sick this meant more to him than anything else.

"He would have found a way with or without you being in the middle of it," she begged, eyes searching my face, and her feet bringing her another step closer.

Maybe he'd been waiting. But I'd served him the ammunition on a silver platter.

I gripped the smooth wooden railing where I stood on the third step down. "You want to know what Anthony just told me, Shea? Why CPS showed up here and took her? They took her because of *me*. Because they believe I'm dangerous and because of that, Kallie is at risk."

"You would never hurt her."

Biting laughter rocked from me, because no, I'd never purposefully hurt her. Never. But that didn't mean my mere presence didn't beg for trouble. Chaos and mayhem and violence attached to my name.

"Look at me, Shea." I stretched my arms out to my sides like an offering.

Shea knew what was underneath. All the scars and hardened body that came from living a hardened life.

It was the truth of who I really was.

"Look at me," I said again. Defeat filled the words.

Tears Shea hadn't been able to stop the entire night rolled faster down her angel face.

Did the fact I had the urge to cross to her make me a sick bastard? Push her against the wall and kiss the hell out of her until neither of us could remember our lives had just gone to shit? Get lost in her sweet touches and soft seduction?

But maybe it was time both of us started facing our reality.

She took me by surprise when disappointment coursed from her. "You think I don't see you?"

Slowly, she shook her head. "Do you want to know what I see when I look at you, Sebastian? I see someone who takes the burden of the entire world and places it on his shoulders because he somehow thinks he deserves that weight. The one who'd bear it all if it meant those he loves would suffer a little less. I see someone who's made mistakes just like the rest of us. Just like *me*. I see someone who maybe on the outside looks a little frightening. But what I'm frightened of most is how intensely he makes me feel."

She touched her chest. "I see a man who's loyal. Devoted. One who opened himself up enough to a love a little girl who isn't even his. I see the man who caused me to fall so hard I didn't know what hit me. I see a man I'd needed so badly, yet hadn't even known it until he showed me what I was missing. I see the one I *love*."

Shea's words assaulted me, battered me with her unending belief and light. Like she was lifting me above the dark she threatened to drown me in.

An enigma. This girl I had no clue if I even knew. My savior. My ruin.

She didn't stop. She just kept firing away.

"I see the only one who I want to do *this* with. Am I scared Jennings is using you to take Kallie from me? Yes. I'm terrified for her. But I also know he would have found another way, and I know it's time I faced it, and I want to face it with you at my side. I don't care what the rest of the world sees. All I care about is what you mean to me."

My chest tightened, welling with emotion. Because fuck, I wanted to believe that, too.

"What if none of this is good enough?"

"What if it is?"

Trying to block it, I shook my head.

No.

God, she made me weak.

My voice grew quiet. "How could I put Kallie's future on the line, knowing what I've done? I'm guilty, Shea. All those accusations…they're true, and there's nothing I can do to dispute them."

They went so much deeper than the courts had record of, too. All the bullshit I'd gotten away with when I was nothing but a punk kid out trying to make it big, me and the rest of my crew out to conquer the world one fucked-up mistake at a time.

Worst part?

Jennings knew. Didn't matter he was the dirtiest crook there was. He held all the cards.

I just didn't know how deep his deck went until tonight.

"It doesn't matter," she whispered, her voice all wispy with hope and faith.

I looked up at the fucking gorgeous girl who, with just a glance, swallowed me whole.

Annihilated me with a touch.

The one I was willing to lay it all down for. My life and my heart and my future. But I was willing to break my own damned heart if it meant she got her little girl back.

I forced myself down the stairs, turning back just in time to watch as I broke Shea a little more. Always knew I would. Disappointment and hurt amplified her fear. With all of me, I wanted to wipe her pain away.

Expose her beauty and belief.

Live in it.

But I didn't know how to stay.

Things had spiraled since the fateful moment when Kallie had almost drowned two days ago. It felt like a fucking lifetime, worn tatters of days strewn across too much time.

This goddamned perpetual tragedy that just wouldn't quit.

I turned away.

"Sebastian…don't leave me. You promised me…you promised you'd never leave me again." Desperate feet pounded on the steps behind me. "Please…look at me."

I couldn't. If I looked back again, I would only cave. Give in, because I was already *gone*.

"Look at me!" she begged from behind. Fingers scraped down my back, trying to latch on.

Pain.

I fisted my hands, trying to catch a fucking breath, to drag the air in and out of my punctured lungs.

April sat on the couch with her face in her hands, crying. She jumped to her feet when I tore open the door. Tears soaked her plain face, plain brown eyes dulled and dimmed. Like maybe she got it, too. Why I couldn't stay and break Shea any more than I already had.

"Sebastian…*see* me!" The tortured cry erupting from Shea's mouth nearly dropped me to my knees. I slammed the door shut behind me and rushed out into the waning storm.

The sky was dark and ominous.

It felt like a warning of what was to be.

two
Shea

PAIN ENGULFED ME. IT crashed in from every side, pummeling and beating and battering until I was being swept away by the vicious undertow.

I gasped over the sorrow, and I grappled at the railing in an attempt to stay upright when my body almost gave.

Kallie.

Kallie.

Kallie.

I felt as if I were shattering. Splintering. My soul fragmenting as it screamed for the pieces that had been ripped away.

Kallie.

Fear consumed me.

What did Martin want with her?

Why now, after all this time?

And Sebastian.

Without him, I no longer knew how to breathe.

Warily, April looked at me where I held onto the railing at the bottom of the stairs. Her wide, frightened eyes were stained red, cheeks wet with her own misery.

"I can't believe this is happening," she whispered, as if she didn't want to speak the words, because if she did, it would make them real.

But I could. I'd always known. No amount of lies or hiding or pretending could have kept this day from coming to pass.

Martin Jennings had been sitting back, lying in wait for the perfect opportunity to strike. The precise time to swoop in and tear my world apart. The circumstances didn't matter. Martin had promised he would find a way to make me pay.

And now I was paying the greatest price.

My head spun, my entire being reeling with the aftermath of everything he threatened to take from me.

Kallie. My baby girl.

Sebastian.

Hadn't Martin already taken enough?

"He would never have just let me go." The raspy words scraped like razors up my sore throat.

Her voice was small. Scared. Just like me. "What do we do?"

A flurry of adrenaline whipped through me. A frenzy fueled by the fear and resolution to do anything and everything I had to do—just like I had before. I lifted my chin. "We fight."

She swiped under her eyes and laughed a soggy laugh that held zero humor. "I can't believe I almost forgot about him. So much time has passed and I'd pretended he didn't exist…it felt like he didn't."

"I know."

And I was to blame. Pretending was so much easier than living with constant anxiety. So much easier than waiting for the switch to flip, for the shoe to drop, for my world to implode like it'd done tonight.

I'd let Sebastian believe there was no one there to claim Kallie. No father to love her or protect her or stand by her side. There was. But Martin would never do any of those things. No. He didn't love.

He used and manipulated and abused.

A rush of nausea swam in my belly as my mind flashed to Kallie's trusting face. Only this time, that face was painted in terror and confusion and desolation.

That sickness coiled like an agitated asp with the thought of her being at his mercy. Because mercy was something Martin Jennings did not grant. There was no doubt in my mind he cared absolutely nothing about her. He viewed her as an obstacle he couldn't pass, as hard as he'd tried to get her out of his way.

Now my daughter was subject to his malicious will.

Sorrow squeezed my chest.

I hated I'd hurt Sebastian.

Hated I'd hidden it from him for so long.

Hated most I'd allowed that monster to steal away my baby girl.

April cast me the saddest of smiles and then dropped her attention to the side. "I know I don't have much to offer, but I'll be here, Shea, fighting with you, until we bring her home."

Tears streaked down my face. "Don't ever say that. You have always been the sanity in all of this. Supporting Kallie and me in every way. I'm not sure I would have made it without you."

She shook her head, eyes blurry and unfocused as they drifted to the far wall. "All the time I've lived here with you and Kallie, I hoped you'd find a guy who would fall head over heels in love with you. With both of you. Someone kind yet strong. Someone who would always stand by your side and do whatever it took to make you happy."

With her focus still faraway, she sucked in her bottom lip.

"When I found Sebastian in our kitchen that morning…I instantly disliked him. I didn't trust him. I was sure he wasn't anything but trouble."

She gave a fierce, regretful shake of her head. "I just *knew* he was going to hurt you. I was scared because I saw the way you looked at him. I figured he wasn't anything but a player out looking for fun while he passed time in Savannah."

She looked at me simply. "I was wrong. I want to blame him for all this…but I can't do that. I'm pretty sure he's the guy who would do *anything* to make sure you're happy."

Simple, simple dreams.

They moaned from within.

A simple girl who loved a simple boy.

How ironic the one thing I'd ever hoped to want with him was being dangled right in front of me.

A family.

But both Sebastian's and my situations were the furthest from *simple*.

April glanced back at the door Sebastian had disappeared through. "Why didn't you tell him?"

I swallowed over the lump of emotion locking my throat. "I was going to…the night when I found out who he was. When I finally admitted I loved him. I was ready to tell him everything. Ready to *trust* him with everything."

He was the first person I did.

Trust.

Sadness tugged at one side of my mouth. "As much as knowing who he was scared me, it felt like it was meant to be. Like maybe no one could understand us the same way we could understand each other."

I gave her a helpless shrug. "He left me before I had the chance. Then he was back and everything happened so fast. Kallie almost drowning…the paparazzi…the pictures. I tried to tell him again tonight."

Right before the social worker showed up at my door.

But now that I knew his connection to Martin, I found I couldn't open my mouth to tell him everything. The things he clearly demanded to know. He thought I didn't trust him. That was a light year from the truth.

I was scared for him.

I *knew* Sebastian. And I also knew the things Martin was capable of. The wicked things he'd done. At least some of them. Surely my knowledge barely dipped a finger in a bottomless barrel of malevolence.

Even when no proof had been found, I carried no delusions. Martin had been responsible for what was done to me. Every self-preserving part of me was certain. And I knew if Sebastian knew what he'd done, it would shred the last of his paper-thin control. In his compulsive need to protect and defend, he'd destroy everything important to both of us. I couldn't risk that. Not for him or for me.

I held too much hope that what we shared was bigger than all of it and together we'd *fix* this, just like Sebastian had said.

Softly, she tilted her head to the side. Telling. Comforting. "He's shocked…scared. But the only thing clear in this horrible situation is that man loves you."

"Yeah," I quietly agreed, because I didn't question that either. I just hoped I hadn't hurt him so deeply he could no longer see it.

three
Sebastian

IN THE DISTANCE, LIGHTNING flashed as the storm headed north out of Savannah. The roads were wet, and streetlamps glowed in the foggy haze. My headlights glinted through the mist, creating the illusion of misshapen stars that shone too bright against my eyes.

I shivered, still fucking soaking wet, my insides just as cold as my skin.

I rubbed a hand over my face and tried to focus.

The river walk was almost deserted. Quiet at this time on a Sunday night.

It seemed ludicrous my first damned instinct was to go to *Charlie's* to seek the reprieve offered within those old walls. But it, too, was closed for the night. The face darkened, as if the hope I'd found there had also been shut down.

Nowhere else to go, I headed back to Tybee Island. Twenty minutes later, I pulled into the drive in front of Anthony's beachfront vacation home.

Sighing, I cut the engine and stepped out into the night. My boots crunched on the gravel and thudded up the seven steps leading to the sweeping entrance. I unlocked the door and entered, having no fucking clue where to go from here, because God knew this wasn't where I wanted to be.

Inside, floor-to-ceiling windows took up the entire wall facing east, the waning storm eclipsing the stars in the sky. The main room was open to the lavish kitchen in the back where Ash, Lyrik, and Zee stood around the island, nothing else to do in this town that was locked down tight on a Sunday night. The smiles on their faces dropped when they saw the expression on mine.

Ash frowned. "Back already?"

Last thing they'd known, the pictures on the Internet had been taken down, and I was heading back to Shea's with my heart on my sleeve. Wondering if she would kick me to the curb once she realized being with someone like me was too much to deal with, the paparazzi hounding us at every turn, making up lies to satiate their thirst for drama.

Little did we know what was *actually* waiting to bring us to our knees.

Agitated, I drove my hands through my hair.

"...and?" Ash prodded.

"And it turns out I don't know two shits about Shea."

Perplexed, Ash set his beer on the counter, and Zee and Lyrik straightened as they caught onto my agitation.

I exhaled heavily, finding it hard to speak. "Earlier tonight… Child Protective Services showed up to take Kallie away…apparently that bogus article and picture was enough to call into question Shea's ability as a mother."

"Bullshit," Lyrik hissed. Ash and Zee both blanched.

Total, complete bullshit.

I bit my bottom lip, doing my best to contain some of the anger working to break free. "This social worker, she just walks right in, picks up Kallie, and carries her right out the door, saying they're placing her with next of kin."

Pain hit me again. The memory of the terror on Kallie's face a punch to the gut.

"We follow her out, trying to make sense of what the hell is goin' on…" I swallowed down the bile. "Martin Jennings is waiting on the curb." I gripped my hair, the words sliding from me like I wanted to purge their truth. "He's her father. Shea lied to me. Told me Kallie's father was dead. She's *Delaney Rhoads*."

"No fuckin' way." Ash stared wide-eyed.

"Who's Delaney Rhoads?" Zee asked, confused.

Ash coughed out some stunned laughter. "Country star…popular six, seven years ago. Up and disappeared with a ton of scandal surrounding her name." Ash had the nerve to smile. "Dude…Shea is Delaney Rhoads. That is crazy cool. Can't believe I didn't recognize her, but hell, that was a long time ago."

"Don't even start, Ash," I warned. I definitely wasn't in the mood to deal with the fact everything was a joke to him.

"What?" He shrugged. "Don't tell me you don't think that's the hottest damn thing to ever cross your path. Shea's fucking beautiful…give her a mic and a guitar." Blue eyes gleamed. "Hell yeah."

Hadn't even let my mind go wandering that direction. I was too caught up in the fact she'd lied to me and Jennings was a key in both our lives. That Kallie was gone.

"Martin Jennings has Kallie?" Zee's voice shook, and he rubbed a disturbed hand over his face.

Finally somewhat got the fuckin' consequence of the situation. "Yeah."

Stunned, he dropped his gaze and cursed.

Ash bounced around. If possible his demeanor grew cockier than normal. "So, let's go get her back. Bust some faces. Make it right. No chance in hell are we leaving that little thing with that piece of shit."

Ash made it sound so simple. *Appealing*. Because I wanted nothing more.

A curl of aggression wound through Lyrik. I could feel it, him feeding off me, the intense need I felt to track down that bastard Jennings and finally right all the asshole's wrongs.

Lyrik was just like me. When you get pushed up against a wall, you push right the fuck back, fists and fury and uncontained aggression. Pair that with Ash spouting his mouth wherever we went? The three of us asked for trouble then turned around and kicked its ass.

But if we gave into that craving, we were only going to make things worse.

"Anthony's on his way. He has an attorney lined up. We're going to set this straight."

"Okay?" Ash drew out as he set his hands on his hips, staring me down.

"Okay, what?"

"Then what the hell are you doing here?"

Running.

I gave a harsh shake of my head. "Martin's using the assault against her. No question the asshole is the one who got the courts involved. I won't be a liability."

Just like Shea had said, he'd been waiting to strike. Bet the sick fuck had been watching us these past months.

Two birds with one stone and all that.

Lyrik swore, while Ash grew livid. "Are you kidding me, Baz? Did she ask you to go?"

I didn't answer.

"Unbelievable," he spat toward the ground.

Yeah. It was. All of it.

"You're an idiot." Ash kept on like the fucker he was.

Didn't have it in me to go toe to toe with him, to debate what was *right* when every goddamned thing was wrong.

Feeling like I might crawl out of my skin, I turned my back on the disappointment rolling off the three of them, because they *didn't know*, didn't know how fucking bad this hurt or the lengths I'd go in order to protect Shea and Kallie.

I escaped out the glass-paned doors leading onto the deck.

Outside, the night was thick. Humidity clung to the sky in the wake of the storm that rolled away like the receding tide. It'd left the slightest chill. A dampness that sunk down to my bones.

My boots thudded on the wooden planks as I marched down toward the sea.

Drawn.

Lights glowed from the windows of the house behind me. Two stories were lit up like a torch, casting the beach in darkness.

I inched down the smooth sand where the tide had been pulled out to sea. I wanted to shout and rant and rave about how fucking unfair this world was.

Always stealing the *good*.

Blotting out the beauty and light when the vile was allowed to run rampant.

I stretched my arms out to my sides and let *his* presence crawl over me.

Julian.

He was always there, waiting for me.

I closed my eyes and let the unending regret consume me.

I froze when I sensed the presence behind me, and I slowly turned to find the lone figure hugging his knees to his chest. He was hunched over, obscured from the stretch of lights from the house where he sat at the base of a dune.

Lost to the dark.

"Austin," I whispered. The sound was eaten up by the wind. I edged toward him, somehow cautious, hating the fact I'd had little time to take care of my baby brother over the last couple of days.

In the texts I shared with Lyrik after what had gone down with the paparazzi and those fucking repulsive pictures, he promised everything was cool. Said they had Austin covered.

Yeah, the guys were family.

But I wasn't sure that could make up for my absence.

Only I could understand what kind of brutal blow the incident here on the beach with Kallie had been to Austin.

The memories it'd evoked.

He was back to covering his head with that goddamned hoodie.

Fuck, I hated it. Hated that he continued to hide from the past just the same as he allowed it to eat him alive.

I had the urge to shake him.

To tell him again *it was not your fault.*

I didn't. Instead, I slumped down beside him. I pushed out a breath and scrubbed a hand down my face.

"What are you doing here?" he asked, digging his fingers into the sand where they dangled between his knees.

I gazed out over the sea. "You know when you think things are finally coming together…that you know you've finally touched on something good? Hurts that much worse when it's ripped from your fingers."

Eyes peered intently at me from the side.

"Knew I was going to bring her down, Austin. The first night I saw her?"

My heart sped with the memory—the energy that'd surrounded her—the need to get lost in all her sweet and soft enough to make me lose my mind.

He just watched, waiting for me to explain.

"Thought she had to be the most gorgeous girl I'd ever seen. There was something about her I couldn't shake…not a damn thing I could do to stay away from her, even though I knew when I went back to that bar I was gonna end up hurting her."

Confusion wound through his tone. "Thought you two had it all worked out? That's why we came back here, right?"

I raked the back of my hand over my mouth, unable to contain the bitterness breaking free. "I've been fooling myself it ever could. Since we came back from L.A., I thought if I let all those walls down...let her in...everything would be okay. That somehow we could make it when my life was nothin' but a disaster. But these last two days? It was like they were a warning I couldn't keep up the charade and everything was going to fall apart. That I was still *pretending*."

I blew a strained breath toward the sky, before I cut my attention to my baby brother. "She lied to me, Austin. Kallie's father isn't dead. Martin Jennings is her father."

Quickly, I filled him in on the events of the night, every wicked word bleeding from my mouth.

With each one, Austin's distress seemed to increase. He jumped to his feet and gripped his shaggy brown hair. "What? Shea is Delaney Rhoads?"

I was surprised he even knew the name, considering he would have only been thirteen when Kallie was born.

He paced the sand, back and forth in front of me, like a partner to the wind. More upset than I ever expected him to be.

He turned his grey stare back to me, his face twisted up in confusion. More disappointment. "So you just walked away? Left her there to deal with all this shit on her own?"

"The shit *I* caused, Austin. She wouldn't be dealing with this right now if it wasn't for me."

"The shit you caused?" Incredulously, he snorted. "Everything you do is to get someone else out of trouble. If this is anyone's fault, it's mine."

"Not your fault," I grated.

I'd told him what felt like a million times.

When was he ever going to start believing it?

"You know what, Baz? You act like you're the only person

around here strong enough to shoulder any blame. You go around protecting and protecting and protecting until it's *suffocating*. You won't even let me take responsibility for what *I did*." Twice, he struck his fist against his chest to punctuate it.

I winced with the bite of his words.

Then he softened, remorse seeming to seep through. "And you know how much it means to me. All you've done. What you've given up. You became my entire world. My mom, my dad, my brother, and my *best friend*. You made sure I ate when Mom couldn't get out of bed, put yourself in Dad's line of fire to protect me. Fucking hauled me around, this little kid thinking he was on top of the world because his big brother allowed him to tag along."

"That was the worst mistake I ever made." My rough voice clashed with the air. "Dragging you into all that."

"Really? Where do you think I'd be right now if you hadn't gotten me out of that house? I'm pretty sure I wouldn't still be breathing."

Pain clenched my heart. "I did it all wrong."

"You were a kid, too. You think I don't know you were doing the best you could?"

Disgusted, he shook his head. "We've had a whole lot of bad in our lives."

His words echoed like my own. *Have so much shit, Shea.*

"And now you finally have something *good*. I don't care who she is or what lies she told you, it doesn't mean what brought you back here in the first place counts any less. She *needs* you. Fuck... she *needs* you, Baz."

Hurt wound through me. Gutting. I ground my teeth.

He tilted his head, looking at me. Discerning eyes speared me in the shadows, the kid far more mature than I'd ever given him credit for.

Always watching.

"The way Shea looks at you? One day...one day I want someone to look at me like that. And guess what, you look at her the exact same way. And you're really going to let *that* go because of an asshole like Jennings? You've fought for everyone your entire life, and now you're going to step down—bow out—when you finally have something worth fighting for? Fight for *her*."

"Austin." I wanted to beg him to stop.

He just continued right on. "My entire life, I've looked up to you. Thought you *knew* everything. Even when *I* gave up, I somehow knew you were going to be there to save me. But if you think giving up on that girl is what's right, then you're a fool."

He gazed back out over the sea, gentle waves lapping at the shore. The haze of clouds had begun to dissipate. A scatter of stars bled through.

He turned his face to the sky, before he glanced at me from over his shoulder. "I saw something better in you."

Then he turned and left me there.

I dropped my face into my hands, rubbing my palms up over my head, too many voices clattering inside.

I saw something better in you.
I saw something better in you.
I saw...you...
I see you.
I see you.
I see you.

Shea had seen more in me than I could ever have imagined. Something better than I ever hoped I could be.

And it rushed me.

That sweet, soft girl.

Because the truth was?

I saw her, too.

four
Sebastian

MY HEART SLAMMED AROUND in my chest and my sight narrowed on one singular goal.

Her.

It felt like a lifetime to get to her house, and there was nothing stopping me now. Unlocking her front door, I charged up the stairs. I didn't pause at her bedroom door. I threw it open. I needed to get to her.

With her back to me, Shea was curled around a pillow on the center of her bed. She startled with the sudden intrusion and jerked up to sitting. Caramel eyes blinked at me through the dim light, confusion and hurt and sorrow.

Motionless, I stood in the doorway as the silence hovered over all our uncertainties.

On all the questions.

But Shea was right.

None of that mattered.

And *this* was enough.

"Shea." My voice broke on her name.

I took a step inside and latched the door shut behind me.

Shea's chin quivered, and she lifted it because I knew this girl wanted to be brave. I knew she was playing through a million scenarios. Mentally going through all the ways I was going to let her go. How I was going to let her down. I knew the words she expected to spill from my mouth because for too long I'd been a coward and a fool, thinking sacrifice was the only way to make this right.

Because every time I turned around, I lost someone I loved.

Not this time.

I swallowed hard. "You want to know what I see when I look at you?"

When the intensity in my voice hit her, Shea choked out a tiny sob.

I took one step closer as I began to speak. "I see someone who's so fucking sweet and kind that every time I look at her it just about knocks me from my feet, because I've had so much bad in my life I don't know how to stand in her presence. I see someone who I know I don't deserve, so every time I turn around, I'm runnin' scared because I'm terrified of ruining everything she is."

Slowly, I approached her, and she watched me in the shadows. Her hands trembled in her lap as I neared.

"I see someone who deserves the greatest kind of joy."

Another step closer, and Shea crept toward the side of the bed. She drew a single leg up to her chest. Clinging to it as if it could protect her from any more pain. Everything she felt and wanted and feared was exposed in the expression on her face.

I stopped at the edge of the bed and dropped to my knees.

A small cry escaped her mouth.

Reaching out, I gripped her face in my hands, my fingers burrowing in soft, soft hair.

"I see someone, who even though there's not a chance in this world I could ever be good enough to have her...good enough to hold her...that's all I want to do. I see someone I want to protect and love and fight for."

Tears streamed down her cheeks. She edged even closer and let her legs slip over the side.

I settled myself between her knees and met the storm in her eyes.

"I see beauty and light."

Those eyes flashed, and emotion crushed my ribs. This girl had me twisted up in every way possible.

Shea gasped when I grabbed her by the waist and pulled her to me. I shifted so I sat on the floor with my back propped against the bed.

Shea was straddling my lap.

Warmth enveloped me. Her heart was pounding, all tucked up against me, right where she belonged.

Her skin felt so soft. Mine lit on fire.

She searched my face and I kept on.

"I see the most fucking gorgeous girl I've ever had the pleasure to lay my eyes on." My voice dropped as I leaned up so I could brush my mouth across her ear. "The pleasure to *touch*."

A shiver rolled through her, and I gathered one of her hands between us, threading our fingers. I studied them as I struggled to form the words.

I lifted my gaze and spoke with the most honesty I'd ever allowed myself.

"When I look at you, I see a future I never thought existed, Shea."

Everything went serious. My mind and my heart and my words. "I see my *wife*. I see the mother of my kids. I see all the shit I never wanted until I met you. I see everything I thought impossible."

The corner of that perfect mouth trembled, and she watched me with hope. Hope that up until this moment, I'd continually tried to crush.

But this girl just kept bringing it back to life.

Refusing to let it go.

Her fingers were still woven with mine, and I brought the back of her hand to my mouth, as if I could seal my declaration with a kiss.

A promise.

She put her weight on her knees on either side of me. She rose up.

Hovering.

Her hands found their way into my hair. Gently she sifted her fingers through it.

It felt so damned good I wanted to moan.

I rolled my head back, getting lost in that face, my hands roaming up and down her sides. "You changed me, Shea."

Soft, sad laughter tumbled from her, and cautiously she peeked at me. "You changed everything about me, Baz. You changed everything I wanted because what I ended up wanting was you. You and Kallie. That's all I need."

I sat up higher and took her mouth. My hands bunched in her hair. Forcing her closer. She opened to me as if she'd just found her lost supply of oxygen and was taking in a saving breath.

That's what I wanted.

To be her breath.

She pressed up higher, rocking over me as her hold tightened in my hair. She muttered between kisses, "Don't leave me, Sebastian. Don't leave me."

Words poured out against my lips, each one uttered between scrapes of her teeth as her kisses became more and more frantic.

"I just got you back and I won't survive losing you again. Promise you'll fight him with me...because you love me and this is where you always want to be."

My fingers dug into her thighs. Squeezing. The promise came on a breath. "Yes."

Palming her ass, I couldn't do anything but rock her against my cock that was straining inside my jeans.

I shouldn't have been hard. Our baby girl was gone.

But curls of lust twisted in my stomach and greed took over my kiss.

When she whimpered into my mouth, I took it upon myself to devour her sweet little tongue.

Because, *yes*, I needed this.

Yes, Shea needed this.

Maybe it was indecent.

But neither of us could stop.

We were drowning in desperation.

Dying in need.

Dying to love.

Seeking reprieve from all the misery and pain.

I was desperate to show her I'd never leave her. Not ever again.

Shea was still wearing those satin pajamas, and I couldn't get through the buttons of the long-sleeved blouse fast enough. I pushed the fabric off her slender shoulders, letting my hands explore the expanse of soft skin as I dragged it down her back.

Hair tangled and wild, wild, wild. Her expression was just as desperate as the heat of her hands that yanked at my shirt and tore it over my head.

Hot palms pressed to my bare chest.

"You're beautiful, Sebastian." She felt along my shoulders. "My beautiful, beautiful man."

"Baby," I whispered, kissing her more. My teeth tugged at her bottom lip, then I set it free with a little pop, before I kissed her hard at the corner of her mouth. I didn't slow down, just dove down to her chin, forcing it up as I went to work on the delicate slope of her neck.

Her fingers dug into my shoulders as she leaned back, keeping herself from falling as I kissed a path down her chest that heaved with every erratic beat of her heart.

Those perfect tits begged, nipples pink and pebbled tight.

I flattened my tongue across one.

So fucking sweet.

I drew it into my mouth.

"Sebastian."

I cupped the back of her neck, forcing her to look down at me.

"Sweet girl, I'm gonna take care of you."

In every way.

"Stand up," I commanded. She kept her hands braced on my shoulders as she slowly pushed to her feet. She was bent at the waist, her face hovering a foot above mine.

The tether that tied us together stretched taut.

Slowly, I dragged her pajama shorts and the lace hidden underneath down those long, long legs.

"Shit," I hissed, watching the action as I revealed every delicious inch of this girl.

She was a vision.

Salvation.

A deliverance from my own personal hell.

Fire and light.

Shea stepped out of them, and I tossed them aside. Never letting go of my shoulders, she stared down at me, my head kicked back against the side of the bed.

I rushed through the buttons on my fly, toeing off my boots in the same second I pushed down my jeans and underwear.

My cock sprang free, and I shrugged my jeans the rest of the way off my legs.

That energy was glowing bright, this girl commanding every last one of my senses.

"Make me crazy, baby."

Shea slowly dropped back down onto her knees, but those hands never let me go.

She swayed forward, and the inside of her thighs brushed my ribs.

I jerked.

"I need you," she said.

And I totally fucking got it. Truth was, I needed her too.

"You have me."

Her tongue swept along her bottom lip, and she sucked in a shaky breath as she eased back a fraction and wrapped her hand around my cock.

Our eyes locked as she slowly lowered herself on my length.

Fuck.

For the flash of a moment, I buried my face in her neck to cover my groan.

One touch.

One touch and my *body* was shaking like a teenager. But my soul had arrived somewhere far in the distance, in a future I'd never imagined.

Where this girl was always going to belong to me.

I took her by the hips.

Guiding her as she began to move.

Sliding sure up and down my dick.

A whimper fell from her when she edged back, our focus going to where we were connected.

My cock slick with her arousal.

Bare skin.

Perfect pussy.

She took me whole again and again.

"Shea." I wound a fist in her hair. I tugged hard and nipped at her chin.

With both hands, she returned it with a fierce tug of her own.

My scalp prickled with tiny spikes of exquisite pain. They skimmed down my spine, gathering low where a knot of pleasure built fast.

Quickly, I shifted, needing control. I held her around the waist as I shifted, crawling to my knees and taking Shea with me.

I laid her on the rug and I found myself wrapped up in miles of perfect legs as she locked herself around my waist. Fingertips dug into my back.

Pushing up on one hand, I looked down on the girl who'd shattered my world. Caramel eyes, dark and deep, and so fucking sweet.

"Don't let go," I warned, the demand gruff as I pulled out, the wide ridge of my head just barely hanging on. Then I slammed back home.

Shea cried out as her walls gripped me tight.

"Fuck…baby."

I pulled in a breath, trying to keep my shit together. A furor of energy lifted high, dipping low, saturating our skin in sweat. Pulsing and pressing, a force neither of us stood a chance to resist.

And I knew if I ever lost her I'd no longer know how to survive.

I moved in her.

With her.

Neither of us gentle.

Every touch rough, every thrust and bow of our bodies sharp and severe.

I slipped a hand between us and began to work Shea's clit.

And I could feel it, the way every inch of her tightened, how she started to glow.

Heat covered us, ripples of energy, this girl a summer storm.

Fierce and turbulent and beautiful.

"Come, sweet girl," I whispered, when I felt her hanging on, like maybe she didn't know how to let go. I increased the pressure, increased my pace.

She was staring at me when she came undone.

Splintering.

Her focus went hazy, as if she were floating with the stars.

She took me right along with her.

We stayed there for the longest time.

Elevated.

Absent.

Present only to each other.

Finally, I slumped down on top of her. I propped my weight on the bend of my knee and an elbow so I didn't crush her. I pushed back the mounds of her mussed hair, just needing to see her.

This girl who was so gorgeous and broken and scared.

The woman who'd become my responsibility.

My future.

Because I'd be damned if I remained a prisoner to my past.

One I'd never walk away from again.

I loved Shea Bentley and she loved me.

It's where it started and where it ended.

Nothing before or after or in between mattered.

"Do you think this is wrong?" Shea's muted voice broke into the heavy silence.

Where we lay under the covers in her bed, I pulled her closer. She curled her back into the den of my chest. "What?" I asked.

The house was quiet and the hour was late. Darkness clung to most of her bedroom. Only slivers of moonlight slanted in from the window.

"Me being here, finding comfort in your arms, when Kallie is alone."

My heavy exhale scattered the hair on her shoulder. I understood her guilt, but I didn't want her feeling it. "Let me ask you something. If you could be doing absolutely anything right now that would get Kallie home sooner, would you be doing it?"

"Of course," she answered without hesitation.

I pressed a tender kiss behind her ear. "Then I think you already know the answer to that."

Shea pulled in a shaky breath. "I hate she's with him and has no idea what's happening." The air hitched in her throat. "I hate I have no idea what she's going through. What could be happening. Hate I'm lying here, useless to help her. Unable to protect her like I always promised I would."

She shuddered and I held her closer.

"She has no clue who he is, Sebastian. She doesn't even know *about* him. The only thing I've ever told her was she didn't have a daddy. I told her it was just her and me and that was all there was ever going to be." Her voice trembled and rolled. "She has to be so scared."

"I know," I murmured back.

I let myself imagine what Kallie was going through right then. The quiet terror she must be feeling. Let it wreck me a little more, knowing Shea was imagining the same thing.

I played with a long strand of her hair. "I trust in my team, Shea. Anthony and Kenny have always been there for me, and they're going to find a way to set this straight. They've never let me down before and I know they're gonna do everything in their power to fix this. And I'm going to be there every step of the way. Fighting. Giving it my all until that little girl is in your arms. You understand what I'm telling you?"

It meant I wouldn't sleep, wouldn't eat until Kallie was safe.

She choked. "What if he hurts her? What if we're too late?"

"No…he won't. He's not that stupid."

Even with my promise, rage boiled beneath the surface. Ready to be unleashed. Because if he did? That rage would come like a destroyer.

She snuggled a little closer, and her voice clogged with a restrained sob. "It's an awful feeling being so thankful I don't have to go through this alone and knowing Kallie has to."

"No, she's not alone, baby. She feels you right here." I placed my hand over Shea's heart.

Slowly, she rolled over to face me. "Earlier…you said you wanted to claim Kallie as your own." The words became almost urgent. "What did you mean?"

A pensive smile tugged at my mouth. I pulled my head back far enough to allow the subdued moonlight to illuminate Shea's face. "I told you what I see when I look at you. I see a family. Always thought family to me would construe something fucked up and broken…just me and the boys and Austin. But I want it to include you. I want it to include Kallie. When she's sad or scared or just needs someone to tell her she's loved, I want to be that guy."

Something both brilliant and fractured passed through Shea's expression. And I knew she was seeing it. The same thing I saw. And somehow I'd gotten lucky enough that this girl wanted it, too.

Hard thing was, both of us were wondering how the fuck we were gonna get there.

"You know…" My voice was rough. "Earlier tonight I took you bare." I frowned. "Twice now, actually. You want to know the truth of what hit me? I was hoping that maybe…just maybe together you and I were making something beautiful."

Shea jerked back an inch. Bewilderment lit on her face. "You'd want that?"

"I don't know…probably would be a bad fucking idea right about now, but sometime, yeah."

Intense emotion held fast in her eyes. "Since the first night you took me out, I couldn't help but think about experiencing those things with you, Sebastian. A life and a home. A family for Kallie." A somber smile fluttered around her mouth. "You surprise me in really wonderful ways."

"Guess I've been surprising myself a lot lately." Smiling softly, I brushed my thumb along her jaw. "Might have something to do with this amazing girl I met. After she came into my life? Don't recognize myself anymore."

Shea cupped my cheek. Tenderly. Everything written on her face adoring and filled with all the love I didn't think I'd ever deserve. She looked at me that way for the longest time, like I meant something, this girl *seeing* me in a way only she could.

"I'm on the pill," she finally said, obviously needing to set that straight.

I gave a slight nod. "I figured as much. But it doesn't mean the thought wasn't there."

The desire.

"I should've asked you though." Regretfully, I shook my head. "That's something I should have talked with you about first, and I'm sorry I let myself get lost in the moment."

I caught her around the wrist of the hand she had on my face, shifted forward, and pressed a kiss to the inside of her elbow.

"You know I'd never purposefully put you at risk," I murmured into the soft skin, and I wrapped her arm around my neck so I could get closer.

All the possible consequences and scenarios I'd allowed my own needs and wants to obscure. But I guess I wasn't coming close to thinking of it as a *consequence*. But instead something good and pure—a kind of gift I never thought I wanted until all of a sudden *it* was there—something profound inside me aching to be filled with every part of Shea.

"I would have stopped you if I was worried. If I didn't trust you," she whispered. "I know you wouldn't hurt me."

"You put so much faith in me."

"Yes," she said simply.

Affection tightened my chest.

"We're going to figure this out," I promised. "We're going to send Jennings straight to hell and then I'm gonna pack you and Kallie up and take you around the world. We're going to show Kallie all of it, and you and I are gonna make love in every country we step foot in. And at night? I'm going to be singing about it… about what you do to me and how you make me feel."

I knew I was dreaming, doing what I could to fill Shea with hope for an escape from this hell.

Eyes shimmering, she choked over the emotion in her throat. Still, she played right along. "It seems like Kallie and I might cramp your style."

I grinned at her, needing to lift her spirit. Our chins touched as I smiled at my girl. "Got a new style, baby."

Shea tightened her hold. "Is that so? And what is this world you're going to be singing about me to going to say?"

"I'm sure they're going to be saying all kinds of things. But I don't give a shit, Shea." My tone grew serious. "Tomorrow they're gonna know what you and Kallie mean to me. They're going to know I will be fighting for you both, and I won't be backing down."

"I'm so scared, Baz," Shea quietly admitted as her mouth quivered with another round of sorrow.

"I know, baby. I'm scared, too."

Yeah, I wanted to fill Shea with hope. But I figured honesty mattered, too.

"I can't believe he has her." She said it so softly, I barely heard her. Misery seemed to steal her breath. "What kind of a monster would come in and rip a little girl from her home? I think somewhere inside me, I had hoped he had changed."

All the questions I wanted to ask Shea about how she was tied to Martin Jennings bubbled to the surface, forced up by the seething anger burning in my veins at the thought of the two of them together.

I started slow, a little bit of awe weaving into my words. "You're Delaney Rhoads."

"No." The word flew free with vehemence. "Martin Jennings made Delaney Rhoads. I never wanted to be her, Sebastian. Yes, I love to sing...love to play...but never at the cost of being *her*. I've spent so much time pretending she didn't exist. Please believe me. I never meant it to hurt you. But I've never told *anyone* about it. Charlie and April are the only ones who know because they helped me through that time. All of us have pretended she didn't exist...that Martin didn't exist...since the moment I returned to Savannah."

Shea hesitated, then continued, "You can imagine now why finding out who you were affected me so much. I'd had that lifestyle and I wanted as far away from it as possible. But in the end, what I really wanted was you."

She gave me a wobbly smile. "Wanted you to love me and hold me, and all of a sudden none of that other stuff mattered. All that mattered was you. I was ready to let you in, the first person I'd *ever* told the truth to. The first person I *trusted*. I wanted you to know it...to share it with me...to understand, because I was pretty sure there was no other person in the world who would understand it better than you."

Her face pinched. "But you ran...and...and you broke me. I've never hurt more than that night until..."

She trailed off. It was as if I could hear what she thought. Her daughter's sweet voice echoing through my mind, mixing with the brutal agony of her cries as she'd begged for her mommy when Martin ripped her away so violently.

Begging for someone to save her when we'd been completely helpless. Hands tied. Knowing using them would only make it worse.

"Until tonight," I finished for her.

"Until tonight," she agreed. "I knew before we went public, you had to know, and I was ready. Tonight…what we shared…"

Meeting my eye, she reached out and brushed trembling fingertips down my jaw. My eyes dropped closed as I let myself lean into the promise of her touch.

Her voice was a soft rasp. "I knew you would forgive me for keeping this from you. I knew you would accept me because I knew you'd always seen me the same way I see you. We see *this*."

Pulling back, she placed her hand over her heart, like she was begging me to understand our hearts were the only things that mattered.

I hooked a finger under her chin, lifting her face to me. The words grated from my throat. "How's it possible to love someone so fucking much and not know the first thing about their past?"

No doubt it sounded like a concession.

Like surrender.

Because neither of us were immune to *this*, this strange connection that billowed between us. What tied us together when neither of us knew the paths that had brought us to this place.

This place where it was *us*.

"Remember when I told you I didn't even know you but you felt like one of the most significant people to have ever come into my life?" she asked.

"Yeah."

"Maybe there was a reason neither of us could let this go."

I moved to hold that sweet face between my hands. "I'd do anything for you, Shea. Give up anything…" My hold tightened in emphasis. "Give up *everything* if it means we get that little girl back."

I finally let myself ask one question that'd been nagging me. "Why'd you quit?"

Shea paled, and she spoke softly. Sadly. "My entire childhood was spent priming me for one singular goal. I spent my days in endless lessons and chasing countless auditions. My momma was going to make me a *star*."

Sarcasm dripped from the word.

"That's the only thing she wanted. The only thing she could see. It got to the point where I knew she didn't care how she made that happen, just as long as it did. All those years, my mother had worked her magic with manipulative words, getting me in front of anyone in the industry who would give me the time of day."

She winced. "When Martin came into our lives, she allowed him to take over everything. Including me. He…he…"

If it were possible, her voice got rougher, dipped into fear. "He controlled everything."

She wavered. Like she needed to decide how much she should say. How much I could tolerate.

"Let's just say Kallie didn't fit into that picture. So I ran."

Guess the girl knew I couldn't tolerate much. Just that bit of history hit me with yet another urge to jump from this bed and hunt the fucker down. That urge was almost irresistible.

She shook her head like she was shaking off the memories then tipped her chin back up to focus on me. "How did you get messed up with him?"

I almost laughed. It was definitely a *mess*.

I played with a few strands of her hair. "I knew the second I met Martin Jennings he was nothin' but a snake, but at the time, none of us cared. The only thing that mattered to the guys and me was *Sunder* making it big. We didn't give a shit about how we made that happen. Anthony had hooked us up, asked him to come check us out at a bar we were playing at. Jennings made us big promises we were quick to jump on. It became clear real fast the guy had his fingers dipped in all kinds of illegal shit—"

With that tidbit of information, her bottom lip trembled. More fucking worry added to this unbearable torment. With my thumb, I smoothed it out, hating dragging all this out into the open. Ripping Shea's wounds open wider. But we didn't have a whole lot of options.

Not if we were going to start being honest with each other.

No more secrets and lies.

"But it wasn't so far off base from what my crew had going down, so I didn't exactly think we had any right to judge. Even though I'd gotten clean, it didn't mean the rest of the guys had. You know what I mean?"

Shea nodded like it hurt.

"It all came to a head a few months ago when Austin overdosed. There was no question in my mind Jennings somehow had a hand in it. I saw him coming out of our tour bus that night. But Austin wouldn't fess up, so I'd gone to Jennings's place and confronted him. While he never admitted involvement, he basically told me my brother was nothing but a punk and the world would be a better place without him in it. I lost it, Shea. Fucking lost it and now he looks like the good guy who was attacked by some deranged delinquent out for blood."

I pressed on with my explanation, doing all I could not to spit the words. "We were supposed to come to some kind of bullshit terms. My attorneys thought I could pay off the asshole, he would dismiss the charges, and I'd get a lesser sentence…fines and community service or some shit like that. But the bastard hates me as much as I hate him. Things escalated at the mediation we had last week and there was no keeping my hands off him. He warned me I'd regret fucking with him."

At the time, I'd wanted to laugh in his face and just beg him to bring it on, that any consequence I had to pay would be well worth it.

Now I knew that debt was too steep.

Not if Kallie was the cost.

Guess I'd thought I couldn't hate him more until I saw that pompous ass driving off with her. Stealing that baby girl from her mother.

From her home.

From me.

"He was after revenge tonight," I confessed. The words were so choppy they vibrated in my chest.

"On both of us," Shea said.

"That douchebag is nothing but a narcissist. Can't believe he'd use a little girl as retaliation. Fuck him," I gritted out, my rage threatening to boil.

Shea blinked slowly, like she didn't want to hear her own words. "He's a sociopath." Her voice grew desperately quiet. "A psychopath."

I pushed up onto my elbow so I could see her better, and Shea rolled onto her back. Her face pinched up in pain as if fighting whatever she was feeling inside.

"Tell me." I couldn't stop the same earlier demand from leaving my mouth.

"I'm not ready."

This was what was haunting me most. What was written all over Shea. Her outright fear of the man I hated most and the possibilities of what had put it there.

"Know you told me you weren't ready to give me details, but, baby…just…just tell me one thing. Did he hurt you?"

Everything shook—my spirit and my body and my words.

She squeezed her eyes closed. A thousand shadows played across her features. A horror of memories. A nightmare that had been her past.

I saw all of it there, marring that gorgeous face.

The rage I'd been fighting took hold.

My hands curled into fists as I watched tears seep free at the corners of her eyes. They raced into her hair.

Shea nodded tight, as if it could block what should never have to be remembered.

Or maybe she was just passing them on to me. Because my mind seethed with them. With the idea of Jennings hurting my girl.

I'd seen it.

Witnessed it.

The malice in his eyes.

The greed fed by something vile.

An unknown fury slammed me.

I'd kill him. If he hurt either one of them again, I'd kill him. This time there'd be no one there to stop me.

Slowly, Shea opened to me, staring up at me while I stared down at her. I felt as if I were coming unhinged, coming apart, torn between bolting from this bed and tracking Jennings down and forcing myself to stay here with her wrapped in my arms.

I knew if I succumbed to the first, it would be the end of me and Shea. I'd lose her forever because there wasn't enough money in the world to keep them from locking me up and throwing away the goddamned key.

Every part of me rejected that idea while all of those same pieces knew any sacrifice would be worth keeping them safe.

Shea fluttered her fingertips over the scar cut deep into my ribs.

Another battle I'd fought for my family.

A lash I'd been happy to take.

In her touch, I felt as if she were tying herself to me. Telling me to stay. The girl saw right through me to that place where the truth of who I really was reigned. She knew what I'd be willing to do.

What I was capable of.

She was keeping something from me not because she wanted to hide it. But because she wanted to protect me.

Observant eyes searched mine with both hope and dread, as they trailed down to where the memory of Julian had been permanently etched onto my side.

"We're so much alike, Sebastian. You just wear all your scars here. On the outside."

I shivered, so fucking transparent beneath the weight of her gaze.

She tugged at my hand and placed my palm flat over the quickened beat of her heart. "While I keep all of mine here."

My spirit thrashed, and I sank down lower, whispering a hair's breadth from that soft, soft mouth. "One day, I need you to show me. All of it."

"I know," she breathed.

Slowly, she rolled to her side, and I curled around her back. Shea nestled her head into the crook of my shoulder and I wrapped my arms around her. Covering her. Protecting her.

"Hold onto me," I demanded.

"Don't let me go."

"Never."

Silence enveloped us, the darkness alive with our turmoil.

There'd be no sleep tonight.

When Shea began to quietly sing, I clutched her to me.

I strained to make out the words that passed languidly between her lips, a tickle to my ears, something like heaven and honey and all things sweet.

So, so sweet.

My heart clenched as I swam in the power of the words.

She was singing *Lullaby* by The Dixie Chicks.

I only knew it because my mom had loved the record it was on. She had listened to it constantly before everything had gone to shit—before my family had lost it all.

As I held on to Shea and listened to her pour the words out into the night—like mourning, like praise—I had the intense urge to weep.

Instead, I buried that feeling with my rage, made it count, added it to the debt Martin Jennings was going to pay.

But Shea?

Shea wept.

Wept unlike anything I'd heard since my mother had wept when the sea stole Julian.

A mother's pain.

A torment I'd prayed I'd never hear again.

And I just held her. Held her and held her and made a million silent promises that I'd never let her go.

"I sang that to Kallie every single night. I don't ever want to stop," she finally managed to whisper before she slipped back into silence.

Long moments passed with just the sound of our breaths, before I pressed a soothing kiss to the top of her head. "Tell me a story, Shea from Savannah."

She stumbled over a soggy laugh, and pulled my arms tighter around her. "What kind of story do you want to hear, Sebastian from California?"

"I want to know who taught you to sing."

five
Shea

Six years old

HEAT PERMEATED THE SMALL church. It was stuffed full of people and Shea was all dressed up, wearing a frilly white dress and white patent-leather shoes. A matching ribbon was tied in her curly hair. Little pebbles of sweat beaded at the base of her neck.

But Shea didn't mind.

Her grandma squeezed her hand where she stood beside her in the pew, and Shea began to sing with the choir.

Amazing Grace,
How sweet the sound
That saved a wretch like me.

Her grandma had taught her how to play it on the piano, had taught her all the words, and it felt like *their* song. Somehow, standing there in church singing it beside her grandma, Shea got the feeling she was doing something really, really important.

I once was lost, but now am found,
Was blind,
But now I see.

Pride filled her as she let the words free.

Drowning to Breathe

Let them float, high and lifted up.

Just like her grandma had taught her to do.

Her grandma was always telling her she had the prettiest voice she'd ever heard. Just like a morning bird, she'd say. She told Shea that God had given it to her as a gift, and nothing pleased Him more than hearing it used to praise His name.

So Shea sang her praise, thanking God she got to be right there, because Shea's favorite places were the ones where she got to be with her grandma.

After they finished singing, the pastor said a prayer before ending the service.

Shea was sure her grandma had to know just about every person who lived in Savannah, because countless people stopped them to say their goodbyes as they made their way out of the busy church.

"Look at you, precious girl," her grandma's friend said. "I could hear you singing all the way across the sanctuary. Just like an angel."

Shea felt the blush rush to her cheeks. She swayed softly as she held onto her grandma's weathered hand. She whispered, "Thank you, ma'am," because her grandma taught her to do that, too.

"We'd better get you home," her grandma said, excusing them from the little group congregating around them. She helped Shea slide into the worn leather backseat of her car, pressed a kiss to her forehead as she helped her buckle in, then smiled down at Shea.

The wrinkles crisscrossing on her face got deeper and deeper the bigger she smiled, and Shea smiled right back.

A map.

All those lines on Kalliana Whitmore's face made up the map of the life her grandma had lived.

At least, that's what she told Shea.

Shea wasn't exactly sure what that meant, but sometimes when she traced the lines on her face right before she fell asleep at night—when she got to spend the night at her house—her grandma would tell her the best stories about how she got those lines. Those stories made her laugh and smile. Sometimes they made her sad, too, but no matter what, they were her favorite.

She promised Shea one day she'd have all her own stories that would line her own face. That was the best part.

Shea couldn't wait.

Her grandma climbed into the driver's seat and started the car.

"Take me to your house, Gramma," she begged through a toothy grin. Her grandma's house was her favorite place in the whole wide world.

"Not today, sweet girl. I have to get you home. Your mother has big plans for you this week."

Shea frowned, but didn't say anything while her Grandma drove them across town and pulled to a stop in front of the small blue house where Shea lived with her momma and daddy.

For some reason, though, her daddy hadn't been around all that much lately.

Her grandma shut off the car and got out, held open the back door, and Shea scrambled out. Shea took off up the sidewalk and up the two concrete steps, hoping her momma was happy today.

Hoping to see her smile.

Her momma was so, so pretty. Shea was going to be just like her one day.

Shea burst through the front door. "I'm home!" she called.

Her grandma emerged behind her. She handed her the small bag Shea packed when she went to spend the night at her house. "Go on and put your stuff away in your room."

"Okay." Shea grinned and ran down the hall, tossed the bag on her floor, and flew right back out.

Though she slowed when she heard the voices in the kitchen.

Those voices were upset and low.

Shea slinked quietly across the living room and pressed her

back against the wall close to the kitchen, wondering why her gramma and momma were so mad.

"You can't go putting your dreams on the shoulders of your daughter. She's too young for you to be pushing her into all that mess."

Her mother huffed, and Shea could hear things banging around in the kitchen, like her momma was angry and just needed to throw something.

"She's the one who *ruined* those dreams."

"You're going to blame a child for you not making it? That has to be the most selfish thing to ever come out of your mouth, Chloe Lynn. It wasn't her fault you went and got yourself knocked up doing anything you could to get your foot in the door."

Her mother's voice dropped real deep. Angry. Angry. Angry. "Don't you dare," her mother seethed.

Shea pressed her hands to her ears and wished she could drown it out.

But their words were still there.

"Then don't you dare treat that little girl as anything less than the gift she is. Maybe God put her with you to keep you from continuing down the destructive path you'd been following for too many years. Maybe it's time you *listened*."

"I'm not a little girl and I definitely don't need to listen to your naggin' anymore. She's my daughter, and I'll damn well do with her as I please."

A beat of silence. In it, Shea's tummy filled with something sour.

Then her grandma's voice got quiet. "Do with her as you please? She's not a possession."

Her momma laughed, but it wasn't a pretty sound. "Really? She belongs to *me*, so I'd say that pretty much sums it up."

Shea pressed herself closer against the wall, wishing she could disappear. She always wanted to make her momma proud, but lately, she always seemed to be so mad.

Her momma said it was Shea's daddy's fault.

Shea sucked in a deep breath and closed her eyes real tight when footsteps creaked across the kitchen floor. She opened them when she couldn't help it any longer, because she felt someone close, and she found her grandma kneeling in front of her.

Her grandma looked sad, and she tilted her head to the side, her voice soft.

"I want you to remember something, sweet girl. You sing when you feel it in here." Her grandma placed her hand over Shea's hammering heart.

"When it feels right and good and makes you happy. Don't ever do it for any other reason."

Then she stood and walked out.

six
Sebastian

DOWNSTAIRS, THE FRONT DOOR rattled. It jarred me from where I'd crawled along the periphery of sleep. Never quite grasping it. Hovering somewhere between reality and a dream. A dream where I'd been haunted by a little girl with a mane of unruly blonde hair and the voice of an angel.

Couldn't make sense whether it was Kallie calling out for me to save her or if the little girl chasing me in those dreams was the woman who now lay safe in the security of my arms.

Still curled around Shea, I blinked and tried to orient myself to the muted morning light. Last night, neither of us could sleep, so I'd thrown some of Shea's things into a duffle bag and driven her over here to the house on Tybee Island. I'd told her Anthony would be here, and it'd be good for us to be here first thing in the morning so we could get straight to work on getting Kallie back.

But really, I knew Shea couldn't be there in her grandmother's house without Kallie in it. The walls ached with her absence.

Sucking in a breath, I attempted to clear the cloud in my head and the ache clinging to my chest.

Everything inside me demanded I stand up for them.

Stand for them.

It was time.

Careful not to wake her, I untangled myself from her and slipped out of bed. I tucked the covers up over her shoulders.

I pulled on the jeans I'd left discarded on the floor. Tiptoeing as quietly as I could, I edged out the door and softly snapped it shut behind me.

A blaze of reds and oranges lit the horizon where the sun climbed up from the edge of the ocean, the emerging day stretching its fingers through the wall of windows that took up the back of Anthony's beach house.

And I knew it'd be Anthony's arrival that had pulled me from my shallow sleep.

I ambled downstairs, trying to rub some of the exhaustion from my eyes. I hit the landing and rounded through the living room to the open kitchen.

In a suit, Anthony stood facing away at the far kitchen counter. He fumbled with the buttons of the Keurig machine as if his life depended on the brew.

Taking in a deep breath, I pressed my hands onto the top of the island separating us.

Had no idea what to expect from my agent and friend.

No doubt, this shit had to be getting old.

Dragging my ass out of every disaster I got myself into.

Taking flights clear across the country in the middle of the night.

Still, he did it time and time again.

When he felt my presence, Anthony looked over his shoulder. "Baz."

It sounded weary. Just about as weary as the expression on his face.

I forced a grin, needing to break up some of the tension clogging the air. "You look like shit, man."

Shooting me a smirk, he turned around to lean up against the counter. "And I wonder why that might be?" he drew out, all sorts of incredulous.

With my palms still pressed to the counter, I gave him a shrug. "Dunno. Could have something to do with the fact one of your asshole clients once again got himself in deep and you had to pack it up and race halfway around the world to dig him out of it."

Although maybe this time…

Maybe this time getting myself in deep was exactly where I was supposed to be.

A short chuckle rumbled from him. "Could have something to do with that."

Anthony sighed like he knew it was time to toss off the lightness passing between us, because fucking around wasn't going to get Kallie back. He focused on pouring a shit-ton of sugar into his coffee and dousing it with cream.

"Thanks for being here," I muttered honestly.

"It's my job," he said like there weren't a whole lot of other options, but then he looked at me seriously as he took a tentative sip of his coffee, his tone changing. "And I want to be here. You know I'm not going to leave you high and dry in the middle of this."

"I know. You know how much I appreciate you being here, don't you? I don't *expect* any of this from you."

Yet, he was always willing.

There as a friend.

"Of course I know that." He pushed out a strained breath and set his coffee aside. "This is messy, Baz."

"You think I don't know that?" It came out sounding more bitter than intended.

But fuck, this was a disaster.

Like he was searching for an answer or maybe restraint, he looked to the ceiling, before he dropped his attention back to me, gaze penetrating.

"You have to be straight up with me, Baz. Did you know Jennings was Kallie's father? The press is all over this shit this morning."

Just the thought of Kallie belonging to that piece of shit spiked my pulse.

"No. Not until CPS showed up and handed her over to him last night."

Glancing at his feet, he shook his head as his tone filled with disbelief. "So you're telling me you've been seeing this girl for what…close to two months…and you never thought to ask her who the baby's daddy was?"

He kept right on talking as he began to pace, like each step would help make each piece in this fucked-up situation add up.

"One minute you tell me you're back in California permanently because you can't stay in Savannah for a second longer…during which time you're acting like a fucking bear because you're so miserable. Next thing I know, you're packing the band up again and heading back here because of a girl I know nothing about."

He paused and pinned me with his stare. "Which is all fine. I've already made it clear I want that for you. But I didn't even know there was a kid involved until my phone started ringing off the hook at 4:00 a.m. yesterday about the pictures on the beach that had hit the tabloids. Then last night?" The words dropped flat.

He huffed in frustration. "Every time I turn around, I'm blindsided by something else involving you, Baz. I can't keep up. How am I supposed to protect you and this band if I don't have the first clue what's going on?"

There was no missing the edge biting his words.

Anthony knew next to nothing when it came to Shea. Guess it was no surprise considering Shea and I were just finally breaking down the walls that'd kept us separated.

Exposing us.

Even though Shea was right.

We knew everything that mattered.

I swallowed hard. I knew how this was going to sound. Anthony didn't understand Shea the way I did, and I knew this sounded fucking *bad*. I had to push the words out. "She told me Kallie's father was dead."

Anthony blinked back at me in a *you've got to be kidding me* way.

I inhaled, doing my best not to get all pissy with him, because not one goddamned part of this situation was his fault.

"Look…things were complicated between me and Shea. Neither of us were looking to start something up."

I gestured between the ceiling and myself. "We never expected *this*, and we both went into this the wrong way, thinking things were only going to be temporary, so we didn't get into all the shit complicating our lives."

Both of us desperate to feel something good.

I'd thought all I wanted was for that gorgeous girl to make me forget…just for a little while.

Little did we know how our lives were getting ready to be ripped up and reshaped.

"She and I have both been keeping enough secrets to sink a ship. This lands on both of us. She only just found out who I really am the night before I ran back to California the week before last…"

We all knew how that ended.

When I remembered the blow I'd received last night, my throat grew thick. "It was only last night I found out she was Delaney Rhoads."

My brow twisted with all the restraint it took to admit this aloud. "Found out Jennings was Kallie's father in the same damn second."

"God," he swore below his breath, rubbing his index finger

back and forth over his top lip.

"You can't put any blame on Shea for this, Anthony. She did it because she was protecting her little girl. Trying to survive and live a normal life. I promise you, there was zero malicious intent behind it."

Questions took hold of the silence.

Another shock of realization slammed my mind, and I finally muttered, "All of this can't be a coincidence."

A heavy sigh blew from him, and he raked a flustered hand through his hair. "No, Baz, you're right. It's not a fucking coincidence."

My stomach churned with nausea, and I clenched my fists on the counter.

Waiting.

Feeling it coming—the need to tear something or someone apart.

He looked me square in the face. "I had no idea who your girl was, Baz. But yesterday morning when we got the pics, I couldn't shake the feeling she looked familiar. About halfway through the day, it finally dawned on me she was Delaney Rhoads. I was tied up in knots wondering if she was playing you…stringing you along as a way to get back into the business, wondering how in the hell I was going to break it to you because I knew how messed up you were over her."

"What?" I gripped my hair. "Fuck…no, Anthony. It's not anything like that. She doesn't want anyone to know who she is."

Relief slid across his features, but his words were filled with speculation. "Are you sure you really know this girl? You really trust her?"

Anger surged at the insinuation, but I curbed it. Anthony was only looking out for the band. Looking out for me. I knew that well enough. Just like I knew Shea.

"Yes," I said without an ounce of hesitation.

Anthony chewed at his lip.

"Tell me." I'd known him long enough to know when he was holding back.

Regret radiated from him as he began to speak. "I first stumbled upon *Charlie's* years ago, back when Angie and I first bought this house. Charlie was a cool guy, plus I was still looking for clients back then, so I made it a habit of going whenever I knew there would be a new band playing."

Clearly uncomfortable, he cleared his throat, sending a round of agitation curling through me.

"This woman…she was always hanging out there with the bands. Gorgeous, but she gave off the vibe she was looking for someone to sink her claws into. At first I thought she was some kind of groupie. You know the type, desperate for any kind of attention, any kind of fame, even if it meant she was getting it from the small, unknown bands playing there. I think it was probably the third time I saw her when Charlie finally introduced her as his sister."

Shit.

I rubbed my hand across my mouth as if it could wipe away the bitter taste.

Shea's mom.

Someone I knew absolutely nothing about.

Shea never talked about her. The mystery surrounding her another fucking secret.

All I had were the hints and innuendos Shea had alluded to last night, and this story didn't do anything to quell the flickers of hate igniting for a woman I'd never even met.

Anthony continued, "There didn't seem to be a whole lot of love lost between her and Charlie, but still, she and I chatted over the next couple times I ran into her, even though I remained leery.

I didn't want to give her the wrong impression, because I definitely wasn't out looking for someone to step out on my Angie with."

He hesitated, then shook his head as he lowered his voice. "She wasn't looking for sex, Baz. She was looking for a way to get her daughter's foot in the door. The first couple of times she talked about her, I humored her. Talked with her a little about the business. But I didn't give it a whole lot of thought. One night she convinced me to listen to a demo. The girl's voice on the recording was...unbelievable. There's no other way to describe it. I would have snatched her up in a heartbeat, but Chloe was already acting as her agent."

"Chloe?" I asked.

"Charlie's sister...Delaney Rhoads's mother. Shea's mother," he amended a bit quieter, like he was catching on to how little I really knew about Shea.

I bit back the hostile laughter that worked its way up.

Nice.

They were on a first-name basis.

He shrugged, though it was laced with remorse. "I figured, what the hell could it hurt? I never wanted to be one of those guys who only did things to benefit himself, so I sent her to Jennings. That was right when I first began working with him. Back before I knew the kind of trash he was."

His sigh was heavy with implication. "That was only a year before I sent Jennings to the bar to check you and the guys out."

With both hands, I palmed the back of my head, trying to beat back the anxiety clamoring through my insides.

Eating me up.

God.

Anthony di Pietro, my agent, but more than that, a friend, a guy I considered an honorary member in my fucked-up family, was the tie.

Of course, I knew it was Anthony who'd sent Jennings to check out *Sunder* that night we were playing in Tennessee. That was no secret. How many times had Anthony vocalized his regret? Wondering if we'd have been better off if he'd never sent Jennings our way?

But none of us could have foreseen the trouble he would bring.

"The word was, Delaney Rhoads couldn't cope with the stardom, and she'd tucked tail and ran back home. Sure, there were rumors circulating about an affair between Jennings and the emerging star, but we learn fast in this industry to ignore all of that unless it's something that affects one of our clients directly. Most of it's all bullshit, anyway. You know this well enough, Baz. I had no clue Delaney Rhoads even had a kid. She disappeared off the face of the earth. Forgotten in days. I never thought to ask Jennings about what had happened to her. I wasn't representing her.

He shook his head. "Hell, I'd never even met her. Initially, I did it thinking it was a favor to Charlie. In all the times I went back over the years, Charlie never once mentioned his niece had moved back there or that she was working in his bar."

He shrugged. "It never crossed my mind."

Of course Charlie never mentioned her.

Secrets.

Secrets.

Secrets.

Secrets meant to protect and defend, yet here they were, threatening to ruin everything.

"I'm sorry, Baz. When I suggested you go to *Charlie's*, I never imagined something I set in motion years ago could possibly affect you now."

Yeah, I was pissed. Some kind of unknown hurt wound through me as I came to understand how this web had been spun together.

Shea and I unwittingly tied to the bastard who wanted to destroy both our lives.

But how could I regret it?

Because that would have meant never losing control with Shea.

And never losing control with her just wasn't an option I could entertain.

I pressed the heels of my hands into my eyes. "What the hell are we going to do? He was here because of me, Anthony. He looked me straight in the eye when he took Kallie and reminded me I was going to regret fucking with him."

A wave of helplessness washed over me, and that was not a feeling I took kindly to. How the hell did you fix something when you had no clue what went down in the first place?

Anthony gave a quick nod. "The second you mentioned his name when you called me, I had no doubt the asshole had ulterior motives."

He always did.

But I knew it went deeper than that. This muddled maze was more than just about *me*. He'd hurt her, and clearly he was aiming to hurt her again. But why? To get back at me? That's what made no fucking sense.

"Shea's terrified for Kallie." The words cracked on my own fear. Because the truth was? I was, too. "We can't just leave her with him."

Sympathy filled his eyes. "I get that, Baz. You know I'd throw myself on a bomb for my own kids. No, I don't know Shea, but I can only imagine the hell she's going through right now. But the one plus in this whole thing is I don't think Jennings is witless enough to hurt a little girl who's recently been placed in his care. He's always meticulous. Covering his ass and letting everyone else take the fall."

I pressed my hands to the counter and blew out a breath. "Yeah...thought as much myself. He's devious, but not a fool."

His tone grew cautious. "You have to ask yourself how far

you're willing to get involved in this. Every time we turn around, this mess gets deeper and deeper."

I gave one fierce shake of my head, cutting that shit off. I knew he meant well, that his intentions were always good. Anthony taking up our backs to protect the guys and me.

But this was one truth he needed to understand. "I'd give up anything for them. All of it. Every last cent to my name. My freedom. My life if that's what it takes."

Silence hung heavy in the air as he stared across at me. Searching for sincerity. Then a satisfied smile pulled at his mouth. "So she's it, then."

That affirmation struck home.

Taking hold.

Filling me full.

My voice was rough. "Yeah. She's it."

He nodded like the game had changed. "All right, then. You're going to need to make a statement. The paps are going to be hounding you as it is. Better to clear this up now and let them know exactly where you stand."

"I stand by Shea."

A smirk ticked up at one side of his mouth. "I think you've made that abundantly clear, my friend."

I started to laugh, when all the air got sucked from the room. Heavy and soft and blinding light.

My spine stiffened in awareness as the girl stole a little more of my breath.

Filled me right up with hers.

Slowly, I turned to look over my shoulder.

Standing near the wall, Shea peered over at us.

Eyes brimming with fear and hope and love.

So fucking gorgeous that this girl once again threatened to drop me straight to my knees.

I tipped my head to the side and beckoned her forward. "Come here, baby."

Warily, she glanced at Anthony, and I wondered just how much she'd picked up of our conversation, before she shuffled forward and nestled into the safety of my side. I curled my arm low around her back and pulled her as close as I could get her.

Anthony's attention jumped between us.

"Anthony, this is my girl, Shea Bentley."

I leaned down and kissed her temple, whispering at the sweetness of her skin, "Baby, this is Anthony Di Pietro. My agent and friend. He's going to help us get Kallie back."

An expression of understanding crossed his face. Lacking judgment. Like he saw all the torment swimming in Shea's eyes.

He moved around the island and extended his hand as he neared. "Shea Bentley. If it isn't an honor to meet the woman who finally took this one down."

He cast me a sly glance then smiled softly at her.

Redness warmed Shea's cheeks, Anthony easily putting her at ease when he wrapped up her hand in his.

"It's great to meet you, Anthony," Shea said, all genuine and real, real, real, returning his handshake. "Thank you for everything you've done to help us. You can't imagine what it means to me."

Everything about him turned warm, like maybe in the course of their brief interaction, Anthony witnessed it, too. The beauty and life. Something pure in her shining light on this wicked world.

"Of course. I wouldn't have it any other way."

"How are you this morning?" I murmured.

A weak smile lifted just one side as she looked up at me, her voice hoarse from the many tears she'd shed last night. "As well as can be expected. I'm just ready to get started on whatever we need to do to get her back."

Anthony nodded reassuringly. "We have a meeting with the attorney at nine. Kenny assured me he is the best family attorney in Savannah. We'll be on this first thing and we won't stop until Kallie is back safely in your arms."

"Damn right, we won't."

Shea and I both jerked our heads to find the source of the voice coming from behind us.

Ash.

He slanted a cocky grin Shea's way, dude all dimples and rumpled blond hair.

Lyrik and Zee bounded downstairs behind him, Lyrik dragging a shirt over the mess of black on his head, Zee watching with the unique concern that followed him wherever he went.

Didn't miss that my baby brother edged down the stairs, too. Lagging. Slower than the rest. Wearing that same damned hoodie like maybe he was pretending he could hide away.

Still, he was here. Present.

A partner to my fucked-up family.

Anthony's eyes widened in surprise. "Uh, you guys do realize it's not even seven in the morning? Don't think I've seen any of you even cracking open an eye before noon in all the years I've known you."

Ash just grinned. "No chance in hell we're going to sleep away the day when we have business to take care of. And by business, I mean taking that motherfucker Jennings down. We were all there and know exactly what went down that day. Not about to stand for that kind of bullshit."

Zee came forward and leaned his forearms on the island. He clasped his hands together as he looked up at us. "Yeah, man. You know whatever we can do...whatever we can say...we'll be there. We know where Kallie belongs."

Shea drew in a sharp breath, like she was gaining strength from their encouragement, each word building a steel armor of courage.

Lyrik lifted his chin toward Ash and Zee as he rolled into the kitchen to grab a cup of coffee. "Like they said, whatever you need, it's done."

Silently, Austin made his way in, too, surrounding us like the rest. He seemed agitated, which wasn't abnormal for him. But still, he cast me a look like he was telling me it was a good damned thing I'd finally come to my senses.

That walking away from Shea wasn't ever gonna be the noble choice.

Not when this girl needed me.

Ash hooked his arm around Shea's neck and dropped a swift kiss to her head. "See. You don't have to worry about a thing, darlin'. We've got this covered."

"Thank you," she said on a broken breath.

"Watch it, man," I warned, letting a chuckle slide. "That's my girl you're kissing on."

Ash smirked. "What? Good friends share and all of that."

I reached around Shea and punched at his shoulder. "Not on your life, asshole."

A giggle slipped from Shea, all self-conscious and shy and every shade of perfect, and those expressive eyes peeked up at me, swimming with faith, hope, and beauty.

My life.

I turned and gathered her face between my hands. I pressed the softest kiss to that even softer mouth.

Anthony cleared his throat. "I think that settles it then." He let his gaze fall on Shea. "Let's get your daughter back."

seven
Shea

MARTIN JENNINGS SAT ON the witness stand. Dark eyes gleamed back at me, the man intent to control my gaze as I faced him from where I sat at the table next to my attorney.

The way he'd always attempted to control me.

His expression conveyed every threat he'd ever dealt me, all under the guise of concerned parent.

"You are mine now."

"I always get what I want, no matter the means to attain it. You'd be wise not to forget it."

"I will guarantee your silence."

A rush of fear trembled through my spirit, and I shifted on the hard chair. Painfully, I twisted my fingers together as if it could bind me with courage. My stomach felt as though it was tied in a thousand knots as I listened to the false sincerity woven in his tone, and a part of me wanted to cower and cave.

But when it came to Kallie, I never had, and that definitely wouldn't change now.

If anything, I was stronger.

And I had Sebastian now. I wasn't alone.

The thought bolstered me, renewed with a charge of determination and fortitude.

Martin sat making a plea as to why he should be granted longer-term full custody of my baby girl.

Each word passing from his mouth only made me sicker.

Ill with the idea this monster could once again take that control. But this time...

This time I refused to give it to him.

"And why is it now you're just interested in obtaining custody of your daughter?" his attorney asked.

Playing devil's advocate.

How ironic.

Still, he was asking all the questions I wanted to demand answers to.

Even knowing every single answer was a lie.

The attorney, Mr. Carbellero, represented the state, though it quickly became clear he was under Martin Jennings's dime, pressing an issue that wouldn't have been an issue at all had Martin not spearheaded it in the first place.

"I never sought any form of custody earlier because I respected Ms. Bentley's wishes to step away from the limelight of the business to raise our daughter in her hometown. It's a decision I've often regretted. When I saw the pictures of paramedics attending my daughter on the beach, I knew I had no other choice than to step in and intervene."

He settled his soulless eyes on me. "Especially when I found out Shea was allowing my child to be exposed to someone as dangerous as Sebastian Stone."

My daughter! I wanted to scream. How could he sit there and try to claim her? After what he'd done? What I'd told Sebastian had been true. I'd foolishly hoped Martin had changed. That some sort of conscience had grown within the warped confines of his evil heart.

From where Sebastian sat directly behind me, I could feel the anger roll from him at Martin's insinuation—the hardness of his breaths and the restraint radiating from his body.

"And you know from experience how dangerous Sebastian Stone can be?" More propaganda from Martin's attorney.

"I've been involved in Sebastian Stone's business dealings for some time now." Martin went on to paint Sebastian in the most awful light, a strung-out addict prone to violence. Violence propagated against him.

Just as I knew Martin to be. A liar. A manipulator. Saying whatever needed to be said to get his way. To build himself up while he tore everyone down around him.

Using them as steppingstones.

My heart lurched with the memories.

A masochist.

A destroyer.

Martin acted out his role so perfectly, giving details of the assault, as if there had been no inciting factors. He implied Sebastian had assaulted him for no reason at all. Martin played himself out to be nothing more than an unsuspecting victim in Sebastian's premeditated fit of rage.

It was just as Sebastian had warned. Martin had the edge. The law on his side. They presented the assault charges against Sebastian as the ugliest kind of blemish—almost as bad as the time he had served in prison four years ago.

My fingers twisted tighter, and I tried to decipher the judge's expression as she listened to Martin's testimony. I knew she could easily look at Sebastian in a negative light—view the rest of the guys in that same light—making judgments on appearances and assumptions.

It made me sad few would blame her.

But she didn't know Sebastian like I did. She didn't see beneath all the hard lines and scars to what burned bright below.

I guessed her to be in her late fifties, and she wore her hair in a smart gray bob. Thin and tall. Yet everything about her felt powerful and strong.

Stoic.

Giving nothing away.

God, I was just thankful she wasn't the judge who'd issued the emergency injunction in the first place.

From behind, I could almost feel Baz's apology pouring from him. Could almost hear the words of self-flagellation churning in his head. He was probably pleading for me to forgive him. Asking me to heed the many warnings he'd given me that he would never be enough, that he would always drag me down and leave me in shreds.

But, I wouldn't listen to those words. Especially when he'd been the only thing that had held me together over the last two days.

Two days I'd been without my daughter.

Two days of torment.

Two days of agony.

Two days of not knowing where she was. If she was scared or if she was safe. If she understood I was fighting for her or if she simply wondered if she had been abandoned.

Two days of Sebastian holding me through it all.

Promising he would *fix* this.

Somehow I knew his thoughts now. The energy traveling between us was alive, and those devoted places in him flared with doubt, the man thinking he would have been doing me a favor had he just walked away.

But in those days, while he'd kept me sane, he'd also filled me with faith. And I felt it now—sure in my heart Kallie would find her way home today.

Certain Sebastian was exactly where he was supposed to be.

Because somehow I knew he needed me just as desperately as I needed him. That the hollow place he had revealed in me had been created with the sole purpose of him filling it.

And I knew…

I knew there was a matching one inside of him.

When Martin's attorney finished, Nigel, our attorney, declined asking Martin Jennings any questions of his own. He had told me earlier our job wouldn't be to prove Martin an unfit father. That would come later if he sought some sort of future custody.

Instead, our job was to disprove the pictures, citing them as the lies they were, and bringing Kallie home.

As his first witness, Nigel called Lyrik. Lyrik strode to the stand, wearing a tailored dark suit, the tattoos on his hands and neck standing out in stark contrast against the obviously expensive clothing, everything about him menacing yet confident.

Nerves curled through my stomach.

Nigel did nothing more than ask him what happened that day, where I had been, where Sebastian had been, gathering his firsthand account.

"We were getting ready to grill some steaks. We'd been out playing on the beach all day, and Shea and Sebastian had just come back from a walk."

He lifted a dark, dark brow. "Kallie had been with us during that time, playing in the sand, burying Zee…"

He gestured with his chin toward Zee who I knew sat behind me with the rest of the guys.

With Charlie, Tamar, and April.

Those who'd come together to support us.

To bring Kallie home.

"When Sebastian and Shea got back from taking that walk," Lyrik continued, "Sebastian and his little brother, Austin, started tossing the ball around on the beach. Kallie was all excited, jumping around and begging her mom to take her out to play in the water."

His tone grew serious. "I remember hearing them both laughing out there, playing in the waves, and then all of a sudden, Shea was screaming she'd lost hold of her. Kallie wasn't ever out there in the water by herself. Never. None of us would have allowed that."

"What happened then?" Nigel asked.

"Sebastian went running to the water. Dove in." He swallowed hard. "It felt like forever, but I doubt more than thirty seconds or so could have passed when he got hold of her. Pulled her out of the water and onto the beach. By then, I was already dialing 911."

"Thank you," was all Nigel said before he took his seat.

Martin's attorney approached and basically asked him the same questions, but with his own innuendo, trying to cast doubt, to catch him in a lie.

Lyrik's story remained the same.

Nigel called Ash, then Zee.

Austin wasn't here.

Nigel had assured us we didn't need him, and Sebastian didn't want him in the same room with Martin unless it was one-hundred percent necessary.

I didn't blame him. God knew, I didn't want to be around him, either.

Each of them gave their testimony, affirming I had been in the water with Kallie and she had in no way been neglected.

Each time Nigel finished, Martin's attorney would approach them, doing everything he could to discredit them, calling their character into question, to chalk it up to their ties to the band.

A pact of deceit.

Last, Sebastian was called.

The power of the man's presence stole the air from the room as he made his way to the stand. Filling it up with something all his own.

The weight of his gaze almost crushed me as he looked across at me, every admission, apprehension, *and* desire blazing in his eyes. Every reason he'd ever given to walk away and everything that had him running back played out in the depths of the roiling grey. A fire that flamed free and bold.

My heart beat frantically as he recounted the story from his perspective. The fear he'd felt was clear. There could be no denying how he cared for my child.

Most of the questions Nigel asked were the same he'd asked the rest of the guys, but he pushed a little deeper, gaining greater detail. It seemed as if Nigel were wrapping up his questioning, walking back toward the table where I sat, when he paused and looked back at Sebastian. "What is it exactly Shea Bentley means to you, Mr. Stone?"

Sebastian looked directly at me, something softening in the severity of his stare. "She's my girl."

His answer was simple, though his expression was anything but.

Yesterday, Sebastian had made a public statement.

Claiming me.

Claiming Kallie.

He denied our relationship had anything to do with the fact Kallie's father was the same man who Sebastian had been arrested for assaulting. He'd calmly stated there was no bearing or connection, and it was just a twisted coincidence that had led us down this cruel yet exquisite path.

These two, they're it for me, so as soon as we clear this mess up and get Kallie back home where she belongs, that's where I'm gonna be.

That's what he'd said before he pulled me a little closer and dropped a tender kiss on the top of my head, told them *thank you for your time*, and turned us away.

They'd rushed, firing question after question at us.

But Anthony had stepped in and corralled them as Sebastian quickly ushered me back inside Nigel's office, saying we wouldn't be available to answer any questions and making a plea for them to respect our privacy in this difficult time.

Nigel nodded. "One last question, Mr. Stone. How long has it been since you've used any illegal substances?"

Sebastian raked a hand down his face and blew a heavy breath from his mouth. "I've been clean for four years."

"Thank you, that's all."

Nigel sat back down beside me, and Martin's attorney approached. There was no missing Sebastian's discomfort, the way he struggled to hold himself back, to keep himself in check, rage barely constrained as the man dove right in to undermine his testimony.

To undermine him as a man.

No doubt, just being in the same room as Martin Jennings was almost more than he could bear. Forcing him to sit through this attack was nothing less than cruel.

And make no mistake. It was an attack.

Mr. Carbellero asked the expected questions, before he shifted tactics and launched into his own agenda.

"Isn't it true you came to Savannah knowing Martin Jennings had ties here?"

"No."

"Isn't it true you sought out Shea Bentley as a way to get back at Martin Jennings with whom you're involved in both criminal and civil suits?"

"No." That time, his answer was harder.

The judge cut in with a lift of her chin. "Mr. Carbellero, please keep your questions pertinent to the event taking place this past Sunday," she warned.

In annoyance, the attorney's lips thinned, and he offered her a clipped nod.

Sebastian fidgeted in the stand, hostility clear, before he was excused.

From the side, Nigel gave me a reassuring glance, confidence clear in his eyes, and I tried to temper the overwhelming emotion pricking at my eyes.

Climbing down from the stand, Sebastian looked at me warily as he passed, big body eating up the ground as he crossed through the short gate and took his seat.

A storm of turmoil ricocheted between us, all our hope clouded with fear and uncertainty.

My fingers twitched, wishing I could go to him. Comfort him the same way he'd been comforting me.

Nigel stood and called my name.

I pulled in a breath and shuffled toward the stand. I was sure my feet would give out as I approached, my breaths shallow and my heart erratic as it pulsed frantic beats through my veins.

Emotion pressed fervently at my chest, and my little girl's face swirled through my mind, her sweet voice an echo in my ear. As if she were near, her spirit fluttering through me on her tiny butterfly wings, brushing across the vacant places where she remained just out of reach.

Calling for me.

I fumbled as I sat down on the chair.

Martin Jennings smiled across at me.

Pleasantly.

As if he'd perfected the act.

As if he held the fate of the world in his pompous hands.

A placating expression that oozed arrogance.

Vile, disgusting man.

Hate hit me like the crack of a sonic boom.

If only everyone here knew what he was truly capable of.

What he'd done.

No. I'd had no proof.

But I knew his guilt as well as I knew his game.

My gut had screamed it. Claimed it. A natural intuition that had risen from inside. An instinct insisting we survive.

And for so long I had.

Survived.

I was sworn in and Nigel Trondow asked me the same questions he'd asked the guys. Only with me like he had done with Sebastian, he went into more detail, beginning from the moment Sebastian and I went on the walk down the beach.

"The pictures that allegedly took place while Kallie was left alone. You claim they took place down the beach without Kallie present?"

"That's correct."

I knew no matter what, those images shed me in less than stellar light. The pictures appeared dirty and lewd. No doubt, they gave pause to my judgment as a mother.

My voice quieted as I swallowed around the lump at the base of my throat, my explanation shaky. "We thought we were completely alone…there wasn't anyone on that part of the beach. That never would have happened in front of my daughter, or in front of anyone else for that matter."

I realized my statement came across as a plea.

For the judge to understand I would never intentionally place my daughter in harm's way.

Nigel strode back to the table and pulled out the images he'd marked for evidence that morning.

"Your Honor, these are the pictures taken without Ms. Bentley or Mr. Stone's knowledge last Sunday, on private property, no less."

He stated the date they were taken and passed them to the judge.

They were the pictures of Sebastian touching me beneath my

bikini top, our passionate kisses, the ones of Kallie from a distance with her face blurred out and surrounded by paramedics.

He handed her more prints. But these…these were the rest of the pictures. The photographer who had sold the condemning pictures had captured moment after moment of that afternoon. There were pictures of me playing in the water with Kallie. Close-ups of her smiling face. The wave. Me screaming when I lost her. Sebastian running in to save her.

They were all there.

I wasn't entirely sure how this stunning reel of evidence had been obtained.

Sebastian had said he would spare no cost and clearly Nigel had dug until he'd found the proof.

"You'll see by our own pictures that Ms. Bentley and Mr. Stone's intimate encounter on the beach did not take place in the same spot where Ms. Bentley lost hold of her daughter behind Mr. Di Pietro's beach-front home."

There could be no question.

They were two separate events.

The judge perched her reading glasses on the narrow bridge of her nose. Quietly she perused them, saying little. The bit she did, she directed at Nigel, asking how and when the second set of images were obtained. Bile worked its way through my stomach.

Because no matter how much proof we believed we had, it still came down to perspective. To the way the judge would see, read, and interpret.

When she finished her inspection, the judge pulled off her glasses, and Nigel turned his attention toward me. "Thank you for your cooperation, Ms. Bentley, I have no further questions."

Mr. Carbellero stood.

He didn't hesitate to tear into me.

Twisting his questions.

Slanting innuendo.

Casting an illusion of neglect and disregard and possible abuse.

Finally I could take it no more and there was nothing I could do to keep the tears from breaking free. They streaked down my face as my words cracked on the appeal. "I would never intentionally place my daughter at risk. She's my entire life."

I was sobbing by the time I was excused, no longer able to stand beneath the pressure, beneath the possibility of losing my daughter.

I broke in front of them all.

The judge adjourned for a fifteen-minute break.

Those passing moments were nothing less than excruciating.

Sebastian stood behind me, rubbing my shoulders, pressing gentle kisses to the back of my head while I felt as if I stood at the cusp of eternity. Two paths tangled. One that would lead me to perpetual torment, and the other directly to deliverance.

How daunting that a woman I'd seen for the first time today held the fate of my daughter in her hands.

An unparalleled position of power.

If only she could have seen the years I'd given Kallie. If only she'd been there to watch my sacrifices. The hours of loving her and protecting her and nurturing her.

Always keeping her safe.

She would know I'd never hurt her or put her in harm's way.

We all rose when she reentered from her chambers, and sat when directed to do so.

It seemed as if the entire room held a collective breath.

She looked in my direction. "I find no evidence of neglect on Ms. Bentley's part."

Her words spun through me, tempting and teasing at my understanding.

She turned her gaze in the direction of Martin. "Mr. Jennings, if you have any true interest in forming a relationship with your daughter with joint custody, then I would suggest you do it through the normal channels and not through a stunt like this."

She lifted the gavel. "I find in favor of the defendant and hereby lift the emergency injunction in the care of Kallie Marie Bentley. Care should immediately be reinstated to her mother."

Wood cracking against wood thundered through the courtroom as she slammed the gavel down, and I was hit with a violent jolt of relief.

Resonating.

Pulsating.

Taking hold.

I gasped. My shoulders dropped in the same second I dropped my head into my hands. And I sobbed. Only this time…this time it was out of thankfulness. Out of joy.

Simple, simple dreams.

They cried out from within me.

Finally.

Finally.

They were within my reach.

A barrage of flashes went off the second the door swung open.

Click.

Click.

Click.

I ducked my head and Sebastian pulled me closer to his side, and I could feel the way every inch of him hardened in defense.

Resentment and hostility.

"Don't even acknowledge them, Shea," Sebastian hissed against my head as he sought to protect me from the swarming onslaught of paparazzi questions.

They pushed and pressed in, vying for position, to be the first to grab our attention.

My head spun with the sudden intrusion. It was a sharp contrast to the rest of my body that felt lighter than it ever had. My arms and legs tingled, my heart stampeding hours into the future when I would hold my baby girl again.

As if I were flying there, more desperate for that moment than for any I'd ever lived in the past.

Over the last two days, as the shock had worn off, the sadness had grown. We'd never had a day apart. It had been utter agony. As if a tangle of roots had sprouted in my insides.

Spearing.

Tunneling.

Burrowing.

Cutting through muscle and bone and marrow.

Piercing me to the core.

To the most vital part of me.

They say our children are made of us. Essential to our being.

It's never so apparent until they are ripped away, and now all those places resonated with the void only my baby girl could fill.

Now I couldn't wait to get to that moment when she would fill it.

But we needed to make it through this crowd first.

A bristle of fierce energy rumbled through Sebastian. His tone was hard as he spoke near my ear. "This is the same bullshit they pull at every turn, and you don't need to deal with it now. They have no right to be here."

But they were.

And this was part of Sebastian's life.

A part I had accepted to be with him.

Although now some of the obsession was directed at me.

We were hit with a firestorm of questions.

Most laced with assumptions.

Lies and hurt and morbid intrigue.

A warped and skewed truth to feed the fascination.

"Can you tell us the verdict in your daughter's custody hearing?"

I cowered closer into Sebastian, part of me wanting to shout victory and adoration, the other determined to keep my mouth closed. Understanding the game because I'd had to play it before.

"Mr. Stone, is it true *Sunder* is currently seeking a new lead to replace you?"

"Sebastian Stone, has your relationship with Hailey Marx officially come to an end?"

Grunting, Sebastian shoved through the swelling crowd, his anger throttled, the restraint he barely hung onto quickly unraveling as he pulled me tighter.

"Ms. Bentley, how do you respond to the breach of contract between you and Mr. Jennings?"

My eyes immediately flew the reporter's direction, and I could feel my brows pinching with the question he hurled.

Breach of contract?

Never before had it been claimed.

Was he claiming it now?

A jumble of voices fought for our attention.

"Now that you're out of hiding, will Delaney Rhoads be making a comeback?"

I wanted to scream, *Not a chance in hell*, but instead I held my tongue and allowed Sebastian to haul us forward, his body a battering ram driving through the throng.

"Sebastian Stone, it's no secret you and Martin Jennings remain at odds. It seems obvious you're using your relationship with Shea Bentley to get back at him."

Sebastian growled, "We told you what we had to say yesterday. Now get the hell out of my way."

Rage vibrated from his bones. It was enough to send the lesser of the photographers scampering out of his way.

But some remained bold, and a microphone was shoved in my face. "Is it true you hid your pregnancy from Martin Jennings, and now he is seeking full custody?"

Nausea rolled in my stomach.

They had no clue, no idea the secrets I'd kept inside or why I'd kept them.

No idea the lengths I'd gone to protect my daughter.

Another voice at my ear. "Your estranged mother is quoted as saying, 'I've never been faced with greater disappointment and discouragement than in my daughter's betrayal.' Can you comment?"

As if I'd been kicked in the gut, I gasped, and angry tears pricked at my eyes. I wanted to lash out, just as Sebastian had done outside the hospital on Sunday night.

Because. This. Hurt.

How did she still shock me with her vitriol?

Didn't they understand what we had already been put through? The pain?

This was the life I'd run from.

One I'd hidden away to protect myself, but most of all, to protect my daughter.

Burying Delaney Rhoads.

But shallow graves are so easily uncovered, and I wasn't sure I was ready to deal with her resurrection.

For a second we broke free, and we darted across the street to where the Suburban was parked. Running lights flashed as we neared it, the locks disarming, and Sebastian yanked open the passenger door, quick to help me inside.

He slammed the door shut behind me.

I watched as he fought back through the reporters, as he rounded the front, this time not quite as amicably as he'd been with me at his side. Three seconds later, his door flung open and he jumped in. Immediately he slammed it closed, cutting off the frenzy of voices.

Panting, my breaths wheezed from my too-tight lungs, and I tried to calm my thundering pulse.

From across the space, Sebastian searched me for injuries he knew would not be visible.

"Those bastards." His rugged face winced, his voice a hard rumble. More regret.

"This is exactly what I was trying to protect you from all along. Never wanted to drag you and Kallie into this kind of life. It's no good, Shea. No fucking good."

I stared at him and my head tilted to the side. My voice was soft but packed with emphasis. "Life with you is *good*, Sebastian. As long as we make it that way. I don't care what lies they tell or what they believe. Just as long as it means I get to spend my life with you."

He exhaled and shook his head, a hint of a smile playing at the corner of his pretty, pretty mouth. "Where'd you come from, baby?"

"I've been right here all along, waiting for you."

Outside, we were surrounded.

But here?

It was just the two of us.

That strange energy still intense and profound.

But different.

Maybe it was the overwhelming relief, the weight that had been lifted, but the air had shifted. A glimmer of sweet. A suggestion of desire. Sebastian slanted me a smile—all flirty and sexy—gaze brazen, as he looked me up and down where I sat in the passenger seat while he readjusted his tie. His gray fitted suit only amplified the bulk of his stunning presence.

"So fucking beautiful," he moved in to murmur near my face, "still can't believe I get to call you my girl."

Heat climbed my neck and I could feel it radiating from my cheeks.

God.

One thing about Sebastian?

He never balked at finding comfort in the other's touch, and over the last two days, he'd sought me out time and time again. Taking me. Soothing me. For a few blissful moments, lifting me to a place where I was detached from everything in this world.

Except for him.

A place where we existed only in the other.

Tied.

Tethered.

Bound.

Hearts and minds and bodies and souls.

After everything that had happened, it seemed impossible only four days had passed since he'd come back to me.

Since he'd torn all those barriers down and chosen to stay.

Even though deep down, in the places we didn't want to acknowledge, we both knew he would eventually have to go.

This life would take him places where I couldn't always physically follow, whether standing up for his little brother would land him back behind bars, or if the call of his spirit would take him back on the road.

At the thought, my heart thrashed a severe beat of defiance, and I flinched as I attempted to block the injustice of it all.

Sebastian frowned when he noticed the shift in me, his touch gentle as he hooked his index finger under my chin.

A simple promise.

You belong to me.

It didn't matter where the road took him. How much time or

distance existed between us.

It didn't hold the power to erase what that promise meant.

"You did it," he finally whispered just above our slowed breaths, and he reached out and cupped the side of my face.

"She's really coming home."

But what would be Martin's next step?

I forced off the grim thought.

"Yeah, Shea, she's really coming home." Sebastian started the truck and put it in gear. "Think it's about damned time we go and get her."

He jerked the long black Suburban out onto the road. Paparazzi scattered. A tumble of bodies rushed to get out of Sebastian's way as he gunned it onto the one-way street and headed away from the courthouse.

Inside my purse, my phone rang.

I dug through my bag and pulled it free.

Nigel.

"Hello?" I answered. There was still a tremor in my voice, unable to shake the worry that in the ten minutes since I'd last spoken with the attorney, something had gone amiss. That I'd misunderstood or misconstrued.

That my mind had played the cruelest kind of trick.

"You can pick up Kallie at 4:30."

I breathed out and glanced at the dashboard.

Four o'clock.

My chest fluttered.

In only thirty minutes, Kallie would be in my arms.

"Claribel Sanchez," he continued with his instructions, "the case manager, will meet you at the house where Martin Jennings has been staying with Kallie to oversee the exchange."

I blanched.

It sounded as if we were bartering goods.

I swallowed down the residual bitterness. Even though I hated that was precisely what Martin had done—using an innocent child as a tool in a failed coup—I would only be thankful she was coming home.

He rattled off the address and I scribbled it down so I could plug it into the navigation.

"Got it," I said.

Of course, the monster had not only taken her from her home, but removed her from her hometown. Placed her in the midst of everything foreign more than thirty miles away.

Every piece of me prayed she was truly okay.

That she would recover and this trauma wouldn't leave her with scars that would never heal.

I bore enough of those for the both of us.

My mind swam with questions.

How had he treated her? Fed her? Cared for a child he didn't even know? What lies had he fed her? How would I answer her thousands of warranted questions?

A chill skittered down my spine.

What would I do if I found out he'd harmed her?

Nigel pushed out a relieved breath. The no-nonsense persona he typically wore veered into something warm. "Congratulations, Shea. I was confident this case would come out in your favor, but I can't begin to describe the satisfaction I feel with getting your little girl back where she belongs. I know my job made a true difference today, and I want to thank you for placing your trust in me."

"Thank you for putting everything you had into it. I will forever be in your debt."

I ended the call, and Sebastian turned and headed north out of Savannah.

He hit the freeway.

Trees hugged the roadway, interspersed by buildings that

opened up to small towns as the sun beat a path west and we continued silently toward our destination. The entire ride I fidgeted in my seat, picking at the hem of my shirt as I incessantly checked the time.

Urging it along.

Ten more minutes.

Sebastian reached across the console and took my hand. "We're gettin' close, baby."

I squeezed his hand and attempted to steady my breaths, to calm the escalation of my heartbeat. But it only increased with every passing second. "I can't wait to see her."

Every emotion I'd felt over the last few months seemed to gather right at the base of my throat. A lump derived from the blinding bliss Sebastian had brought into my life and the pain and torment that had followed, building and weaving and breaking and strengthening until I stood right here.

On the cusp of where it all manifested as my future.

A future with her.

A future with him.

All muddied with a cataclysm of unknowns that would make up our lives.

Unknowns I couldn't wait to experience.

Exiting the freeway, Sebastian made a right, then a left.

Sitting forward in my seat, I clamped down on his hand.

Wave after wave of yearning washed me through.

My beautiful, frightening man cast me a reassuring smile as he made another right down a street, then began to slow as we approached the address.

He pulled up to a stop in front of a single-story home.

My gaze was immediately drawn to the windows framed by white shutters, wondering if Kallie stood behind one, peering out, just as anxious for my return as I was for hers.

Did she know I was coming? Did she know I would have come for her two days ago had it been possible?

For the rural area, the house was on the nicer side. A manicured lawn adorned the yard. Two mature, lush trees flanked the walkway lined with rows of recently planted fall flowers.

Still, it didn't come close to touching the extravagance of Martin's Nashville residence.

I realized this was little more than a holding cell. A place to keep Kallie, because he hadn't been allowed to move her out of state until I'd been in front of a judge.

A palpable rush of agitation burned through Sebastian, and he gripped the steering wheel, his attention also locked on the face of the house where my daughter had been held.

The clock read four twenty-eight, and the same small blue car that had been present the night Kallie was taken pulled up behind the Suburban as the sun slid slowly toward the horizon.

In discomfort, Sebastian cleared his throat. "Think it's best I wait here. Last thing we need is me bringing more trouble on you two. Took about all I had not to lay that smug bastard out back in court. Not sure how things would go down without a building full of cops to deter me."

I gave a quick nod. "Yeah."

I knew with Sebastian, it was vastly more than just an idle threat, which was precisely why I could never let him know just how depraved Martin truly was.

He smiled a brilliant smile that cut through his intensity. Something beautiful beneath his hardened scars. "Go get your girl."

Through the rearview mirror, I watched Claribel Sanchez step from her car. I did the same. Although my movements were rushed and shaky, filled with the culmination of my anxiety, fear, and relief.

This was it.

I attempted to steel myself against the idea of facing Martin in this setting. One without the screen of intercessors. No attorneys or judges or officers there to act as a buffer. Only this lone woman, who knew nothing of Martin, and Sebastian who knew too much.

I flattened my palms down the front of my blouse, nervously straightening it, needing something to do with my hands.

She approached me with a cautious smile on her face. "Ms. Bentley." Sympathy flashed across her features. "I'm glad I can be here to help with the transition."

In her eyes I saw an apology. As if maybe she'd felt it in her gut she'd been making a mistake the night she'd torn my daughter from our home.

Or rather, the judge had made one, because it was clear she'd only been doing what she'd been commissioned to do. The lines marring the woman's face obviously told of the countless hours she devoted to her job with very little thanks, but rather case after case of heartache and abuse and broken homes.

I twisted my hands as I glanced at the house, making a vain attempt at controlling the moisture clouding my eyes. "I'm just thankful this transition is taking place."

Her smile turned knowing, and she gestured with her head toward the house. "If you'll just wait here, I'll go inside and get your daughter and bring her out to you."

She looked to the Suburban. "And with Mr. Jennings's and Mr. Stone's history, I'd like to ask he remain in the truck."

Apparently Sebastian wasn't the only one who viewed himself as a danger.

"Of course, thank you," I rushed.

"You're welcome."

She took the walkway to the front door and rang the doorbell. An older woman I'd never seen before opened the door.

Not Martin.

I stuttered over my heightened defenses, a second's ease in

knowing I wouldn't have to face him. I absolutely hated the power he still held over me. The utter fear I felt at just the mention of his name.

Although it was no longer just for myself, but for my daughter.

Nodding, the older woman extended the door open and welcomed Claribel inside. Then it closed.

I stood there with my heart in my throat. Restless, I tried to force myself to stand still and wait, when the only thing in the world I wanted was to beat down the door and find my daughter.

Five minutes later, the door opened again.

A tiny girl with a mane of wild blonde curls stepped out, and my heart, which had been in my throat, felt as if it burst. As if it exploded with a balm filling my chest too full, overflowing into my veins. Touching and soothing and inciting where it brushed through every inch of me.

Swallowing hard, I shook more as my gaze met with those sweet brown eyes, love and belief and innocence still shining through.

Without even making sense of it, I was moving, taking two hesitant steps forward, knowing I was supposed to stay.

To wait.

I broke out in a sprint. Awkwardly. My heels clattered against the sidewalk, and my pulse thundered and spun, a frenzy urging me forward.

Claribel stopped at the bottom of the three steps that led to the house. Kallie's hand was still secured in hers.

A foot away, I fell to my knees. Concrete ripped at my stockings and cut into my skin.

But none of that registered.

The only thing I felt was the desperate ache to hold my daughter.

Kallie.

I choked. Tears fell fast and free, soaking my face.

I reached for her. Pulled her to me. The warmth of her tiny body pressed into my chest. My face got lost in ringlet curls, and I breathed her in, hugging her close, my mouth at her ear. "I missed you, Butterfly. I missed you."

God, I'd missed her so much it was frightening.

Terrifying.

My body wept with the residual pain and torment crashing violently with this welcomed remedy.

Little arms wrapped tightly around my neck. "Mommy." She said it so quietly. As if she were testing if it were true. Wondering if I really was there. Then she breathed out her own relief, letting go of some of her fear while she clung to me.

"It's okay, sweet girl. I have you. I have you."

Slowly, I climbed to my feet, taking Kallie with me.

Claribel Sanchez inclined her head down the walk. "We should go."

Nodding, I wrapped my arm tighter around Kallie, my free hand pressed to the back of her head. She buried her face in my neck, and her little heart beat so hard against mine. Frantically, I kissed the top of her head. "I have you," I whispered again as I followed the social worker down the walkway.

Claribel Sanchez opened the back door of the Suburban and placed a bag inside, one that had not belonged to Kallie two days ago. Part of me wanted to rip it from where she set it on the floor. To throw it to the ground. To trample it into dust. To erase any memories of the past two days.

For Kallie as much as for myself.

Instead, I edged around her and reluctantly settled Kallie in the booster seat, loathed to let her go. I buckled her in and kissed her on the forehead, moved to her temple, then to her tiny nose.

On the tiniest giggle, she lifted her trusting face to me and a smile whispered at the corner of her red-bow lips.

I could feel Sebastian, the gravity of his stare, the power of energy that glimmered in the confined space. I looked up and met his strange grey eyes, saw the heavy swallow that bobbed his throat as his gaze drifted to my baby girl.

Affection.

Love.

Adoration.

My head spun with the magnitude of it.

"Hi, Baz." Kallie's timid voice broke into the charged air, her sweet little drawl tugging at me from all angles. A hint of that unending exuberance bled through her greeting.

A soft smile edged Sebastian's mouth.

"Hey, Little Bug. You ready to go home?"

Her smile grew and she kicked her feet. "I so, so, so ready."

"Let's get you out of here," I said, and I kissed her forehead again, unable to stop, before I finally forced myself to step back and shut her door.

Claribel Sanchez stood there waiting, before she gave me a slight tilt of her head. "I will need to follow up in a couple of weeks. Take care of her."

"Always."

She got into her car and drove away.

I started for the front passenger's door when I *felt* the presence behind me. Mouth going dry, I froze with my hand clamped down on the door handle.

Sickness crawled across the surface of my skin.

He inched closer. My instincts kicked in. My body shrank away, my eyes squeezed tight, and my lungs sealed off.

Cringing.

Cowering.

I hated he still evoked this reaction in me.

Greed and conceit and spite pressed into my senses, and my

lungs burned with restraint until I could do nothing but take in a sharp breath.

That smell.

There would never be anything I could do to erase it from my mind.

A noxious spice that under any other circumstances should have been pleasant.

But pair it with something vile, the memories of his body dictating mine—that scent soaking my nose and clogging my throat—and it was as if I were suddenly eighteen again. Just a scared little girl with a voice so many proclaimed adoration for…yet never really heard.

Regret curled my stomach with nausea, and Martin Jennings laughed, low and malignant.

I refused to bend to him. Slowly, I turned around and lifted my chin, my eyes narrowed as I took in the man who'd sought to take everything from me.

Using me up.

All too happy to hang me out to dry.

It was the same second I heard the driver's side door click open.

A shimmer of violence pitched through the darkening day, a crack of aggression struck the dense air.

From behind me, I could sense every step Sebastian took as he carefully approached, making his way around the front of the Suburban.

Slow.

Purposeful.

Poised to protect.

I latched onto his controlled disdain, allowed it to multiply—to be enough for both of us—and stared at the face I wished I could forget.

My voice wavered, but I held strong. "If you hurt my daughter…in any way…I swear to God, I won't stop until you wish you were dead."

Martin Jennings tsked. "So angry, Delaney. Funny, I always thought you a pushover."

His breath spread across my face as he inched closer. Eyes, so dark they were almost black, glinted with contempt.

A sneer curled his mouth. "You'd always been so anxious to please. Stumbling all over yourself for a little praise. You surprise me."

Every cell in my body squeezed as memories of the mistakes I'd made surged forward.

Taunting.

Reminders of a past I had never wanted to live.

"You don't know anything about me," I spat, holding my ground while I felt as if it might crumble out from beneath my feet.

Memories of myself as a teenager swamped me. Growing up, every path I'd ever traveled had been with my mother at the reins. Leading me. I strove to conform to who she wanted me to be, always hungering for her attention. Anxious to make her proud. Desperate for a soft touch or a gentle hug or some kind of affection, rather than bearing the brunt of all her hateful dissatisfaction.

Sadness closed over me.

Both she *and* Martin had used that to their advantage.

Took advantage of me.

She had allowed him to take over everything in my life. Changing my image. My name. The songs I sang. I had been nothing more than his pretty little puppet, there to do with as he'd wished, which quickly included him claiming me as his own.

Just an ignorant lamb willingly led to the slaughter. Blind to what was waiting around the corner.

Until I'd discovered what was lurking behind it.

I could feel Sebastian edge forward. Tension wound in the

force of his breaths, and Martin's gaze darted over my shoulder at him, before it flitted back to me. He sent me a mocking smirk.

"I see you've gone digging through the trash for a little of that attention you've always been so desperate for," he taunted with a chuckle. "Such a shame. A *waste*."

The last dropped with slow insult, and I could feel Sebastian's rage pulsing at my back, the man at war with himself to keep from attacking.

Air shot from Martin's nose, and I knew he felt it, too.

"By all means, Mr. Stone, come at me. There would be no better way to end this day than watching you get hauled away in cuffs."

"Stay away from us," I warned through a barely heard whisper.

Martin laughed. "Do you really think you won today, Delaney? You think this is over?" His voice dropped. "Had you forgotten?"

Dread prickled across my skin.

Dark eyes glinted malevolent satisfaction and his mouth twisted in a morbid sneer as if he found glee with it. "Besides, I'm just getting to know *my daughter*."

My daughter was uttered on a deviant's tongue, yet came off with pure disdain. I wanted to puke.

"What do you want from us?" The words cracked. I knew it sounded as if I were begging.

Sebastian wound his arm around my waist, his hand firm across my stomach as he pulled me against him.

"Shea, don't," he urged, attempting to drag me back and keep me from getting sucked into the cesspool that was Martin Jennings.

Offhandedly, Martin lifted a shoulder, ignoring Sebastian, his tone deceptively sweet. "Come now, Delaney. Did you really think I wouldn't return for you? I promised I would. And I never break my promises. You do remember what you cost me?"

He looked at me pointedly. Reminding.

But the underlying reminder wasn't about how much money

had been lost by my desertion. But what he'd planned to do with that money. Money effectively stolen from me because of the contracts I'd been pressured to sign. Contracts where almost all royalties went to Martin and my mother. My eighteen-year-old naivety had once again gotten the best of me.

Lester Ford was a name I'd wanted to forget. For years I almost had. But briefly hearing his name on the news about a year ago had caused everything inside me to seize. The announcement the Tennessee tycoon was throwing in a bid to run for governor tripping up my feet.

Ignorantly, I'd pushed the importance of it aside. Pretended some more.

Anger pressed at my chest. "I owe you nothing."

He laughed as if I was ignorant, then glanced at the blackened back window of the Suburban. "Don't forget she's my daughter, too."

It came across as another threat, this revolting man using my child against me.

Expendable.

A belonging.

A possession.

Just as my mother had treated me. The same as she'd passed me on to him.

Sold me, really.

I'd just been too blinded by my desire to please her to see it for what it really was.

But I wasn't that frightened girl anymore.

He lifted his chin in a gesture toward Sebastian. "And you can't imagine the pleasure it will bring me to take down the two people who owe me most in one fell swoop. I suppose I should thank you for slumming it with this piece of trash, Delaney. I couldn't ask for a better scenario."

He leaned in close as he mouthed at my ear. "I *will* guarantee your silence."

I choked and Sebastian growled.

As Martin backed away, his smile curled the hairs at the back of my neck, fierce and shameless and somehow knowing. He turned on his heel and stalked toward the house.

There was no question he'd not forgotten *my* promise, either.

The shaky, foolishly bold promise I'd made when he'd come to the hospital the day Kallie was born.

The one stating I would expose both him and Lester Ford if he didn't let Kallie and me go, implying I had securities in place that would destroy him if something happened to me.

He'd promised I was nothing but a fool for thinking I had any control, and he'd be back for me when the time was right.

Maybe he knew I'd been bluffing. Doing anything in my power to protect my daughter.

Still, I was certain we'd danced around those threats for years. Each of us reliant on what one held over the other.

But why now?

"We'll fight you," I claimed on a broken shout.

Martin stopped. Slow to look over his shoulder.

I did everything I could to steady the words, to keep from conceding and yielding the way I'd always done. "And I promise, I'll do everything to make sure you go down in flames."

He began to turn back around, when I said, "And my name isn't Delaney. She died a long time ago."

The smile on his face appeared satisfied, and he shook his head as if pleased, muttering as he walked way, "You surprise me again, Delaney Rhoads."

eight
Sebastian

THE SUN WAS JUST sinking behind the trees when I rolled to a stop in front of Shea's house.

Kallie had long since fallen asleep.

Shea climbed right out, immediately going to her daughter. Taking her. Holding her. Protecting her.

I was just as quick. I went to her side, my hand at the small of Shea's back as we made our way up the walkway.

A couple paparazzi were staked out down the street, snagging pics, but I was thankful for the most part they were wise enough to let us be.

The front door flew open and April came rushing out, hands pressed over her mouth.

Relief.

All of us. We reeled in it.

Even if my hands twitched with the need to rip Jennings to shreds. Limb from limb. Slowly. Meticulously. Permanently.

That encounter had left a furor of violence demanding action and a load of new questions demanding answers.

Felt it coming. And soon.

Shea climbed the three steps up to the porch, and Kallie stirred, head poking up, brown eyes confused before they flashed recognition, joy and sweet and solace, the child immediately soothed by her surroundings.

Shea kissed her temple. "You're home, Butterfly," she whispered.

Kallie held tight to Shea's neck, squeezing just about as tight as my chest squeezed with everything I never thought I could feel.

The emotion about more than I could bear.

Too fucking much, so fucking light and good. Blinding. All that beauty pressing in.

April touched Kallie's face as Shea passed. Kallie looked up and smiled that precious smile.

"Auntie April." Her voice was small, but the love shining from her eyes was *enough*.

April let out a quiet sob. "Kallie."

Didn't think Kallie was ready for the questions that needed to be asked.

It was clear in the way she clung to her mom. Quiet. Subdued.

Reeling from her own relief.

Instead, Shea sat down with her on the couch and rocked her, murmuring a thousand reassurances.

You're safe.

I have you.

I won't ever let anyone hurt you.

"You can ask me…tell me anything," Shea said quietly at the top of her head. "Whenever you're ready."

God, the woman was the most incredible mom, and a pang of significance formed when I looked at the two of them together.

Mine.

Kallie's tiny angel voice cut into the tension. "Can we watch Nemo?"

Shea couldn't hold back the quick, soggy laugh, because asking if she could watch a movie didn't come close to the direction of what Shea was suggesting.

But maybe there was some comfort in that, too.

That Kallie just wanted to do something normal.

"Yeah, sweet girl, we can watch Nemo," Shea answered softly, hugging her more.

We all settled on the couch with the lights dimmed. April quietly stole upstairs after she pressed a kiss to Kallie's forehead, then one to Shea's, before she cast me a look that was both wary and filled with appreciation. Same way she'd been looking at me since I'd returned. Like she knew as well as I did that I'd brought trouble into Shea's life.

Same way as we both knew Shea needed me.

Almost as badly as I needed her.

Shea shifted so she was nestled into my side, her legs angled along the length of the couch, Kallie all twisted up in her arms and resting her back on her mother's chest.

I let my arm wind around Shea's shoulders, my fingers softly twisting through Kallie's hair, curls wild, wild, wild.

And you'd think it'd be impossible, but somehow this little girl managed to steal yet another part of me.

Didn't know if it was just because she belonged to her mom.

That she was a piece of Shea.

This fucking gorgeous girl, who with just a glimpse had caused me to fall.

I knew it. The second I'd felt her standing there my life had been altered.

I never anticipated I would fall so fucking hard, and that when I finally landed, I'd no longer look the same.

The television flashed and flickered. Bright blips against the dark as the movie played on.

Shadows and silhouettes lit up their expressions.

My girls.

Shea tilted her head back and peered up at me. Her storm alive, subdued yet savage.

Dark.

Light.

Heavy.

Soft.

Everything got so fucking tight, like I couldn't get air.

Like I was just beneath the surface.

Drowning.

Yet I felt I was floating through it all, on all that warmth and life and light.

Love was cruel like that.

A monster.

A savior.

Both anguish and ecstasy.

Because I knew right then, this life wouldn't be worth living if I wasn't living it for them.

In the darkness, possessiveness swelled.

Like a shroud wrapping them with my promise.

It didn't matter the circumstances or the consequences.

The result would be the same.

I'd do anything, give it all, make any sacrifice to keep them safe.

To keep them happy.

To keep them together.

No matter the cost.

"Be careful, Little Bug," I warned over my shoulder to a wiggling Kallie, as I stood at the sink filling a huge pot with water. Perched on the butcher-block island that rested in the middle of the country kitchen, her little legs kicked and arms flailed as she danced around to Van Morrison's *Brown Eyed Girl* playing on the small radio sitting next to her.

Nothing in the world seemed more appropriate.

"I know, Baz." She said my name like a ballad, lifting it high and pitching it low. A wide grin split her face, exposing her perfect, tiny teeth. "I'm so, so big, you know. I'm gonna be five in only six more months. *And* I'm bein' super safe."

Okay, I drew out in my head, little thing none too shy to set me straight.

Kallie didn't miss a beat and launched back into the song.

Afternoon light spilled in through the windows. Hazy rays struck against the untamed mound of her curls. Lighting her up. Like some kind of halo followed her around everywhere she went.

And damn, the kid learned fast.

Second time she heard the song?

She was singing those lyrics like that was exactly what she was made to do.

Shutting off the faucet, I moved to the stove, lit the burner, and placed the pot full of water over the flames. I turned around and crossed the short space to Kallie's side and went back to slathering butter onto two halves of French loaf bread.

Yeah.

Apparently I'd become all kinds of domestic.

Lyrik and Ash were going to have a field day.

I eyed Kallie, attempting not to smile when she gave me another one of those grins and clasped her hands together. "Oh, Momma is gonna be so, so excited when she gets home and we have dinner all ready for her."

She waved her hands in the air when she said *all*, tone oozing with innocence and a dash of country.

So fucking cute.

I lifted a brow. "You think so?"

"Uh-huh, I know so. Momma likes surprises. Almost as much as me."

I chuckled, thinking Shea was going to be surprised, all right. Kallie and I'd managed to trash the kitchen in about three point five seconds. Kallie was nothing less than a whirlwind and I wasn't exactly what one would call skilled in the kitchen.

We made quite the illustrious pair.

"Did you know I'm gonna have a surprise party one day?" she chattered on, shaking a shit ton of garlic salt on the bread I'd just finished buttering.

"I'm going to have butterflies all over and a butterfly dress and a butterfly cake. Oh, oh, OH, *and* butterfly face-paintin', just like at Paige's birthday party 'cause it was so pretty and I want everyone at my whole party to look just like a butterfly princess."

Garlic salt was flying all over the place. Kallie's attention was more focused on the faraway fantasy she was conjuring than the task at hand. She said birthday like 'burfday', and another one of those hardened parts inside me melted.

Swore to God, the kid wielded some kind of magical princess powers—tossing around some glitter and sparkly shit, casting a spell to bring the next man who crossed her path to his knees.

Pretty sure her mom possessed that power, too.

I was in deep, deep trouble.

Another chuckle rolled off my tongue, and I tapped Kallie's button nose. "Not sure it's considered a surprise party if you plan it yourself, Little Bug."

That precious nose scrunched up with confusion, before an idea clicked. "How 'bout you plan one for me, Baz?" she asked. Caramel eyes went wide with their hopeful plea.

There was nothing entitled or assuming about it. It was all awe and hope and imagination.

Yep, I was completely and utterly fucked.

Owned.

Hoped to God I wasn't supposed to be resisting all the cuteness, because it was just not gonna happen. Figured there were all kinds of rules set in place about not spoiling a kid rotten, but there wasn't one bratty bone in Kallie Marie Bentley.

She was an untamed, fiery ball of pure sweetness.

Guileless.

Genuine.

Sincere.

Guess she got that from her mother, too.

Like I had to think really hard about it, I twisted my face up in contemplation. "Hmm...I don't know."

Anticipation had her clasping her hands again, and she pressed them up under her chin, those tiny teeth exposed as a bright smile split her face. "Oh please, oh please. I'll be so, so good and listen to every'fing you and Momma tell me!"

I broke out in a grin. "In that case, I think maybe something can be arranged."

"Yes!" she squealed. Excitement blazed from her, her entire being lighting up like a sudden burst of sunshine.

Basking me in it.

Pretty sure that was going to be the best damned party this town had ever seen.

She danced around on the counter some more, going right back to singing her song and dousing the bread in so much garlic salt I was sure Shea and I were going to be choking it down.

Two and a half weeks had passed since we'd got her back. We'd settled into a routine. That *routine* basically meant me spending every waking second I possibly could with them. Every sleeping second, too. Binging on their time, feeding and fueling myself for the time when my life was going to call me away.

But this time?

This time it'd be done with the promise I'd be back, no matter how long the shit in my life stole them from me.

When she'd first got home, it'd taken a couple of days for Kallie to really begin to relax and start acting like her normal self again. The first week she'd had a couple nightmares.

Fuck, they'd been one of the most heartbreaking scenes I'd ever seen.

Shea had asked her gentle questions, never pressuring her, but always encouraging her to open up. To talk and get it out rather than holding her fear inside. Promising any secret she needed to tell would forever be safe with us.

Still blew my mind Shea trusted me with all of it. With her daughter. With the care, effort, and love that went into it.

Raising her.

Neither of us had stated or uttered it aloud, though we both knew well enough that's what was happening. I'd slipped into the role like I'd been purposed to do it all along.

Taking on Kallie as my own.

Did I still worry? Wonder if my being a part of their lives was only going to drag them down? Cause them more pain and suffering?

Hell yeah.

Every fucking second.

I guess I just worried more about what their lives might look like without me in it.

Or maybe it was just my own selfishness and greed that had me here, refusing to let them go.

But in moments like these? When I was here with Kallie, making her smile, being a partner to Shea, someone there to support and bolster and ease?

I had to believe I had more to offer. Believe everything Shea saw in me was real. Who I could really be. That maybe I could be better than all the shit I'd allowed to run my life for too many years.

Shea was right.

It was a choice.

And I was choosing them.

One of the only comforts we'd had in the whole situation was that bastard Jennings hadn't been around much while he'd held Kallie at that house. As Kallie had started feeling comfortable enough to begin telling stories, divulging little bits of what'd gone down, it became clear the old lady who'd answered the door was the one who'd done all the caretaking.

Asshole didn't give two shits about Kallie.

Not as if it'd come as a surprise.

She'd been nothing more than the pawn. A tactic in his self-righteous game.

Sick part? We were still unsure if it was for entertainment or gain.

I arranged the loaves of bread on a metal tray and slipped them into the oven. I punched numbers into the timer and glanced at the clock.

Any time now, Shea would be walking through the door.

My heart rate ticked up a notch. Was it ridiculous she'd only been gone for four hours and I was already anxious to see her again?

I shook my head at myself.

Never.

Things were so fucking good. But that didn't mean we weren't constantly on edge, waiting for the other shoe to drop. Jennings hadn't pushed the custody issue since the day Kallie'd come home. One could hope he'd given up.

But Shea and I knew better. He was just biding his time.

Lying in wait.

The way all predators do.

Kallie belted out the last of the chorus to *Brown Eyed Girl*, sweet, sweet voice dancing in my ears. She grinned so wide it stretched out to touch me.

"That one is my favorite, FAVORITE, Baz."

I ruffled her hair. "Pretty awesome, right? Song kinda reminds me of a couple girls I know."

"Who?"

Just then, the side door rattled, and Shea came fumbling in, all soft seduction and radiant smile.

Fucking gorgeous.

I searched for the air that suddenly felt thick. Didn't even try to hide the way I let my gaze take all of her in, eyes caressing up and down.

A curl of lust consumed me in the same second a rush of calm settled in the center of my chest.

Chaos and peace.

She floated in, all summer breeze and bouncing curls and joyful grin, today my girl light, light, light.

Sometimes I didn't know how to make sense of her. It was like a constant war raged within her, crushing deep butting up against irresistible brilliant bright.

Kallie flapped her arms. "Momma...surprise! Me and Baz are makin' s'ghetti for dinner. It's gonna be so, so, so good! You better be hungry."

Shea slanted me the sweetest, most appreciative smile before she turned toward her daughter with a feigned gasp. "Oh my goodness, did you make me dinner? And spaghetti is my favorite. How did you know I've been craving it the entire day at work?"

Shea edged around the island. She planted a kiss to Kallie's forehead. Kallie lifted her face and gazed at her with unconditional adoration and love. Shea poked her chubby belly, and Kallie squealed, grabbing at Shea's hands, little shoulders going up to her ears.

These two were going to be the death of me.

"Silly Momma, I already knows it's your favorite. S'ghetti's my favorite, too. 'Member?" Kallie's voice turned scolding.

Shea laughed a throaty sound that had my eyes tracing her again. "Of course, I remember. Do you think I'd forget something as important as that?"

"No way." Kallie shook her head.

After taking some time off to readjust with Kallie, Shea had gone back to work a week ago. She'd taken some lunch shifts to get back into the swing of things before she returned to her regular schedule this coming Tuesday.

Three days away.

Should have known the uproar it'd cause when I told her I'd take care of her. Asked her straight up if she just wanted to stay home and forget about working at *Charlie's*.

She was having no part of that. Again she'd told me she wasn't in this for my money or what I could give her.

But that was the thing. I wanted her to have it all.

Worst part was knowing my days here were fleeting. Part of me was working through every scenario, trying to figure out how I could convince her to come along with me. At the same time, I knew I couldn't just roll in here and displace Shea and Kallie from their home.

Shea caught me staring. I swallowed heavily when those knowing eyes latched onto me. This time it was her turn to track me. Hunger and need and slow appreciation.

Fuck, the girl knew exactly how to undo me.

She stepped forward till her tits were brushing at my chest, hiking up on her toes to steal a kiss.

The second her mouth met mine, I grabbed her by the hips, all too eager to give her one back. I kissed her sweet and slow, keeping it PG considering we had little eyes for an audience.

Still, Kallie giggled like it was the most scandalous thing she'd ever witnessed. "You give Momma too many kisses."

I pulled back, fingers still burrowed in Shea's hips. "What?" I teased, voice going deep with disbelief. "There's no such thing as too many kisses."

"Uh-huh," Kallie countered.

I passed Shea a smile, before I released her and took two measured steps toward Kallie.

"What, like this?" I grabbed her by the face and peppered loud, smacking kisses all over her angel face.

Kallie squealed, thrashing limbs and quivering chest that rolled with rasping laughter. "Stop, Baz! Those are tickle kisses!"

"Can't...stop," I drew out between kisses, making her squeal more.

Kallie retaliated, tiny fingers latching onto my ears, and she scattered her own noisy kisses across my cheeks. She jerked back, mischief and joy swimming in her eyes. "Got you!"

Laughing lightly, I nudged her chin with my index finger. "You got me."

Got me good.

Wasn't ever going to be the same.

I turned my attention back to Shea and got tripped up by the adoration shining from her face.

Still didn't understand how I got lucky enough to be on the receiving end of something that beautiful.

Easing toward her, my voice dropped as I wound an arm around her waist and pulled her to me. "How was your day?"

With a contented smile, she stared up at me, tired but totally at ease. "Busy, but good."

I planted a few more kisses at the edge of that delicious mouth. "Good."

"Hey," Kallie objected through a huge grin.

With my mouth still running along Shea's, I sent Kallie a mumbled, "Watch yourself, little woman."

"Little Bug," she corrected, and damn, my heart went a little crazy.

Haywire.

I was completely unaccustomed to all this good when I'd been existing for so long in the bad.

On a laugh, Shea untangled herself from my hold and finally took in her surroundings. She seemed quick to take note of the disaster that had befallen her kitchen. Other than Kallie? This room was basically her pride and joy.

She raised a brow at me, words a playful accusation. "And how was your day?"

"Busy, but good," I shot back as I snagged her by the belt loops and gave her a good tug.

She smirked. "Looks like it."

A new song came on, and Shea glanced at the radio. Until that piece of electronics and I met, I was pretty sure it had only known old country songs.

Shea's attention darted to Kallie who again started wiggling around on the island.

Shea cut her eyes back to me. A look of mock horror stretched across her face. "What in the world are you letting my daughter listen to?"

I tossed her horrified expression right back, though mine probably didn't come across quite as feigned.

"What? Thought I'd start Kallie here off on some of the classics." I lifted a shoulder. "The Rolling Stones. Led Zeppelin. You know, ease her in slow. Then maybe move on to some old school punk, get her primed before I introduce her to the real stuff."

So maybe I thought the kid needed a little variety in her musical tastes.

Dismay widened Shea's eyes. "And the *real stuff* would be?"

I scowled a little, playing with her, just a little prod. "I don't know…I might know of a couple bands I could introduce her to."

"Are you trying to lure my kid to the dark side?" Her tone was nothing but flirt and tease, and she wound a fist in my shirt, yanking and making me stumble forward a step.

I didn't mind a bit. I found the base of her neck and tipped her head toward me. My other hand hit that sweet spot at the small of her back, bending her back. I whispered close to her face, lips hovering an inch from hers. "Never would dream of it, baby."

Her eyes darted to mine, and that energy swelled. It was always this way. One touch. One murmur.

Fire.

That bell-like voice had me jerking my head back enough to catch the grin lighting up Kallie's face. "All morning when you went and seen your *brover*, me and Momma were listening to you singin', Baz. Momma turned it up way, way loud."

Slowly, I slid my gaze back to Shea who was still leaning back, completely reliant on my hold. "Is that so?" I demanded.

A deep blush skated right up Shea's neck and throbbed on her cheeks.

So maybe I shouldn't get off on the idea of my girl listening to me while I was away.

Crazy how just a few weeks ago, I'd felt ill over the idea. I didn't want my sweet, soft girl witnessing the way *Sunder* had to look on stage. All that hostility and hard and aggression that beat through our songs.

But now…

Now I wanted her to be a part of it.

Every aspect.

Every facet.

Because Shea got that it was me.

"You miss me while I was gone?" A smirk ticked up at one corner of my mouth.

Shea wet her lips, voice raspy with the admission. "Always."

"Good girl."

Teeth clamped down on her bottom lip, so hard it blanched, and damn if I didn't want to haul her upstairs, toss her onto her bed, and sink into her warmth.

To taste and play and fuck.

To get lost in her sea of light and dark.

Just for a little while.

But the water was starting to boil on the stove and we had a little one watching us with rapt attention, innocence needing to remain intact.

Priorities and all.

I dropped a swift, closed-mouthed kiss to Shea's tempting mouth, then righted her on her unsteady feet. "Come on, let's finish up dinner. We just need to throw on the spaghetti and we can eat."

Shea shook off the desire skimming along her honey skin. "Sounds good."

I angled in and scooped Kallie from the counter. She released a high-pitched shriek, throwing her arms out, flapping them around as I made her soar through the air.

Butterflies and contentment and ease.

I slung her onto my back and helped her dump the box of spaghetti into the boiling water.

This was the way it was always supposed to be.

The way *we* were supposed to be.

The three of us sat down at the table and shared the meal.

And I knew I'd never experience anything better in my life.

"You are a mess." Shea rubbed her nose against Kallie's as she pulled her from the chair and into her arms.

Spaghetti sauce was smeared across Kallie's face, clumps stuck to the front of her shirt, pieces decorating her hair. It looked like more had dropped onto the floor than had made it into her mouth.

"Bath time."

Shea adjusted Kallie on her side, her lithe body slithering toward me where she dipped down and fixed a kiss on me where I still sat at the table. "Thank you both for dinner," Shea said quietly.

Gratefully.

Truly.

Affection squeezed my ribs.

"Anytime," I answered back, meaning it. "Go on and get this little one cleaned up and I'll work on getting the kitchen back in working order."

Upstairs, water ran, and I got up and cleared the table. I dove into the pile of dishes in the sink, quick to rinse through them and load them into the dishwasher. I wiped down the counters, swept up the floor, cutting through the mess Kallie and I had made earlier while wondering again how it was possible my life could change so drastically in just a few short months.

Sunder was still supposed to be on our European tour, filling up dark, rowdy music halls, raising hell, reveling in debauchery and sin. And here I was in this quaint city, cleaning my girl's kitchen.

Talk about a mindfuck.

Finished with the kitchen, I walked through the swinging door and living room. Wood creaked beneath my steps as I edged upstairs. Laughter rang out from the bathroom, the sound drawing me forward.

I nudged the door open wider and leaned my shoulder against the jamb.

Kallie splashed around in her bath, covered to her chest in bubbles. Shea sat on the edge of the tub. She'd torn off the sweater she'd been wearing, and now was in nothing but her jeans and a skin-tight tank, the front of it soaked with water.

Damn.

She glanced up at where I was sucking the flawless sight down, eyes locking on me.

Warm.

Honest.

Pure.

"What's going on in here?" I asked like they were causing all sorts of trouble, making Kallie laugh and giggle. I edged forward just in time to catch Kallie cupping a big mound of bubbles in her hands. She blew them into Shea's face.

Shea yelped then laughed, wiping it off, a few streaks still clinging to her face. "I think I'm under attack by the suds monster."

"The suds monster, eh?" I asked, eyeing Kallie who started shaking her head, guilty playfulness written all over her.

"Nuh-uh." A grin spilled from her. "I not a monster." She stuck some of the suds to her chin. "I'm Santa Claus."

Shea looked over at me. The expression on her face touched me from across the space.

Joy.

Joy.

Joy.

Shea's cell rang from her bedroom. "Mind if I grab that?"

"Nope. Go ahead. I've got her."

She grazed my hand as she passed, a simple touch that felt anything but.

Significant.

That's what Shea and I had, even in the effortless moments like these.

Trust and certainty.

I took Shea's spot at the edge of the tub. "Hey there, Little Bug. Did you get cleaned up?"

Kallie nodded. She held her hands up that were wrinkled and pruned. "All done."

Chuckling, I leaned over and grabbed a towel from the rack then dunked my hand in the water to pull the plug.

Water swirled as it began to drain.

Kallie scrambled to standing, and I wrapped the towel around her and lifted her from under the arms, taking a shit-ton of bubbles with us. "Out you go."

As I stood, I swung her around. Of course, it made her laugh hysterically, because the kid had to be the happiest thing I'd ever known.

I sat her on the counter, her feet in the sink, tiny body all wrapped up, arms free and tucked in close as she hunched her shoulders.

I stood right behind her to keep her from falling.

Water dripped from her hair, and I grabbed a second towel, figuring the disaster on her head was going to take more attention than anything else.

I began rubbing it through the mess of ringlet curls.

God, she smelled like strawberries and baby, and that protective place in me swelled.

It was the same place that worried incessantly about my little brother.

The same place I'd thought had long ago been filled to capacity.

Somehow broken and faulty, composed of guilt and regret. A distorted obligation.

But that place had transformed.

Expanded.

More, more, more.

I ran the towel through her hair again, gripping the mass and gently tugging her head back as I made a last pass. She peered up at me, and I pressed a kiss to her forehead. "There we are."

I grabbed a brush and ran it through Kallie's dampened hair.

I could feel eyes on me as I worked, this little girl's attention trained on me through the mirror.

I glanced up at her, seeing the wonder there, something brewing in her eyes.

She brushed her teeth, then after helping her down, she ran to her room with the towel around her, the bottom dragging on the floor.

Pausing at the doorway, I listened to Shea's voice traveling from her bedroom, carefree and airy. "No problem, Charlie," she said, and I continued on toward Kallie's room.

By the time I made it there, she'd already dug through her dresser and had pulled a nightgown over her head.

She hopped right into bed.

Chuckling, I crossed the room and sank down to my knees next to her. I helped her adjust the covers, and those shoulders lifted up to her cheeks. She released a timid giggle, her expression shifting back to the way she was watching me through the mirror.

One arm snaked out, and she tentatively ran the pads of tiny fingertips along the ink scrawled over my left forearm, my hard and scarred and tainted a stark contradiction to the purity of this kid, snowy flesh up against all my dark.

Her voice was a whisper. "I wanna have butterflies painted all over my arms just like Momma has on her side."

Instantly, I was picturing this little girl grown. Eighteen or more. As beautiful as her mom. Tattoos swirling in bright, distinct patterns down her arms. Another flash with skin unmarred.

A piece inside me broke at the same time as it lifted.

Would I get to be around for that? To witness who this incredible kid became?

"Just like you, Baz." She said it in that sweet voice, mouth pulling at every direction, her smile so fucking overpowering I was nothing but a puddle in the middle of her floor. "I want lots and lots."

A rough chuckle rumbled from me, and I tugged at one of those unruly curls. "What do you think your mommy would think about that?"

"Momma likes yours."

Another chuckle, this one deeper. She sure as hell seemed to.

"Can I get one right now?"

"Uh…no." I tried to contain my amusement. "You have to wait until you're big. Like your mom."

"What if I asked her pretty please?"

"Pretty sure that'd still be a big huge no." Didn't need to get into the fact it wasn't even an option.

"How about if you were my daddy? Would you let me?"

I fucking froze, my mouth going dry.

I swallowed around the rock at the base of my throat when I finally caught up.

Had seen those wheels turning in her head, kid as clever as they came as she hedged a subject we'd been skating along for weeks.

God, I was treading on thin ice. Walking a fine line.

Knew I was about five seconds from a fall.

I cautioned my response. "If I were your daddy, then I'd tell you no, too, because little girls aren't allowed to get tattoos. And then when you got big, I'd encourage you to do whatever makes you happy, as long as it doesn't hurt you or anyone else. As long as it's good, just like you."

Cheeks going red, she grinned wide, gripping the covers and holding them at her chin. "I think I would like that."

"What would you like?"

"If you were my daddy."

My heart lurched. And I tripped.
Falling.
Falling.
Falling.
Going under.
Sinking deeper.

I felt the presence behind me. The billow of her storm. A fierce squall of energy pressed into the room. Drawn, I looked over my shoulder. Our eyes met, a thousand words passing in a glance. A vision of a future I'd spend my life working to deserve.

Shea lifted her chin, giving me the go. Passing on her unconditional support and belief. *In me.* The answer I gave was entirely my choice.

But there was no missing the intensity behind her consent. The vehement zeal she protected her daughter with.

If I was in, then I was all in.

This wasn't a fucking game and there would be no turning back.

Slowly, I swiveled my attention back to the little girl who'd changed everything.

Kallie just grinned more, like it was the most natural thing in the world and she hadn't just shifted the axis of mine.

But that was the thing. It was natural. Meant to be. Because even though the words hadn't been said, we'd been heading this direction all along.

When I'd started my pursuit, this was the road I was getting led down, even though at the time I'd no clue of the destination.

Because Shea didn't have time for distractions or diversions.

Both of them deserved it all. Something solid. Permanent.

A tremble rolled through me, because I still had so much shit. So many demons, regrets, and consequences yet to be paid.

But just like me, Shea was all in.

She already knew the deal.

What I was up against and where I could go.

And by the grace of God she was willing to stand by me through it all.

The words came raspy as they passed from my mouth. "I think I would like that, too."

nine
Shea

A MISTY GLOW DRAPED the enormous room. Bodies were packed wall to wall in the carefree atmosphere. For years, *Charlie's* had been a staple in Savannah. A place people converged to cast away their worries and concerns. To let go and feel free. Unfettered by the day's tribulations. The entire city seemed to flock here for a reprieve. They let themselves go within these old, rustic walls that always seemed to hold a million secrets. Like the old wood echoed with them, keeping them safe and protected.

Sebastian's and my secret had begun here.

An unrelenting attraction that had grown into something magnificent.

I felt the smile edge my mouth, and I tried to focus on my job rather than the man who refused to leave my mind.

A week had passed since I'd returned to my normal schedule here at *Charlie's* where I worked nights so I could be with Kallie during the day.

But our lives hadn't come close to returning to *normal*, and our days were the furthest from being ordinary or mundane. The familiar pattern I'd grown so accustomed to—one of Kallie and I surviving alone—had been eradicated. Replaced with a passion that threatened to consume me. To burn me alive with the vibrancy and intensity.

Chewing at my bottom lip, I pushed those thoughts aside and delivered drinks to a booth close to the stage. The three guys sitting there were all business, suit jackets removed, sleeves of their button-ups rolled up casually as they relaxed at the end of the day.

Two bands were scheduled to play tonight, and we were on a break between the two. Our sound guy, Derrick, was playing one of those new upbeat country songs, and it blared from the speakers.

People swarmed the dance floor at the base of the stage, couples gliding into a two-step, getting lost in the easy vibe.

I delivered drinks to a couple more tables, then stopped to take the order of a group of five barely legal girls who'd just made their way in and grabbed an open table in my section. All of them were out to celebrate the youngest girl's twenty-first birthday. Dressed in next to nothing, clearly begging for attention, overdone hair and makeup, bare skin for miles.

I only knew it was the youngest's birthday considering I'd double-checked her ID about five times because she looked like she couldn't be a day older than fifteen.

Each of them ordered a frilly drink. They were giggling and whispering as if they were in middle school, and I shot them a quick grin. Even if I couldn't relate, I was never one to judge anyone for their fun. I jotted down their order and said, "I'll be right back with those."

I shouldered back through the throng gathered around the high-top tables set up in the open space in front of the dance floor, and worked my way back to the ornate bar floating like an oasis in the center of *Charlie's*.

My uncle Charlie stood behind it.

His never-ending smile peeked through his ratty beard and my heart throbbed in appreciation. He was mixing drinks in shakers while chatting with an old man who appeared to be doing a stand-up job of drowning his sorrows. Knowing Charlie, he was giving it his all to build the poor guy up.

That was the thing about Charlie.

He was one of the *good* guys.

Everything he did was for the benefit of someone else.

He caught me grinning as I approached and tossed me a wink. "Hey there, Shea Bear. You doing okay? Looks like we have some wild ones out there tonight."

Tamar sidled up beside him, long hair the most vibrant kind of red. Her lips were dyed even redder, and she quirked them up in a sexy grin as she snatched the bottle of vodka from Charlie's hand. "Pssh. You don't know wild, old man."

Laughter trickled from me, and I shook my head as I slid the napkin where I'd written the five girls' drinks on across the bar.

"What, is Savannah getting too boring for your L.A. blood?" I teased her, lifting a brow at my friend who stood out in this bar just about as bad as Sebastian had the first time I'd seen him hidden in his corner booth.

"Never," she shot back with a smile. "I like *boring* just fine. Why do you think I've stuck around so long?"

"Uh…pretty sure that'd be because of me, darlin'," Charlie supplied, stretching his arms out like he was the obvious gift of living in Savannah.

No doubt, he was a bonus.

He'd been taking care of Tamar and me since we'd walked through *Charlie's* doors years ago, each of us escaping here for our own reasons. I'd been running home and Tamar had been running *from* home.

An ironic expression slid across Tamar's face as she poured the vodka across three shot glasses. "Now who's full of himself?"

Charlie had been giving Tamar crap about being full of herself since she started working here. Neither of us had ever seen her not completely put together, not a piece of hair out of place, makeup thick yet flawless, clothes just like she'd stepped out of one of those motorcycle magazines, tattooed skin for days.

She was a force.

Unwilling to allow anyone to mess with her.

I had my suspicions she'd been messed with enough.

But she was the kind of force to be welcomed, the girl proud yet profoundly loyal.

Charlie's expression turned sly. "Just tellin' it like it is, sweetheart. And for the record, my bar isn't anything close to boring."

With a laugh, I shook my head.

Cocky old man.

His smile faded, and he looked at me seriously. "But for real, how's it goin' out there, Bear? You doing okay tonight?"

The smile I gave him was soft and appreciative, and it only just hinted at an eye-roll because my burly, softy of an uncle had taken all that fatherly concern he typically watched me with to a striking new level.

But I completely understood it. His concern wasn't just for me. He was worried about Kallie's welfare, just as much as the rest of us. He was thinking of her future and the threat of what may come to pass.

Martin Jennings's resurgence lurked like cobwebs in the corners of my mind.

Weeks had passed without a word. It left me in a state of disquiet. Constantly on guard. But I refused to give my life to a worry that for the time I couldn't control.

I would relish in this moment's harmony and savor the love I'd been given.

No, I was no fool. There was so much to worry about, concern flying at us from every direction. But that was another thing my grandmother had taught me.

You take what you're given and make the very best of it. Live life to the fullest even when it might feel empty. Live like there are no barriers when there are walls towering in front of you. Be prepared to fight, even in times of peace. And be willing to live in peace when there are wars raging all around you.

And God, this was going to be a war.

I could feel it.

Felt it to the deepest places in my spirit. In that instinctual place born the first time I held my daughter in my arms. A mother's knowledge. A gut feeling that whispered and warned and told me to prepare.

Part of me had been preparing for years, because I knew Martin would never forget what I knew.

But in the meantime, while I lay in wait, I wouldn't be shirking or shrinking, and I refused to give into the misery that simmered like a threat in the darkest fragment of me.

For now, I chose to live.

And when this life called me to fight, I would fight.

"I'm just fine, Charlie. Really," I promised.

"That's my girl."

Tamar began filling my drink order when the double doors swung open. Even though there'd been a constant flow of people traipsing in and out tonight, my attention immediately sought out the source. As if there was no other place in the world I could possibly look.

Expectation.

A bond absolute.

A tension only I could feel.

Sebastian stepped through the door, all strength and mystery and damaged beauty. The lamp swinging from the rafters above him amplified it, striking against the bold, powerful lines of his face. Those strange grey eyes made a pass through the room. Hunting. They were quick to lock on me.

Chills skated down my spine. A scatter of butterflies blossomed in my belly, fluttering just under the surface of my skin, lifting my flesh in a rush of goosebumps.

It made no difference how many times he had me.

He always held me.

Captive.

Ensnared and bound.

Without conscious choice, I was moving, as if my feet weren't even touching the ground. Erasing the space between us.

Sebastian stood there in the rays of muted, hazy light, emanating that almost frightening, masculine glory. An old black T-shirt stretched tight across his solid chest. The mural of intricate ink scrawled down the entirety of his arms, the story written there jumping and twitching with the bristling muscle.

His expression was somehow both cruel and dripping with affection.

Devastating.

And I thought perhaps I'd lost a piece of my mind, a part of my soul, because my mouth watered and my body hummed with need that bordered on unhealthy.

Vivid.

Violent.

Dangerous.

I didn't even acknowledge the rest of the guys who stepped through the door behind him.

Instead I was pushing up on my toes and wrapping my arms around his neck, and his arms were closing around my waist.

Warmth and relief.

That pretty, pretty mouth came closer and closer until it met with mine.

Heaven.

"Hi," he mumbled at my lips, his tweaking up at the corners beneath our connection.

God, I loved when I could feel him smile under our kiss.

"Hi," I answered. Reluctantly, I pulled away. "I thought you guys were practicing tonight?"

Not that I was going to complain.

"We finished early," Sebastian supplied quickly. Something passed through the savage expression that stuttered my heart with a slick of apprehension.

He forced a tight smile, and I tore my gaze from him, allowing my eyes to travel to the guys.

A rowdy pile of rock star filled up *Charlie's* doorway.

Almost angtsy.

Anxious.

Wild and unruly and so obviously out of place.

"Hey, guys."

Lyrik hazarded a hand through the mess of black atop his head, tattooed fingers flashing in the light, dark eyes in a constant blaze as he lifted his chin to me in greeting.

Zee leaned in and dropped a swift kiss to my cheek. "Hey, Shea," he murmured lightly, casting a quick glance at Sebastian.

Wary.

A short ribbon of dread unfurled in my belly.

Something was up.

Distracting me, Ash was quick to step forward and hook his arm around my neck, flashing me his dimples. "Sitting at home on a gorgeous Tuesday night with all that *Charlie's* has to offer? Now that just seems ludicrous. The temptation is too great to resist. What man in his right mind would pass up good music, great drinks, and beautiful ladies? So here we are to take advantage. You should be honored by our presence."

As always, Ash was all too keen to lay it on thick.

The guy was larger than life, more arrogant than anyone I'd ever met, but even I had to admit it was all part of his charm. Without a doubt, he'd left a trail of dropped panties all across the world.

He kissed the top of my head, grinning as he turned us out to survey the landscape of *Charlie's*. "Tell me you saved our favorite booth for us."

Ash's favorite booth?

I glanced to the booth secreted away in the darkest corner of the bar. The place I would forever think of as Sebastian's.

As ours.

A place Ash, in all his arrogant grandeur, had decided to claim as his own.

The brave, bold side of me wanted to set him straight. Let him in on exactly what had transpired there. The self-conscious side said *no chance in hell*.

I felt the eyes on me, and I glanced over to catch Sebastian's burning gaze, swimming in mischief and simmering with sex, and my teeth latched onto my bottom lip in an attempt to snuff out my reaction, the embarrassment and heat that instantly smoldered on my cheeks.

Without a doubt, his mind was exactly where mine was, back in that night when he'd broken me.

Marked me.

Tainted me.

I'd thought it was the end, when in reality, we were just beginning.

A couple was snuggled up in our booth, the girl playing coy and the guy looking as if he was getting ready to dive in and devour her.

Apparently it was catching.

I glanced up at Ash who still had his arm locked round my neck. "Ah…no. I'm sorry, but I didn't think you guys were coming.

You're going to have to make do with a table down front. Do you think you can handle that?"

Ash huffed out the fakest sigh. "Fine. But that means you have to slip us some free drinks."

He winked.

"Ha. You wish, rich boy. Just for that, I'm going to announce to the bar an entire round is on you."

"Rich boy?" Horror lashed across his face. "Now that's just plain cold, Shea."

A short burst of laughter rang from me.

I had never met a group of guys more mortified by their wealth. It was kind of endearing and sweet, and there was something about it that made me love the lot of them just a little more.

Love.

It was true.

I'd come to think of Sebastian's unorthodox family as my own. Just as he'd come to fall in love with mine.

With the one.

My child.

Hearing Kallie call him *Daddy* was one of the most terrifying, marvelous things to ever fall from her sweet mouth. Like the first time she said *Momma*. So pure and full of undying trust.

Those simple, simple dreams were making a valiant attempt at becoming my reality.

Kallie kept testing it, tasting how it felt on her tongue, and Sebastian would be blatantly overcome by emotion every time she asserted it.

We were moving fast. As if we were caught in a tunnel of speeding light. Flashing forward. Velocity hurtling us toward the future.

It was exhilarating and wholly unnerving.

Because neither of us knew where we would land. So many

unanswered questions remained, but there was no stopping the momentum that had us flying.

Again, I got swept away by the feeling my feet weren't touching the ground. As if I were suspended just above it, drifting through the most sublime kind of dream.

Around my neck, Ash squeezed his arm a little tighter and leaned forward to look at Sebastian. "Tell your woman here we work hard for our money."

Amusement played at Sebastian, warm eyes heating me up.

I bumped Ash with my hip. "Oh, I bet you work *hard*, all right."

Ash feigned a shocked gasp. "Are you speaking in innuendoes, beautiful, innocent Shea? I believe our boy here has corrupted you. And now I am most definitely *hard*."

He tossed me a playful smirk, one that looked a whole lot smug as he slanted it toward Sebastian.

A threat clouded Sebastian's striking face, and I sucked in a breath.

God, looking so good should be criminal. I guess maybe it came with the territory.

"Hands off my girl, asshole, or you won't have the capacity to work *hard* at anything."

Laughter ricocheted around the room, Ash's and mine.

Unwinding myself from Ash, I made a move toward Sebastian, grinning wildly, and I let him wind me up instead.

Wound.

Wound.

Wound.

With him, that's where I remained.

Insides twisted and twined. Restless and edgy.

A strong, deliberate hand skated down my back, firm palm gripping my ass over my cut-off shorts.

Aroused.

Yes.

Let's not forget I was always, always aroused.

Sebastian nuzzled his nose into my cheek, grazing up and over the seam of my ear. He inhaled, exhaled, his expelled energy spinning through me like a tempest. "Missed you, baby."

"I missed you, too."

It didn't matter that little more than eight hours had passed since I'd last seen him, it was true.

That fact was a little terrifying, too.

I was in deep.

Somewhere bottomless.

Fathomless.

Lyrik bypassed us. He glanced back over his shoulder as he headed for the riot of bodies congregating in the bar. He lifted his voice so we could hear him over the noise. "We gonna drink or stand around like a pack of bitches watching Baz feel up his girl all night?"

He headed deeper into the fray, menacing strength striding through the crowd. He was so tall I could see the tilt of his head as he turned to consume Tamar in his fiery glare.

She basically snarled at him from her post behind the bar.

Tension ricocheted between them. Maybe Tamar had warmed to the idea of Sebastian and me, but it did not apply to the rest of the guys.

Especially Lyrik.

I couldn't tell what she wanted more—to rip off his face or his clothes. I'd asked her point-blank if something had happened between them, and she'd just grunted a slur about *cocky assholes think they can take whatever they want* and something about how happy it'd make her to *cut off his dick and cram it down his throat.*

Whatever was going on? She was fighting it with teeth bared.

Sebastian didn't let me go as we followed Lyrik, who apparently knew exactly where he was headed. He was already taking a seat on a stool at one of the high-top tables close to the stage.

"Make yourself at home," I teased.

I forced myself to untangle my limbs from Sebastian and he slid onto his stool.

You have a job to do, I reminded myself, because the only thing I wanted to do right then was crawl onto his lap.

One cavalier brow arched, Lyrik all kinds of smug. I swear, these guys were too much, my hands full every single time they walked through the door. "Figured we had an in and all."

Zee and Ash took the remaining stools.

Ash let out an exaggerated sigh, and he sat back, blue gaze probing the crowd. Calculating. Ready to make a move. It was clear what was on his mind.

As much as I hated it, I couldn't stop the prick of jealousy that jabbed at my consciousness.

There was no missing the way the women seemed immediately drawn to them. Heads turning. Attention seeking. None immune to the aura that glimmered around the whole of them, a bristle of sex and dangerous beauty and lust.

It was this way night after night, and it became ever more obvious that Sebastian was *wanted*. That he was and would always be the target of many affections. I couldn't help but wonder how many times he had been in a bar just like this, staging his own move.

Pain needled at my skin. Was it crazy the idea of him with anyone else hurt? But it felt as if I'd been waiting for him my entire life. I'd never been the jealous type, but Sebastian held the power to evoke the most foolish kinds of reactions in me. He made me feel things I'd never felt before. Experience the impossible and suffer the exquisite.

I shoved off the useless thoughts. "So what is everyone drinking tonight?"

Everything about Ash gleamed. "Bring us our usual, darlin'. But make them doubles. We have cause for celebration."

Sebastian flinched. In my periphery, I caught the glower in his expression. One that warned he was about two seconds away from reaching across the table to rip Ash's tongue out.

That feeling was back, the sense I was being propelled forward by a rushing tide of joy, while at the same time, was about to be ensnared in an unseen undertow.

Threatened to be washed out to sea.

Sinking.

Sebastian's voice was soft. Almost afraid to, I slowly turned to look at him.

Grey eyes caressed me softly, almost as soft as his voice. "Just get us our regulars, baby."

"Okay."

I walked away, though there was no distance where I couldn't feel the weight of his stare as I struggled through the bottleneck to get back to the bar. The next band had struck up, and the already ear-splitting noise had escalated to deafening.

Tamar frowned at me as she slid drinks for the five girls I'd all but forgotten toward me. "You look green," she shouted over the music.

"I'm fine."

She released a chuckle of disbelief. "Liar."

Arranging drinks on my tray, I fumbled through an incredulous laugh. "Am I that transparent?"

"Yep." She gestured with her chin in the direction of the guys' table. "When it comes to him, you've always been. Since the first night he showed up here."

I lifted a shoulder. "Honestly, it's nothing. I just got a…weird feeling." I shook my head. "For so long my only focus had been coming here to earn enough to support my daughter and myself and then going home to her. It's a little unsettling having my life so unsettled."

She snorted. "Love has a way of *unsettling* you. Just be careful it doesn't knock you off your feet."

The warning hit me strange, inciting that ominous feeling that had been trying to make itself known for weeks. One I'd shoved down time and again, unwilling to give voice or time because all I wanted was this *time* with him.

The problem was, I didn't want that *time* to end.

Tamar was on top of it, passing me the guys' drinks, already knowing what they would order.

I smiled in appreciation. "You're a rock star."

"Ha. Not so much, but I'm pretty sure you have a table full of them waiting for you right about now. Get going, woman. You can't leave them alone for long or they'll incite some kind of riot. Lord knows Charlie will have a meltdown."

Light laughter rumbled from me, because it really wasn't that far from the truth. Trouble followed them everywhere they went.

I balanced my tray with drinks for both tables, careful not to slosh anything as I weaved my way through the throbbing crowd. Everyone had begun to move, energy alive as the upbeat country band roused the already over-eager crowd.

By the time I cleared a mob of guys blocking my path, all five party girls were standing around Baz's table.

Hanging off the guys.

Smiling and flirting and making something I didn't even recognize rise inside me.

God.

This wasn't me.

Not even close.

But I had the overwhelming urge to throw the tray of drinks in the redhead's face, because she was rubbing up against my man, whispering something in his ear, getting friendly in a way that made me want to rip her arms from her body.

But Sebastian.

Sebastian was just staring across at me, those severe eyes still caressing up and down, like they hadn't stopped. Something like a smile ticked up at the edge of one side of his pretty, pretty mouth. As if he could read my thoughts like they were written in a book, a play-by-play of the possessiveness that crested in me, wave after wave.

But I felt his promise.

It was always going to be me.

Tamping down my insecurities, I approached, brow arched as I took in the raucous members of Sebastian's pseudo-family. "Looks like you've all suckered in a little company. Guess you're trying to make my job easy on me tonight. Shall I drop all of these here?"

Ash took an appreciative glance around the table surrounded by too much skin. "Sounds like a damned good plan to me, Beautiful Shea."

I shouldered in between Lyrik and Baz and set my tray on the table. Maybe I shouldn't have felt so smug when I jostled the redhead toward Lyrik, but hell, I was only human.

Who could blame me?

I passed shot glasses to the guys, frilly drinks to the girls, all the while gritting my teeth and trying to cling to some kind of maturity, because I was long past playing games. Ironic, considering I was feeling about as petulant as a fifteen-year-old girl who's daddy told her she wasn't allowed to go to the prom and the boy she was crushing on had asked someone else.

An arm snaked out, wrapping around my belly, hot hand splaying wide as I was dragged back onto the lap I'd had a fantasy of climbing just minutes before.

My body was awkwardly draped across his, my back to his chest and one of his knees sliding up between my thighs to keep me attached to him. One of my booted feet was planted on the ground and my other leg was pushed up under the table by the force of him.

A shocked sound left me, and his breath was rough at my ear, words hoarse. "Do you know how damned sexy you are when you're jealous?"

I squeaked.

Caught.

Guilty.

I didn't even have it in me to be ashamed.

"You think I want that girl?" he continued on like a threat, and a shudder rolled through me with the groan that rumbled in his chest. His voice went lower. Darker. "Only thing I want right now is to drag you down the hallway and into the bathroom, rip these shorts off your fucking insanely long legs, and sink into you from behind. I'd like nothing more than to watch you through the mirror as you shake and tremble."

His hand wandered farther down, cupping me over my sex.

I whimpered, thanking God the evidence of what he was doing was obstructed by the height of the table and the shadowy darkness surrounding us.

"Watch you come undone," he rumbled.

My blood pulsed and raced, and a flush sprinted across the surface of my skin. Mouth parted, I tilted my head to the side, so close his stubble rubbed at my cheek.

Intense eyes peered down at me.

Desire.

Want.

Lust.

There was no mistaking it.

No disguising it.

Guess the redhead got the message, too, because I caught just a glimpse of her pout before she turned her attention to Lyrik who already had the birthday girl crawling all over him.

He didn't seem to mind, and normally I'd roll my eyes because, wow, that really was just ridiculous and cliché. Nothing like a rock star getting greedy and taking two.

But I was too busy trying to control the way I shivered and shook as Sebastian let his fingers go trailing beneath the frayed hem of my cut-off shorts.

Good Lord, he was bold. His brazen confidence all too eager to set me straight on my wayward worries.

"You got that?" He ran his thumb just under the edge of my panties. "Don't make me prove it."

Was he serious? I was about five seconds from begging him to.

Struggling for air, I gripped the edge of the table.

I was being every kind of unprofessional. Flustered and hot, I forgot where I was because Sebastian Stone had a way of making me forget everything except for him.

Peeling myself from his lap, I straightened myself. I hoped it wasn't blatantly obvious how outrageously turned on I was.

Lyrik watched me with outright humor, raking his teeth along his bottom lip to contain his amusement, just as both girls got a little more comfortable. Ash grinned like a fool, Zee with a shake of his head and a slightly embarrassed smile.

Um…obvious. Very, very obvious. Flustered, I tucked a thick lock of hair behind my ear. "Anything else I can get y'all?"

Ash lifted his shot. "Stay…I'm about to toast."

He looked around the guys, first at Lyrik who raised his chin at the same time as he lifted his shot glass, as if he already knew exactly what they were celebrating. He moved on to Zee who lifted a drink of his own, creases of discomfort appearing at the corners of his eyes. Then he moved to Baz who dug his fingers into my side. As if he were holding on for dear life because he felt it slipping away.

Felt me slipping away.

Ash lifted his shot glass a little higher. "To a future that's looking bright."

And I should have found comfort in it, because Ash was pure smiles and uncontained satisfaction.

But I didn't, because those fingers at my side tightened.

Almost painfully.

Regret.

Regret.

Regret.

It stormed around us.

The group of girls lifted their glasses, having no idea what they were toasting, but eager to play along. "To the future."

As if any of them would be a part of it.

And the unease in Sebastian left me wondering if I would be, either.

I did my best to focus on work and not pay attention to the way Sebastian watched me throughout the night. It was virtually impossible.

That piercing gaze followed me, seeking and searching me out, the constant flickering and changing emotion almost too much for me to bear.

I wanted to beg him for reassurance, for the night to pass quickly so he could take me and wrap me in his arms, provide encouragement that whatever I was feeling was unwarranted.

The second band was still on stage, working through their final set. A haze of indistinct faces filtered through my sight as I went through the motions, my concentration focused on the single table that stood out in the limelight. Prominent above all others.

When I emerged from the kitchen through the swinging doors and back into the bar, it was again immediate. I executed my own hunt, seeking him out.

Only this time, he was no longer there. The same five girls surrounded the table, Lyrik and Ash more than pleased to entertain them, Zee straddling the sidelines, as if he didn't want to be a part of their games.

Sebastian's chair was empty.

Blood pumped heavily through my veins. On edge, I moved through the crowd, taking care of my customers up close to the dance floor in front of the stage, faking smiles and tossing out counterfeit pleasantries.

I delivered appetizers to a table and began to back away.

An erotic shock burned through me with the arm that wrapped around to my front from behind.

Sebastian had surfaced from within the mass, and he was quick to pull me back into the center of the clash of bodies that surged and swayed on the dance floor, an agitated crush that rolled with the beat.

Sebastian's movements were completely at odds with the frenzy, each action purposed, steady and strong as he slowly turned me in his arms.

"Dance with me," he whispered so close to my ear I could hear him above the clamor.

And it was so sweet, the constant contradiction to all his hard and brash and scarred. This beautiful, torrid man proceeded to secure me in the strength of his arms. His heart beat hard, a boom, boom, boom supplied by his own unrest.

Completely enfolded in him, I pressed my face into his collarbone. Breathed him in. Desperately, my fingers fisted in his shirt.

"Tell me what's happening."

The resigned breath he released filtered across the top of my head, stirring my hair. He drew me closer. "They want us back in California on Thursday."

Sorrow flamed from the pit of my stomach, licking up to touch me everywhere.

I clung to him tighter, my arms bound between us, fists in his shirt, powerful arms hugging and hugging and hugging.

I couldn't breathe.

Sebastian spoke at the top of my head, the words vibrating my bones, unheard yet understood. "Kenny pled down the assault charges."

Relief blasted through every cell of my body.

"No jail time," Sebastian explained. "Community service and a fucking fortune in fines, but that's it. I have to appear in front of a judge to finalize it all, but the criminal shit is done. Martin can still come after me with the civil suit, but he's not taking me from you."

Then why did it still feel like he was?

The overpowering relief I felt in his freedom was a strange sensation. Yes, Martin may still try to exert control over me, but he no longer held that control over Sebastian—the threat of jail time for standing up for his brother. For protecting and preserving. It clashed with the realization that the call on Sebastian's life was finally calling him away.

Even though I knew it would come to this, it didn't make Sebastian leaving me any less difficult.

Strobes flashed from above the stage, and a chaotic ring of bodies circled us while Sebastian slowly swayed, moving us at half the pace of the strident beat.

Clearing his throat, he continued, "With the news, our label wants us back on the road immediately after my court appearance. They're putting together a short tour, mostly western states, getting us out to a few cities to build a buzz, before we're back in the studio to record the new album. Guys are fuckin' relieved, baby. This is what we've been waiting for."

He pulled back, hands framing my face. Sadness crawled across his defined features. His jaw clenched as he dealt with the jumble of emotions. Thumbs stroked beneath my eyes, fingers firm as they dug into the back of my neck. "Fuck…just looking at you breaks my goddamned heart. Everything I'm feeling right now is written all over your face."

He squeezed in emphasis, searching me, slipping inside, under, and all around. Stealing more.

"Is…is moving there…permanent?" I stammered over the question, because this…this is what we'd avoided. We'd evaded talk of the inevitable and instead jumped right on that speeding train.

He gave a quick, uncertain shake of his head. A steely frown tipped down the crooked side of his mouth. "I don't know."

Taking my hand trapped between us, he wove our fingers together. He lifted them and gently brushed his lips across my knuckles. The promise was muttered on fierce words. "All I know is that *this…this* is what is permanent. The rest of my life…I don't know. What the hell I'm gonna do with my baby brother…the guys…how long I can keep living this kind of life. The only thing I'm certain about is you. But I also know for now I *can't* change this, Shea."

"I told you I would never ask you to give it up. It's a part of who you are. What makes you wonderful and a piece of what truly makes you happy."

He dropped his face into the side of my head and nodded, because he knew it, too.

An impossible silence enveloped us in a cocoon of unknowns and apprehension and insecurities.

"What does it mean for us?" I finally managed to ask. His heart pounded beneath the thin fabric of his shirt.

Pulling back, he pinned me with an unflinching stare. "When we finish up touring the west coast, I want you to come to California."

My spirit danced with the idea, before reality came crashing down. Because just like Sebastian, I had my own responsibilities. "I can't just leave here, Sebastian. Uproot Kallie. This is our home."

"I'm not asking you to pack up all your stuff and move right now. I'm asking you to come out for a while. Check out L.A. See where I live and what I do. We'll figure out the rest of it from there. One day at time, as long as each of those days lead to you always being at my side."

Still clutching him, I almost laughed. "I hate L.A., remember?"

Face turned toward the ceiling, he chuckled, before he leveled me with the most brilliant kind of smile. "Not a big city kind of girl, huh?"

This time my soggy laughter bled free as we both went back to that first night when he'd coaxed me onto the back of his bike, when he'd teased and played and taunted me against the outside wall of my house, tempting me in all the ways a man had never had the power to do before.

When I'd fought, refusing to give in, a fool to think *this* was escapable.

"Savannah is just fine." With lightness woven into my tone, I parroted the answer I'd given him then. My voice went quiet with sincerity. "But only when you're in it."

Now…now I wasn't so sure I could ever see this place the same after he was gone.

Because I wasn't the same.

And when you change, it's impossible to stay in the same place.

ten
Sebastian

I SHIFTED UNCOMFORTABLY AGAINST the hard, wooden chair, my nerves frayed and frenzied. Just because Kenny had this all wrapped up, the plea accepted by both parties, didn't mean I was sitting easy. Furthest from it.

Being in the same room with Martin Jennings was punishment in itself.

My knee bounced a million miles a minute, and Kenny cut me a glance. *Calm down.*

I couldn't.

An itch slithered along my skin. Did it make me sick I wanted nothing more than to stand up in the middle of court and take out Jennings?

He sat across the room, also facing the judge. That didn't mean his arrogance wasn't filling the room. Polluting the air. Felt like I was suffocating in it.

I tugged at my too-tight collar, fiddled with my tie.

"Mr. Stone," the judge asked, the old man crotchety and bald, "you're in agreement with the plea accepted by the state prosecutors?"

"Yes, sir," I said, throat raw.

He nodded and peered at the papers through wire-rimmed reading glasses. He didn't look up at me as he read the terms, the fine, and the probation.

I knew I should thank my lucky stars I wasn't going to find my ass behind bars again, but hell, this shit stung. Jennings sitting over there cool as a cat, the prick kicked back like he was squeaky clean and not the bottom feeder he was.

Somewhere along the way, these bogus assault charges had taken the backburner to whatever corrupt intentions he had with Shea and Kallie. Yeah, I wanted out of this legal mess. Mostly because it meant I'd be free, better equipped to take care of my girls.

The judge kept reading, "The defendant may not come within one hundred yards of victim…"

Right.

They were telling me to stay away from Jennings. If only that would keep him away from Shea and Kallie.

The judge finished and we stood as he did, the man quick to exit to his chambers. The moment he did, Kenny turned to me and clapped me on the back. "Congratulations, Sebastian." He narrowed his eyes in warning. "Let's stay out of court, shall we?"

I shook his hand. "I'll do my best."

Dry laughter rolled from him. "I think you might want to *dig deep* to find that best."

He knew me well.

I followed Kenny through the short gate where Anthony waited, doing my best not to look in Jennings's direction. I probably deserved a pat on the back considering I could feel his pretentious glare burning into the back of my head.

Anthony shook my hand. A satisfied smile held his face. "I told you we wouldn't allow you to go to jail for this. This is good, Baz. Really good."

"You never let me down."

His smile warmed.

Kenny led the way out of the courtroom, down the hall, and onto the courthouse steps.

A barrage of flashes went off.

No surprise.

The paparazzi descended the second I stepped out the door.

"Mr. Stone, can you tell us the outcome of the assault charges?"

"You made a public statement confirming your relationship with Delaney Rhoads…or Shea Bentley, yet you're back in L.A. while Ms. Bentley remains in Savannah. Has that relationship ended?"

I knew it was a bad idea to engage them, but that one? Couldn't keep my mouth shut.

"Ms. Bentley and I are still very much together."

Anthony grabbed my upper arm, the same way he always did when he went into business mode. "Mr. Stone won't be answering any further questions this afternoon. You can direct inquiries to my office."

We crossed the street and headed for my truck parked in the adjoining lot.

I'd left both my car and the Suburban back in Savannah with Shea. Couldn't help it, wanting to leave something with her, like a promise this time apart wasn't really a separation, that I'd be coming back to her and Kallie as soon as I could.

Only five days had passed and I was already missing the hell out of them. Missing the laughter and joy. The ease of their house that felt like a home.

Anthony and I said our goodbyes at the curb as he climbed into the back of the town car he had waiting. I clicked the fob and opened the door of my truck.

An ominous presence crawled over me like a disease.

Fuck.

I raked a hand over the top of my head, hesitant to turn around, knowing who I would find. Did it anyway, because what the hell was I supposed to do?

Martin Jennings stood about one hundred fifty feet away. A whole ton closer than the hundred yards the judge had just ordered, the bastard taunting me. Attempting to incite the rage I was doing my best to control.

What was the protocol here? Questions raced. It wasn't like I'd tracked him down, but I really didn't have the first clue what the court order entailed. Seemed I should figure that shit out.

Stat.

I released a bitter chuckle as I completely turned around, standing at the open door of my truck. "And to what do I owe the displeasure?"

"You think you got away with this?"

"*I* got away with this?" My words were teeming with implication. With all the shit I knew about him. So maybe some of it wasn't first-hand, but God knew my baby brother had witnessed plenty.

Austin had admitted enough for me to know it was Martin's guys who had supplied both him and Mark. Didn't give a fuck if it made me a snitch. If it kept Kallie and Shea out of his grips? I'd give myself the damned title.

Go down in flames.

As long as it meant I could protect my family. Every last one of them were tied to this piece of shit.

"I warned you you'd regret fucking with me, and I always make good on my promises."

My fists clenched. "You like fucking with little girl's heads? Keeping them scared and wondering what the hell is going on with their lives? Kallie spending two days in your presence was payment enough. One second was too much."

Cruel and unjust punishment.

Torture.

For all of us.

He scoffed. "That was a mere warning."

"What do you want?"

"What Shea owes me." Dark eyes gleamed conceit and contempt. "Everything."

He set his shoulders back, lifted his scarred chin that I'd really like to scar up some more. "Like I told her, taking you down with her is just a bonus."

He stared me down like the world owed him something and he was out to take it back.

Scratch that.

Like he owned the world.

Untouchable.

My insides nearly cracked, a knot of aggression throbbing to be unleashed. "Shea owes you nothing," I growled.

"I think you'll find that's not true. Her money-hungry mother assured me in the contracts she was so eager for Shea to sign. Shea breaching them solidified it, and that kid guaranteed it."

Kallie.

Kallie.

Kallie.

My chest heaved at his disregard because *that kid* had become *my kid*.

"Stay away from them. Stay away from my family. Stay away from me." The words sounded like gravel as I forced them out, holding onto the last threads of my unraveling control.

Last thing I needed was to give into his baiting. I knew this asshole wanted me in jail. Out of his way.

Was that what this was about?

Gettin' rid of me?

A shot of air escaped his nose.

Incredulous.

Scornful.

"Shea had obligations. She reneged on them. That doesn't mean I don't expect restitution. Just like Mark." He said the last like a threat.

Mark.

I gripped my head.

Pain.

Dread.

Questions.

Too much.

I tried to stand beneath the blow, because it felt like I was under an all-out attack.

Shea.

Kallie.

Mark.

Austin.

How can one man be linked to all the people in my life?

Fuck.

My hand clamped down on the inner door handle of my truck. God knew I was about to come loose.

"You won't touch her," I warned. "Even think about it and you can consider the little party we had the last time I showed up at your house a prelude to what's coming for you."

Punks kids like your brother aren't ever going to make it, anyway.

I'd never forget what he'd said.

Like Austin hadn't mattered. His life worthless. I'd lost all sanity, all restraint, just like he seemed to be begging me to do now.

Jennings laughed, twisted mirth in his eyes. "Did you forget who I am, Sebastian Stone?"

Money.

Power.

Greed.

Pretension.

He busied himself by adjusting the cuffs on his suit jacket, head tipped down to watch the action while he slanted an eye up at me like the cocky bitch he was.

"I will take whatever I want. Shea is mine…she was the second her mother came groveling at my feet, willing to sell her soul and her daughter's for a little taste of stardom."

Shea was right. He was a sociopath. A psychopath. He got off on power. Off on exerting whatever morbid control he held over the people around him.

I felt sick—mad with the need to show him who *I* was.

"You're wrong. She's mine."

Never had I spoken anything truer in my life.

"We'll see about that."

I held my ground, throwing daggers I wished were real at the fucker as he gave me one last glance over his shoulder before disappearing around a big SUV.

I climbed into my truck, both hands shaking as I clung to the steering wheel and tried to steady my breaths. They came hard and fast, fueled by pure, unmitigated hate. Asshole knew my hands were tied, bound up by all this court bullshit. Both of us knew if I gave into the urge to wipe him out, my ass would be back behind bars faster than I could kiss Shea goodbye one last time.

My gut told me that's exactly what he wanted.

I turned over the ignition. The engine rumbled deep, almost as deep as the questions and anger that rattled me to the core.

Twilight was already taking hold of the smoggy Los Angeles sky as I pulled onto the congested street. What seemed like an unending train of cars fought to make their way home, me right in the middle of it, wondering just where *home* was.

By the time I was driving up the road to the place I shared

with the guys, the sun was dipping below the horizon. The massive house in the Hills was tucked and hidden away behind tall, dense trees and lush vegetation, Hollywood stretched out below. Cars lined the street and filled up our drive.

Shit.

Last thing I needed was a houseful of people I didn't want to see. All I wanted was to talk to my baby brother then crawl through a phone to get to Shea.

But today was our last day in L.A. before we hit the road tomorrow, the guys taking one last day to relax and unwind, one last day of freedom before it was constant road, city, and stage for the next four weeks.

None of my crew had gone to my court hearing because it was supposed to be routine. But nothin' about what transpired this afternoon felt *routine*. I felt agitated and disturbed.

Hatin' Jennings.

Hatin' the fact he was again spouting shit about Mark and Austin.

Hatin' that my girls were alone in Savannah and vulnerable.

I squeezed my truck into the drive and parked where I could, killed the engine, hurried up the walk. I threw open the double-doors.

Inside, the house was jammed full of people. A lot of the faces I knew. Others were strangers, no doubt a slew of friends of friends of friends. Ash and Lyrik always took it upon themselves to welcome in every dirt bag in the city.

They loved this shit—people packed wall to wall—the two of them always out looking for a good time, the faked-out chicks all too eager to give it to them.

Did it make me a prick that not so long ago I loved this shit, too, and now I wanted to throw everyone's asses to the curb?

No question, I loved all the guys. They were my brothers. There for me through everything. I mean, with all the shit with Kallie going down, that bogus trial they had to sit in on—I couldn't thank any of them enough.

They'd rallied.

Supported me when I needed them most.

Stepped up and acted like men when they preferred to stay firmly in the realm of juvenile delinquent. Not that I had the right to say much about that. God knew my ass was just as guilty, every chance I got dipping my toes in a murky vat of sin.

But I couldn't escape the feeling I was outgrowing *this*.

Images of Shea and Kallie swirled through my mind.

Some things just meant more.

Looking for Ash, I worked my way through the groups mingling around the oversized living room overlooking the sprawling city below, a twinkle of lights as far as the eye could see. Beyond the wall of sliding glass doors was the pool, water making a slow transition from blue to purple to pink and back again. Overeager women hung around it with cocktail glasses dripping from their fingers, doing more of that schmoozing that ensured my gag reflex was indeed intact.

Ash was hanging out just inside where those doors sat, throwing back a shot. Katrina, a chick who'd made her rounds through the band one too many times, was tacked to his side like a three-day itch.

"Ash," I said, not able to contain some of the irritation from bleeding through.

He paid no mind I was annoyed.

"Baz, dude, it's about damned time you got here. Karl Fitzgerald has been waiting for you in your office for the last…like thirty minutes. He showed up stating he wants a…" Ash lifted both his hands in the air, shot glass still clasped in one hand as he air quoted, "'word' with you. Talk about a fuckin' buzz kill. Here I am, entertaining all these beautiful ladies."

He stretched his tattooed arms out wide, like if given the chance, he'd take every last one of them. Asshole probably would. No question, they'd all come running.

"Doorbell rang and here I'm thinking I'm going to open it to another gorgeous girl, and there stood that slimy bastard, asking for you. Almost shut the door in his face, but I wasn't so sure how well that reception would be accepted. Figured it was time to play nice with the money-man. I'll leave the getting us in hot water up to you."

He shot me a wink, and I cut off my laughter. God, Ash was nothing but outrageous.

But he sure as shit got that much right.

Slimy bastard asking for a *word*.

That's the way the Mylton Records CEO always staged himself, showing up in moments when we were least expecting him, ready to assert whatever control he wanted over us. Sometimes I wished they'd have just cut us free back when the assault charges were hanging over my head.

But thinking like that? That was no less than a betrayal to my crew. A disregard to the blood and sweat and fucking turmoil we'd trudged through to get here.

Disrespect to Mark.

I owed all of them my loyalty.

"Thanks, man," I told him. "I'll see what he wants."

He gave me a salute. "Not a problem."

I turned back into the crowd, Ash's amused voice hitting me from behind. "Kiss some ass for me."

"Not a chance," I hollered back, shaking my head as I shouldered through the crowd, sending out a few hellos to people I knew and diligently avoiding those I didn't, because I was in no mood to be making friends. Especially those of the female orientation.

Fuck, Shea was the best. A girl unlike any I'd ever met. Sure, she'd shown a couple flashes of jealousy, which was hotter than all hell the way she wanted me only for herself. But even sexier than that was the astonishing faith she placed in me, the way she sent me off to live the life I love.

Music.

She knew that's where I was free. What I was created to do.

Even though leaving her and Kallie behind was the most excruciating thing I'd ever had to do.

Damn, I missed them.

Was pretty sure *these* withdrawals I was feeling were more brutal than any drug I'd ever had to kick. Every night I crawled into my bed alone and questioned that decision, wondering again just how much longer I could go on living this life when I was just as equally being called to live another.

I slipped down the hall and passed by the den currently playing host to depravity.

Sex, drugs, and rock 'n' roll, baby.

I cringed, doing my best to ignore the spectacle, and entered through the very last door.

Karl Fitzgerald sat behind my desk with his shiny dress shoe propped up on it like he owned it.

He angled himself to stand when I entered, extending that greedy palm my way. "Well, Mr. Stone, I hear congratulations are in order."

Reluctantly, I shook it. "I suppose they are."

"You did well to get Martin Jennings out of your life."

I curbed a sarcastic snort. Right. As if Jennings wouldn't just keep coming back. Making Shea's life hell any way he could. It was like I could smell it. Feel it coming in the distance. A tremor of malice rippling through uneven air.

Considering Fitzgerald was in my chair, I plopped into one of the plush chairs facing the desk and hooked an ankle over my knee, going for casual while I ignored the unease his presence sent sliding over me.

Obviously, this meeting wasn't anywhere near over.

I rocked back.

Waiting.

Challenging him with my stare.

Because I could feel he had just a little more bullshit to throw my way. You'd think I'd had enough of it today.

"Is *Sunder* prepared for this tour and prepared to go into the studio as scheduled in four weeks?" The man minced no words.

"Yeah, of course," I said with a casual lift of my shoulder.

"Good…good." He nodded, straightened his tie before he sat forward. "You know we need you guys at your best."

I lifted one hand like I was asking him to continue.

And your point is, asshole?

My expression pretty much felt like a dare.

"And are you sure *you're* ready?" he prodded with a telling lift of his brow. "We don't need to be concerned about this woman you've been making a scene with over the last couple of months?"

A scene?

Contention oozed through the words. "What's that supposed to mean?"

"It means you seem to be easily distracted of late."

"What I do with my personal life is none of your concern."

"I think you know that's not the truth."

I jerked forward in the chair. Anger that continually boiled just beneath the surface threatened to erupt, and after the confrontation I'd had with Jennings this afternoon, I had little reserve left. I swallowed some of it back and tried to make sense of what he was suggesting.

My eyes narrowed, just as tight as my voice. "First you want me to clean up my act and now you don't want me to settle down. Just what the hell is it you want from me?"

Bitterness fueled the question, because there wasn't a place inside me that wanted the answer.

He shrugged like he had the right to utter what came next from his greedy mouth. "We want a brand. The troubled rocker we signed without the jail time. And we sure as hell don't want a daddy."

I flew out of my seat, palms flat on the desk as I glared across at him.

"I'm not a fucking brand."

The chuckle rolling from him pissed me off more.

His eyes gleamed. "Ah, there he is. The one who can't help find a little trouble. That's who we're looking for."

I gritted my teeth. The words I bit out were hard. "What I've got going with Shea is none of your business and it's not ever gonna be. You want *Sunder?* Fine. You have us. But when I walk off that stage, you don't have anything to say about it."

I pushed off and stormed toward the door. His next statement had my steps faltering at the threshold, but I refused to give him the courtesy of looking back.

"You settle down with her and you're going to destroy this band. You know that, don't you?"

Something fierce bristled inside me. The feeling I was being torn in two directions, ripped and shredded and scored.

God, there was no wiping out the desperate desire to play, to create, that feeling of complete freedom I felt on stage when surrounded by my crew. By the crowd. Energy that roared with a reckless peace.

All of it was at war with Shea.
Shea.
Shea.
Shea.

Her energy brighter.

Bolder.

A rending force.

I pushed the rest of the way out of the room and stalked down the hall.

I cursed when my cell started ringing from my pocket. I dug it out, then nearly crushed it in my hold when I saw who it was.

Another fucking leech.

My piece-of-shit father who no doubt was calling to take a little more.

A parasite no different than Karl Fitzgerald.

No different than the slew of assholes presently taking up my house.

Everyone wanted a piece of Sebastian Stone.

I was sick of it.

Silencing the call, I charged down the hall—cutting along the edge of the living room and bypassing as many people as I could—ignoring the rest who shot me titillated looks. I drove through the huge kitchen inhabited by more insipid faces who thought they saw me, but didn't know me at all.

Surface.

That's what they wanted.

The desire for the superficial.

The fake.

A *brand*.

Fuck that.

I flew out the side door that landed me on the terrace at the side of the house. Here, the vegetation was lush and thick. Instant isolation. Hidden behind bushes was a narrow, winding wrought-iron staircase. I went straight for it, ascended two stories of exterior stucco wall, and climbed onto the soaring roof.

Noise filtered up from the party below. But up here it felt as if

I were in another world.

An escape.

Guess I shouldn't have been all that surprised to find Austin hiding away here, too, dark hoodie over his head where he sat close to the edge of the roof, staring over the vast city. A haze billowed around him as he expelled the smoke from his lungs, joint poised between pinched fingers as he prepared to take another drag.

Fuck.

I rubbed a hand over my face to calm myself before I cautioned my feet as I eased toward him. His back stiffened as I approached. Neither of us said anything when I settled down at his side.

Lights stretched on forever, a beautiful mess of city and a stunning mass of souls.

Austin pressed the joint to his lips, pulled it in, held fast before he turned his head to the sky and slowly let it out. He trained his attention back over the urban sea.

"Was wondering where you were," I finally said.

For the longest time my introduction remained unanswered. I felt the hesitation before he allowed the words to bleed free. "You ever wonder if there's anyone out there as fucked up as we are?"

Air puffed from my nose, my tone subdued. "Don't know, Austin. Sometimes it seems like that would be impossible, but I've got to figure there's a ton of people out there so much worse off. People completely alone. Rejected. Not sure there's a lot of people out there who've got what we do."

I wasn't talking material shit.

Knew well enough none of that mattered.

"You know," he said, voice pensive and rough, "you set me up with all of this."

He waved the hand holding the joint in the air. "Give me everything I could possibly want. And none of it's ever enough because I have no clue what it is I really want."

He drove out an incredulous laugh. "All those people down there? And I've never felt more alone."

"That's because you don't belong here."

He laughed again, an acidic sound before he was sucking in another lungful in an effort to soothe all the shit that'd been haunting him his whole life. Anytime we were in L.A., it was always amplified. Always waiting to drag him under in its seedy grips.

"And just where is it I belong?"

"Austin." It was a plea.

He shook his head. "I know you're dying to launch into me, Baz."

He held out the joint, twisting it around to draw attention. "Tell me I shouldn't be up here *indulging*. But I just walked in on three chicks doing lines off each other." He chuckled darkly and spears of fear pierced me. "Pretty sure you'd agree this was the better alternative."

Fucking Ash.

This shit had to stop. I did my best to keep Austin clear, hide him away from all the garbage that went down, but it was impossible when he was thrown right in the middle of it.

None of us should have been around it.

Not after Austin's overdose.

Not after losing Mark.

This was nothing less than an insult.

A disregard.

And it wasn't as if we were welcoming it. It just always came with the territory.

The bullshit side of this life I no longer knew how to handle.

My shoulders bunched. "I'll kick them out. Get rid of everyone. You don't need to deal with this shit."

"But that's the thing, I need to *deal* with something, Baz. You don't get it. All this protecting you do. I've got to figure this out for myself or I'm not ever going to make it."

My hand went to his neck, and I squeezed. "Yes, you are. I'm not going to let you fail."

He cut his face to me, grey eyes pinned on mine.

Intent.

Open.

Hopeful but resigned to what he didn't know how to control.

The kid hardly looked like a kid anymore.

Words broke on the emotion. "I have to be the one responsible for not failing, Baz. I've failed everyone. Julian. Mom and Dad. You. *Mark*." He swallowed hard. "If I'm going to live, then I need to figure out how not to fail myself. You can't keep saving me."

Mark.

Fear struck me again, and I tightened my hand that rested on the back of my brother's neck. "After my court appearance this afternoon, Jennings followed me out to my truck. Started tossing out a bunch of garbage about Shea...about Mark."

I stated it like the question it was. *What the fuck is going on? Do you know?*

God, what I wouldn't give to know why Jennings had been coming off our bus that night. But Austin had sworn he had no clue, that he'd texted for the pills and it was Jennings who'd shown up rather than one of the scumbags the asshole normally had doing his bidding. Woke up the next day in the hospital.

Every inch of him stiffened, and he dropped his attention to the shadows playing from the tree branches against the roof before he finally looked at me. "You're done, right? You signed the plea?"

"Yeah. It's done."

He nodded harshly. "Good. Just stay away from him, Baz. Take Shea and Kallie and get as far away as you can. Put all of that behind you."

Resentment seeped from my pores. "Don't think that's going

to be possible."

We all knew we hadn't seen the last of Jennings.

Austin pressed the heels of his hands into his eyes. Rocking. Scared. Words a plea. "If I could take it all back, you know I would, right, Baz?"

"Take what back?"

"All of it…all the way back to the day I ruined both our lives. Every mistake I've made since. I fucked everything up. Fucked it up bad."

I gripped his neck again, trying to get him to look at me. "You didn't ruin our lives, Austin."

"Stop making excuses for me. I took Julian's and I've done nothing but ruin lives since."

God, when was this kid gonna see it wasn't him? That it was *me*. I'd been the one responsible. The one who was supposed to be watching them instead of fucking around with some girl.

My fault.

But he still couldn't see it.

My phone started ringing in my pocket again. My heart rate ramped up with the thought of it being Shea, before it went hard when our father's number again marred the screen.

Damn it.

Austin caught it before I could hide it.

Hurt blazed from his skin as self-deprecating laughter trembled out. "See what I mean? I'm still ruining everything. What's he want? More money? To keep holding something you didn't do over your head?"

Shaking his head, he frantically stubbed out the joint and scrambled to stand. "Fuck him and fuck this. I'm going to bed."

Jaw clenched, I killed the call, listened to the cackle of laughter floating up from below, the retreating of Austin's footsteps.

That whole feeling I was being torn in two?

I got the sick feeling my world was about to come apart.

Finally I tore myself from my spot and back into the house. I didn't even consider joining the party. I headed upstairs toward my room.

Lyrik was just starting down as I approached the top of the landing. He cocked me a smirk. "Hiding now, are we?"

"How'd you know?" I tossed him a guilty grin.

He laughed, rubbed tattooed fingers over his chin. "Because I *know* you. Known you most of my damned life. Whatever you wanted? You were all in. Fighting for it with all you have." He tilted his head toward the stairs. "And I know you don't want that anymore. Not all that hard to figure out."

Unease shifted my feet, and I glanced away before I gained the courage to look back at him.

"Don't sweat it, man," he said. "Maybe you didn't know it, but you were always looking for something. You found it in Shea."

I stared at one of my oldest friends. Knowing he got me. That just like the rest of the guys, they'd take up my side, no matter what it was I asked of them.

Just like I had to do for them.

He lifted his chin in parting and bounded downstairs.

Feeling emotionally exhausted, I hauled myself to the end of the hall and entered through the double doors set across from Austin's room. They led into the master suite. Inside, the room was dark and void. More so with the party playing on from below.

Thank God it was Monday and Shea was off. I fell into the center of my bed, pulling my phone from my jeans pocket. I dialed my girl.

It took her a couple of rings to answer.

"Sebastian."

Relief hit me hard when I heard that sweet, seductive voice come across the line. My spirit did some crazy thing, something physical, a whole-body tremble that started from within.

"Shea, baby, miss you so bad."

A soft giggle rolled from her. "I think these have been the longest five days of my life." Her voice quieted. "And we're just getting started."

She was right. The coming four weeks would be excruciating.

"It'll go by fast," I promised.

"Says the guy who's going to be out on the road in front of his fans night after night with endless parties to keep him entertained, while he leaves his girlfriend bored out of her mind and alone all the way across the country."

It was a sulk filled with pure tease. I could picture those full lips pulling into a sultry pout, and I tried to stop my thoughts from rushing south, right along with my blood.

Laughing lightly, I rolled onto my side. "Hardly. After being on that bus for a few days, I'll probably be hitchhiking my way back to you. I'll be riding shotgun in some big rig, giving him a sob story about my girl I left behind and how I have to make it back to her."

"Mmm…I like the sound of that. Just watch out for the creepers."

A warm chuckle flowed from my lips. "Nothin' to worry about, baby. Don't you think I look like I can take care of myself?"

She giggled. "Oh, I'm sure you can. I have seen you in action before. Unless someone has a death wish, no one is going to stand in your way."

I could almost see the roll of her eyes, before an edge of seriousness wove into her tone. "So…how did everything go today? You're finished?"

"I'm done." Tried to keep it out, but I knew she didn't miss the shot of anger that found its way into my answer.

She wavered, before she whispered, "Was Martin there?"

I pushed out a strained sigh. "Yeah. He was there."

"And…?" she prodded when I didn't divulge more details.

I roughed a hand down my face, not wanting to get into it, wishing I could erase the conversation from my head. Really, I wished I could erase the conversation from my reality. "And he's still an asshole. Followed me out to my car, started talking all kinds of bullshit about you and my family. Basically he said he's just gettin' started."

From across the distance, I could almost see the expression on my girl's face. The worry and fear she felt every time Jennings was mentioned. The way she wished she could erase it, too.

"I'm sorry, baby," I murmured.

"No, don't say that. You don't have anything to be sorry about. This…we're doing this together, whatever may come. Until then, we can't give him any part of us. Any of our time or our thoughts or our energy. I refuse to *give* him any more."

God, she was a fucking miracle. A positive light shining bright, bright, bright.

I rolled onto my back and stared at the ceiling. What Jennings had said about her mom was nagging at my consciousness, every part of me needing to know more. I got the phone as close to my ear as I could, wishing there was a way it could get me closer. My voice went tender, because fuck, this girl eclipsed all my hard.

"Tell me a story, Shea from Savannah."

eleven
Shea

Twelve years old

HER BLACK PATENT DRESS shoes clicked on the wooden stage floor that was nearly as black as her shoes, except for the scuffed-up spots where Shea could only imagine instrument boxes had been dragged or where shoes had danced.

She knew she should have been looking up instead of studying that floor, but today the butterflies she normally got felt more like bees. Nerves droned in her ears and swarmed in her belly.

She just wanted to make her momma proud.

Coming to a stop at the front of the stage where a piece of tape made a line at the microphone, Shea forced herself to finally look up.

She could do this. She'd had enough lessons and enough auditions to know what was expected of her.

A spotlight blinded her from above. She squinted and tried to make out the few faces in the front row of the almost-empty music theater. It was impossible, but she knew they were there.

At the ready to critique, judge, and assess.

She was used to it by now.

Well.

Almost.

She wasn't so sure she'd ever get used to some of the mean things people would say.

The rejection.

But it was the disappointment on her momma's face that always bothered her most.

And this one was important.

During the entire car ride from Savannah to Memphis they'd made just for this audition, her momma had drilled it into her. *It's big, baby. You land this and we're set. You have to be at your best and nothing less.*

Her momma had purchased a brand new dress for this audition, the lacy material tight at her neck and wrists. It landed below her knees.

Her momma said it was modest and pretty. Just what they were looking for.

Shea scratched at the itchy material when those bees buzzed, and she shifted on her feet, feeling she might be sick while she waited for instruction.

A deep voice rolled through the milky fog. "Can you tell us your name, please?"

"Shea Bentley," she drawled quietly into the microphone, having to hike up onto her tippy-toes to reach.

"Okay, Shea Bentley, you can begin."

From where she sat at the piano, Shea's momma looked at her from over her shoulder and played a single chord. A cue that went along with her stern look.

Focus.

And Shea did.

Just as her momma dove into the music, Shea dove deep and found that place inside where she *felt* it. Where she *felt* it right in the center of her heart.

Just like her grandma had told her to do.

Even though she sometimes didn't feel quite right—and so many times felt like crying instead of smiling because she always seemed to mess everything up—standing there, singing this song?

Shea felt right.

She gave it everything she had. She allowed herself to rise above this place and imagined she was standing beside her grandma in church. Her grandma was holding her hand, squeezing it in quiet encouragement.

And Shea sang. Opened up her lungs the same as she opened her mouth.

It felt beautiful and important.

Significant.

The piano blinked out at the end of the song. Shea carried the tune on her voice, not needing the accompaniment to hit the highest note.

When she finished, Shea had to reorient herself, having forgotten where she was. Awkwardness filled her as she stared unseeing at the hidden faces in the front as the light continued to blare down on her.

"That was beautiful. Simply beautiful," the same man's voice said from behind the shimmering fog.

Her momma was suddenly at her side, pushing her forward, offering her like a prize.

But his voice changed when he said the next, "Unfortunately, we're looking for someone who is just a little older. A little more mature. I have no doubt this young lady has a bright future ahead of her."

At her side, Shea's momma went rigid, and Shea got that sour feeling in the pit of her stomach.

"Thank you for your time," her momma said gruffly, before

she was hauling Shea by the arm off the side of the stage. She shoved Shea's things into a bag, and Shea struggled to keep up when she again grabbed her by the arm. Her momma flung open the side door. Shea blinked off the blinding light and tried to adjust herself, this time because the afternoon sun blazed from above.

It seemed as if Shea could never keep up.

The hand on her forearm squeezed, the words grated as her momma stormed through the parking lot. "Can't you do anything right? You manage to fuck up everything, don't you? Every single time. Just like your deadbeat dad. Worthless. Do you know how much I've invested in you, Shea? The money? The time?"

Shea flinched when she felt the sting of nails digging into her skin. Tears pricked at her eyes, and she struggled to hold them back.

"I tried, Momma." The quieted words wobbled from her aching throat.

Her momma flung the bag into the backseat of her old car while Shea eased into the front seat and buckled up, wishing she had someplace to hide.

Her momma started the car and jerked it out of the parking spot, peeling from the lot.

Embarrassment and shame had Shea's head tipped down, face turned so she could see the blur of buildings as her momma turned her anger to the street.

The tears she'd been trying to hold finally fell. They made her throat feel full and her eyes burn, and all she wanted was to go home. To go to her grandma's house where it was safe.

She tried so hard to hold it back, but a sob heaved free, and she felt a shudder shake her shoulders as she tried to sink into the door and disappear.

Her momma released a muted curse, before she started talking quick. "I'm sorry, baby. It was that damned dress. You looked like a little girl. Should've gotten you something more mature."

She felt the same fingers that had been digging into her arm softly touch her shoulder. "We'll find something better for the next one…do your hair up real nice and make you look as pretty as you are. I bet you could pass for fifteen. How's that sound?"

Hesitating, Shea turned to face her. Wiping her tears with the scratchy sleeve of the dress, she nodded in hope. "Okay, Momma."

Her momma smiled. Her momma was so pretty when she smiled.

"That's my shining star."

twelve
Shea

"GO, BEFORE I HAVE to drag your skinny ass on that plane myself." Tamar held me on the outside of both shoulders, giving me a slight shake, a shot of annoyance and a ton of mischief playing in her blue eyes.

I glanced down at Kallie who just grinned up at me with all her joy as she swayed her stuffed butterfly clutched to her chest.

Nerves rushed me again.

The only nights I'd ever spent without her had been the two Martin had had her in his clutches. Just the thought of leaving my baby girl now terrified me, something innate within me warning Martin was still out there, waiting for the next opportunity to strike.

But even without that threat, I'd still worry.

This was my daughter we were talking about.

April crossed her arms and huffed.

Charlie chuckled.

"She's going to be fine, Shea Bear," he encouraged with his hands stuffed in his pockets. He cast a slight grin my daughter's way. "You really think we're gonna let a single thing go wrong when we have this little one in our care? Not a chance. Now go. Have fun. Live it up a little. Act your age. Las Vegas is calling your name."

It wasn't Las Vegas calling my name.

It was Sebastian Stone.

My eyes drifted to my daughter again. Hesitation pressed at my ribs.

With a wide smile, she flashed me a row of tiny teeth. "Momma…you *have* to go or *my* daddy is gonna be way, way, WAY sad if he doesn't get his *burfday* surprise and you got to give him his present for me."

She said it with all her country flourish and little girl slur, the words rushed and jumbled with excitement.

She took a step forward, shoved the lanky stuffed brown monkey my direction.

She'd seen it in the window of a boutique shop near our house and insisted he would love it, declaring *monkeys are his favorite* as she'd rambled on about the green monkey tattooed on his side. Of course my sweet daughter had no idea the significance of the ink he'd permanently etched across his ribs, a reminder of a life he would never forget, the love of a brother he'd lost too soon.

Accepting it from her, I hugged it to my chest. "He's going to love it, Butterfly."

He would. I knew he would. Simply because it was a gesture from her pure, innocent heart.

Her smile grew and she swayed a little wider as a giggle erupted from within her.

"We have her," April promised as she set a palm on Kallie's head.

"Yes, we do," Tamar added as she tossed a sly wink at my daughter. "We have nonstop fun planned for this little one. We're gettin' our girl on and are getting manis and pedis and are having us a pajama party, aren't we, Kallie?"

Kallie jumped around. "Yes! Yes! Yes! I can't wait. We're gonna have so, so much fun and I'm gonna stay up all night until the sun comes up and have popcorn and watch all my movies and Auntie April and Auntie Tamar are gonna stay up all night, too."

I held my laughter. Someone was a little excited.

"Don't have too much fun without me," I told her playfully as I brushed the back of my fingers down her soft cheek.

"Oh, I'm sure you'll be having enough fun for all of us." This time the wink Tamar tossed was at me, innuendo thick.

My stomach tightened in anticipation. The truth was, I couldn't wait to get to him. Being without him was getting harder and harder every day.

April burst out laughing. "Oh, there is no question about that."

Picking up Kallie, I hugged her tight and whispered in her ear. "I'll see you in two days. Be a good girl while Momma is gone, okay? I'll be thinking of you every second. I love you so much."

"I know, Momma. I love you more than the whole wide world." She squeezed my neck, her stuffed butterfly pressing into my face, my emotions on overload with my own excitement mixed with the flickers of fear from entrusting her to someone else's care.

I set her down and passed out quick kisses to each member of my unconventional family. Those who again stood at my side, helping me surprise Sebastian on his birthday while the band played a show in Las Vegas. The short four-week tour was more than halfway in, and Sebastian and I had plans for Kallie and I to go to California as soon as they were finished.

But I couldn't wait that long.

All the guys were in on the surprise.

It was his birthday, after all, and I wanted to be there to celebrate it with him, as hard as it was leaving behind my daughter, even for a short time. But Charlie had convinced me it was okay. That I wasn't neglecting her or harming her in any way, but instead giving her coping skills, the ability to be separated from me without suffering anxiety.

Funny, I was the one with anxiety.

Of course, it was the ever-present worry about Martin that made it understandably more difficult to leave her. It made it harder to quell the innate need to wrap her up in my protection, to hold her in my arms forever and never let her go.

But this wasn't me letting her go.

This was me investing in the future we had with Sebastian.

I set one last kiss to my daughter's forehead and headed toward the security line. I twisted and lifted my hand in a small wave.

My own excitement flared as I boarded the plane and fastened my buckle. I sent Lyrik, Ash, and Zee a group text. "I'm on my way."

I settled into the seat, lay my head back, and closed my eyes as I breathed in deep.

I'm on my way.

Horns blared within the heavy Friday afternoon traffic. A river of people streamed the sidewalks lining the busy strip. Groups traversed from one extravagant hotel to another, clutching tall colorful frozen drinks, stumbling and joking as they hopped from one indulgent destination to the next. Even within the confines of the town car, I could hear the riot of voices, the excitement that held fast to the air as people flocked to the City of Sin to indulge in exactly that.

You could *feel* it. A tremor of lust and letting go, all cares stripped away as abandon was cast into the wind.

Reckless and rash and wild.

The car made a quick right and wound into the lavish hotel's passenger pick-up and drop-off, its towers reaching toward the sky where they peered down over the fountains of The Bellagio and the stunning replication of The Eiffel Tower—a bit of Paris brought to the dry desert of Nevada.

Anticipation clenched my stomach, and I fumbled out of the backseat as a ripple of anxious need tickled through my nerves and quickened the beat of my heart.

My phone chirped. With shaking hands, I clicked into the message where Lyrik sent instructions on where to find them. *Lobby, north side.*

I left my suitcase with a bellman. Sucking in a breath, I entered into the sensual oasis of glass and lights and nude silhouettes that flashed behind fogged glass, everything about the upscale hotel a sensory overload of suggestion and sex.

My feet moved across the shiny floor in his direction, my pulse increasing with each step. By the time I rounded the corner, every inch of me was shaking with the need to see his face. To feel his skin and soak in his presence.

An eager group of people were congregated around them, video cameras poised as *Sunder* stood answering questions about the show tonight and the upcoming album.

I'd made it just in time to catch the last of their scheduled press conference. The vibe was casual as the four of them posed for pictures and openly answered questions. Behind the media, a ring of onlookers had gathered, snapping pic after pic with their phones. A few called out to them, vying for a little attention from the group of guys who stood out even in the mess of this erotic wilderness, all of them oozing sex and disorder and a taste of delicious wickedness.

Sebastian was like a beacon among it all. The brightest light that was still the darkest dark.

Both hands were stuffed in his jean pockets and he rocked back on his heels, the way he always did when he didn't know what to do with himself, his head angled to the side as his pretty, pretty mouth moved with whatever he said.

Tingles flooded me from head to toe.

I remained just in the distance of the crowd so I could take him in, my eyes roaming over him with hunger and need.

The man was the most beautiful thing I'd ever seen, so perfectly imperfect as he flashed his imposing grin for the camera, everything about him intriguing and mysterious and a little bit frightening.

I watched as he interacted with the press and his fans, engaged yet somehow reserved, the man giving them what they expected, the surface and the show.

But I saw everything written beneath.

Mid-sentence, he trailed off and for a moment he froze. Grey eyes lifted.

Seeking.

As if he felt the weight of my gaze upon him—the same way I always felt his.

When they latched onto me, I full out shook. His strange intensity filled the air, powering into me, wave after crashing wave.

We were locked in a stare.

Shock and confusion sifted through his expression.

But I saw it the second it hit him. The realization I was really there. The relief as he forgot everything else happening around him.

All except for me.

Abandoning his circle of admirers, he wove his lithe body through the crowd, shouldering through, ignoring everyone who tried to get his attention.

With every purposeful stride he took in my direction, my heart hammered harder, the quiet gasps slipping in and out of my lungs coming shorter and sharper until they were gone.

Breathless.

And I was in his arms, swept from my feet.

He twirled us once in a staggered spin, before he twisted a

single hand up in my hair, the other firm and secure as he held me around my lower back.

I clung to his shoulders as every inch of me glowed.

That mouth was suddenly overtaking mine, all tender lips, eager intentions, and stunning man.

He whispered between kisses, "Shea…baby…Shea. Fuck…I missed you…missed you so fuckin' bad."

My hands found his face. "I missed you…more than you could know."

He let my body slide down the hard length of his, but he didn't release his hold. If anything, he held me closer as my old red cowgirl boots touched the floor, even though I was still soaring in the clouds.

He dropped his forehead to mine and breathed me in. "Finally get what that old sayin' 'sight for sore eyes' really means."

A small giggle rippled from between my lips, where his still hovered, the air between us charged. "Happy Birthday."

He grunted, fingers digging into my sides. "Best. Birthday. Ever."

"Yeah?"

"Hell yeah. How long will you be here?"

"Until Sunday."

I pulled back to look up at his gorgeous face, all hard lines and defined jaw and full, full lips.

God. How was this man mine?

I raked my teeth across my bottom lip, going for a tease. "You're not disappointed I just showed up here unannounced to crash your party? In some circles, that might be considered rude."

He laughed a disbelieving sound. "Uh…no. Pretty damned sure you just made my entire year. About to lose my damned mind without you."

He hugged me again as he exhaled in relief, taking me in a gentle sway, a slow dance in the middle of a barrage of camera flashes and subdued whispers and a few catcalls coming from none other than Ash himself.

Sebastian suddenly pulled back, attention jumping all around me. "Where's Kallie?"

"At home."

He frowned.

"Charlie promised to man the bar while I was gone and Tamar took the weekend off to help April with her." I arched a brow. "I didn't think bringing a four-year-old to Vegas to celebrate a rock star's birthday would be the best parenting choice I could make."

He feigned a horrified gasp. "You left my daughter in the care of Tamar? We are talking about the woman who looks like she wants to cut every guy's balls off simply because he's a man? I'm not sure how I feel about that."

My daughter.

It was the first time I'd heard him refer to her that way. The sound of Kallie calling him *daddy* was already enough to twist me up inside with hope and dreams and love.

But this? This was overwhelming and pure, offered without a second thought. All those places inside me slipped a little further into Sebastian Stone.

His.

There was no question about it.

I gave him a coy smile, letting my hand go running up his strong chest, over the tee stretched across his wide, wide shoulders where my palm caught onto the firm beat of his heart. "Getting protective, are we?"

On a chuckle, he slanted me a smile that lifted on the crooked side. "Just a tad."

Then that playful smile took on a tone of wistfulness. "Can't believe how damned bad I miss her."

"I know." I dug around in my bag and pulled out the present Kallie had picked for him. Tentatively, I held it out. "She misses you, too."

Sebastian stilled, hesitating as his attention darted between the stuffed animal and me, both confusion and recognition flaring in his eyes.

"She saw it and insisted you have it. She told me again and again to make sure you know it's only from her for your birthday." I lowered my voice to a hopeful whisper, letting my fingertips trail over the spot on his side where the green monkey was hidden below his shirt. "She thinks monkeys are your favorite."

His hand trembled as he accepted it, and he pressed it to his nose, eyes dropping closed, breathing it in as if it brought him closer to her.

"God, I can almost smell her, Shea. Miss her so damned bad."

Slowly, he opened to me, voice deep and sincere. "She is the most amazing kid. After all the shit I've done, don't know how I got so lucky. That you came into my life…bringing that little girl with you."

Yeah. My hard, tainted man was so sweet and soft. I saw it, felt it beneath his scars and turbulence and dark demeanor.

Ash's laughter rang out from behind us, breaking up the heaviness that had woven into the moment.

"Beautiful Shea! What's up, darlin'? Lookin' gorgeous as ever."

I turned just in time to catch him rushing me, all dimples and thick, tattooed biceps and heartbreaker smile. I gasped when he picked me up off my feet, swinging me around like a rag doll. Laughter erupted from me. I clutched his shoulders, sure this crazy boy was going to drop me in his exuberance.

"Oh my God, Ash, put me down."

"Not a chance, darlin'. I missed the hell outta ya."

"Really," Sebastian said like a warning, earning a smirk from

Ash and a chuckle from Lyrik who stepped in to save me. He gave me a quick hug as he muttered quietly at my ear, "It's good you're here. He's been missing you and in a bad way."

In appreciation, I nodded at him, glanced at Sebastian who watched our exchange with mild curiosity and a whole lot of happiness.

Zee stepped in for a quick hug, too.

It seemed a little nuts how much I'd missed them all, how this group of guys had become such a mainstay in my life.

Eyes twinkling, Sebastian shook his head. "Should have known you assholes were up to something. Been acting all sketchy and skittish all damned morning. You could have saved me a ton of misery if you'd have given me a clue my girl was on her way."

"What?" Ash chided in amused disbelief, "and ruin all the work Shea put into making this a surprise? Not a chance, my friend. Suck it up and be thankful she's here."

Sebastian wound an arm around my waist, pulling me flush, bringing us chest to chest, both our hearts still wound and beating fast. He pushed his nose into my hair.

His whispered reply along the shell of my ear sent a swell of goosebumps along the back of my neck. "Oh, believe me, I'm thankful, all right. Gonna be showing you all weekend just how *thankful* I am."

Lust rolled through me, fluttering low, the dull ache I'd been feeling for weeks flaming to life.

A low chuckle rumbled in Sebastian's chest, the man all too keen and aware, but not ashamed in the least to press a little closer to show me the evidence of just how badly he'd been missing me, too. His mouth was at my ear. "Can't wait to get you alone."

Lyrik rubbed a tattooed hand over his chin. "Hate to be the one to break up the happy reunion, but we're out of here in half an hour. Need to get to the venue by five."

Sebastian groaned, then lifted his chin in a gesture of understanding to Lyrik, swung his attention right back to me as he wove his fingers through mine. "Where are your things?"

"I left them with the concierge."

Eyes narrowed, he chewed at his lip, then gave a clipped nod as if he'd come to some kind of resolution.

"Perfect." He pulled our entwined hands to his mouth, kissed along my knuckles, before he tugged me into motion.

I couldn't stop the tiny squeal from escaping my throat when a frenzy of butterflies staged an assault to my belly, this moment so carefree, all our worries and troubles and fears cast aside.

Charlie was right.

I needed this.

We needed this.

I held onto his wrist with my free hand, doing my best to keep up with him as he hauled me toward registration and straight into the VIP line.

But he didn't allow me to remain behind him.

No.

Instead he pulled me forward and spun me around in one fluid move. The cool, smooth marble of the counter pressed into my upper back as he pinned me to it, the man bold, dictating my every move.

He didn't hesitate to wedge one of his knees between my thighs just as he stretched his arms out on either side of me, holding me captive between him and the registration desk.

Trapped.

And there was no part of me that wanted to be set free.

Those butterflies went wild—a craze of lust and desire that amassed as this insane, stunning love.

I knew the way he made me feel was nothing short of a gift.

Big body towering over mine, he leaned over my shoulder and

spoke to the receptionist while I peered out at the mass of people watching us with curious glances and jealous stares.

"I need to upgrade my room," he said.

The receptionist tapped at her keyboard. "Current room number?"

"1653."

"Do you know your preference for the new room, sir?"

"Best suite you have for me and my girl," he replied as he nuzzled into my neck.

"Sebastian," I hissed, trying to stop him from doing something so over-the-top, because my intention had never been for him to splurge on me.

Any old bed would do.

"Bite your tongue, woman," he hissed right back, although everything about it was playful. "Know exactly what you're gettin' ready to say, and the answer is no. It's my birthday, and this is what *I* want. Got it?"

"Are you trying to guilt me into getting what you want?" I shot back with a smile, hiking up onto my toes so I could plant a small kiss on his chin.

He smirked. "Whatever it takes."

The receptionist worked quickly, and a few seconds later she discretely slid a small envelope with keycards our way. "You're all set.

"If you could have my luggage transferred from my old room and Ms. Bentley's delivered to the new," he added.

"That will be no problem. Enjoy."

His voice came across like a growl, the severity of it directed only at me. "I definitely plan to."

Oh God.

I was in the best kind of trouble.

With that, Sebastian whisked me toward the bank of elevators across the lobby. Anxious, he jabbed at the button. With a ding, the door slid open, and he mumbled the room number to the attendant at the same second he pushed me up against the wall in the far back corner.

Pinned again.

Hot hands palmed my neck and he dove in for a kiss.

I gave in, before I giggled and pulled back, considering there were about fifteen other people crammed in the elevator with us.

"Um…do you not see we have an audience?" I murmured toward his face that gleamed with a smirk he couldn't seem to shake.

"Can only see one thing, baby."

Was I too old to swoon?

Apparently not, because my knees knocked, my insides quaked, and a rush of lightheadedness swayed through my senses.

Light.

Light.

Light.

He gave it to me when I should be drowning in dark, lost to the fear of my past catching up to me. But no, this miraculous man held me close. Lifting me up before I crashed to the ground.

The elevator stopped at seven different floors before it finally opened to the top floor.

Yes, I counted.

Sebastian tipped his head at the attendant, rushing us out into the foyer and to the double door. With the hand clutching Kallie's monkey, he fumbled with the key card, refusing to let go of my hand. He managed to swipe the card and buzzed us in. One of the doors swung open, and he swiftly turned, mouth back on mine as he dragged me into the immaculate room.

Even though he was kissing me mad, I couldn't keep one eye from opening and peeking at the opulence around us. "Oh, wow," I mumbled as he pulled me deeper into the living area. "I think this place is bigger than my house."

And my house wasn't exactly small.

Or modest.

But this suite made it look like a dump.

Sebastian pulled away just enough to survey the space.

The luxurious living area was decorated in whites and blacks. Dashes of royal blue were strewn about, giving it a splash of color. A large U-shaped couch sat in the center of it, surrounded by plush lounging chairs set up in front of a TV that took up most of one wall, while a formal dining room set for eight took up the back side. There was a bar that wasn't so mini and an office area. A wall of two-story windows looked out over the strip, a breathtaking view of city and sky.

Our attention was drawn to a winding staircase that led upstairs to what I could only assume was the bedroom.

His demeanor turned predatory, a gleam of grey and a twitch of his body. He reached out and touched my face. "Gonna fuck you everywhere in this place. On every surface. In every room." He edged in, breath whispering across my face. "And then I'm going to do it again."

He set the monkey aside, tossed the keycards down with it, then lifted me, forcing me to wrap my legs around his waist.

I had on a pair of short cut-offs and my boots.

Yeah.

I'd worn them for him.

I knew he liked the shorts, the boots, loved the way his gaze trailed up and down my legs every time I wore them.

He crossed the room and set me on the edge of the glass table, let his hands go trailing up and down my thighs as he rubbed his heavy cock to my center.

I purred as he cupped my neck in both hands, kissing me slow.

"Been too long, baby. I want to tear into you. Tonight I'm going to devour every inch of this sweet little body."

"Like you haven't already?" I nipped at his mouth, my insides turning molten, his fingers like fire.

I'd done things with Sebastian I'd never dreamed of doing with another man. Let him fill me, explore me, and fuck me every way. Let him touch me in ways I'd thought were dark and ugly and depraved.

But, no.

It was pure, unbridled pleasure.

A candid trust.

A beauty found in the rawness, and a bond found in the vulnerability.

"Like I could ever get enough of you," he murmured back, rough, just as rough as his hands as he tugged me closer.

Knuckles rapped at the door.

Sebastian looked to the high ceiling and let out a strained groan. "Shit."

Laughing, I pushed him back. "We need to get going anyway. I don't want to be responsible for making you late."

He pressed a closed-mouthed kiss to my lips.

"*Later*," he promised.

"Yes, please," I said as I grasped at his tee a little greedily in the same second he was pulling away.

"Woman," he growled as a warning, diving in for another quick kiss, and I laughed again and hopped onto the floor as he went to answer the door.

A bellman breezed in with our things, propping an acoustic guitar case against the wall and taking the rest of our luggage upstairs to the bedroom, then coming right back down.

Sebastian dug his wallet out of his pocket, producing another large bill like he always did, the man so generous, so contrary to all that brash intimidation.

He locked the door behind him.

"I need to change," we both said at the same time, with the same reluctance, and we both stilled and stared because we seemed to be playing the same tune. Sebastian released an affectionate laugh.

"Come on, let's get out of here or we're never going to make it." He took my hand in his and we bound upstairs. He shrugged out of his clothes and dug into his suitcase, the same as I did mine.

"Damn it," I cursed, digging around more and cursing myself again.

"What?"

I glanced up to find him in his underwear, and my eyes stayed there a little longer than necessary.

The gorgeous man was bent over as he pulled the second leg of his jeans off his foot then reached for a fresh pair, and a shiver rolled through me as I was struck with both the best and worst kind of temptation.

Just a glimpse of that body derailed me from the task at hand, and *that* was the one thing the guys had made clear when we'd set up Sebastian's birthday surprise.

They had a gig.

And the gig came first.

Under no circumstances was I allowed to make him late.

For a pack of unruly rockers, they sure had tossed out a lot of *rules*.

Which I totally understood. But there was a needy, desperate part of me that wanted to ignore all obligations, the part that wanted to lock us in this room and let him start the devouring he promised to do.

Catching my libidinous stare, because, God, there was no concealing it, he tossed me a cocky grin, and once again mouthed, "Later." Then he inclined his head toward the disaster I was making in my suitcase.

"Damn it, what? Looks a little like you've let Kallie unpack for you. That child is nothing but a hurricane."

Soft laughter rolled from me at the sweet, sweet thought, my baby girl in all her vigor and life, then I shook my head at myself again. "I can't believe it…I forgot my toiletry bag."

"You don't need makeup." A wry smirk ticked up at the corner of that flirty mouth as his voice dropped to a rumble. "Or clothes for that matter."

The playful roll of my eyes was unstoppable. "Don't get too excited…I have clothes for days. I just don't have anything else. Everything was in there…makeup, toothbrush, curling iron, pills."

Helplessly, I dug around again, searching for what I knew wasn't there. I suddenly had a clear picture of it packed and sitting on my vanity back at the house.

"Shit…shit…shit," I muttered.

Sebastian waltzed forward, bare-footed in soft, worn jeans, the sexiest thing I'd ever seen.

He pressed a tender kiss to my temple. "Don't worry about it. I'll call down and have them send some stuff up. Sound good?"

I sent him a resigned smile. There was nothing I could do about it now. "Yeah, that would be nice."

Sebastian finished changing, jogged downstairs, and made the call to get some of my stuff replaced, while I quickly dressed in the outfit Tamar helped me pick out for tonight—another pair of torn-up, cut-off shorts, a flowy cream top with thick, crocheted lace edging, and super high-heeled brown suede booties that made my legs look long, sexy, and sleek.

Country Chic.

"Don't fix what ain't broke," Tamar had said with a flip of her red hair while we'd shopped, telling me I'd already perfected the look so I should just go with it.

I walked into the extravagant bathroom adjoining the bedroom, where the suite's opulent theme overflowed seamlessly. I grabbed a tissue and allowed myself one more irritated groan for forgetting my stuff, then leaned toward the mirror and dabbed at my eye makeup to smooth out the creases, and wipe some of the sticky airplane residue away.

At least I had my face powder and some clear lip gloss in my purse.

It was going to have to do.

Sebastian appeared in the doorway, tattooed arms stretched across it, the man stealing a little more of my breath. "Just got a text. Boys are downstairs. We need to run."

"I'm ready." I followed him into the bedroom and grabbed my small purse from the bed, situated the strap over my head and shoulder. "Is Austin coming?"

"Nah…he always hangs back at the hotel. Shows aren't the best atmosphere for him," he said with a tinge of regret. Then he hefted a shoulder. "He seems pretty content though, so I guess it's good."

"It is good," I promised, knowing how much he worried about his little brother, wishing I knew more and there was more I could do.

But I also understood there were things shared only between the two of them.

We rode the elevator down and walked hand-in-hand through the lobby and to the back entrance where the guys waited.

Lyrik's cocky expression fell when he saw us. "You've got to be kiddin' me."

Zee broke out in some kind of rebel celebration. "Pay up, bitch."

Lyrik punched at him and Zee jumped out of his reach, howling with laughter. "What…can't handle it when someone half your age is again taking some more of your dough? You are losing your touch, old man."

"Says the punk kid who's barely old enough to make it into the casino? Don't make me teach you a lesson, boy," Lyrik taunted right back.

Sebastian's eyes narrowed at Lyrik as he opened the back passenger door. "Don't look so happy to see me, asshole," he said with one brow lifted.

Lyrik dug a one hundred-dollar bill from his wallet and slapped it into Zee's waiting, gloating hand. The irritation on his face appeared a whole lot like he'd rather be slapping it across Zee's face.

With Zee still cracking up, Ash and Zee climbed into the third row of the long, black Escalade, Lyrik hopped into the front passenger, and Sebastian ushered me into the middle row and climbed in behind me.

Lyrik looked over his shoulder. Dark eyes gleamed with amused disbelief. "That's because seeing your ass come waltzing out of that hotel any less than half an hour late cost me a Benjamin, Baz Boy."

"Bettin' against me now, are we?"

Ash leaned forward, arms wrapped around my headrest as he poked his head forward. "Don't sit over there acting all surprised, man. If I had a girl that looked like Shea…"

A low whistle dropped from him as he let his gaze travel down my legs. "You could bet your last dollar I'd be walking out of there late, too."

Um. Wow.

I could feel the heat rush up my neck, the smile pulling at my face. Because they were too much, larger than life, every kind of right, Sebastian's miss-matched family that had somehow become my own.

"Hey now…hey now," Zee contended. "Don't go demeaning my faith in my man, here. I knew he wouldn't let the crew down. Got your back, Baz."

I squeaked in shock when Sebastian suddenly hauled me from my seat onto his lap, draping me across him. He nuzzled his nose along my neck and palmed my exposed thigh, giving it a squeeze that wasn't so gentle.

"Or maybe I just plan on taking the time to lay my girl out right. Doesn't have a thing to do with any of you fuckers."

Oh God.

That redness climbed all the way to my cheeks. The desire Sebastian had lit back in the room had barely just settled to a simmer, and here he was, stoking it again, the promise in his words enough to send a chill slithering through my body.

"This isn't an awkward conversation or anything." I widened my eyes at all of them who had no shame at all, eyes watching Sebastian and me as if we were the best kind of entertainment.

Considering the bets, apparently we were.

Ash cackled and smacked my now vacant seat as the driver pulled out into the heavy traffic congesting the strip.

"Come now, sweet, innocent Shea. You're part of the band now, baby. There are no secrets between us and there's not a subject that's gonna be off limits. Can you handle it?"

It was all tease, but I could feel the caution behind it. The guy was always so cocky and smug, but there was a loyalty about him, too. Just like Sebastian, something good beneath all the brash. I knew he was warning me about what we were about to head into, wondering if I could handle it, the lifestyle they lived, the abounding outside forces Sebastian had wanted to shield and protect me from.

I snuggled further into Sebastian's hold.

As long as Sebastian loved me the way he should, the way I loved him, there wasn't anything I couldn't handle.

Draping his arms over the middle seat, Zee leaned forward and began to tap out a beat on the black leather, quietly humming the tune.

Ash picked right up, singing the words under his breath as he began to bob his head along with Zee's impromptu song. Maybe I shouldn't have been surprised, but Lyrik chimed right in, the man who exuded menace and mayhem tapping his fingers on the thighs of his ripped-up skinny jeans as he joined in with Ash and Zee, as if they did this all the time.

Were they serious?

I looked up at Sebastian. He slanted me a rogue grin, dipped that gorgeous face down toward me as those full, full lips began to move.

That beautiful, beautiful voice for a beautiful, beautiful man singing that soothing sound, his mouth hovering an inch from my lips as if he were singing to me.

But those intense eyes glinted and gleamed, swimming with mischief and ease as he played along with the guys, those four big, bad rockers going retro.

They were singing *Leaving Las Vegas* by Sheryl Crow.

Giggling, I clutched Sebastian's neck. Something giddy washed over me as the air in the car went light. The effortless bond between the four talented men filled me with joy, because I knew this was such a huge part of Sebastian's life, being on the road with them, their day-to-day.

For so many years I'd silenced my voice. As if it were a part of my secrets locked tight. As if the words that danced on my tongue had been buried with Delaney Rhoads.

But today…today I couldn't help myself…because I felt free.

Vindicated.

And I let it go.

Lifted my voice and joined in just as they hit the chorus, belted it out as I sang to Sebastian who sang right back. His hands clutched my sides. The joy in his eyes was something I felt all the way to my soul.

We trailed off and the rest of the cab was conspicuously silent. As if a strange disturbance had stamped out the easy air.

Embarrassment held my tongue, my teeth gnawing nervously at my bottom lip while I buried my face in Sebastian's neck, wishing there was a way to disappear.

What was I thinking?

Then Ash hooted. "Holy hell, woman. Did that really just come out of your mouth?"

I buried my frown in Sebastian's neck, feeling the vibration of his chuckle as he held me a little tighter.

"Told you, man," Sebastian muttered, scattering a bunch of kisses over the crown of my head.

"Told him what?" I finally got the courage to ask, peeking up at him as he dipped his chin down to meet my eye.

Typically, I wasn't the shrinking-violet type. But when it came to singing, it brought back my childhood insecurities. The fact I'd been a constant disappointment to my mother. The pressure she'd exerted. The expectations I never met. Her never-satisfied hunger for more.

More fame.

More money.

Without a thought to the dire consequences that would result from her shortsighted intentions.

"That you, sweet girl, make me sound like a hack."

"Hardly," I whispered seriously.

He squeezed my thigh again, becoming playful. "Just do me a favor and don't go singing backstage tonight or anything, okay? Don't need you going and outshining me, especially on my birthday. Don't think I can handle that kind of blow to my ego."

I rose up so I could press a kiss at the center of his strong throat, my words soft and rumbly where I murmured them at his

Adam's apple. "I could never outshine you."

This dark, mysterious man had become my brightest light.

With a slight grin, I pulled back. "Besides, I'm not sure I could pull off all those growly screams you're so famous for."

Deep, seductive laughter rolled from him, and he hugged me closer, wrapping a single hand in my hair and murmuring low. "You scream just fine, baby. Just make sure what you're screaming is my name."

A slow ache settled between my thighs.

Later.

The venue was off the strip, and the driver made a couple turns before he pulled into a lot and rounded to the back entrance of the music hall. Everyone was quick to climb out. Sebastian never released my hand as we followed the guys into the dingy, dusky theater, up three concrete steps to a blackened-out door manned by a burly guard.

The second we stepped into the darkness, I could feel the sizzle of energy snap in the dense air. As if that magnetized energy drew strength from the guys who breathed it in, and radiated it back out. It only increased as they lifted their chins and sucked it down, as if they fed into the frenzy. A buzz of hyped eagerness seemed to come naturally, as their minds shifted gears in preparation for the show.

My eyes darted around, capturing everything.

It was strange because I was so accustomed to live music at *Charlie's*, the energy that would hold fast to the air, an anticipation unlike anything other as someone took to the stage and brought a song to life.

But this...this seemed entirely different. The way roadies bustled around backstage, carrying gear and setting it in position, the test of the soundboard, the hustle and scramble to get everything set in place, the directions being shouted, an adept chaos I couldn't imagine transpiring any other way.

Added to the feel was the deafening level of rock music that seemed to dictate every move and beat.

Sebastian squeezed my hand, leaned in close to my ear, and lifted his voice. "You all right?"

There was no missing the concern swirling in the depth of those attentive eyes as they peered at me, the man searching for any discomfort I might feel. For flickers of the regret and betrayal I'd sustained in a world so similar to this.

We'd only touched briefly on the hurt, the dreams I'd had that had never quite been my own, but were still seated so deeply within my spirit. I still ached for it every day.

The truth of how much I loved to play.

What Sebastian didn't know was none of that could ever be worth the cost I'd been asked to pay.

I'd be lying if I said I hadn't been nervous when I'd boarded the plane this morning, that I hadn't wondered what it might feel like to stand backstage again and know none of it would ever belong to me. Just an outsider looking in on something magnificent and inspired.

But, no.

There was no discomfort or ugly memories or pangs of regret.

"Better than all right," I told him truthfully. "I'm just excited to see you play."

His expression softened with a tenderness I was sure he only allowed me, and he wound me into the safety of those strong arms. His voice was hoarse. "Can't tell you how damned happy I am you're here. Hope you know that, baby. Want you with me. Always."

My hands clung to his sides. "And I'm here because with you is where I want to be. Always."

Deep satisfaction flashed across his face. "Come on...I've got a bunch of shit I have to take care of before we go on. Opening band's gonna be hitting the stage soon."

Sebastian led me down a dim, hazy corridor to a large reception room on the left. The light within was subdued but brighter than out in the hall and the areas backstage.

I peeked inside at the overstuffed, worn couches. Guys who screamed sex, drugs, and rock 'n' roll lounged on them, slinging back beers and laughing loud, talking shit like all these guys seemed to love to do.

Really, the atmosphere seemed almost laid-back except for the glimmer of lust that seemed to cling to the air. Thick, dark, and ominous.

Girls who'd barely made the transition into women hung on the sidelines, chatting and clearly waiting to be noticed. Most fit in, as if they'd been drawn into the chaotic vibe, clothes as dark as the makeup painted around their eyes.

But I guess it wouldn't be a real concert if there weren't a few who looked as if they'd forgotten groupies went out of style in the eighties. Or maybe they were just giving it a good go to bring it back.

Sebastian introduced me to a couple of people, some of the road crew and his tour manager, and a few friends who followed them show to show.

He took it upon himself to hoist me onto a table where my boots swung a foot from the grimy floor, before he handed me a beer and sealed my mouth with a possessive, perfect kiss, then sent a look around the room at everyone who was watching us.

Off limits.

It was cute and sweet and protective, and I couldn't help my own buzz of excitement that rippled through me as I sat back and enjoyed my time. Even though I missed Kallie, that beneath everything was the unending fear of the fight I knew was coming, tonight I felt liberated and unrestrained. There was no question my daughter was safe, that she was having a blast, playing butterflies and princesses and living in her fairy tales.

Showered with love and care.

So I let my reservations go. Let my body sway as the opening band took to the stage, and my mind wandered to the fans I could hear screaming through the walls.

I sat by myself for a long time, every so often making idle chat with the few people who approached me, all of them men. The only attention I received from the women were a few sneers and jealous stares.

An hour later, Sebastian appeared in front of me, all smiles and child-like exuberance. "We're getting ready to go on, baby. You ready?"

"Absolutely."

He helped me down, and I followed his long strides back down the hall where he led me to the side of the stage.

VIP.

"This is you."

I grinned up at him, teeth going to my lip as I tried to hide the rush of emotions I felt. I couldn't believe I was here, experiencing this with him. All the videos I'd watched of him onstage, night after night when I'd been missing him like crazy, wondering how he was and what he was doing while out on the road.

And here I was.

"Sebastian," Ash called from where he stood with the rest of the guys across the space. "Get your ass over here."

"Be right back," Sebastian promised.

I watched as he sauntered away, my stomach twisting in knots at the raw, striking beauty of the man.

I turned and peered out from behind the long curtain where I was hidden in the shadows. Energy vibrated from the crowd and another round of nerves rustled through me. It seemed insane I was here, back in the midst of music from which I'd run so far. I'd almost forgotten what it felt like to stand backstage while that fervor held fast to the air, anticipation building strong as fans waited for their beloved band to take the stage.

But this was different than anything I'd ever experienced in my days as Delaney Rhoads.

There was an underlying charge here, a furor in the crowd that spoke of lawlessness and disorder.

Kerosene just itching for a match.

Bodies were crammed into the cavernous, hollow space, the ceiling high and the slanted floor bare. It was set at an incline, the floor high on the entrance side and tapering down the entire way until it met with the elevated stage. Standing room only, a riot of youth vied for a better position closer to the stage, pushing and shoving to get closer.

Darkness covered the crowd, and the sound of the roadies testing the equipment only made the rowdy atmosphere rise.

I felt a partner to it. Fuel for it. As if *I* was more desperate to see Sebastian on that stage than every fan combined. Even though I'd binged on posted on-line videos of *Sunder*, it didn't come close to comparing to this.

No wonder he needed this.

Thrived on this.

Loved this.

Soon I'd be returning to Savannah, and I wanted to take this experience home with me. To tuck this memory deep with the love I had for Sebastian, so I would have something to sustain me in our separation when he went back on the road.

I wanted to be able to close my eyes while he was away and picture him onstage, knowing first-hand what he would be experiencing night after night.

A roadie beat on a drum.

Adrenaline rushed, and I sucked in a breath as I reveled in it all.

My body trembled in recognition when hot, needy hands gripped my waist from behind, and the breath I'd breathed was suddenly *him*.

Sebastian buried his nose beneath my hair. He ran it along the nape of my neck and up behind my ear. My flesh prickled in the most delicious way, every nerve alight at his touch.

I shook.

"It's time," he whispered against the sensitive shell of my ear.

He planted a lingering kiss to my neck. "Don't move from this spot," he warned against the skin, then he wrapped his arms completely around my waist. "Remember every last one of the assholes hanging out back here are exactly that. Assholes. Especially those punks who opened for us. Don't want to have to come off the stage during the show to kill someone."

Knowing Sebastian, he was one-hundred percent serious.

I almost laughed. As if I didn't know how this went down. The predators on the prowl, backstage their den, where they hunted and gorged and devoured.

But that was the thing with Sebastian. He never looked at me as the girl who'd been there or the one who'd seen it all—the one who'd allowed herself to become prey.

To him, I was the innocent country girl from Savannah, the one he did everything in his power to protect.

Was it wrong that fact made me love him just a little more?

"I'll be right here waiting," I promised, swaying in his arms.

"Good girl," he whispered low, breathing me in, nose trailing and hands feeling.

"Mmm…why the fuck do you gotta smell so damned good?" he grumbled through a groan.

Hands went sliding down the front of my thighs, skin to skin. He pressed his face into the hollow where my neck met my shoulder, suckling and kissing and making me weak in the knees. "Feel so good," he muttered, voice rough. "Driving me right out of my mind."

In reality, it was him who made me lose mine.

"Wait till I get you back to that room."

"Maybe I just want to keep you coming back to me," I taunted a little, letting my weight fall against his pounding chest.

"I will always come back to you."

The slap Ash landed to the back of Sebastian's head jarred us from the little cocoon we'd created.

Blue eyes blazed with laughter. "Focus, man. We're on and you're over here looking like you're about to drag your girl into a dark corner. Bros before hos. You know the code. Don't break my heart by making me kick your ass."

Sebastian threw an idle punch at him, as idle as the threat. "Whatever, dude. We both know I'd drop you in a second flat."

Ash bounced around on his toes as if he were going to prove him wrong, fists throwing mock punches in Sebastian's direction. "In your dreams, Stone. Are you gonna make me have to embarrass you in front of Beautiful Shea, here? You know the only thing that's gonna do is make this fine woman fall in love with me. No one could blame her. I'm irresistible."

Sebastian growled through the laughter he was holding back. "About to cross a line, asshole."

Laughing, I pushed him off, that sweeping, free feeling racing through me again. "Go."

On a groan, he began to follow Ash, before he seemed to think better of it, and rushed back and pecked my lips in that sweet, sweet way. He pointed at me as he walked backward toward the rest of the guys huddled just out of sight offstage. "Don't move."

In amusement, I shook my head, making a silent promise I would *always be right here*, wherever he was, and mouthed, "Impress me, rocker boy."

He smiled an earth-shattering smile.

Rocking my world.

My chest squeezed.

The imposing man finally dragged himself away, turning his focus to where it should be and to the band.

Heads leaned in, they formed a circle, unheard words spoken, claps to the back as they hyped themselves up.

Together, the four of them were a force.

Bold and intimidating and beautiful in the most daunting way.

Listening to the chanting roar of the crowd, exhilaration spiraled through my belly. Zee ducked through the curtains and onto the stage. Fisting drumsticks in his hand, he thrust them over his head, looking out over the crowd that screamed like a squall beating at the ocean.

Ash and Lyrik strode out behind him.

That roar turned wild, energy billowing, threatening to spill over.

Sebastian stepped onstage.

Everything erupted.

Screams filled the air as Sebastian slipped the strap of an electric guitar over his head and shouted, "Good evening."

He edged toward the mic and tapped his foot on a pedal on the floor before he dove right into one of their hard, reckless songs. He strummed a manic beat, skilled fingers sliding in precision up and down the neck of the guitar.

Brilliant and captivating and so talented it shook me to the core.

But it was when his mouth met the mic that his powerful voice tore through me.

Every cell in my body came alive, my heart pressing at my ribs, as I looked at the man I loved more than any other. At the man who was my baby's father in every way. At the man who'd come with a violent force to upturn my life.

To shake it up with joy and love, with something deep and profound.

The rest of the guys were just as intent on their parts. Lyrik played another electric guitar, all that mess of black on top of his head flying as his body crashed with the beat, Ash's head lifted toward the sky as he played the bass line, lost to the music, while Zee pounded frantically at the drums on a riser behind them.

On the floor, bodies thrashed.

Untamed.

Slamming and uncontrolled.

Free.

The four looked so much like the first time I'd witnessed them, when I'd locked myself away in the office of *Charlie's*, in that moment when I was unsure if I could continue down a path that would lead me right back into the type of life I'd fled.

But I should have known any path I took would lead me straight to Sebastian.

It didn't matter Sebastian screamed the lyrics, that I *felt* the words more than I understood them.

His voice still melted over me.

Sinking in and becoming one with my bones.

The words indecipherable yet so clear.

That energy surrounded me, again making me feel as if I were elevated. Riding wave after wave of Sebastian Stone.

From the side, he turned his head with his mouth still pressed to the mic. He was searching. Searching for me.

Those eyes met mine and he swept me away.

The entire show enraptured me.

Lost in his spirit.

Drowning in his presence.

Where he was my air and my hope, the one who'd breathed

belief into the hollow loneliness of my heart.

The one who'd filled it.

Tears welled in my eyes as an onslaught of emotion engulfed me, stringing me out, this man devastating in the most stunning way.

When their set came to a close, Sebastian tossed his pick into the crowd, and shouted a last "Goodnight" into the mic. He sauntered offstage as if he were riding that palpitating emotion, too. That intensity went wild, just as wild as those strange grey eyes as they sought me out. A surge of his energy nearly knocked me from my feet the second they landed on me.

There was no hesitation in his step. His stride was long and confident and determined on one singular goal.

Me.

He crashed into me, pushing me up against the nearest solid surface, hands and teeth and tongue.

I grunted when my back hit the huge speaker, and he just kissed me harder, deeper, as if he were trying to climb inside, a dark halo vibrating from his spirit and desperation in his touch. With each needy caress, it was as if he were transferring it to me, lighting me up, inciting and stirring—a provocation that went so much deeper than just the surface.

"Shea," he moaned in something that sounded like relief. My fingers wove through his hair, bringing him closer, kissing him deeper.

Falling.

As if there was no end. No beginning.

Just us, now, and forever.

"You about done?" Lyrik's voice broke the connection.

"Not even close," Sebastian muttered at my mouth, still clutching me tight.

A dark chuckle slid from Lyrik. "Show's over, man."

Obviously, he was referring to more than *Sunder* being on stage.

God, I lost myself with Sebastian, forgot where I was and who would see.

Sebastian just grumbled at him as he continued to kiss me. "Go away."

"Not a chance, my friend. You need to shower...we have plans. Remember?"

Sebastian glared at him from over his shoulder, still holding onto me as if he were going to dive right back in. "That was before my girl showed up and altered my *plans*."

Lyrik looked at me. "Shea's all part of the plan, aren't you, Shea?"

I was almost reluctant to nod, because I wanted nothing more than Sebastian to finally get me behind closed doors.

But somehow I forced myself to agree. "Yep...part of the plan."

A grin pulled at one side of my mouth when he narrowed his eyes in my direction.

"You just showed up to torture me, didn't you, woman?"

"Don't be a pussy, man. A little anticipation never hurt anyone," Lyrik spouted off as he raked a hand through his hair.

"Wouldn't call four weeks a *little* anticipation." He turned back to me with the suggestion of the demand twisting on his lips. "Tell me how you're gonna make it up to me."

Hands eager and teasing at the hem of his shirt, I pressed one more kiss to that pretty, pretty mouth. "Any. Way. You. Want."

"Now you're just asking for trouble."

No doubt. But I was willing to take whatever he wanted to bring.

Sebastian ripped himself away and helped me right myself on unsteady feet.

Again, Sebastian left me in the little room, promising to be right back. He was gone for little more than five minutes before he was there. Changed, brown hair damp and darkened, he wore a long-sleeved button-up shirt with the cuffs rolled to just below his elbows, his undeniable strength revealed in the bristling muscle beneath the intricate ink etched on the exposed skin of his forearms.

There was no missing the heads that turned, the desire evident in the blatant stares as eyes were drawn in the direction of this magnificent man. Dripping of sex and darkness. Shrouded in mystery. A riddle only I had the answer to.

A freshly showered Ash waltzed in right behind and clapped his hands once in front of him. "Let's do this."

Sebastian gathered my hand back in his while Ash talked to the small group of friends who were meeting us at the club. The five of us headed out the back door and into the night, the November sky cool, the sounds of revelry riding on the air.

The SUV that had dropped us off sat waiting, but it was a black Maserati convertible parked behind it that Sebastian went straight for.

My steps faltered and my mouth dropped open.

I was supposed to be dishing out the surprises this weekend, not the other way around.

At my reaction, Sebastian just gave me an offhanded shrug and tugged at my hand as he walked out ahead of me, turning to face me and taking a few steps back. "Made a call when I ordered your stuff for the room. Figured we might want our own ride for the weekend."

"I would hardly call that a *ride*."

"What? It has wheels."

And I knew without a doubt this was for me, because Sebastian's tastes so obviously leaned toward the mean, blacked-out cars with big engines and muscle and guts. This car was sleek, small, and fast, pretentious luxury at its finest.

"You're insane, Sebastian from California."

His laughter was free and full, and filled me whole, my lungs pressing firm at my ribs as I relished in the sound.

"Can't blame a man for taking care of his girl."

"More like spoiling her."

He tugged me hard, making me fall into the warmth of his chest. His heart beat steady and strong. Fingertips brushed along my jaw as the words went soft. "Don't mind doing a little of that, either."

I relinquished, and Sebastian helped me into the soft leather of the front seat, ambled around the front, hopped into the driver's seat, and started the car.

We followed the SUV to the club Ash had arranged for Sebastian's party, back when Sebastian thought it was just going to be him and the guys and a few of their friends out for a night on the town.

A kaleidoscope of lights blazed from the strip. Every casino and hotel was lit up like a torch that promised gratification found in no other place than this city. The top was down and the air was cool, and my heart beat a thunder of contentment in my chest. One of my hands was secured on Sebastian's thigh, the other weaving through the rushing air where my arm was draped over the windowsill.

Ten minutes later, we pulled up to the valet right behind the Escalade, and Sebastian ran around and helped me out. He kept his hand in mine, his head lifted without the reservation he typically wore around the media, as a volley of camera flashes erupted the second we stepped into view.

A red rope held back a line of partygoers dressed to impress, hopeful to make it inside. A few of them called out for *Sunder* as the band strode right toward the entrance. Some singled out Sebastian, calling his name to grab his attention, as they lifted their phones and snagged pictures. He smiled in their direction—the man all happiness and excitement—without an ounce of bristling hostility that normally accompanied being in the public eye.

And I realized sometimes love soothes some of that anger away.

I clung to his side. The force of my smile, this joy inside me, was more than I could understand.

"Delaney Rhoads," someone shouted from the line.

On instinct, my eyes flashed that direction, not sure what to do. Whether I should run or hide or lift my chin in pride the same way Sebastian seemed to do.

Sebastian hugged me a little tighter, quiet support, voice casual when he called out, "Her name's Shea, man. Don't forget it."

Someone laughed and hollered, "Shea," and I just smiled and offered a timid wave, allowing Sebastian to lead me through the entrance of the overflowing club.

Inside, it was darker than night yet brighter than day, bodies lit up like silhouettes in the strobes of light. Professional dancers were suspended from the high cathedral ceiling in cages as the crowd raved below, coves of booths and tables tucked out of sight around the dance floor.

Led upstairs to a private room, we were seated on plush sofas. A myriad of lights glowed from the mirrored ceilings and glass-paned walls, giving us an unobstructed view of the writhing dance floor below.

Sebastian was quick to pull me down beside him, and I curled into his side as he fastened an arm around my shoulders.

More of Sebastian's friends piled in, some who I'd met at the show, others completely unfamiliar, arms draped around girls wearing next to nothing as they filtered in to wish Sebastian Happy Birthday.

But none were as eager to get the party started as Ash.

He ordered a round of shots for everyone, and the two cocktail waitresses assigned to our party delivered them a couple minutes later.

Ash stood and lifted his glass. "I do believe it's time for a toast."

Sebastian muttered, "Uh, oh."

A round of hoots went up, and everyone lifted their tiny glasses of tequila rimmed in salt and garnished with wedges of lime.

I followed suit, smiling up at Sebastian.

Playful eyes glinted down at me.

"We all know I've been putting up with your sorry ass for a long time now…" Ash began his toast in a tone that sounded regretful, but by the smirk showing up on every line on his face, everyone knew it was anything but. "Years just keep flyin' by and you keep getting' older and uglier while I somehow manage to maintain all my boyish good looks. No surprise there, right?" he offered while he raised his arms out to the sides in that cocky way, nodding his head around the room as he tried to get everyone to agree with him.

Laughter rolled.

Sebastian just chuckled quietly and rubbed his palm over his mouth, amusement clear as he let his friend razz him the way he always did.

No harm given.

None taken.

While he continued to gloat, something genuine edged the creases at the corners of Ash's eyes. "We've been through some really horrific times, man…some really fuckin' good ones, too. And my hope is those good ones just keep coming and coming, because I don't know of anyone in this world who deserves them more than you. Happy Birthday, Baz."

They shared a silent moment before Ash raised his glass higher and toward Sebastian.

"To Sebastian." A racket of voices lifted. "Happy Birthday."

Shots were downed.

All except for Sebastian's and mine. Because he turned the intensity of those eyes to my face, passing the moment Ash and he had shared on to me. I felt drawn, and I shifted in the same second Sebastian was turning me, urging me forward.

I straddled his lap.

I didn't care there were a bunch of people here I didn't know, who didn't know me. Didn't care about the women who were probably thirsting for my man, thinking I was just another passing craze, a fling or a fuck or whatever they wanted to believe me to be.

When the truth was, I was his.

Sebastian glanced his thumb over my bottom lip, eyes trailing the action, before he took a wedge of lime and ran it over the same spot.

I could feel the blood rush to plump my lip.

He then ran it over the top, the sensitive skin tingling with the touch, wet by the trickle of juice.

The scent of citrus filled my nostrils.

I sucked in a shaky breath, and he lifted the shot glass to my mouth, the taste of salt hitting my tongue right before the tequila followed it.

Sebastian leaned forward to gather his own taste. His tongue was soft as it rimmed my lips, before it softly slipped inside.

Savoring.

Tempting.

Teasing.

A promise of what was to come.

I wrapped my arms around his head while he kissed me and I whispered, "Happy Birthday."

"Best birthday ever," he whispered back.

The atmosphere was easy, carefree, and Sebastian refused to let me off his lap as he talked with those who'd come to help him celebrate.

The mood became elevated as more drinks were tossed back. Ash and Lyrik let go, the way they so often did at *Charlie's*, joking around, living their lives on their terms.

Somehow they'd managed to create their own dance floor upstairs in our private room, people coming and going as more and more unfamiliar, star-struck faces appeared.

I could only assume most of them were willing women they'd raided from downstairs.

"Dance with me." Sebastian's smooth words licked through me like flames. Unlike when he'd uttered them to me that night at *Charlie's*. The night I'd worried this hope was slipping away. Now, none of the sadness or fear held me.

I should have known better, then.

Should have known this was real.

Unstoppable.

Unbreakable.

Sebastian helped me off his lap, and pushed to his feet. That strange, intense energy brimmed to life as he gazed down at me. He said nothing as he wove his fingers through mine. He took me by all kinds of sweet surprise when he didn't lead me into the mix of his friends in the private room. Instead, he led me slowly down the stairs to the main floor of the club.

With each step, I could feel the rate of my pulse increase, the boom, boom, boom of my heart escalate as he led me into the manic fray that thrummed with the electric beat.

Sebastian's movements were slow. Intentional. Sensual and sexual, causing stuttered breaths to gasp from between my lips when he aligned us front to front. His heat, his heart, and his eyes upon me, shutting out the rest of the world, while he wrapped me up and lifted me out of it.

His hands slid down my back, cupping my ass before he ran them down the outside of my thighs, our own thrumming beat swirling around us. Our bodies moved in sync. In the key we always struck. Rough and desperate and needy.

He kissed me and kissed me and kissed me while one song transitioned from one to another and then another.

Until I was breathless, hot and wet, and sure I couldn't take a second more.

"Let's get out of here," he finally murmured at my mouth.

"God, yes."

A chuckle rolled from his tongue, and he was suddenly striding through the crowd, my hand in his as I struggled to keep up with a man who was most definitely on a mission.

I giggled and clutched him a little tighter, more than ready to go along for the ride.

He gave the valet the slip for the car, and went right back to kissing me while we waited, neither of us concerned about the cameras or gawking eyes.

Because none of that mattered except for this incendiary moment.

When the car came to a stop in front of us, Sebastian handed out another one of his outrageous tips, snatched the keys, and led me to the passenger side. He helped me in, leaning in to grab another kiss.

Lust and love fought for dominance in his expression when he tore himself away, and he slammed my door shut and ran around to his side. I didn't hesitate to shift in my seat, my hand going to the flat, rigid planes of his abdomen as he shifted hard, tires squealing as he took to the street. I kissed at his neck and teased at his ear, fingers toying with the waistband of his jeans, while he groaned and tried to focus on the road.

"You tryin' to kill me, Shea?"

I gasped when the car jerked and Sebastian made a sudden, sharp turn, and then another. He screeched to a stop on a deserted side street.

A fog of lust clouded my mind as I was yanked back onto his lap, my knees on either side of his legs, his needy cock grinding at the seam of my cut-off shorts as his mouth overtook mine.

Oh. God.

I moaned, fingers digging into his shoulders.

I arched up and pressed my breasts to his chest. They ached with just a glimmer of the need throbbing between my thighs.

Hot hands gripped the outside of my hips, forcing me back down on his dick that strained from his jeans.

I might have been on top, but he was definitely in control.

"Fuck, baby…what have you done to me…what have you *done* to me? Dying to be inside you. Have to feel you. Need you so bad."

"You have me."

He palmed my ass, hands running up my sides as he lifted me higher, his head rocking back as he moved and grasped the back of my head, forcing it down as he continued that frenzied assault of tongue, teeth, and mouth.

"Need you forever. Need you wearing my name and showing off my ring." It was all a slur of desperation.

Shock sifted through me, and I froze as what he said penetrated.

I edged back a fraction, still holding onto his shoulders.

It felt as if the world were trembling around me when I took the chance to peer down at him.

He met my gaze.

Raw and severe and honest.

"Marry me."

Hope flashed like wildfire, image after image of a fantasy life I'd never thought possible.

Simple, simple dreams.

They burned from within.

I swallowed around the emotion lodged in my throat and forced out the words. "Are you serious?"

"With all I got…with all I have to offer. Marry me, Shea Bentley."

I blinked frantically. "Right now?"

"Right now. When things settle down, we'll do the big ceremony thing. Have my guys stand up as my best men. Make April and Tamar wear the ugliest dresses you can find."

One cheek twitched as he said that. Breathing quickly, I tried to catch up to what he was asking me.

The words just got rougher as he continued. "We'll have our Kallie tossing petals down in front of you because she'll be the cutest damned flower girl to ever walk an aisle. Have everyone we care about there to witness it. I want all of that, Shea," he emphasized as he grasped me a little tighter. "I want to give it to you. But now? Celebrating my birthday? Want to make you my wife. Just you and me and a future that's wide open in front of us."

Hopeful eyes searched my face. "Tell me you want that, too."

"Yes." It rushed out from somewhere deep within.

"Yes?"

"Yes…yes…yes," I whispered almost frantically. Or maybe it was just my frantic kisses I couldn't stop. Kisses of joy, something whole and beautiful and absolute.

I could feel him smile beneath my lips.

Find love and bring it here. My grandmother's voice echoed through my mind.

I found it, Grandma.

I found it.

He pulled back. "I promise you, Shea, I'm gonna love you forever. I'm going to protect it and never let it go. Be the husband you deserve and the father Kallie needs."

"Sebastian," I breathed, and he cupped my neck, thumb brushing under my jaw.

"You are the one I've been waiting for."

My thoughts flashed to my Kallie.

Without a shadow of a doubt, the wonderful things Sebastian wanted, the things *I* wanted, she'd want them, too.

No questions lingered.

This was right.

He kissed me hard, then moved me to my seat, slanting me a lopsided grin as he threw the car back into drive, and made a quick U in the middle of the road. He pressed the voice recognition on the navigation for the Marriage Bureau.

He drove quickly and purposefully while I flew, my spirit far and fast in front of us.

Touching that future wide open ahead.

We found a spot to park, and Sebastian jumped out and ran around to meet me. Again I found myself struggling to keep up with him as we ran into the building, filled out the form, and paid the fee for a marriage license.

All of this seemed so insane, yet so entirely perfect.

I was getting married.

To Sebastian Stone.

We raced back out to the car. Sebastian's melodic laughter clashed with the night as he threw the convertible back into reverse, and there was nothing I could do. I was back on my knees in my seat, leaning across the console, kissing his face. His neck. Touching him everywhere.

I bounced when he slanted the car into a lot. My smile that seemed unending somehow managed to grow.

We didn't even get out of the car. Sebastian just maneuvered around to the drive-through lane where we paid another fee and handed over our license. The officiant began to speak. We nodded our understanding as he asked a couple questions to ensure we understood we were entering into a legal marriage.

Yes.

Yes.

And yes.

When he began with the vows, a peal of laughter erupted from me when I was abruptly drawn back onto Sebastian's lap, straddling him again.

The officiant's words faded away when Sebastian gripped my face and spoke his own vows to me.

"I'm gonna love you forever. Respect you. Protect you and hold you and always stay true to you."

My hands trembled where I cupped his jaw.

"I will never give you up or let this love go. My forever is forever. My life yours to keep."

We were a flurry of "I dos" and kisses and husband and wife.

Just as fast, we were back on the road, pulling into the hotel valet, hearts pounding and spirits dancing as we rushed through the lobby to the bank of elevators.

We stumbled from the elevator. Sebastian's hands were on my hips as he edged me backward toward the door. His mouth never left mine as he fumbled with the key to our suite.

He swept me off my feet and into the cradle of his arms.

A bride carried over the threshold by the man who promised to hold her.

Protect her.

Love her.

Sebastian slammed the door shut with his foot. His heavy footsteps echoed across the marble tile. He didn't waver or stop. He just went straight for the staircase, never breaking our connection as he wound us up the steps to the bedroom above.

"This is real…this is real," he mumbled between his bid to get me closer. His hold tightened as his mouth went roving down the column of my neck. "Baby, tell me this is real."

"Yes…it's real. All of it…it's real."

We were real.

My heart crashed around in my chest.

Free.

Joy and light and life.

Our touches were frantic as we tore at the other's clothes, our mouths never far as we kissed across the skin we revealed. Our hands were desperate as we pared each other down until we were nothing but naked, heated flesh.

He tossed me onto the center of the enormous bed. My gorgeous man stood at the side, staring down at me with a smile of utter amazement. The gleam in those steely eyes predatory.

There had never been a time before, or would there be a time in my future, when I would feel quite like this.

Desired.

Absolutely adored.

So deliriously happy I didn't know inside from out or up from down, because he'd come in and painted a new beginning. Crushed my walls and altered my realities.

Tonight I had become Sebastian Stone's wife.

"I can't believe you're really mine," he said, like an echo of my own thoughts.

"I'm yours…husband." I felt the catch at the corner of my lips, a tremble that wavered somewhere between playful and wonder.

The sound he made was something akin to a growl.

"Husband."

He said it as if he were testing out how it sounded on his tongue, before he suddenly pounced on me. "Come here, wife. I'm about to take what's mine. You ready for me?"

Laughter tickled from between my lips, and I arched my back as my need swelled, coalescing as a sweet, exquisite ache low in my belly. "Always."

Sebastian ran a hand down the outside of my thigh. "Do you have any idea the fantasies I've been having about being wrapped up in these legs, Shea? All the nights I've spent alone, dreaming about them? About how fuckin' amazing they feel every time I have them wrapped around my waist? Wondering how someone like me got lucky enough to be with someone like you? Now I'm gonna be wrapped up in them for the rest of my life."

He ran his nose along my jaw, arms wrapped around me tight. "You've made me the happiest man alive."

Energy zinged like a live wire. A billow of joy and a bolt of desire.

I looked up to meet the promise in his gaze, fingers grazing over his pouty bottom lip. "I never knew there was happiness like this. And then there was you."

And then there was you.

The smallest smile played at that pretty, pretty mouth. Words I'd whispered months ago that had finally sent us burning down this collision course of passion and need, leading us to this unending devotion neither of us could have imagined we'd ever see.

Then his smile turned sly, eyes glinting in joy and churning with the dirty, delicious deeds he was getting ready to enact on my body.

A ripple of pure desire trembled through me, and he chuckled as I released the well of giggles trickling up my throat, because there was no suppressing my elation.

He pressed his mouth all over my chest and I clung to his shoulders, my head rocking back as he captured one nipple in his hot, hot mouth. He sucked and played and toyed, while his hand wandered down my stomach, a stir of anxious butterflies quivering within.

Anticipation screamed through my veins.

He dragged a knuckle over my clit, and I laughed through a moan when he chuckled, loving the look of infectious delight on his face. His expression danced in the shadows. Greed and pride and lust, awe and devotion and love. It all merged into this euphoric moment created just for us.

He pushed his weight to one hand, and with the other, he drove two fingers inside me.

Sparks flew, little glimmers of pleasure lighting up at the outside of my eyes.

He slid them in and out of my sex, his body a live wire as he shifted over me. "So wet," he said as he climbed onto his knees. He kept himself low as he crawled forward and nudged my legs up as he went, spreading me wide as his fingers touched me even deeper. "Someone's anxious, isn't she? Want me just as bad as I want you, don't you, Mrs. Stone?"

A rush of blissed-out joy rolled through me when he used that name. His name. The name he'd given to me. I dragged my nails down the defined ridges of his strong back. "You have no idea, Mr. Stone, just how desperately I want you." I lifted up, brushing my mouth along his ear. "How much I need you."

Sebastian grabbed his cock and aligned himself, smirking as he raked his teeth over his bottom lip and stared me down.

I groaned when hit with the errant thought. I grinned at my husband, basking in all the light he was shining my way, while I gave a gentle shove to his shoulders and whispered like my life depended on it, "Hurry...find a condom. I forgot my pills, remember?"

Missing them for a couple days probably wasn't a big deal, but the risk was always there.

Sebastian chuckled a little more, running the thick head of his dick between my folds. "No. And why the hell would I have condoms?"

Oh. Right.

I giggled, still riding that dizzying wave, my head rocking back and forth on the sheets while he drove me mad with temptation.

"Sebastian, you're going to get me pregnant."

It came out with the raspy rumble of a laugh.

It was swallowed by the sudden intensity that choked all levity from the room.

Thick and silent and heavy.

His severity consuming.

As if the idea of the words from my mouth had knocked him from his foundation.

My heart thudded in my chest, raced and sped as I tried to catch up to the erratic acceleration of his.

Eyes went dark as they locked on me, and he moved to run shaky fingers through the length of my hair, expression going soft, soft, soft as his head tilted to the side.

"Let's make a baby."

A silent, shocked gasp parted my lips. Again, I felt as if I were in that tunnel of flashing light, on a speeding train propelling us toward a future coming faster and faster and faster.

"That's a lot of big decisions for one night," I finally managed to say.

His hold tightened. "When it comes to you, all my decisions have already been made."

He gave a slight, unsure shake of his head. "I never thought I'd get *this*, Shea. Never thought I'd find someone who touches me the way you do. Believes in me the way you do. Thought being alone was going to be the cost of the band making it. But, no. Here you are, filling up all the hollow spaces in my life."

I blinked back tears as this amazing man mirrored my thoughts from just hours ago.

An old sorrow passed through his eyes. "Time doesn't sit still and I want to make every second I get to spend with you count. Don't want to wait for the right time when *all* of time is right with you."

Emotion spread through my chest, warmth stretching out to touch every place inside me, and euphoria spilled over, the same as the tears in my eyes. "All of time. Every minute. Every second."

A gush of air rushed from his lungs and he pushed up on both hands, this stunning man hovering over me. "Do you see me, Shea?"

I took his face in my hands. "I will never look away."

And neither of us did as Sebastian slowly filled me, the man always so rough and desperate and raw, handling me as if I were glass.

Time given to cherish this moment.

For all of time.

My body took his as he stretched me in the most exquisite way.

Deeply.

Completely.

So full he stole my breath.

Just the same as this man had stolen my heart.

I blinked against the dark, just shimmers of light breaking through the satiny drapes that hung across the glass doors leading to the balcony. Faint sounds of the bustling city echoed from far below.

I awoke to an empty bed. Though I wasn't alone. I could feel his presence surrounding me. Sitting up, I heard the distant strains of an acoustic guitar rising from downstairs, that beautiful, beautiful voice for a beautiful, beautiful man quieted.

Yet it was the only thing I could hear.

I climbed from the bed and wrapped myself in a sheet, padded quietly out the door. I paused at the top of the stairs.

Sebastian sat on the floor with his back propped against the couch, facing away, shoulders bare, guitar cradled in his lap.

Words floated up. The soft pluck of the strings and a mellow melody stretched out to touch my soul.

Slowly I edged down the winding staircase, one hand on the smooth rail as I clutched the sheet to my chest with the other.

The muscles in his back tensed and bowed when he felt my approach, but there was no hitch in his song. Just the sweet, sweet sound urging me toward him.

Barefoot, I stepped onto the cool marble at the landing, and shuffled deeper into the living space. Inch by inch. I rounded the side of the couch and came to a stop three feet in front of him.

Eyes slowly lifted to mine, this stunning man capturing me in the heavy weight of his stare.

Lights flashed and glowed from the windows overlooking the city. Colors flickered across his face, those bold, beautiful lines striking in the night.

And it was like instinct—like magic—when Sebastian halted the song he was composing, just long enough to lift the guitar from his lap and welcome me onto it.

He'd pulled on a pair of old jeans that had been worn soft, and he parted his legs just enough to make me room. I settled on the floor between his legs with my back to his bare chest, the cool, thin sheet against his warm skin sending goosebumps across my flesh.

He exhaled a harsh breath at the contact, his heartbeat a deep, steady thrum. He situated the guitar on my lap and wrapped me in his hold.

The intricate color engraved over his arms seemed to whirl across his skin. Muscle flexed beneath as if it ached to tell its story.

Or maybe it ached to write a new one.

His breath tickled along my neck, blowing strands of my hair around us as he leaned over my shoulder. His hands caressed the back of mine as he carefully set them on the guitar.

My fingertips pressed the strings down onto the fret as Sebastian lightly covered them with his own. A gentle guidance. A quiet encouragement.

Our spirits one.

As if he understood my own ache. As if he were the only person with the capacity to feel the hole left when I'd given up my dreams because I was never willing to pay the price.

Not when the price was my daughter.

But that didn't mean the need to create, to compose, and to play didn't burn from within.

And I knew. And I knew. And I knew.

Sebastian Stone had been created for me.

A thrill rushed through my nerves, because I hadn't made music in so very long.

Together we strummed.

Sebastian's voice rasped at the shell of my ear, the lyrics broken and unpolished as he whispered the beginnings of a soul-baring song.

You.
Came like a storm.
In the distance.
Coming closer.

I felt comfort and surety in the choice we'd made.

The jump we'd taken.

And together, we fell. Fell into the song, our fingers finding our own perfect rhythm on the strings. Fell into the words, our spirits and tongues coming together to tell our story.

Fell further into beauty.

Fell into a sea of stars that blinded my eyes. Where we floated in a high place that belonged only to us. A place that didn't belong to this world.

In a place where Sebastian and Shea Stone would never end.

thirteen
Sebastian

ANXIOUSLY, I POUNDED ON the hotel door. I paced two steps one direction and then two steps in the opposite, before I rapped my knuckles on the wood again.

"All right…all right…cool your fucking jets, man, I'm coming," echoed from the other side.

Metal scraped before the door opened enough for my baby brother's face to come into view, brown hair a mess, baggy boxers sagging on his narrow hips the only thing covering up his tall, lanky body. "Where's the damned fire?"

Upstairs, still asleep in my suite.

I shouldered into his room. "What, I can't just stop by my baby brother's room to say hi?"

"At seven thirty in the morning? Uh…no." Slanting a hand through his bedhead, he narrowed suspicious eyes on me. "What's up?"

"Who said anything was up?"

He barked out a knowing laugh. "I don't know…you come in here at the ass-crack of dawn, day after your birthday, mind you, cheesy-ass grin on your face and a bounce to your step. Looks like something's up to me."

He was right. Couldn't wipe the fucking grin from my face even if I wanted to.

Which I didn't.

Never felt so good in all my life.

"Yeah…you're right. Something's up, and I wanted you to be the first to know."

Ten minutes later, I was letting Austin's door slam shut behind me, and hauling ass back to our suite.

With all of me, I needed to get back to my girl.

Sliding the keycard through the slot, I unlatched the door and slipped inside. A stilled quiet echoed back as the sun climbed past the horizon. Rays of morning slanted across the city. Right now, it was probably the most mellow it could possibly be.

Crazy, considering I was the most wound up I'd ever been. Last night I couldn't catch even a wink, hadn't even skated in the direction of sleep as I let everything that'd transpired over the night catch up to me.

Fuck, was I floating on air. Riding on the commitment and music we'd made, something so fucking brilliant and intense and real that I'd felt it sinking in, becoming one with my bones. Same way as I felt that girl sinking deeper into my spirit last night, holding me hostage with her voice and freeing me with her words.

Sure. People were going to say we were rushing things. Say both of us were nothing but irresponsible fools diving heart first into this unending ecstasy that could only shift. Trouble just waiting to swallow us whole.

I didn't give two fucks about that.

Wasn't like I'd ever been known to play by the rules, anyway.

And when it came to Shea, I was ready to break them all. Bust up all the presuppositions and projections, those stating we were setting ourselves up to fail before we ever got the chance to fly.

She was the answer for my soul.

I headed straight for the stairs, footsteps light, not wanting to wake her. Unlike me, Shea'd been snuggled in my arms, long lost to sleep when I'd finally untangled myself when I couldn't ignore the nagging feeling I needed to talk to my brother.

At the top of the stairs, I paused when I looked at the bed on which we'd done all that consummating.

Empty.

Blankets shoved to the floor.

Water ran from a faucet in the bathroom, and my heart skipped an anxious beat.

Shea.

In four steps, I cleared the bedroom floor and nudged open the bathroom door.

My chest tightened, need and love and devotion washing me through.

She stood in front of the dressing table mirror with her back to me.

One glimpse and every inch of me grew hard.

My wife.

Still couldn't believe it.

That same silky white sheet was tucked under her arms. It dipped down low enough on her back to reveal that delectable expanse of creamy skin, draping the rest of the way down to pool like liquid ivory on the floor. Waves of blonde spilled and spilled, those locks falling free over her delicate bare shoulders and framing her face, just begging for my hands to get wrapped up in it.

Fucking gorgeous.

Shake the earth kind of gorgeous.

Outshine the stars kind of gorgeous.

Yeah, that kind of gorgeous.

And. She. Was. Mine.

Caramel eyes flew up to meet my gaze when she caught my reflection in the mirror. Slowly I advanced. Her storm gathered strength. All that dark and light and life crashed over me. Like this girl was surrounded by electricity, a current sparking in the air.

Second I'd seen her, there was no doubt in my mind she held the power to turn my world upside down.

Should have known better.

She'd shattered it.

Redefined who I was and who I wanted to be.

Stripped me of all control and left me bare.

Found a way to seep through those cracks inside my scarred heart and somehow made it whole.

"There you are." Her voice was rough with sated satisfaction, still groggy from sleep.

My footsteps echoed across the floor as I edged up behind her. My hands went to her flat belly then roamed over the soft curve of her hips, traipsing right back again, the silky fabric the only barrier as I tugged all her soft against my hard.

"Did you miss me?" I mumbled at her ear.

Tongue darting out to wet that lush bottom lip, she released a tiny moan into the thick tension holding us captive in this room, that invisible tether that tied us together once again drawing taut.

"Always. I woke up to an empty bed and thought maybe you'd gotten cold feet."

One side of her mouth curled with the tease, and a low chuckle rolled from me as I nuzzled along the slope of her neck.

Running my nose from her ear to the cap of her shoulder, I whispered my truth. "Never."

Longing searched for a way out, intense and visceral. Something instinctual. A harsh breath pushed from my lungs, and I took a step back and toed off my shoes. Intent becoming clear.

Shea's stare was just as heavy as mine as we watched each other through the mirror, like she fed from my every move, little earthquakes vibrating through her as that energy collected like a palpable mass.

Suffocating.

Reaching up to my collar, I dragged my tee over my head and tossed it to the floor, took another step back as I ticked through the buttons of my jeans. Shea's attention tracked the movement. My pulse volatile and wild.

I shrugged off my jeans and my underwear. Baring myself. My cock, eager as ever, sprang free of its confines, at the ready and beggin' for more, more, more.

Wasn't ever gonna get enough.

Desire swirled through her eyes as they traced across my skin like she would give anything to consume me. To sink inside and disappear.

But I didn't think she had the first clue the way she possessed *me*.

That she was already there.

"Turn around," I ordered, words scraping like a lash from my throat.

So slowly she spun to face me, anticipation thick, and I knew she was waiting for me to strike. To take and take and take.

But, no. Instead, I climbed down onto both knees and knelt at her feet.

Figured one just wouldn't do.

Not for Shea.

Not for my wife.

I was going to give it all.

A halo of light shone around her, hair lit up like white fire, my girl wrapped loosely in that silky sheet.

Lust cut a path through my veins and knotted in my stomach. Shea stared down at me like the temptress she was.

An angel.

A goddess.

Slipping my hands beneath the sheet, I ran them up the outside of her legs, chasing the tremors that rolled beneath the surface of her skin. Palpable and alive. Slipping from her and sinking into me.

I sucked in a breath and cupped her ass, pulling her forward in the same second I pressed my nose to her silk-covered sex.

Closing my eyes, I inhaled, relished in her heat and desire while my girl gasped, that sweet, seductive sound spurring me on.

Meeting her eyes, I slowly parted the sheet and revealed smooth, honeyed skin. I gave it a firm tug and pulled it free. Fabric floated to the floor.

And there she stood with me kneeling at her feet, my hands on the outside of her thighs.

A vision.

Dark.

Light.

Heavy.

Soft.

Fucking perfect.

My wife.

"So fucking beautiful, Shea. Every inch of you. Got the best everything. Now I'm gonna spend the rest of my life cherishing it. Adoring it. Adoring you."

Protecting you and loving you and giving it all.

Would lie, steal, and defeat.

Kill.

Die.

Anything it took, just as long as this girl lived the life she deserved.

Wrapping my hands farther around to the backs of her thighs, I spread her, just enough to gain room to press my tongue to her clit.

Fuck. Would never grow tired of the way she tasted.

Ripples of pleasure shook through her, and I delved a little deeper, running my tongue through her slick flesh. Her hands fell back to grasp the counter, perfect round tits jutting forward as her head rocked back.

"Sebastian."

My chest tightened with my name begging from her mouth, and I spread her more. Gave and took, fingers pushing into the well of her tight, hot body, mouth sucking and licking and feeding on that sweet spot that had her writhing, desire running wild.

"Please," she whimpered, and I knew she was already close, gaining speed, a flutter of her walls and a quiver of her thighs.

"I know, baby, I know. I've got you."

I've got you.

Shea broke and her entire body convulsed when her orgasm came with a vengeance. Fingers ripped fistfuls of my hair, and God, if I didn't love that, too. Loved it rough, loved it when Shea gave just as good as she got. Those pricks of pain sent chills skating down my spine.

Lust.

Flames licking my insides.

Dick so fucking stiff it was hard to breathe.

I rode it with her, continuing to lave her with soft sucks and deep pulls, as I drew out every last ounce of pleasure I could. Her fucking insane body trembled and shook around me, before my girl slumped back, breaths panting and searching for air she couldn't seem to find.

I pushed to my feet and dug greedy fingers into her hips, quickly hoisting her onto the edge of the counter.

A throaty sound rumbled from her when I ran my hands up

and down the backside of her thighs, her hands propped back on the counter to hold her weight.

Shea gave me a look that was pure and utter destruction. This girl so damned sexy laid out under the bathroom lights, all aglow, flushed with remnants of pleasure still rippling through her body. But her expression promised she was ready for so much more.

Trouble.
Trouble.
Trouble.

This girl was gonna be the end of me.

Grasping her by the knees, I spread her wide. My lips latched onto the sensitive skin at the inside of her thigh, the intense urge to mark her taking over as I let my itching fingers go trailing back through her perfect pink pussy.

Shea whimpered and writhed as I sucked at her flesh while my fingers staked their claim.

"So fucking wet," I groaned, pressing my cheek to the spot where I'd just left my brand, and she jerked when I ran my stubble all the way up the inside of her thigh.

Damn it all if I wasn't dying for another taste.

I ran my tongue from the cleft of her sweet little ass all the way to her clit.

"Oh God," she whimpered. Trembling fingers rustled through my hair. "One look and I forget who I am. One touch and I'm gone. You are my everything."

Urging me to straighten, she leaned forward enough to trace along my jaw, dragging slow down my neck to my chest, glancing softly over my scars.

Love.
Belief.
Beauty.
Trust.

Trailing a path down my body, her fingertips brushed over the green monkey immortalized on my side.

This girl was so damned in tune with who I was. Like she shared in this loss without needing insight to the details. Shea just got every bit of me.

My heart lurched when I thought of the brown monkey laying on the entry table downstairs, that baby girl just as sweet.

I deserved none of it.

And here I stood, covered in Shea's light, cloaked in her darkness, surrounded in her scent of satisfaction, lost beneath the surface where she became the air. *My air.*

Drowning to Breathe.

"God, I love you…so much…so much," I said, hand going to her cheek while the other continued to wind her right back up, because if I was going, then I was taking her along with me.

"I know." She said it like she'd received a gift, her words again taking on that reverent tone, seeing through all my bullshit to what mattered underneath. "I love you…with all of me."

She continued tracking down, fingertips gliding down my stomach that jerked beneath her touch.

She wrapped her hand around the base of my cock.

So damned soft.

I grunted through a groan.

Pure seduction kicked up at the corner of her mouth as she gave me one good stroke, thumb running around my throbbing head.

"Shit," slid from between my clenched teeth, and I wrapped my hand around hers, let her pump me once more, before I took over and pressed the tip of my dick to her drenched center and nudged in an inch.

Sweat gathered at the nape of my neck and my entire body twitched with restraint.

"You ready for me?" I bit off. Everything about it came across like a threat, because every cell in my body screamed at me to *take* my wife. My guts were twisted with need and my thighs shook like a goddamned leaf.

Wanted to fuck just about as bad as I wanted to adore.

"Yes," grated from her mouth.

I surged forward and Shea screamed out as her body adjusted to mine. Streaks of pleasure rippled from my body as I drove into her.

"Every time…every fucking time," I muttered, trying to recover my composure considering I'd lost it the second I'd walked through the door. There wasn't anything in the world that felt better than this. Better than her.

Shea.

She whimpered and dug her fingers into my shoulders, holding on when I began to move, every move frenzied with my body's demand. Miles of long, toned legs were wrapped around my waist, and each greedy thrust jarred her back.

Wrapping an arm around her back, I held her by the base of the neck to keep her steady, my hips meeting hers as I continued at the savage pace.

Needed to consume.

To take it all.

With my free hand, I dipped two fingers into the warm, wet well of her mouth. Shea moaned, then sucked, cheeks hollowing out as her tongue pulsated around my fingers.

Fuck, she was a dream, this girl a fantasy. Like she'd been offered to me. Wrapped up with a big red bow. But tucked inside was more. Something fragile and soft, her love a guiltless trust that struck me deep. Just drove me a little madder, crazy for this girl who owned every part of me.

I pumped my fingers in and out of her mouth while strangled

words tumbled from my own. "You have no idea how sexy you are. You are amazing."

Withdrawing my fingers, I slid my arm under her thigh. I dragged her farther off the counter and ran my fingers around where we were joined. My breaths turned ragged when I turned course, and moved to run them up and down the crease of her ass, everything going silent when I started making circles at that tight little hole.

Lust clouded her features, caramel darkening the darkest dark. A slow slide of desire. A glimpse of fear immediately was eclipsed by the fire lapping between us. Her lips parted and her energy swelled. Lifting us higher.

"Love it all," I murmured rough as I pushed those two fingers inside.

"Sebastian," she cried. Fingertips scraped at my skin as she clung to the bunched muscles of my back, a sharp, pleading gasp falling from that sweet mouth, my girl simmering sex yet entirely innocent at the same time.

Vulnerable.

Entrusting all her pleasure to me.

I began to pump them in time with my cock, and with every stroke, I took her deeper. "Love that you let me touch you…love you know I'd never hurt you."

She wheezed sharp breaths. Everything tightened to a pinpoint around us, our pants and our future and the air. The girl dragging me beneath the surface, pulling me under. Her head rocked back and I took the opportunity to latch onto the dusky nipple of one of those perfect, round tits.

I bit down and she screamed. She clenched hard on my cock and my fingers, and we both let go. Let the world shatter around us. Pleasure burst, strobes of fragmenting color and light. The ground fell away and the sky drifted into nothingness.

For a moment, we got lost in it, in the depths of that place that belonged only to us. In the shadows and the light. In the power of her undying storm.

She whimpered again and again. *My name. My name. My name.*

My hips jerked and my body spasmed as I poured into her, praying it was taking hold. Thinking maybe I was a fool to think for even a second I deserved something like *this*.

But it was a true fool who rejected the gifts they were given.

"Shea...baby...Shea."

On a shuddered breath, she slumped forward and buried her face in my chest, and I buried mine in her hair as I slowly eased out of her.

"You are incredible," I mumbled at the top of her head. I kissed across that invisible crown, running down to her temple where I felt the strength of her pulse beat.

Inclining my head back, I studied the lines of her face. "You okay?"

Her expression one of awe, she mindlessly chewed at her bottom lip, as if she couldn't make sense of the connection we shared any more than I could. Her tone brimmed with emotion. "I would never describe what I'm feeling right now as *okay*."

I chuckled then kissed her mouth. "Come on...let's get you cleaned up."

I swept my girl into my arms—holding her like I was always gonna do—and strode toward the shower.

Giggles rang through the room, and I felt the carefree sound bang around somewhere in my chest. Shea's grin brightened the entire room as she fought to break away, jerking this way and that, but totally failing considering she was wrapped back up in that sheet.

Right where I'd tossed her in the center of the bed after we'd showered.

Didn't bother letting her get dressed.

Figured that was nothing but wasted time.

Besides, she looked damned good rolling around in that bed with nothing but a flimsy piece of fabric outlining that killer body.

"Not a chance, buddy," she warned on a gush of exerted air when I narrowed my predatory gaze on her. She rolled, having another go at skirting my advances, but I shifted farther to the right where I stood at the end of the bed.

My hands were on the mattress, my body bent as I tracked her movements, my dick already pointing to the sky.

She shrieked when I grabbed her by the ankle and flipped her onto her back. I scrambled onto the bed, climbing over her, putting just enough of my weight on her to hold her down.

"What?" I smirked when I pressed her hands into the bed above her head.

More giggles erupted from her. Was going to be sure I coaxed that sound from her every goddamn day.

Raving, she shook her head, wet hair flying, but that grin provided me her tell. "Sebastian, you're going to kill me," she wheezed. "I can't take any more."

"What can't you take?" I teased.

"Uh..." she groaned then laughed when I rubbed my cock against her belly. "Stop it...you're way too tempting for me to resist."

"Then why are you resisting?" I dipped down, pressing a smattering of kisses under her chin, causing her head to rock back and those perfect tits that were already puckered tight to press into my chest, the beat of her heart running wild against mine.

"You sore, baby? I'll be gentle," I cooed, trying to bite back laughter when she gave me a look that promised she knew I was nothing but a liar.

"You're never *gentle*."

"Oh, come on, Shea. I can be gentle."

Teasing eyes went wide. "Pretty sure that's only reserved for special occasions."

I let that laughter roll, then pressed her hands a little deeper into the bed, rocking over her, tone going harsh. "Tell me you don't like it."

A seductive sound rumbled at the base of her throat, and she arched, lifting her chin. "I don't like it."

I began to frown, before she brushed her lips along the shell of my ear. "I love it."

"That's what I thought. Besides, we have something kind of important we need to work on, don't you think?" I said with a suggestive raise of my brows.

Shea drew a shoulder to her cheek, like she was swimming in the thought. "There's always next month."

"And the next," I murmured back, "and the next."

And the next and forever.

Didn't mean I didn't want it now.

She flashed me another grin. "Don't get your hopes up, rocker boy. This is probably going to take some time."

I growled, diving in for a kiss. "And I'll gladly oblige all the hard work it's gonna take. Starting. Right. Now."

She giggled again. "Pretty sure you started last night. Right here in this bed. On the bathroom counter this morning." With each spot she called me out on, her voice grew deeper. "How about that shower?"

Hell yeah, we'd gotten a good start.

"Doesn't mean I'm finished with you."

Apparently my girl didn't remember the promise I'd made her yesterday when we'd first rolled into this ridiculous suite. Seemed as good a time as any to remind her.

A shrill ring bleated from the nightstand, and my phone vibrated on the glass.

I groaned, leaned down, and nipped at her nose. "Don't move."

That smile only widened, and she rolled to her side to face me, clutching the sheet to her chest, watching me with deep affection while I fumbled for my phone.

Lyrik.

I flopped onto my back, couldn't contain my own smile because I was so damned happy.

Accepting the call, I pressed it to my ear. "Lyrik, seriously, man, can't this wait? I'm trying to get my wife pregnant."

"Your what?" There was no missing the shocked disbelief through the phone, then his silence. For a few awkward beats nothing was said, before I felt the dark smirk slide to his face when he spoke again. "Tell me I didn't just hear what I think I heard."

"And what is it you think you heard?"

"Think I heard one of my asshole best friends telling me he went and got married without letting any of us know. And I think I heard him saying something about his naked ass doing some kind of filthy deed where his sweet girl would be tied to his ugly ass for the rest of her life."

My grin just grew. "Sounds about right."

"Holy fuck."

"Yep."

Ash's elevated voice carried across the line, like he was shouting toward the phone Lyrik held. "What the hell, dude? Tell me Lyrik is fucking with me, because this shit ain't cool."

Lyrik answered, "No fuckery man…asshole went and ditched us for his girl."

"Holy fuck is right." Ash just got louder. "You over there corrupting my girl, man? Beautiful Shea," he hollered, "I'm coming, baby. I'll save you."

If I didn't know my punk-ass friend was completely full of shit, I would've knocked him a week from Sunday. But that's just the way we were. Giving each other crap every chance we got, acting like we were tearing each other down when we were just building each other up.

Shea played right along, yelling toward the speaker I tried with no avail to cover. "Save me, Ash. I've been taken against my will, by a sex fiend who won't let me out of bed, no less."

She was gonna be tied to it if she kept that shit up.

"On my way, baby girl!" Ash was shouting again, and there was a scuffle, muffled words shouted between Lyrik and Ash, and the faint inclination of Zee coming in on the conversation on the back end.

Knew without a shadow of a doubt my entire crew would have my back. That they'd support this decision I'd made to permanently make Shea a part of my life, because I no longer knew how to go on living without her in it.

Would it affect them? Yeah. You can't make life-altering changes without it altering your life.

A door slammed and the line went quiet before Lyrik spoke again, this time subdued and without any of the prior mocking in his tone. "What are you gonna do, man?"

"Don't know yet."

More silence.

"I get it, Baz. Totally get it. Do what you feel you have to do. Do what makes you happy."

"I am," I said, completely honest.

I glanced at Shea who reflected empowering light back at me.

Happy.

For once, I felt it above anything else.

"We'll figure this shit out."

It was all encouragement mixed up with his own worry. For so long, it'd just been us, the band and me and my baby brother. Nothing else in this fucked-up world had mattered.

Not until now.

"Talk soon," he said, before the line went dead and I rolled to my side, Lyrik's questions raising my own.

A tiny frown bridged Shea's brow, like she caught onto it, too.

Needing the connection, I wove my fingers through hers. "What are we going to do, Shea?"

Unease slithered through her, before she quietly offered an answer that had no solution. "We kind of rushed into this, didn't we?"

Soft, admissive laughter fumbled from my mouth. "Yeah."

No use in lying to ourselves.

We'd rushed.

The reality was we'd been rushing since the moment I'd looked up and found her standing in front of me at that horseshoe booth at *Charlie's*. She'd arrived like a flood to a parched desert, quenching a thirst I'd never realized I felt, my life barren until she'd breathed across it with her life.

My voice went soft with sincerity. "But I don't regret it. Not for a second."

She caught her bottom lip between her teeth, held it there while she gave the slightest shake of her head. "Me, neither. Not at all."

I swallowed over the lump forming in my throat. "You know, you and Kallie were planning on coming to California to stay for a few days after we wrap up this tour."

She nodded like she was following my mixed-up train of thought.

"Right after, we have to hit the studio."

Another nod.

The words grew rough. "I can't stand the idea of you and Kallie not being there. Of not coming home to my wife every night. Want you falling asleep in my arms and waking up there, too. Come. Stay with me for a while. I've got an extra room we can set up for Kallie."

Mark's room. Hadn't touched it since he'd died. The four of us had done nothing more than figuratively board it up, yellow tape and hazard signs posted all around it, because none of us had been ready to deal with the heartbreak we knew would be waiting behind it. Once I'd asked Zee if he wanted to go in and clear out his brother's stuff, but he'd resisted, saying he wasn't ready to go there yet.

But maybe it was time we moved on.

"I'll be sure the guys are all on board. Make sure there's no nonsense going down while we're there. We can stay there as long as we need, until you and I figure this shit out. Figure out where we want to live. Where we want to raise our daughter."

Where we wanted to make a home. Add to it. Make a family.

God, just the thought had both fear and devotion knocking around inside me, the innate need to see it through, to protect and love them, ensure they got everything in this world they deserved.

Joy pulled at every inch of her.

"What?" I asked quietly.

Those eyes flashed. "You don't know how happy it makes me to hear you call her that."

I squeezed her fingers wrapped in mine. "You don't know how happy it makes me to be *able* to call her that. You don't know what you've given me, Shea…bringing her into my life."

"I'd like that," she finally said through the emotion gathered in her throat. "I can't wait to tell her."

I pulled her hand to my mouth and kissed the vacant spot on her left hand ring finger. "First order of business will be puttin' something pretty on this finger. Told you I wanted you to be showing off my ring. We'll go find someone who can design you something special…something different. Something you can show off everywhere you go, so people are gonna know you are mine and I am yours."

Something as unique as my girl.

Sadness traveled through her features that somehow glowed with hope, and her lip trembled as her gaze darted to the wall, before she settled her attention back on me. "I know what I'd like."

"Anything."

"My grandma…"

Second she said it, something deep within me tuned in, quick to listen, because I knew whatever was getting ready to pass from her mouth was important.

"You know she left me the house."

I gave her a slight nod, encouraging her to continue.

"She also left me most of her jewelry…most importantly her wedding ring."

Tears pooled in her eyes, and she got that expression again, eyes creasing with regret and mouth pulling with remorse. The one she got when she shared the painful moments of her past. "He… it was…it was stolen." She winced and forced a smile. "Losing it broke my heart."

My girl fluttered her fingertips along my jaw. "I'd do anything to replace it. To get the spirit of it back so I can wear it to honor her. To honor them."

Her smile trembled, so full of love and loss, and I gathered her closer. "Shea," I whispered, and she just continued on. "She and my grandpa…they loved each other unlike anything I've ever seen, Sebastian. In a way so pure and beautiful that I remember, even as a little girl, hoping someday I'd get to experience a love like that. My grandma always told me she'd been given a fairy tale. She told me to go out and find one of my own."

She drew her head back to look at me. "It was unlike anything I've witnessed…until you loved me."

My chest tightened.

Affection profound.

Wrapping me up, layer after layer.

Didn't think I had the capacity to love like this.

But this girl?

She proved to me I did.

"Nothing would make me happier than giving that to you, Shea." My smile was soft, and I kissed along the line of her temple where it met with the defined curve of her jaw, part of me wanting to jump out of this bed and track down the fucker who'd taken it from her. Take it back.

"We'll recreate it."

Didn't know if I was talking more about the ring or her grandparents.

Knew all along how much she'd adored them. It had been where she'd felt safest.

And that…that was what I wanted. For her to feel that with me. Safe.

To know I would always protect her. Stand up for her. Fight for her.

She took my hand and held it up, like this girl was imagining what it would look like for the ring to grace my finger.

"My grandpa's was simple. Just a platinum band engraved with the word "always" on the inside. And my grandma's…hers was beautiful." She squinted, lost in the memory. "Antique and delicate and somehow striking."

"Do you remember the details?" I asked.

"I will never forget it."

"Then we'll make it happen."

Downstairs, someone pounded on the door. I frowned, hating the idea of breaking up the moment.

"Just ignore it," I told her.

Fists pounded again, although this time it sounded like a herd of wild animals trying to bust their way in.

Shea's smile made a resurgence. "We should get that."

"Do we have to?" I pretended to whine through my grin, and the new onslaught of battering told me we most definitely did.

"Um…yeah. I'm not sure at this point a lock would keep them out."

I pressed a resigned kiss to my wife's mouth and rolled from bed. I grabbed a pair of jeans from my suitcase and pulled on a fresh tee, eyeing my girl while she quickly dressed, shorts and tank and everything sweet.

God, I was done for.

I hooked her hand in mine, knuckles pressed to my mouth, before I gave it up and towed her behind me downstairs to the unruly echo of my crew getting rebellious outside.

Quickly, I undid the lock and let the door fly free.

Ash waltzed in with two champagne bottles lifted over his head, knowing smug smile denting the lines on his face. Zee followed closely behind with a handful of flute stems wound between his fingers, Lyrik riding in on all his cool intensity.

Austin came shuffling in behind.

Ash made himself right at home, popped the cap on a bottle of champagne. "Think this calls for a celebration."

"You think everything calls for a celebration," I told him wryly.

He just smiled my way as he held up a glass and filled it. "And you say that as if it's a bad thing."

We spent a couple hours celebrating with the guys, the mood easy and light, and when they finally left, we texted April and asked her to set Kallie up on Skype.

Told her we had big news.

Through the screen, Kallie grinned at us, blonde curls wild, wild, wild, that toothy smile filling up my heart and my world. She frowned in confusion when we told her we got married and said she already thought we were.

And I wished I were there to wrap her up, take her in my arms, because there was nothing better in this world than a child's innocence. Especially hers. Her belief in what we were long before it'd even come to pass.

A family.

It seemed word traveled fast. Soon I accepted a congratulatory call from Anthony, laced with some frustration about my impulsiveness getting me in trouble, forgetting details like a pre-nup there was no chance in hell I would have asked her to sign, anyway. Guy was always looking out for me. I got a text from Kenny, then fielded a call from Charlie that was chockfull of encouragement and dripping with warning.

Apparently if I hurt *his girl* he was gonna track me down and I'd be pissing from a bag for the rest of my life.

Noted.

But I just smiled, knowing there was no risk at all.

Shea got a snarky text from Tamar, something about being sure she had me by the dick.

Mission accomplished.

I gave Shea some privacy when April called and they sat on the phone for close to half an hour. Both of them had cried. I totally got it, understood the bond they had. They'd grown up together and had dreamed together. Lived together. Mourned together. Now I'd come in and shaken up that dynamic. Both of them knew the way things had been was coming to an end.

Sometimes when you welcome in something new, the old can no longer remain.

But I'd also been around April enough to know she wanted the best for Shea. The best for Kallie. And just like my guys, she would support Shea through whatever decisions she made.

The day passed, and Shea and I ordered dinner in, sat at that big table set for eight and ate over candlelight. We fed each other pieces of lobster and steak and cheesecake, pretty much acting like a couple of lovesick teenagers, which was exactly the way I felt.

When we finished, I pushed our spent plates aside and set Shea in their place. In the gentle flames of the candles flickering across her face and glowing against the vast bank of windows in the backdrop of night, I made love to my wife.

I spent the rest of the weekend taking her in every room, on every surface, in every way. Fucked and tasted and adored.

Then just like I warned her I would, I turned right around and did it again.

Best. Birthday. Ever.

fourteen
Shea

"YOU DON'T REALLY BELIEVE in Prince Charming, do you, Butterfly?" April teased, lifting the to-go coffee cup to her mouth.

Giggles floated on the breeze gentling through the afternoon air, and Kallie kicked her head back and let her sweet laughter free as she held her own tiny cup filled with hot chocolate between two chubby hands.

Her *big girl* drink.

"Uh-huh, Auntie April," she said with all the childish authority she could muster.

She sat on her knees, chair pushed up close to the metal patio table where we relaxed on the wide sidewalk outside our favorite coffee shop in the old part of Savannah. Overhead umbrellas protected us from the sun, and a quaint, peaceful feeling held fast in the atmosphere.

"There *are* so, so, so many princes! I'll show you. I got lots in my books right up in my room. And me and my momma are gonna get on a plane and fly far, far away and go to *Cowiforna* and my daddy is gonna take me to Disneyland and I'm gonna meet all of 'em."

Love filled me so completely it became difficult to breathe. Every time my precious daughter called Sebastian *daddy* it stole my air.

And now it was becoming a true reality.

Permanent.

I'd been home for three days. Married for four. God, it still blew my mind.

I was married to Sebastian Stone.

Did I worry? Fear Sebastian and I had rushed into things too fast?

Of course. I was human…and a mother. A mother who'd lived as a single mother for a lot of years. I'd held onto old insecurities for so long, sometimes it was difficult to let them go, especially after Martin had returned.

But being with Sebastian made me feel freer than I'd ever felt.

And the truth was, I believed in us.

Life wasn't worth living if we didn't take the chance to go after what brought us the most joy. Wasn't worth living if we didn't fight to be with the ones we loved or work for the relationships that brought beauty into our lives.

Sebastian was all those things, and he was *worth* it.

Tamar smirked across at me, blue eyes twinkling as she wrapped her painted red lips around the straw of her iced cappuccino.

She'd been giving me crap about the whole eloping thing since the second she'd caught wind.

I hiked up a shoulder in a *What? And if you even say a single thing I will kill you* sort of way.

Her amusement only grew. "So the infamous Sebastian Stone became your knight in shining armor, isn't that right, Shea?"

April chuckled and Kallie giggled like it was the funniest thing she'd ever heard.

"If the bill fits…" I trailed off suggestively.

"Oh, come on, Tamar, you're just jealous you don't have a superhot rocker there to worship the ground you walk on," April cut in, taking a swig of her coffee and sitting back in her chair.

"Pssh." Tamar rolled her eyes, pure sex and sass. "Like I need some cocky guy to make me feel good."

Uncontainable laughter burst from April and me. I knew we were both struggling to hold back every inappropriate retort itching to fly from our tongues.

"Really? Sounds to me like that theory would get old and *fast*." Over her cup, April wagged her brows, letting her attention dart down to Tamar's hand.

I leaned in closer and murmured conspiratorially, "I'd be willing to make some bets Lyrik would be all kinds of happy to step in and take care of that little problem for you."

I didn't mind getting a rise from my friend. Any time the two of them were in a building together? The flaming sexual tension nearly burnt it down.

"Ha. I have exactly zero problems that need to be taken care of…all except for one. Him. Player doesn't know when to take a hint. Every time he walks into the bar he thinks he's going to get a little piece of this." She shimmied her curvy body on her chair. "Not gonna happen."

"Says the girl who once accused me of being completely blind when it came to what was happening between Sebastian and me."

"So?" she defended.

"So take a look in the mirror, girlfriend," April said with a slap to the table.

"Girlfriend?" Kallie asked in confusion, big brown eyes going wide as she tried to follow the conversation, so sweet and innocent and adorable.

My heart overflowed.

How had I gotten so lucky?

Tamar straightened, hesitated as she played with the straw on her drink. "I really can't believe you're leaving."

The flippancy of our mood evaporated. "I can't believe it, either. It's almost unbelievable, everything that has happened in such a short time."

April slanted me the smallest smile. "Guess I shouldn't have been making all those claims that one day some amazing guy was going to come in and sweep you off those pretty feet. Didn't expect that would mean he'd be sweeping you away to another state."

I flinched at the flash of sorrow in her expression. It was true we'd become our own patchwork family. Kallie was a fundamental piece of April, too.

"You're not giving Kallie or me up, April, and just because we're going out there doesn't mean we're going to stay forever. Sebastian just has to be there right now. And…" I wavered on what to say, "I don't have to be here."

Yes. There was a huge part of me that wanted to be. Here. Home. But the bigger part *had* to be with Sebastian.

Tamar cleared her throat. "I think I speak for us all when we say we just want you to be happy."

April sniffled and glanced away, before she looked back with a smile that was both forced and genuine. "That's all we want."

Tamar's red lips curled. "Well…all except Charlie. I've never heard the old man rant and rave the way he did when he found out you were leaving. I thought he was going to have an aneurysm."

I laughed and shook my head. "He's just a tad protective."

In his mind, we were *his* daughter and granddaughter, and as much as he'd always encouraged me to pursue my heart's desires, I knew embarking on this new journey was tearing him up. The truth was, just thinking about severing even a fraction of the connection we had broke something inside me, too.

When I'd gone to his place on Monday, sat him down and told him I wasn't going back to the bar and was going to California, I'd finally understood what it looked like for a man to blow a gasket. The full effect of his fatherly concern had overflowed in a slew of questions and what ifs and warnings.

In the end he'd pulled me to him, hugged me tight, and whispered, "You go, Shea Bear. Live your life. Love every second of it."

He'd taken care of me for so long, and even though I could tell him nothing would change, we both knew it would. There was a small part he had to let go—the part as my ultimate protector and confidant—as Sebastian had come in to take that place.

"My daddy had to go to wook," Kallie began to prattle, leaning her elbows on the table and clasping her hands together, her smile all tiny teeth and hope and unending faith. "And when he gets all done is when we get to fly way, way, way up high in the sky, right, Momma?"

She looked at me for confirmation.

"Yes, Butterfly. We'll be going soon."

Just a week and a half.

Concern and yearning rolled through me like a lopsided ball. My longing for Sebastian in the days he was away, fighting for dominance with my love of this place.

Desperate for that connection, I reached for her. "Come here, sweetheart. Why don't we send your daddy something to make him smile while he's at work?"

I scooted back my chair, the metal legs screeching against concrete. Kallie grinned and giggled as we pressed our cheeks together and I snapped our selfie on my phone.

So what if I'd already texted him earlier today just to tell him I missed him? I did it again, only this time I went into the photo editor and printed it across the image, sent it to him with all the devotion dwelling in my heart.

Missing you.

I knew he wouldn't respond until very late tonight after the *Sunder* show in Phoenix. But every night, he was faithful to call me, to love me from across the miles.

Faithful.

The truth was I had *faith* in him, gave it to him in every aspect.

Tamar glanced at her phone. "It's getting late. I better go before Charlie gets all riled up again if I get to work late tonight."

She stood and dropped a quick kiss to April's cheek, then came toward Kallie and me and leaned in, smothering Kallie with kisses before she hugged me.

Her voice a tight whisper, she said, "We really miss you there, Shea. It's not the same without you, but we all know it was time. Charlie more than anyone else."

Thick appreciation gathered at the base of my throat, and I swallowed around it as I smiled at my friend who was so rough on the exterior. But I knew better. Underneath the ink that covered her skin, concealed under the sass and sneer, was someone generous and kind and tender.

I fought a smile.

Just like Sebastian.

Without a glance back, she turned and strutted away.

I dug in my wallet and tossed a tip on the table, and April and I held Kallie's hands, swinging her between us as we headed toward where we'd parked along the street.

I lifted my face to the sky. Branches rustled on the changing trees that boasted the most beautiful colors a person could ever hope to see—fiery oranges, golden yellows, and reds so deep they were almost black.

Savannah in fall seemed to possess a certain calmness, a peace and tranquility I'd only found in this place.

How could I leave it?

I clicked the fob to Sebastian's Suburban.

I loved that he'd left it with me. Not because it was a possession or something to take from him. But rather it felt like a promise, a reminder we were one no matter how much time or distance separated us. I helped Kallie crawl into her seat, set a quick kiss to the top of her head as I buckled her in. "All set?"

She threw both her hands in the air with her butterfly flourish. "All set!"

April climbed into the front passenger seat, I climbed into the driver's. We drove the short distance back to my house. The house I loved. The one place that had been my childhood safe haven when my life had been so unsure—the pressure and the burden and the coercion.

As I pulled into the drive, I wondered if I would willingly leave it behind. If I could. If I should. If I would let this beautiful home that housed my most cherished childhood memories go because it no longer had the capacity to house my desires.

Simply because the rest of my heart was waiting for me on the other side of the country.

Find love and bring it here.

My grandmother's words flowed through me on gentle waves. A soft reassurance that maybe *that* didn't have to mean this house. That maybe the only thing she'd wanted was their kind of love *for me*—one she'd shared with my grandfather—one that was never-ending and overpowering.

That *here* was home, wherever that may be.

Here. With her. Where her spirit always seemed to hover, as if I reached out and fluttered my fingers through the dense air I could touch her.

Here. With my daughter.

Here. With Sebastian.

No matter if here meant Savannah or California.

I cut the engine and hopped out, quick to open my daughter's door. In the backseat, she was singing, setting free her tinkling, angel voice, belting out a silly song as she flapped her hands and kicked her feet. I unlatched her buckle and began pulling her into my arms.

Somehow, in that moment, every part of me felt at peace.

I was doing this. Moving on. Putting my past behind me and running for the future I had with Sebastian.

"Shea Bentley?"

I froze.

Dread lifted the hairs at the nape of my neck and I stiffened, like an omen fisted the base of my spine. Holding Kallie close with one arm, I pressed her face into my shoulder, my free hand at the back of her head.

Protective.

Possessive.

Slowly, I turned around.

The man standing in front of my house appeared completely innocuous.

Harmless.

Khaki pants.

Solid blue, short-sleeved, button-up shirt.

But the way my heart rate spiked, my instincts told me he was anything but.

Locking my daughter to me, I lifted my chin in challenge. "Yes?"

He strode forward and produced a large manila envelope. He pushed it my direction, and the air in my lungs suddenly felt like sharp shards of ice.

Panic raged like wildfire. Flames licking at my insides, singeing me. My knees went weak. As if I were weightless. Lost in space that held no form or air or hope.

My world tumbling. Crashing. Shattering.

I stumbled back.

"No."

He shoved the folder into my hand.

No.

April ran to us, took Kallie from my shaking arms, shushing away my daughter's fear while her knowing eyes watched me.

"Let's get inside," she said quietly, leading me with one hand while she held Kallie with the other. The farthest I could make it was across the porch and inside the door before I fell to my knees on the hardwood floor.

Shaking, I fumbled with the metal clasp and ripped open the seal. A stack of papers slipped out.

But it was the little individual piece that fluttered out on its own that captured my attention. Down, down it fell. Landing face up.

Words pressed into the paper in fierce handwriting I recognized immediately.

I will guarantee your silence.

fifteen
Sebastian

"EIGHT O'CLOCK TOMORROW MORNING bus rolls out for Denver." I pointed at Ash, the guiltiest fucker of them all. "Don't be late."

He gave me a mocking salute. "Not to worry, dear Baz Boy. We won't let you down. I'll be sure of it."

Ash in charge?

Awesome.

I sent a pleading look to Zee.

He just grinned and gestured between Lyrik and Ash. "Sorry, man, no can do. Claiming responsibility for these two is like pleading guilty for a crime I didn't commit. No, thank you."

Lyrik smacked him on the back of the head. "I'll be committing a crime in about five seconds if you don't watch yourself, little man."

"Little man?" Zee bounced around, just asking for it. "I'll show you *little man*."

I shook my head as I began to back away, anxious to get back to the hotel so I could call Shea. "Serious…eight."

Not sure when I'd gone and become the voice of reason for the band, when I started taking responsibility for everyone. Guess maybe it'd been a long damned time ago, and I was just starting to see it. Understand the loyalty that went with it.

Lyrik gestured with this chin. *Got it.*

I turned and worked my way through the crowd.

We'd just finished up an outdoor show in Phoenix, which honestly had been cool as fuck. The crowd had been wild, sold out, the night air bristling with near-violent energy the music had stirred to life.

Now, the road crew was moving quickly, breaking shit down to get it packed up and ready to head to Denver tomorrow morning for our next show two days from now. Fans who had passes and some of the press were mingled around.

I was doing my best not to get noticed so I could get the hell out of there with as little fanfare as possible.

I dodged a few questions and even more girls who clearly wanted more than a pic, and rushed out to wait for the car I'd called.

Lifting my face, I pulled in a cleansing breath.

A smattering of bright stars dotted the blackened canopy above, barely peppering what promised to be a gorgeous night sky, although most of it was obscured by the glow of city lights. I was hidden down a small side street, but things were still bustling on the main streets flanking me, a stream of unending cars twisting through the urban maze. In the distance, the drone of cars flying down the freeway filled my ears, semi-trucks supplying the blare of their horn every now and then.

Still, something about it felt calm.

A black SUV pulled to the curb. I hopped in the back and shot the driver the name of the hotel where I was staying.

Releasing a heavy sigh, I relaxed into the leather as he took to the street. Streetlamps flashed through the tinted windows as he merged into the stream of traffic.

A smile curved the edges of my mouth as I dug my phone out

of my bag and flicked into the messages. Knew there would be messages waiting for me.

There always were.

Sure, I had thousands of fans screaming at me night after night.

But these little gestures Shea sent my way? Her simple words letting me know I was never far from her mind? Those rang out so much louder than all of them.

Tonight there were three.

I grinned at the simplicity of the first text message.

Missing you.

God, I wondered if she could miss me even half as much as I was missing her.

Crazy.

I'd only left her at the airport three days before, and I was already back to missing her like mad, counting down the days until she met me in California and we could finally start this life together.

Funny, it was the little things I was missin' most. Being in Shea's kitchen, cooking with my girls, tucking Kallie in at night, waking up slow in Shea's arms.

Yeah, we talked every day, but there was no substitution for the real thing.

The second message had the grin I wore turning wistful. Shea and Kallie were sitting outside with Savannah as their backdrop, heads pressed together, mounds of blonde curls framing their precious faces, caramel eyes warm and sweet. It filled me with a longing that physically hurt. Smiles went on forever, like they were touching me across the space.

Shea'd inscribed the picture the same as the first.

Missing you.

The third was another plain text. *Call me when the show's over. Doesn't matter how late. Just need to hear your voice.*

The driver pulled to a stop at the circular drive at the back entrance of the hotel.

"Thank you," I said, quick to climb out.

Slinging my bag over my shoulder, I headed through the tall sliding doors that spanned the entire backside. My shoes echoed on the white floors flecked with gold. A fountain in the center of the lobby rose tall before water splashed back into the marble bowl.

The hotel was over the top like all the rest, but when you spend most of your time crammed on a bus with a bunch of guys, sometimes spreading out and indulging was a necessity. I was already checked in, so I took the elevator directly to my floor.

I went straight for Austin's door adjacent to my suite and knocked.

A few seconds passed before I heard a rustle on the other side. My baby brother's hair was a complete disaster when he finally cracked it open. Grey eyes squinted out at me. "What's up, man?"

"Just was wondering how you were."

He gave me a half-assed grin. "Same as when you checked on me before you left."

The smile I returned was a little self-conscious. Couldn't help that I worried about him constantly, even when he kept telling me it was time he figured out shit for himself. This kid had become my responsibility a long damned time ago. "You get dinner?"

"Yes, *Father*, I did," he said with eyes bugged out. "Did you want to do a plate check?"

Sarcastic little punk.

Laughter bubbled below the surface. I did my all to contain it.

"Watch yourself, man, or I'm going to be coming through that door to kick your ass instead of telling you not to hesitate to order room service. Next time I won't be so nice."

So what if I loved it when it was like this? When we could just joke around without any strain weighing us down. When I knew things could be good for him and he had the whole world at his feet. It was just waiting for him to get brave enough to take a step. It gave me the kind of hope I thought we'd lost a long time ago.

Back in L.A., I couldn't shake the worry from plaguing me, his mood dark and ominous, expression filled with shadows and memories and suffocating regret. Once we'd left, his spirits seemed to improve, and each day the kid seemed to become lighter and lighter, the smile that was so rare resurfacing on his face.

Just like now.

That smile broadened as the sarcasm grew thick. "Oh, yes. Now there's the big brother I know and love. Some things will never change."

"Whatever."

But both of us knew everything had changed.

I gestured with my chin toward my door as I drummed my fingertips on his doorframe. "I'll be in my room if you need anything."

A grin pulled hard at his mouth. "Ah…figured you might be. We all know how these nights go down now…the rest of the guys out partying, living it up on the town, while you tuck tail and head back to your room. Big, bad Sebastian Stone pussy-whipped. Don't act like I can't see that leash strapped around your neck."

Fighting the laughter rolling around in my chest, my teeth clamped down on my bottom lip.

"Watch it, man, or I'm going to make that ass-kickin' a reality."

Liked seein' the smile on his face. Needed it. Life was coming together in a way I never thought it could, everything important to me flourishing. Thriving. The band and my baby brother and a breathtaking love I never saw coming.

"Bring it on. Wouldn't want you to get rusty or anything," he ribbed, rubbing it in a little deeper as he stepped back and widened his door, just begging for it. "Last thing we need is for you to go and get soft on us."

Taking two steps to the side, I slid my keycard through the

slot of my door, still leaning back so I could toss him a wry smile. "Someone around here needs to be."

"Thought that was Zee's job."

"Touché, little brother, touché."

I opened my door and Austin stepped back in his. "Fine, asshole, leave me for your *wife*. I'm bored as fuck in here."

"You could come in and hang out with me," I hollered.

"And listen to you two going on and on about how much you miss each other, making fucking kissing noises and all that mushy bullshit? Um...no. I'd like to keep my dinner down, thank you very much. We all hear it enough on the bus."

He took another step back and let his door fall closed.

"You're just jealous," I called out with the shutting of my own door.

His muddled answer echoed through the wall. "You might just have me there, big brother."

I was still shaking my head, my face full of a smile, as I crossed the living area and headed into the huge bathroom I really didn't need, then hopped in the shower big enough for five. I lathered up, rinsing off all the sweat from the show, jumped out, and dried just as fast.

Couldn't wait to get to my girl.

Grabbing my phone, I tapped out a text. *Turn on Skype. Need to see your face.*

Two seconds later, my phone blipped. *Okay.*

I frowned, expecting a smiley face or a silly heart or an *I can't wait*, but I guess that would just take more time.

I dragged on a clean pair of boxers, pulled my laptop from its case, and flopped down at the center of the bed. Couldn't wait to catch a glimpse of her.

God, Austin was right.

I was whipped.

Locked down.

Gone for this girl.

I didn't stand a fucking chance.

Shea accepted the call and my heart seized.

Those sweet eyes immediately locked on me. But they weren't shining with happiness. They were fucking tormented. Swollen and red and brimming with tears she was doing her best to keep from falling. Shadows played around her, fed by the tiny lamp glowing from her nightstand. Her face twisted, agony written in every line.

Anger clawed at my insides. It was instant. The essential need to protect and defend.

A sob tore through her when she met my gaze. "Sebastian."

My jaw clenched. "What happened?"

Her eyes squeezed closed and her mouth trembled. "Martin."

The name shot me from the bed. It wasn't like I hadn't been waiting for it. Expecting it to strike from her tongue the second I'd seen the look shrouding her face.

Didn't mean it didn't send rage blistering through me, boiling in my veins, singeing my skin.

Felt like I was burning alive.

I ripped at my hair. Frantic, I looked around the room for my things. My gaze narrowed as I calculated just how long it'd take me to hop on a plane to hunt the fucker down.

Almost six weeks had passed since the last time we'd heard from him, and I'd gone and let myself relax. Took comfort in the time.

Realistically knew it would come to this, but that didn't stop the boundless hate from rapid firing through every nerve ending.

And I didn't even know what the piece of shit had done.

I paced, glancing back at Shea sitting there in the middle of her bed as I made each pass. Both of us coming apart.

"Where's Kallie?" I finally managed to grate out, not sure I could take the answer. My mind tossed through every scenario.

"In her room. Asleep."

Relief slammed me. I scrubbed both hands over my face, dragging them down as I looked to the ceiling. That tiny bit of solace had me slumping down at the edge of the bed, my back to Shea, head in my hands. I was doing my best to rein it in. But those urges were there. The need to fight and defend.

Fists and fury and unrelenting rage.

To stand up for my family.

To make it right.

"Sebastian." I heard Shea's plea clear as day. Knew she felt it, too. What I was itching to do.

Reluctantly, I looked back her.

"Don't," she begged through a whisper.

I swallowed hard. Containing it was almost too much. Violence skimmed beneath the surface of my skin. My hands clenched into fists, released, then fisted again. It was an act I might've hoped would soothe, but it only served to coil the anger tighter.

I shifted to face her. "Tell me."

Quivering lips tugged at one side as she fought emotion, and all I wanted was to reach through the screen to get to her.

I hated we were so far apart.

I wanted to be there.

Holding her.

Protecting her.

Didn't take lightly to the vows I had made.

My attention trailed the bob of her delicate throat as she struggled to form the words.

"I was served this evening." She pulled in a rasping breath and forced it out. "He's seeking full custody of Kallie."

"Fuck," I cursed, jerking my attention to the far wall. Bitterness burned. My knee bounced like a fucking short-circuited jackhammer, every cell in my body prodding me to get up and go. To fucking do something. Because sitting here idly sure as hell wasn't going to fix this.

This was what we'd expected, wasn't it? Relentless nagging that had smoldered low, just out of sight, a warning that the asshole wasn't ever gonna let her live in peace.

A sob tore from her, and her confession tumbled over me like a rockslide as she cried through the slur of words.

"I'm scared. God…I'm so scared. And…and that's exactly what he wants. He wants me scared. To know he's in control. He wants to remind me he knows how to *hurt* me and he won't hesitate to do it."

"Why, Shea? Why the fuck does he want to hurt you so bad?"

Why the fuck did he want to hurt any of us like this?

I was sick of this shit not making sense. Sick of Martin holding Mark and Austin over me like a shrouded mystery. Sick of Shea putting a veil over whatever she thought needed hiding.

But I knew…

Knew whatever lay beneath them both was a fucking nightmare.

Her eyes squeezed closed, her face sodden with tears as she frantically shook her head. "Don't you get it? He knows how to control you, too, Sebastian. He knows your weaknesses. He studies and anticipates exactly how someone will react and uses that to his advantage. He knows you're aggressive. He knows you're willing to protect those you love, and this is exactly what he wants. To *provoke* you so he can separate us."

Humorlessly, she laughed, and her tone went low with significance, as if she were giving me a clue. "And I…I didn't act how he anticipated. He expected my submission and instead I took him by surprise."

I raked my hand over the top of my head. "Then what do we

do? What do *I* do?"

She pressed her hands to her chest. "Stand by me. Fight with me. Don't ever leave me. When I get to California, I'm going to tell you everything that happened. And you're going to protect me by standing by my side, you're going to help me by being there when I tell the attorney and anyone who will listen, and above it all, you will protect me by staying away from him."

My brow pinched, because this fucking hurt. Hurt that Shea had been resisting confiding in me because of who *I* was. A fucking loose cannon. Someone prone to violence. And there it was, right beneath the surface, fire flaming and licking and begging for release.

My voice was tight. "Made you a promise I'd protect you, Shea. Live for you. And that's exactly what I'm gonna do. You and Kallie? You're my life. *My everything.* And I will do anything…give up anything…to make sure you two are together. I won't let him win."

She brushed the back of her hand over the wetness on her cheeks. "He will do anything to break us apart…to separate us. He knows we're weaker alone. All his words about taking us down at the same time?"

Her head shook with bitterness and hate, something so foreign on my girl's face, but I saw it there—the atrocities he'd committed—the things she still kept inside.

The scars she wore on her heart while I wore mine on my skin.

"It's a tactic. A ploy. He thinks he can fill us with threats. Convince our subconscious into believing together we're easy targets. But, no." Her eyes drew together as she refuted the idea, as she spilled her own belief. "He's a coward. A *coward*. Someone who allows others to carry out his crimes and then lords it over them as if he is the one exerting control."

That brave chin quivered. "I gave him my submission for so long, and I refuse to ever be that girl again. I was her, Sebastian. I *was* weak."

Strength filled the profession. "But I'm not weak anymore. And I'm even stronger with you by my side."

Raw.

Bold.

Courageous.

"Promise me you won't let him provoke you, Sebastian. He knows exactly how to ruin people. He finds their weaknesses. He knows Kallie is mine. And he knows the two of us are yours."

I swallowed hard. "I promise, baby."

I promise.

I scrubbed my palms over my face, fisted my hair, some kind of desperation taking me over. "Please, Shea. Need you to tell me one thing right now. Tell me how the hell you ended up with him."

sixteen
Shea

Eighteen years old

SPOTLIGHTS BLINDED FROM ABOVE, and a light sheen of sweat lifted on Shea's heated skin. Her black dress glimmered with the sequins sown into it, covering it entirely, the fabric itchy where it was held in a strapless fashion above her breasts. High black heels adorned her feet, and she tried not to focus on the way they made her feel awkward and compromised, the sexy shoe completely exposed on one side by the slit in her dress that cut all the way up to her thigh.

She'd walked out onto the stage feeling like a blundering fool, although she'd been told she looked like a million bucks.

She had one song.

One song at the country awards show introducing her as Delaney Rhoads.

It was unheard of, she'd been told, coming on the scene that fast, being invited to play this way.

And she'd been told again she was just that good.

Yet somehow Shea felt like a fraud.

Still, the guitar in her hands and her mouth at the mic felt like the most natural thing in the world.

She let her thoughts go and paid no mind to those who filled the music theater in Nashville. It was crammed, the plush maroon seats filled to capacity.

Sold out.

Just like she had.

As if she was ever given any choice.

Today was her birthday.

Eighteen.

She had signed the contract. She'd sat in that big leather office chair with her insides quaking and her mother whispering in her ear, "This is it, baby. We made it. Everything we worked for all these years. We have it. You're a star."

Shea had scrawled her messy signature across the line, unable to still the shaking in her hand, because everything inside her had screamed she should not.

But tonight?

On this stage?

Shea sang. She let her fingers strum away the sadness, and her voice cover the sour taste on her tongue.

She knew her grandmother would be watching her on TV from her hospice bed. The woman she loved most in the world was too sick to be here.

The only thing Shea wanted was for her grandmother to understand that even though the circumstances might have been horrible, when Shea began to play, everything else floated away and she *felt* it in her heart.

Just like her grandmother had made her promise to do when she was just a little girl.

Shea wanted to make her proud.

Not of what she'd attained, or the money promised, or a life of fame. Shea wasn't impressed with any of those things.

Shea just wanted her to know she was using the gift she'd been given, and when she sang, somewhere inside her, it still felt *important*.

Shea's voice trailed off into silence before roaring applause broke through the air. It echoed through the enormous hall as people jumped to their feet to give her a standing ovation.

Tears sprang to Shea's eyes.

Because she'd felt the beauty, too, the same thing that seemed to ride on the energy that filled the space.

It was what was waiting for her offstage that was vile.

Shea whispered a quiet, "Thank you," into the mic before she exited the stage.

Her mother hovered behind the curtains. "There's my shining star." She made sure everyone heard.

Her mother's creepy boyfriend Donny, who'd been tacked to her mother's side since the second they'd rolled into Nashville, was nearly salivating where he stood behind Shea's mother.

"Come here, sweetheart, there are people to meet," her mother said.

Shea did her best to smile pleasantly as she shook hands with those who only wanted her for the things she didn't want to give, like touching her skin gave them a taste of glory when she knew without a shadow of a doubt she'd sold her soul into sin.

No, it wasn't because she desired any of it.

She'd simply been on this train for far too long and had no access to the brakes, the pressure and coercion too much to take, so she'd always given in. For so long she'd simply gone through the motions and never voiced her opinions or concerns because they were never heard anyway. Her mother was in full control and she couldn't find the strength to fight her.

But now she wondered when it would be her who would *break*.

Warily, Shea looked up when she felt the eyes boring into her.

A searing heat of predatory lust. She felt burned by it, and not in a desirous way, but like hell had found its way to her.

She shuddered.

Her mother prodded her back and pushed up onto her toes to speak into her ear. "Go on, girl. He's waiting on you."

When Shea hesitated, she could feel her mother's annoyance, as if she were speaking to a toddler who had no clue what it took to make it in the real world.

Shea wasn't sure she did.

"Achieving your dreams will require sacrifices, Shea."

In that moment, Shea had never hated her mother more. She'd sold her off so easily, using her for little more than personal gain. Shea had spent years striving harder and higher and faster, thinking if she managed to touch the sky her mother would finally see her as the star she wanted her to be. She'd spent so many years being tailored into this *thing*, stitched and patched and sewn into something that had become unrecognizable.

But the outside was completely mismatched with the fabric of who she wanted to be.

"Besides," her mother said with a perverse grin, "the two of you make a gorgeous couple. It's what the world wants to see. A beautiful young girl on the arm of a successful, handsome man. He's put himself on the line for you, and it's time you showed some gratitude for it."

Gratitude?

The simmering bile in her stomach worked into a frenzy, and Shea thought she would be sick.

She knew Martin Jennings was attractive. She wasn't blind. But in the year she'd known him, she also felt something dark lurking around him, something ugly that radiated from his pores like an omen.

Every cell in her body implored she stay away.

Instead, she made her feet move in his direction where he held back like a phantom along the far wall.

She ducked her head timidly when she came to a stop in front of him.

"Magnificent," he said in his smooth, slick voice. He touched her cheek, and she held her breath, trying not to flinch. "Do you have any idea the effect you had on the crowd, Delaney Rhoads? Every single person out there was putty in your hands. You are magic."

Her thoughts went back to her grandmother, a picture of a frail woman lying in the confines of her bed.

Would she have thought the show *magic*?

What would she think now?

The pads of Martin's fingers slid down the outside of her arm and threaded through her fingers. Chills of unease lifted her skin, but she didn't fight it, just like she hadn't fought it two days before when he'd pushed her against the wall in his office and kissed her mouth and her neck.

But tonight when he guided her down a winding maze of backstage corridors and led her into a vacant office hidden in the bowels of the theater, the lights cast low, he didn't stop. He set her on the desk and lifted the skirt of her dress as he went.

Tears soaked her face, and Martin wiped the wetness away. "You're far too beautiful to cry, Delaney Rhoads." He brushed his mouth at the corner of hers and she whimpered.

"Shh...you're mine now."

She shook violently, *no* poised on her tongue, but she didn't know how to release it. Just like she didn't know how to say it with every path her mother had led her down.

Say it, Shea. Say no. Please, say it, she silently begged herself, before she turned to silently begging him. *No. No. No.*

Metal clanked as he fumbled through his belt, and his slacks dropped to his thighs. Shea panicked, her hands shoving and slapping at his chest as her breaths turned ragged with fear.

"Shh," he whispered again, as he shackled both her wrists in one of his hands and forced her closer to the edge of the desk. He wedged himself between her legs.

She cried out in pain when he ripped through her.

She sobbed. Her breaths choked and panted as he moved in her.

Music filtered from above, another act on stage, and she tried with everything she had to focus on those beautiful sounds and not the grunts raking from Martin's mouth. But there was nothing beautiful in this moment.

Sadness and pain crushed her. How ironic that a man was touching her for the first time in her life, and she'd never felt more alone.

And Shea… Shea might have hated this man with all her life. Shea might have hated her mother more than she ever had before. But not nearly as much as she hated herself.

seventeen
Sebastian

I STOOD IN THE hallway outside Mark's door. My chest heaved as I sucked down a steeling breath, hand shaking on the knob. Searching for courage just to open the fucking door.

Quiet echoed down the hall of the huge house. All the guys were gone and Austin was tucked away in his room down the opposite hall.

We'd been back in L.A. for two days and my girls would be here tomorrow. This needed to get done and soon.

We were pressing on with our original plans, refusing to back down to Jennings's threats. Besides, we figured it was safer for them to be here. With me.

God knew I'd sleep better.

Had Kenny, another attorney, and some of their guys here in L.A. digging their heels in deep, trenching through any shit they could find on the pompous bastard. Shit that had nothin' to do with *Sunder* or Shea or any of us. Safe shit that would still send him straight to hell, because we knew where his greedy hands had been.

What Shea didn't know was I had a reserve. A backup plan. That I'd gladly incriminate myself to finally make Jennings go away.

For good.

One way or another, we were going to make sure he had no say about anything in Kallie's future.

Now I just needed to make it through this door. Just didn't know it was going to be so damned hard.

Cold raced up my arm as my hand clutched the metal knob, and I squeezed my eyes, forcing myself to turn it. The door swung open, hinges squeaky from disuse.

The smell clinging to the abandoned room hit me like two tons of bricks.

I squeezed my eyes tighter as I fought it, before I finally released the breath I'd been holding and shuddered through a deep inhale.

It was musty and stifled, but in it was him, like the leather of that old jacket he'd always worn and a hint of the herbal cigarettes he'd always smoked.

Grief that'd been locked up tight battled for escape. Gathering like a thunderstorm in my chest. Slowly building. Enclosing on my throat.

The loss of Mark had been so sudden and traumatic, part of it still didn't feel real. Sometimes I imagined I'd look up and find him rounding the corner—that shy, insecure smile he always wore spreading into something genuine and honest when he looked at me.

God, he'd been a lost soul.

So fucking lost.

But that didn't mean the bond between the five of us wasn't solid. Distorted, warped pieces that somehow perfectly aligned and fit. My fucked-up family. But I thought maybe the bond between Mark and I had been even greater because I'd been so fucking lost, too.

Dazed, I drifted out into the middle of the room as I felt the weight of my friend's loss. Rays of light streaked in from the gap in the blinds, cutting into the gloom. The king bed was unmade, a rumple of sheets and blankets that spoke of a thrashing spirit, sheets of paper strewn about the floor, the words so often silent on his tongue lashed out across the pages.

I wandered over to his desk. My fingertips trailed over the picture displayed in a frame. It was all the guys with our arms slung over each other's shoulders, beers in our free hands, Zee and Austin there, too. It brought on a wistful smile, and I shook my head, wondering how the hell I was ever going to get through this.

But I had to.

Had a little girl who was ready to shine her light on this desolate room.

I tore the linens from the bed and shoved them into a black garbage bag, then grabbed one of the empty boxes I'd left out in the hall and began to clear out his desk. This stuff? I'd just roll tape across the seam of the box. Seal it up. Save it. Knew one day Zee would want to go rummaging through when his broken heart was ready to take that step.

The drawers were filled with a ton of old cassette tapes and CDs, his own words scrawled across them, music we had made. All the scratches and scribbles of paper when we'd jammed, the guy always quick to jot stuff down when we were capturing a moment in a song.

My chest tightened with unspent sorrow.

God. It fucking hurt.

My eyes blurred as I filled one box then another, forcing myself to just forge through.

When I cleared out his desk, I moved on to his walk-in closet, flipped on the light switch. Light flickered before it came to life, and I blinked to adjust to the harshness. It was just a long, narrow path, clothes hung up on either side, old, tattered shoes shoved in the cubbies, and clutter clogging the shelves.

A soft chuckle of affection slipped into the room. Guy couldn't get rid of anything.

I shoved sections of shirts together, pressing them between my hands to lift the hangers free, and threw them out into the middle of the bedroom floor. I continued on till one side was clear, then the other, until there was a fucking mountain of clothes in the middle of the bedroom floor.

Some hipster thrift shop was going to have a field day.

I started pulling out boxes, the anguish oppressive as I struggled to make it through what felt like ridding the last of Mark's presence from our lives.

Knew that's why I'd stalled for so long.

Wanted one last thing to hang onto, even when I hadn't had the strength to step through the door.

Getting down on my knees, I pulled out a few storage boxes Mark had shoved under the shelves at the far back corner. I lifted a lid and peeked inside.

Pictures.

I sat back and pulled out a stack. Nostalgia, darts of regret and pain, and a forever kind of connection I knew could never be severed hit me. Image after image of us as teenagers, hanging out in Ash's garage, back in the days when we were gonna take the world by the balls and there was nothing that could have stopped us from making it big.

Back before we'd let the lifestyle wear us thin and the endless parties take us down all kinds of roads we never should have gone.

My gut clenched at some of the faces, some of the guys we'd called friends who were nothing less than dealers feeding the bloodthirsty frenzy. The need to feel something that in the end just didn't exist.

Only thing there was emptiness.

Pissed me off more because some of these guys were directly

tied to Jennings.

I cringed when I saw a picture of Donny. One of Jennings's right-hand guys. Blitzed-out blue eyes stared back, face tweaked with that seedy fucking grin.

Seemed the second Mark started hanging out with that creep, he'd been sucked into a downward spiral he couldn't stop. Tripped right into the cesspool that would be his demise. He'd gone and gotten in deep. Started hiding shit. Even from me. At that time, Donny had always been lurking, hanging out at every show, acting like it was his place and all part of the gig. I knew better. He'd been plying Mark with his supply.

I dug a little deeper in the box, moving more photos out of the way. I had the sudden urge to understand Mark better in that period of time. Wishing I'd paid closer attention. Done more before it'd been too late.

A thick leather-bound journal was tucked to the side. I pulled it out, feeling like a sick fuck for invading his privacy. But hell, he'd been my best friend. And I *missed* him. Missed him so fuckin' bad it physically hurt, my chest feeling like it just might cave with the pressure in my heart, and I wanted to hang on to a little more.

I unlaced the leather strap and flipped to the first page. Immediately, I recognized his handwriting. The date jotted at the side was close to seven years ago.

The road's tough. Especially nights like these when everyone is passed out around me. I can never sleep. Who would have known the loneliest time in the world is the moment before the sun comes up? Night after night, I meet that moment intimately. I know it like a lover even when there's no comfort in its touch. It's worth it. The band is worth it. But I get the sense I'll never know what it's like to be home.

I rubbed my hand over my face and tried to break up the overwhelming urge to weep. Killed me he'd felt this way. I rifled through more pages. Most of the entries echoed the same, sometimes skipping months. Getting just a little more desperate with each passing year.

I tried. I fucking tried. Baz got out of jail and got clean. I tried. I tried.

Why hadn't I done something? Intervened?

I wavered, part of me wanting to slam the damned journal closed. Close it up and forget. But the other felt compelled. I skimmed through more pages where Mark had recorded just how lost he'd felt.

When I turned another page, my sight narrowed in on the handwriting that had turned messy and frantic, slanting crooked down the page.

I fucked up. Fucked up bad. Donny told me Martin said it'd only be once. Once. That was all it was supposed to be.

What the fuck?

He was talking about Jennings.

My heart rate sped and I sat up higher on my knees, fingers gripping the journal as I scanned for more.

Fucking Donny and his fucking mouth. Always with his fucking mouth. I didn't want to know. I didn't want any part of it. I knew Martin was sick. Both of them were sick. But not that sick. I told Martin so. I told him to go to hell when he demanded the money I owe him. Told him I'd take everything I know to the cops. I was going to anyway, money be damned. I knew what he'd had Donny do to that girl. I knew what he planned to have him do. She was a loose end. A liability. Just like me. Call me a snitch. I didn't care. Let the asshole burn.

A thread of awareness dangled in my periphery, something ominous and dark. Felt like I couldn't grab a breath when I desperately flipped the page. A small stack of snapshots fell out from between the pages, fluttering to the floor. What my attention immediately latched on to was what Mark had written on the page.

Donny's gone. Dead in the water. I'm going to be next. I know it. Feel it coming. Am I scared? Yeah. Terrified, really. I led Martin on. Made him be-

lieve I'd leaked info. Ratted him and Lester out. He thinks I'm blackmailing, but I don't have anything but Donny's word. And Donny's word is about as valuable as a ten-dollar whore. My only intention had been to thwart the plans he had to hurt that girl again. Only this time, make it final. Sick. Fucking sick. Couldn't live with myself if it happened, so I'd rather die stopping it. I guess I finally did something in my life worth a shit.

It was dated two days before he'd overdosed.

Cold dread seized my heart, everything going heavy, like it was attempting to pump ice through my veins.

He killed him.

Oh God. My head spun. *He killed him.*

With trembling fingers, I reached down and picked up one of the pictures that'd fallen face down on the floor, hesitant to discover what was there, but knowing I couldn't look away.

It was a snapshot of Mark and Donny and my baby brother. The party happening around them was clear. All three of them were obviously lost to a bombed-out wasteland.

But it was the woman Donny had draped across his lap that shook me to the core. A face so fucking familiar, that the breath punched from my lungs and left me on a shocked wheeze.

I'd seen that face hanging on Shea's upstairs wall more times than I cared to count. Showcased in old frames, appearing years younger there than in this image. The woman who'd pushed her and pushed her and pushed her, Shea's childhood memories a horror story of manipulation and greed.

Shea's mom.

I gripped my head as I tried to process, swarmed with an onslaught of confusion and anger and utter devastation.

Mark, Jennings, Austin, and motherfucking Chloe Lynn.

She was a loose end. A liability. Just like me.

Who was he talking about? Didn't want to accept the possibility it could be Shea. But I knew…I fucking knew.

I roared and shot to my feet. Another rush of dizziness hit me. My shoulder rammed into the wall, my balance blown, my world shattered. I stumbled over the shit blocking the closet doorway in a frantic bid to get out with one of the pictures fisted in my hand. I charged out of Mark's room and down the hall. Didn't even hesitate at his door, just threw it open. It flew back and crashed against the inside of his wall.

Austin jumped from his bed in the same second I stormed in.

Something livid ate up my insides. Propelling me forward.

"Baz," my baby brother said as his startled expression twisted through confusion and nervous doubt. I didn't pause, just gathered the collar of his shirt in my hands and pushed him up against the wall. My teeth grated where they clenched, and that surprised expression on his face morphed into fear.

"Tell me you didn't lie to me when you swore you didn't know what happened the night Mark died."

Alarmed eyes flashed with recognition. Going back to the day I'd confronted him right here in this room after the failed mediation with Jennings.

The day he started spouting off about Mark being nothing but pathetic.

I shook him, my voice a desperate seethe. "Tell. Me."

No. I wouldn't hurt him. Never. But there was no way I was leaving this room without the truth.

"Baz," he begged.

Releasing one hand, I shoved the crumpled snapshot in his face. "Tell me why the fuck you and Mark are with Shea's mom."

His face went deathly white.

Guilt.

Guilt.

Guilt.

Fear soured my stomach, and the words grated with betrayal.

"You lied to me. This is why you've been so weird about Shea?"

Tears filled his eyes and overflowed down his cheeks. The kid's reaction was like a punch to the gut. I knew he was caught somewhere between the tormented child I'd taken responsibility for and the man trying to make his way out.

But that was no excuse.

"Tell me what you're doing in a picture with Shea's mom, Austin. Tell me what the fuck Mark was talking about in his journal...all this shit about Donny and Jennings and the trouble he was in. The girl he hurt." The last turned into a plea.

He swallowed like he was seeking courage. "I don't fucking know everything, Baz. Promise you." The words began to fly. "All I know is Mark got in over his head. Owed Jennings a bunch of money. Honest, I don't know all the details. I just know it was a lot. Enough that he didn't know how he was going to get out from under it, and it was Donny who'd gotten him involved."

His attention darted to the opposite wall, contemplating what to say, before he turned back to me. "I'd seen Shea's mom...Chloe Lynn...around a few times when we'd partied. I had no idea who she was. Not until one night Donny was all coked up."

Austin's lip curled in disgust. "He always acted like such a badass. Wanted everyone to think he was. That night, he started bragging about all the shit Martin had him doing for him. All the drug runs he headed, the beat downs when someone got out of line."

I struggled to find some control as Austin's eyes pinched closed. "He was laughing when he started talking about how years before he'd been sent to *fuck up* Delaney Rhoads. Said something about 'taking care of it.' Then he'd mocked Chloe Lynn for being the mother of a washed-up country singer."

I wheezed in a breath, my head spinning with hatred. My hands curled tighter in Austin's shirt. My legs were trembling as everything inside me began to break apart.

"He what?" The words scraped with the affliction, horror, and shock, as I barely caught a glimpse of the carnage.

What did he do?
What did he do?
Mark.
Shea.

I'd claimed to know exactly what Martin Jennings was capable of.

Turns out what I knew didn't come close.

"Did Chloe Lynn know what'd gone down…what he'd done?"

His entire face winced with the regretful nod. He looked at me, sorrow pulling at the edges of his mouth. "Mark…you *knew* him, Baz. Better than all of us. As fucked up as he was, he was a good guy. What Donny said got to him. Ate at him. The night he OD'd…I told you before he was acting all sketchy and paranoid. That was the truth. But what I didn't tell you was he was stumbling around the bus, saying something about going to the cops about Delaney Rhoads. Said he couldn't keep quiet about an innocent girl being hurt…and it was a secret he wouldn't keep."

Austin choked over a sob. "I know Martin was responsible for Mark, Baz. I *know* it. Donny disappeared, without a trace, and the next thing I know, Mark's dead."

Outright fear bled from his pores, my baby brother shaking in my enraged hands.

"I was so fucking scared, Baz. So fucking scared. You immediately forced me into rehab, and I wanted it. I wanted to break out of that life. Run from it. I thought maybe…maybe I was finally going to be free of everything horrible I continually let ruin my life. I'd let Mark down. But for once, I wasn't going to let you down. I'd promised myself to get clean and everything would be better. Martin would be forgotten and we'd move on with our lives."

Agitated, his tongue darted out to wet his lips. "But then he came onto the tour bus. Digging. Asking questions about what I knew about Delaney Rhoads. I'd told him *nothing*. His response was to slide three pills my way. He knew I couldn't resist. Knew I was weak."

He knows our weaknesses. Shea's assertion crashed down around me. Anger pumped furiously, feeding the hostility.

"Next thing I knew, I woke up in the hospital. I took it as a warning to keep my mouth shut, and that's what I've been doing all this time."

"Do you know what Mark was talking about in his journal?" I demanded, my nose pressed up to his like maybe if I got close enough, I could fall inside and find out what he'd been keeping a secret for far too long. "About a girl who was a loose end."

I shook him. "One he was willing to die for."

His brows drew deep in question, obviously unaware. It became clear when he came to the same conclusion. His eyes rounded like black, blank buttons of fear.

Like I'd been burned, my hands jerked free, and Austin dropped to his knees on the floor.

Shea.

Head slumping forward, Austin's words slurred together. "Don't hate me, Baz. Please, don't hate me. I was scared. So scared. Please don't hate me. You're the only person I've got. When I found out Shea was Delaney, I wanted to tell you…I did…but I couldn't risk it…couldn't risk you losing it again. I can't lose you, too."

A harsh sound tore up my throat, raged with the flash of fury.

"I could never hate you."

Never.

All I'd given had always been for my family. Standing up for them. Defending them.

I shoved out the door and down the hall to the sound of Austin calling after me. But I couldn't stop from moving. My feet pounded down the stairs.

A red haze colored my narrowed sight. Blinding hate.

What did he do?

He hurt her.

And Mark. My baby brother.

Dizziness spiraled across my vision, and I gripped my head, trying to stay upright.

Jesus help me.

What was this?

Mark was a threat, so he took him out?

Austin a threat?

Shea…a threat?

I reeled with the magnitude.

I'd always believed him dangerous.

But this?

Stunning rage seethed beneath my skin. Every piece of me felt like it was gonna crack, fall to the ground in jagged pieces, as I stumbled out the door and to my truck. I turned the ignition and the engine roared. Slammed it into gear and peeled from the driveway and onto the street.

I blinked and blinked, squeezing my eyes closed then opening them wide. Tryin' to see through her storm.

Dark, dark, dark.

Promise me.

Her words filtered through me like wisps of smoke, and I pressed the heel of my hand into my eye, my mouth dropping open on a silent cry as I tried to focus through the streaks of blinding light.

How could I just turn away with what I knew and with what still needed to be learned? Sit back and hold tight?

That wasn't me.

And Shea…

Shea had always *seen* me. Recognized who I was beneath all the hard and scarred.

And this was *me*.

Guess she'd known it all along.

Promised I would do whatever it took, give up everything to set it right.

And I would.

On pure instinct, I sped down the narrow roads out of the Hills. When I hit the congested West Hollywood streets, I accelerated, weaving through traffic and jumping lanes. Everything around me was a blur except for the focus of my destination.

Tires squealed as I took a sharp right turn into the pretentious Beverly Hills neighborhood. My truck careened to a stop in the drive in front of his house.

Inhale. Exhale. I struggled for composure. For some measure of reason in this fucked-up situation.

Seemed I always found myself in these positions.

Trouble.

It followed me wherever I went.

But this time the fight was ending on my side.

I stepped from the truck, pulled out my phone, and set the recorder before I slipped it back in my pocket. If the fucker was here, I was going to capture every word.

Inhale. Exhale.

Promise me.

Fuck. *I can't, Shea. I can't let this go.*

Inhale. Exhale.

I slipped over the low wrought iron fence and dropped into the courtyard.

Shaking.

Fucking shaking.

Water lapped at the fountain and birds rustled through the

trees.

Peaceful.

The calm before the storm.

But the storm was there, gathering force, igniting the madness that propelled me forward.

My hand went for the ornate latch of the double doors. I was surprised when one side gave.

Through pursed lips, I pushed out a stifled breath. Every muscle in my body was rigid with restraint, my movements guarded and subdued as I slipped unseen into the quiet of the massive house.

The peace, the quiet, the calm was at odds with the rapid-fire sensations gutting my insides. Hate and vengeance and revenge.

White walls and floors everywhere, the ceilings high and color the starkest white.

I'd heard it said it was cold in hell.

I inched through the foyer, shoulder up against the wall, as I rounded the corner and eased along the edge of the formal living room, drawn deeper into the house. I emerged at a tall, wide entryway. Pillars flanked it like some kind of Greek god's castle, precisely like the bastard thought he ruled.

It opened to a large space that boasted the kitchen and another sitting area that looked out over the lawn and pool.

But none of that held my attention.

Jennings. Casually sitting sideways at the high granite bar, rocked back in a stool with his ankle hooked over his knee. *Smug bastard.* His fingers drummed on the counter like the asshole was bored, not a fucking care in his warped, perverted world. In his other hand, a tumbler rolled with amber liquid.

Eyeing me, he took a sip before his head cocked to the side, snide and spite taking over his filthy expression. "I wondered when you'd come. Always have to be the hero, don't you?"

The walls closed in.

Motherfucker.

He knew I'd show.

Just like Shea.

He might as well have laid out the welcome mat.

My fists curled, trying for once in my fucking life to maintain control.

Fix this.

That was a promise I could keep, and it killed me, the thought of being without Shea. Of letting her down. Because I loved her so goddamned much. So much it eclipsed all reason. So much that I'd let it all go, give it up to keep them safe. How many times had I promised it? Just didn't know being struck with the reality of losing them, staring it down through the wicked eyes of depravity, would be so excruciating. A rending crack right down the middle that broke me in two.

"This ends now."

He scoffed, raked his teeth over his bottom lip.

"And how's that, *Mr. Stone*?"

"You're going to tell me what you did to them. What you did to Shea. To Mark. To my brother."

When I said their names, a fragment of the composure I was barely clinging to flew out the window. Exposing what was inside.

Vulnerable.

Martin caught it and smiled a venomous smile. "I always do what has to be done."

"Not good enough," I grated. All I needed was a little evidence. Something condemning, so I could send this asshole straight back to hell where he belonged. Where he could rot. Even if I was rotting right alongside him.

He took another slow swill of his drink.

"What do you want to hear, *Mr. Stone?* You want to hear your best friend wasn't a strung-out addict? That he had some other reason to succumb to the drug running hot through his veins, slowly snuffing the life out of him until he lay there wasted? A heap of decaying garbage face down on the floor? Because we both know that's exactly what he was. Just like your brother."

Fiery dots of hate glimmered across my vision and I felt an earthquake shaking beneath my feet.

I fought to maintain my footing on the rippling ground.

He grinned. Goading. Prodding like a branding iron. "But there are some things people just shouldn't know."

He skirted around the details, luring me into his fucked-up cage-match, forced me into a ring made up of chain links and barbed wire and razor blades where nobody came out alive.

"What did you do?"

He ignored my question with a slow, repeating shake of his head as if he were getting lost in contemplation. "Some would call it brave. Others would call it stupid. Just like Delaney…sticking her nose in places it didn't belong. Trying to use it against me."

He grinned. "Yeah. I guess I'd call it stupid, too."

That malicious grin widened when he saw the shudder roll through me, another reaction I had no chance to contain.

With the glass in his hand, he pointed at me like we were the best of friends sharing an inside joke, tipping it my direction as he chuckled through suggestive laughter. "But that Delaney Rhoads. Mmm. She's quite the fuck, isn't she? Can see why you're hung up on that one. *Those legs*. Of course, she cried like a bitch the first time I took her. Tore her open like a brand new present, just like her *momma* had offered me."

Fury.

Like a strike of lightning to a dry, withered tree.

A force of nature. An act of God.

Unbridled and unchecked.

I didn't even realize I was moving until the moment my body

connected with his.

I flew into him like the crack of thunder. The stool crashed to the floor and we tumbled over the top of it.

Jennings and I were a tangle of limbs and aggression and the foulest kind of hate.

I scrambled to get on top of him. I went straight for the throat, squeezing at his lifeline, because God knew I wanted nothing more than to squeeze the life out of him.

Like he'd done Mark.

My teeth ground.

His depraved eyes darkened, something vile and wicked, sucking me down into the depths of his barren soul.

I squeezed harder, my breaths grunted through the rage dripping from my words. "What did you do to Mark? To my brother? *To Shea?*"

I was desperate.

Fingers dug into the back of my hands as he struggled below me.

He gritted out the words. "Do you know who I am? What I'm going to do to you?"

Not if I ended this first.

"Who's Lester and what was Mark gonna stop?"

That question evoked the first flare of fear in him. A blanched whiteness flashed across his face that had nothin' to do with the air I was repressing from his lungs.

Finally, I found his weakness.

"Tell me…who the fuck is Lester and how's he involved with Shea and Mark?"

Just one fucking word, that's all I needed.

A fist suddenly hooked me at the temple. The hit took me hard enough to stun me, to catch me off guard, and it gave the bastard time to shove me off and stumble to his feet.

But in a second flat I was on mine. With all my weight, I lunged forward.

We collided.

A rain of glass shattered around us as we busted through the sliding door and crashed out onto the patio. Stone dug into flesh, muscles burned with exertion. I barely registered my skin stinging with sharp lances of pain.

It only served as fuel to the fire.

I hit him over and over. One brutal blow after another. "Tell me what you did. Admit it, you piece of shit. Admit it. Tell me! What did you do to Shea? Who's Lester? Did you kill Mark? Did you hurt Shea?"

Bones crunched and blood splattered.

Rage spiraled, spinning and curling and whirling until it sucked me down to a place where all my dark and ugly reigned. That place where Shea had shone so bright it'd been obscured. Nearly forgotten. A place I'd begun to pretend didn't exist. It was a place so dark I couldn't see. A place screaming echoes of pain so loud it erased all logical thought.

A place so foul it wiped out my humanity and obliterated my mission.

The goal I had come to attain.

Because ending him would do better.

"Freeze!"

The command boomed against the static buzzing in my ears. Everything slowed. My mind was just able to comprehend the furor of bodies rushing onto the scene. I became aware of the guns pointed in my direction.

Frantic, I clamored to my feet. Eyes blinking through the haze of bloodlust, I tried to focus on the swarm of officers stepping through the broken door, others coming around the side of the house to surround me.

"Get down...on the ground...hands behind your head," one shouted.

Slowly, I dropped to my knees, hands raised in surrender, before I slumped forward and put them behind my head.

Officers surrounded me.

My face was pressed into the ground, and I reared with the overwhelming violence still skimming through my system.

Nausea swelled.

A knee was forced between my shoulder blades, and my arms were wrenched back as cuffs were slapped on my wrists.

"You are under arrest. You have the right to..."

The reality of what I'd done hit me.

An officer yanked me to my feet, jumbled words vying to press into my senses. "...remain silent. Anything..."

Through the blur of voices and pain and regret, my clouded gaze lifted to Jennings who was sitting up on both his knees, attempting to climb to his feet. Blood smeared across his face.

But there was no shock in his expression. No regret or worry of negative consequence.

Those vile eyes just smirked back at me as he reached for my phone where it lay next to him in the grass. It had fallen out of my pocket.

Fuck.

He held the face out toward me. Shattered into a million splintered pieces. But the red dot could still be seen, indicating it was recording. *The bastard knew.*

Chills cinched my entire body when he leveled me with a baleful gaze.

He mouthed a single word.

"Yes."

A silent admission of guilt that no one was ever gonna hear.

Then he tucked my phone into his back pocket, gestured just as casually at the cameras mounted on the wall.

Cameras probably inside as well.

I wondered when you'd come.

Jennings had completed his mission.

Getting me out of the way so he could get to Shea.

That fucking bogus suit asking for custody of Kallie. Every time he'd gotten in my face. He'd incited and provoked and spurred until he had me ensnared.

He'd removed Mark.

He'd found the best way to remove me.

Shea was right.

He watched for weaknesses.

Knew exactly how to wreck and ruin.

He knew Kallie was Shea's weakness.

And without a doubt, he knew Shea was mine.

eighteen
Shea

LAUGHTER BOUNCED OFF THE walls of Kallie's room. Bold and bright enough to fill up all the aching spaces inside me. Enough to sustain and encourage when part of me wanted to break.

It gave me the courage to shun the creeping fear and push on with our lives.

The kind of life I'd always promised to give my daughter. Only now, that promise had extended to me.

I pushed all thoughts of Martin aside and smiled at April who tucked a big lock of curls behind Kallie's ear, my precious child beaming with all the teasing April had been tossing her way.

"Oh right…I see how it is. The two of you just up and ditch me the second something better comes along." My best friend shook her head in feigned offense and tucked a few more of Kallie's shirts into her suitcase.

I knocked my hip into April, grinning just as wide. "You know you're going to love it. This big old house to yourself for the next who knows how long? Maybe it's time you started doing a little *entertaining* of your own."

While we were away, April would stay here, taking care of my cherished home.

She straightened the pile and added more, shaking her head while she did. "Only if I can find a man hanging around Savannah that looks half as good as yours."

Just the mention of Sebastian spiked my pulse, need fluttering low in my belly at the mere thought of him touching me again. "Um…you have seen my husband? I'm not sure that's possible."

Almost two weeks had passed since the last time I'd seen him. Every day had felt like forever and the next even longer. They'd finally wrapped up the tour and returned to California two days ago. First thing in the morning, Kallie and I would be boarding a plane to reunite with him.

Threads of anticipation and warmth weaved through my chest, an intricate pattern of desire and comfort.

Never would I have thought a man like him could have provided me both.

The man hard and rigid and bold, yet still so impeccably soft.

God, I couldn't wait to get wrapped in the safety of his arms.

Over the last few months, I'd gained another best friend. I also gained some of my confidence back. Since moving back to Savannah, I'd known joy. A true sense of family.

But it was Sebastian who'd completed that family.

That didn't mean my emotions weren't all over the place. This morning I'd hopped out of bed more excited than I'd been in a long, long time, then this afternoon I'd fallen to my knees and hugged a quilt my grandmother had made to my chest while I'd wept. Leaving this house, even if only temporary, felt as if I were leaving a piece of myself behind.

But all great relationships required sacrifice.

And I would make this one, whether if it was for a moment or a lifetime.

Did I hope we ended up back here? In this home I loved with all of me? With the sound of Kallie's voice and the laughter of the children we added to our family echoing through it?

Yes.

But the love I had for Sebastian was so much greater than any place, because there was no way what I felt for him could be contained by walls or floors or ceilings.

April chuckled as she organized more of Kallie's things. "Nice. Go and get my hopes up and then turn around and burst my bubble by bringing me back down to reality. Some friend you are. Take all the good guys and don't leave any for the rest of us."

"Ha. That pack of wild boys? They are far from *mine*."

"Oh, please." She rolled affectionate brown eyes. "Any one of those guys would walk through fire for you. When did that happen?"

I gestured to Kallie who was lost in concentration as she strategically packed her backpack with things to entertain her during the flight. "I'm pretty sure it was *Kallie* who happened. She has every last one of them wrapped around her fingers."

All the guys adored her.

Would it be strange staying with them at the *Sunder* house while Sebastian and I figured things out? Should I be worried I was bringing her into a household of revelry and overindulgence, exposing her to things she shouldn't see?

On some level, yes, but on a higher level, no. Because Sebastian said the guys were ready. They were on board with a new set of rules. Ones they'd promised to uphold for the sake of my little girl.

And if we did decide to stay in L.A., we wouldn't be staying in that house for long.

It'd be temporary until we found a new home. New walls to create a million treasured memories. New floors to build a beautiful, breathtaking life.

I had faith in at all.

That my precious daughter would end up where she should be.

With Sebastian and me. In a family that loved her above all else. Where Sebastian and I loved each other just as much. An indestructible foundation that could never be collapsed or defeated.

A tease slipped into my words. "I'm sure we could put some work in on wrapping one of them around your finger. None of the guys are all that bad to look at."

Understatement of the year. Each of them had their own special lure, an appeal of their own.

She huffed. "Um…no…and thank you. I do believe I prefer my boys a little tamer. If I don't find him in the library, then I don't want him."

I grinned. "Come on…don't you want to add some excitement into your life?"

Her brows disappeared behind her blunted bangs. "You mean trouble?"

I laughed outright. My best friend was spot on.

My cell rang from my bedroom. "I'll be right back, I'm going to grab that."

"No problem. Kallie and I will keep doing our thing, won't we, Butterfly?"

"Yep!" she said from her perch on the floor, shoving as many books into her bag as she could.

I let my fingertips glide over the top of her head as I passed, a gentle, *I love you*, because you could never have too many.

I rushed to my room. A small frown formed when I saw Lyrik's number lighting up the screen, and I felt an unanticipated tremor rumble under my feet.

"Hello?" I answered, both hesitantly and urgently.

"Shea."

Just the tone of his voice dropped me to my knees.

Kallie and I touched down in California late Saturday afternoon. Anthony picked us up at the airport and drove us toward Sebastian's house in the Hollywood Hills.

My forehead rolled against the window, and I stared out at the city that blinked by unseen, a desolate blur of gray and color and pavement that whirled together to form a darkened cloud.

My baby girl sat behind me in her booster, her gaze also tuned to the city that whizzed by, but her constant curiosity and fascinated questions were absent from her tongue.

Everywhere hurt—my head and my stomach and this aching in my chest that made me feel as if I couldn't breathe.

My lungs collapsed.

Right under the rubble that had become my life.

Why did he do it?

An unbearable silence filled up the confines of the car. Questions that begged to be asked were locked up with grief and the wrenching knowledge that none of us had answers.

The mood was such a contradiction to what I'd imagined less than twenty-four hours ago. Instead of the happy homecoming with laughter and kisses and thrumming, ecstatic hearts, I felt as if mine were being crushed.

I pressed my hand to my stomach and tried to still the turmoil, the hollowed out sickness that moaned from within.

Simple, simple dreams.

Why, Sebastian?

Why?

Hesitation rippled through the silence, and I could feel the overt worry in Anthony's gaze as he quickly cut his eyes my way then back to the road again. Finally he spoke, his tone laden with concern. "I didn't know if you would come."

I turned to look at him. My chin trembled. "How could I not?"

In admission, he lifted his shoulders helplessly while still keeping both hands on the steering wheel. "People deal differently. Get scared. Give up. I wasn't so sure where you'd land."

"How could you think that? He's my husband." The words came on a wave of vehemence, the thought of losing him more than I could bear.

And even if he weren't my husband, if his birthday night had turned out any other way, I would still be here. Here with him and for him and fighting with everything I had.

Just like somewhere inside me I knew he'd been fighting for me, too.

Anthony's lips pressed into a thin line, and I knew it was sadness that tipped it down at one side. He cleared his throat.

"Please...don't take that the wrong way. I have seen people bail when I least expected them to. But honestly? I would've been surprised...shocked really...if you weren't right here."

His voice softened and he laughed quietly. "Never thought Baz would love someone the way he loves you."

He glanced in the mirror at Kallie and quieted his voice more. "The way he loves her. I guess that's what shocked me most."

He peered my way, then back to the road, his throat bobbing like it hurt as he swallowed. "And I always wanted it for him. But it did scare me that if he did find somebody—" Another pleading glance. "Someone like you...it would make him more dangerous than ever. With his love comes passion, Shea, and that passion is probably the strongest thing I've ever seen. He's a fight-to-the-death kind of guy. He's always been, and he's always going to be. Those of us who love him? We've accepted it."

My smile was full of grief and awe, my understanding one-hundred percent clear. I'd accepted it. But that didn't mean I hadn't also tried to protect him from it, because that was just a part of who I was, too.

Emotion pressed in from every direction, a spike of desperation slicing through the words. "Did anyone find out anything more?"

The shake of his head seemed regretful. "No. We were all blindsided by this, Shea. Not just you. We haven't been able to get in to talk with him yet and Kenny doesn't think he can make that happen until Monday."

Monday?

He hesitated again, sliding his gaze back to Kallie, to the road, then me. As if gauging what to say. Weighing if he had it in him to hurt me more.

"Just tell me," I begged, because I couldn't stand being left in the dark.

His words were measured and quiet, as if he could shield little ears from the magnitude of them.

"The charges are bad, Shea. He broke his restraining order by going over there, which is probably the least of his worries. It's the assault and battery. Breaking and entering. Felonies that can add up to life, especially with his record. For the first time Kenny's outlook is bleak."

He roughed a hand through his hair, anger and frustration and worry bleeding through. "This is going to be a battle I'm not sure we can win."

Sorrow struck every cell. Invaded every crevice.

Hands squeezing the wheel, his deep voice broke into the torment. "But things that are worth it? They're always a battle, Shea. Everything important comes with a cost. We don't always realize the truth of that because we don't fight for the things that don't truly matter to us. In my experience, the best things come through tribulation. What is forged in the fire always comes out stronger."

I swallowed around the lump in my throat.

Sebastian was the fire.

"Thank you," I whispered, just noticing we'd pulled to a stop in a drive in front of an immaculate home.

"That's what I'm here for. Whatever you need, just ask, okay?"

I nodded.

Anthony helped us take our things into the house. On the outskirts of my mind I recognized it was incredibly beautiful, so different than the sleek, modern lines I'd anticipated. Instead it was a stunning structure of warm stucco, sweeping windows, and dark, homey woods, a Tuscan haven hidden away by lush vegetation in the Hills.

No place inside me had the capacity to appreciate it. All those places had been struck down, chained in a fear and a loss that spun firm and fast and ferocious, all muddled with a hope I refused to relinquish.

I held tight.

The only way I knew how to keep myself together.

Inside, all the guys were there to welcome us, but the mood was decidedly somber.

Zee hugged me for a long, long time, his hold so full of sympathy it made me want to give in and weep. Like he sensed it, he pulled back and took Kallie's hand, asking if she wanted to go for a walk around the pool and gardens, luring her with the many different types of butterflies she would find.

Supportive eyes flashed to me, a look that promised he would take care of my baby. That he was offering me a second's reprieve in the midst of tumult. A moment to catch up to the pieces that were still falling apart.

With a stoic jerk of his chin, Lyrik looked on with sorrow and understanding as he leaned back against the wall with his hands stuffed in his pockets. Beneath that rigid calm I saw it. A gleam of malice and mayhem, the glint in his eyes dark and foreboding and fueled by anger. No doubt he was itching to break out, to go track Martin down the same way Sebastian had done and seek his own revenge.

"Come on, Beautiful Shea," Ash said, with none of the flirt and tease he normally injected into his words as he gathered my bags. "Let's get you settled. You have to be exhausted."

I was.

Absolutely exhausted.

Emotionally.

Mentally.

But I knew well enough there would be no sleep.

This is going to be a battle I'm not sure we can win.

I followed him upstairs. At the top of the landing were two hallways. We took the one to the right. Ash led me to the room at the very end on the left, shut off by high double-doors. He turned the knob and let the door swing open wide.

Sebastian.

His presence hit me like a rogue wave.

Completely unanticipated and knocking the breath from my lungs—all spice and man and dark seduction.

Greedily, my eyes sucked in his space. Natural light glimmered in from the balcony doors that overlooked the pool, and heavy, dark drapes framed them at the sides.

The guitar we'd played together on our wedding night was propped against the wall next to his bed, as if he'd lain there against the leather headboard and his fingers had played the strings.

Thinking of me.

I could almost hear that beautiful, beautiful voice filling the air, deep and rough and brushing across my skin, like the pleasured scrape of nails as we lost ourselves in the other's body.

I pressed my hand to the wall to keep myself upright, overcome with the staggering weight of it all.

Ash eyed me warily. "You okay?"

I shook my head. "No."

There was no use in lying because I was not okay.

Not in any shape or fashion.

He nodded, his discomfort clear. And part of me wanted to laugh, because I thought if I shed a single tear, this rocker just might bolt. Boys like him didn't do well when women cried. But there he stood, his expression so blatantly clear.

He wished there was something he could do. A way to fix the mess Sebastian had gotten himself in.

With none of that flare or grandeur or cockiness, he gestured around the room. "Baz's pad, obviously."

It seemed stupid that I missed his arrogance, but it only amplified everything lacking. Everything missing.

Sebastian.

Sebastian.

Sebastian.

His name turned dizzying cartwheels through my mind.

"Bathroom's there." Ash pointed to the en suite. "Austin's room is directly across the hall and I'm the first on the left, so I'm right here if you need anything."

More hesitation, before he blew out a strained breath toward the ceiling, then looked back at me. "Baz had been clearing out Mark's room for Kallie…it's down the opposite hall, last door on the right. Kallie's welcome to stay in there. Not sure with everything if you two want to be separated and it's still a fuckin' mess, but it's there if you want it. We can help clear it out if you want us to. Nobody's been up to finishing the job."

I nodded. "Thank you."

He twisted his mouth to the side. "You're welcome."

He sidestepped me, and I shifted, moving deeper into Sebastian's room to give him room to pass. At the doorway, he paused with his back to me, before he slowly turned around. "Want you to know you're welcome here, Shea. This is your home now, for as long as you want it to be, no matter what goes down with Baz."

Tears resurfaced in my eyes, because it was so overwhelming, the loss and the love and the unwavering support they showed for each other.

"You're family now." He rapped his knuckles on the doorjamb, as if he were driving home the point.

Then he disappeared through the doorway and left me to the startling loneliness. You'd think it would be impossible for something so barren to feel so alive.

Lost, I wandered to the bed, fingertips tracing along the sheets long since cold, and I gathered up the blanket and pressed it to my nose to take in more of him.

Sebastian.

I wanted to be angry. Curse him for being so reckless.

But I saw him for who he was.

A guardian.

Unsettled, I looked around the empty room, knowing I couldn't sit idle. That I had to do *something*.

The nerves skittering through me promised it was to fight.

I stepped out into the empty hall, somehow drawn toward Mark's room.

Yesterday, Sebastian and I had been texting on and off. Even with the burden of Martin on our shoulders, we'd been excited, flirting and teasing and playing while we anticipated being together again.

The last text I'd received from him had been filled with the same kind of thrill.

Score. Found Kallie all kinds of cute shit for her room. Going to have it ready to surprise her tomorrow. Can't wait to see her face. Getting to work. Love you.

No warning or indication of anything amiss.

Fingertips fluttering along the wall, I slowly edged in the direction of Mark's room as Ash had instructed. Silence echoed back, as if the massive house held still, whispering a hushed warning. My steps slowed in apprehension as I traversed the landing and crossed into the opposite hall.

At the end of it, a pile of shopping bags sat outside the room. I crept closer. The door stood wide open. Holding onto the wall, I peeked around the corner and inside.

A mountain of clothes were piled in the middle of the floor, and a few black garbage bags sat at the end of the bed stuffed full and tied off with a knot.

Warily, I stepped inside. My heart rate sped.

Muted light glowed through the gaps in the blinds, a thick coat of dust covering everything, the sober energy in here dampened even more than throughout the rest of the house.

It must have been so difficult for Sebastian to come in here, my brave, beautiful man.

My eyes jumped around, trying to latch onto something, a feeling or a vibe or the heart of Sebastian that had sent him running from here and into the grips of Martin.

Crossing the room to the desk, I ran my fingers over the few pictures left cluttering the surface, as if those were the things Sebastian couldn't bear to part with. A feeling of sorrow captured my spirit as I strayed into the void Mark's tragedy had left behind. Heaviness weighing me down, I turned from the desk and eased around the pile of clothes, my attention hooking on the yawning closet where a single light still burned from within.

I peered inside. The rods and half the shelves had been cleared out.

Unease trickled into my senses.

A job half done.

I sucked in a breath as a vibration of disquiet stirred through me, and I tentatively took a few steps deeper into the closet.

Boxes lined the floor, some shoved farther toward the room as if Sebastian were planning to get rid of them or store them elsewhere, and a couple were still tucked in the shelves and coves.

At the very back, a plastic storage bin had been dragged out onto the closet floor, the lid balanced at the side. In front of it, a few pictures were scattered about and a journal was turned upside down, pages bent as if it'd been dropped.

I sank to my knees, shaking hands and panted breaths out of control as I reached down and cautiously picked up the journal.

I hated the thought of invading the man's privacy, long after he was gone, but I knew whatever Sebastian had found was now clutched in my trembling hands.

Another piece of me broke for a man I didn't know as I scanned the pure and utter desolation slashed across the pages. Page after page of hopelessness and shame. The heart and mind of a terribly lost soul.

Tears gathered in my eyes as I continued on, searching for anything. *Any* indication of what would have sent Sebastian toward a fate I knew he didn't want.

My attention caught on an entry nearing the back, in a place where his typically messy penmanship had become almost violent. Frantic.

Fucking Donny and his fucking mouth.

Donny?

A sinking feeling washed through me, taunting me with flickers of recognition. Vicious blue eyes I would never forget. I gripped the book, reading as fast as I could.

Always with his fucking mouth. I didn't want to know. I didn't want any part of it. I knew Martin was sick. Both of them were sick. But not that sick. I told Martin so. I told him to go to hell when he demanded the money I owe him. Told him I'd take everything I know to the cops. I was going to anyway, money be damned. I knew what he'd had Donny do to that girl. I knew what he planned to have him do. She was a loose end. A liability. Just like me. Call me a snitch. I didn't care. Let the asshole burn.

That girl.

That girl.

That girl.

That girl.

Oh my God.

Was this me?

A liability. A loose end?

That sinking feeling pulled me beneath the surface, like blackened waters lapping over my head.

I flipped the page. All my breath locked up in my throat, so thick and tight and suffocating. Lightheadedness tilted the room.

Donny's gone. Dead in the water. I'm going to be next. I know it. Feel it coming. Am I scared? Yeah. Terrified, really. I led Martin on. Made him believe I'd leaked info. Ratted him and Lester out. He thinks I'm blackmailing, but I don't have anything but Donny's word. And Donny's word is about as valuable as a ten-dollar whore. My only intention had been to thwart the plans he had to hurt that girl again. Only this time, make it final. Sick. Fucking sick. Couldn't live with myself if there was any chance of it happening, so I'd rather die stopping it. I guess I finally did something in my life worth a shit.

Horror and hate collided in a cataclysm of fear when I locked on the name.

Lester.

And I knew. And I knew. And I knew.

I lurched forward, holding myself up on my hands and knees as I gasped for absent air.

I'd always thought the threat I'd made had saved Kallie's and my life. Allowed us to live the way he never would have let us. But now I wondered if it was the stupidest thing I'd ever done.

And Sebastian…he was so protective, bore so much shame, regret, and guilt over the loss of Mark. One inciting factor would be the match. A combustion of sparks and flames and gasoline that would set him off.

Send him over the edge of the cliff on which he always teetered.

Volatile and explosive.

Just like Anthony had claimed…had asked me to accept.

Sebastian never loved lightly.

This was what Martin had wanted, wasn't it? What he'd counted on?

Divide and conquer.

Isolate and sabotage.

His whole intent was to take Sebastian from me. To leave me the most vulnerable I could be.

Little did he know I would fight him to the death.

Shivers shook through my entire body, and I tried to swallow around the rock in my throat as I reached down and picked up one of the pictures that lay face down on the floor.

My hand shot to my mouth to cover a cry.

Oh my God.

Oh my God.

Mark, Austin, Donny, and *my mother*.

A deep, guttural cry suddenly ricocheted off the walls in the small closet, one that meshed with the devastated sadness of mine.

I jerked to look over my shoulder.

Austin.

He clutched both sides of the doorframe, holding himself up, spirit and body crumpled and broken. Confession barely decipherable, he looked at me as if he were begging me to see him. "It's my fault. It was always my fault."

I scrambled to face him, pushing all the way up onto my knees, my words jumbled as they poured from my mouth. I held out the journal. "Austin…what is this? Tell me what you know."

He winced as if the sight of it caused him physical pain. "We knew, Shea. Mark and I…we knew. Donny told us what Martin had them do to you."

They knew.

Austin shook his head and laughed a spiteful sound. "There's never any fucking proof, right, Shea? Assholes can just keep hurting and hurting and hurting and there's never any proof. But Mark didn't care. He said he was going to the cops anyway. And then Mark was gone… He was gone, Shea," he said with all the implication he could summon.

Oh my God. Martin. He did this to Mark.

Everything spun and dizziness swelled.

Austin kept crying, words tumbling from him like a confession that had been held in for far too long. "Baz found all this shit Mark had kept…demanded to know what the hell I knew. I couldn't keep it from him any longer, Shea. I couldn't. I'm so fucking sorry. So sorry."

I gulped over the reality of what Sebastian had found. Of what he had learned. My last secret. The one I'd kept to protect him.

I staggered onto unsteady feet, unable to process everything he was trying to tell me. My focus would only latch onto one thing. I shoved one of the pictures at him. "When…when was this picture taken?"

"I don't know…maybe a year and a half ago. Not long before Mark died."

Between the heavy, stale air, the disorganized chaos of the room, and the catastrophic discovery, I felt bile rise in my throat. My skin cold and clammy.

I took a desperate step forward.

"Where is she?"

nineteen
Shea

Eighteen years old

THE HEELS OF CHLOE Lynn's high-heeled boots clicked on the tile floor where she paced in annoyance, arms crossed over her chest, dressed in designer skinny jeans and a flowy blouse. Her mother looked poised and ready to conquer the world, while Shea knew she looked absolutely horrible, her eyes stained red and cheeks chapped from crying.

"Please, Momma, I need your help."

She'd hidden it for as long as she could.

Four months, and there was no longer any hidin'.

Shea met the force of her mother's disgusted glare. Cold. Cold. Cold.

Beneath it Shea wanted to cower and shrink, but she refused to be that girl for one day longer. No longer would she bow and submit.

But that didn't mean fear wasn't trembling through her bones.

"What is it exactly you want me to do, Delaney?"

Shea cringed, voice ragged. "Don't call me that."

"Why? It's about time you accepted who you are."

"What if that's not who I want to be?"

Shea cringed again when her mother laughed, bitter, low, and sarcastic. "It's a little late now, don't you think? You have contracts. Albums to record and tours to fulfill. You have *obligations*. I'm not going to tell you anything different than what Martin told you. You're going to suck it up and act like a woman. Wipe those ugly tears off your face and take care of what needs to be taken care of, and that's gonna be the end of it."

Pain sliced through Shea's chest, something physical amassed from many years.

"I did everything for you. All my life spent in lessons and chasing down auditions. Me running faster and faster because you were right behind me pushing and pushing and pushing."

"And you think now that we finally got what we've worked so hard for, I'm going to stand by and let you throw it all away? You go and get yourself knocked up and you think it changes anything? I'm not going to let you ruin my life. Not again."

Shea's face crumpled with the blow. "Is that what I was? A mistake?"

Finally, all her mother's pushin' had driven her right into the ground.

Laughing as if Shea were completely ignorant, her mother shook her head as she lifted the half-spent bottle of wine, red liquid billowing into the well of her emptied glass.

"Time to grow up, Delaney. Wipe the stars out of your eyes. All those dreams about falling in love and happy families you've always been so fond of? The nonsense your grandma filled your head with? It doesn't exist. Go back to Martin. He's waitin' on you."

Then she turned her back and walked through the arch.

Shea stood in the middle of her mother's Nashville kitchen, the fear for her child and the loss of her grandma nearly dropping her to the floor in a broken pile. The opulence surrounding her rode on every song Shea had ever sang, the cost of a life she didn't want to live.

In that moment, she felt the last thread of commitment she had for her mother snap.

Frantically, Shea ripped shirts from their hangers and shoved them into a suitcase sitting on the floor in the middle of the walk-in closet. Adrenaline and terror and the overwhelming urge to run coursed through her veins.

He would try to stop her. She knew he would. But she wouldn't let him.

It was time and *this* time there was no turning back.

She'd overheard what she shouldn't. Martin in a business deal with Lester Ford, the middle-aged man just as disgusting as Martin. Just as pretentious. Just as fake. Crooked. One of Nashville's wealthiest, revered in their circles.

Now Shea knew better.

She'd been sure their business dealings slanted on the seedy side, but she'd had no idea how sordid they went.

Martin was funding Lester's campaign with drug money.

All of this—it was a front. Martin was nothing more than a lowlife drug trafficker, sending money out west while wearing a five-thousand-dollar suit.

He'd caught her lurking in the shadows. Listening. He had pushed her against the wall and pressed his hand to her throat and a gun to her side.

"You think you know what's going on?" he'd spat. "What you heard, you will tell no one. Do you understand? I made you. You owe me, and I will collect my debt. You'll never be without me, Delaney Rhoads. I. Own. You. Open your mouth and all you know and love will vanish. Do you understand what I'm telling you?"

Petrified, I could only nod.

"I will guarantee your silence," he'd whispered with all the menace in his black, black soul.

That's what he'd said and that's when Shea had decided no more.

He'd wanted the money—the money from the record deal she'd signed. The millions that should have gone to her, but instead in all her naivety, she'd signed contracts that awarded virtually all of it to her mother and Martin. He owed that money to Lester... needed it to fulfill a debt.

Her threat to leave had been returned with a threat to kill her.

She didn't really think he would.

He wanted her scared.

Maybe she should have been more fearful.

Or maybe she was.

But she refused to live this life.

Martin thought she'd had an abortion. That she'd surrendered the way she always had.

But no.

No longer would Shea allow herself to be a prisoner to this nightmare. She was escaping before it ruined more of who she was and stole from her the one thing worth living for.

Shea filled the suitcase to bursting, dropped to her knees, and grunted as she forced the zipper closed, another wave of terror pounding adrenaline through her blood.

Desperately, she whispered to the baby growing in her belly, "I'm going to take care of you. I promise, I'm going to be the best momma you could ever have. Just you and me."

Just you and me.

Shea climbed back to her feet and drew her phone from her back pocket. She just needed to hear a sane voice. Someone there to remind her she wasn't completely alone in this world that threatened to rip her apart. A reassurance that what she was doing was right.

Quickly she dialed her uncle Charlie.

He answered on the first ring. "Shea Bear." Relief was evident in his heavy exhale. "You on your way, sweetheart?"

"Almost..."

Shea looked around the closet, gauging what she could grab in the short window she had. "I have to pack a couple more things and then I'll be. I should be there by daylight."

The trip from Nashville to Savannah was just shy of an eight-hour drive.

"Be careful, sweet girl. I'll be right here waitin'."

"Thank you," she whispered, that simple statement filled with so much, so much gratitude to the man who she knew was saving her from this life.

She ended the call, hauling the overstuffed suitcase behind her out into the bedroom.

Moonlight filtered in through the transparent drapes, the darkened room cast in shadows and memories and regrets.

Shea's gaze slid unwelcomed to the plush bed made up of satiny linens. Her stomach turned with nausea at the thought of ever having *shared* it with Martin Jennings.

But she'd be taking one good thing from this awful mess.

In the end, this baby was the only thing that mattered.

She grabbed the large duffle bag she'd already packed and slung it over her shoulder, maneuvered the suitcase over the thick carpet to the dresser against the far wall.

Her jewelry box rested on top of it.

It was chock-full of diamonds, gold, and gems—all tokens of this flashy, false life. But the only things she was after were the heirlooms her grandmother had left her when she'd passed—her ring and the matching necklace her grandfather had given her on their wedding day.

She opened the special bottom drawer where she stored them.

A noise clattered from the other side of the house. At the sound, her head jerked up. Freezing cold slid down her spine.

Then that noise was eclipsed by pure foreboding silence.

No.

Shea swallowed and slowly turned as the hairs at the back of her neck lifted. Craning her ear, she trained her attention out beyond the bedroom.

Listening.

Fear tingled as a flash of goosebumps swelled across her skin.

She could sense it.

Smell it in the air.

The stench of evil.

Something wicked coming her way.

Just outside the door, the wooden floorboards creaked. Shivers vibrated uncontrollably through her limbs, and she fumbled backward and bumped into the dresser.

The jewelry box rattled.

It was as if the sound was the strike to a match.

The bedroom door burst open, and her heart took off in a wild, thundering sprint.

There were three of them, all dressed in black, masks over their faces, wild eyes staring at her through the dingy duskiness of the room. Slowly, they encroached.

A tiny whimper trembled from her tongue, eyes darting between the three of them. One stood out from the others, taking a step in front, and a shocked cry jutted from her mouth when the malicious blue eyes stared her down.

The fierce need to protect her baby shot through her in a panic of survival.

She spun and raced for the bathroom door.

All she had to do was get to that door and lock it behind her.

There was a window—a window to her escape.

Shea pushed herself as hard as she could go.

But the man in front was faster.

He grabbed her by the hair, taking a handful and jerking her around. In the same motion, his opposite fist struck her at the temple.

Pain splintered through her head and blackness closed in at the edges of her sight.

She fought for consciousness, barely aware he was throwing her to the ground.

Yet somehow her wide, unblinking eyes took it all in on a shocked reel that recorded in slow motion.

"Do it." The man in charge shouted his command at the other two who stood gaping at her where she had crumpled in a ball.

A voice so familiar.

"Do it!" he shouted again.

The two moved into action, tearing the covers from the bed she hated and ripping the drapes from the windows, yanking open dresser drawers and strewing clothes across the floor.

The ringleader landed another punch to her eye, and she gasped out at the agony of it.

But it was the kick to her stomach that nearly killed her.

Physically.

Emotionally.

She was sure the pain went deep enough to touch her soul.

Shea wailed.

Darkness tried to suck her under, and she wanted to succumb, to give up, but she knew she couldn't give in.

Fight.

And she did.

She struggled to bring up her knees, to guard herself with her arms and hands, all the while praying harder than she had in all her life.

"No," she whimpered. "Please."

She dug deep to find the strength to curl herself into a tight ball.

And the man…he kicked and kicked and kicked.

Battering until she could feel the cuts and wounds he inflicted on her arms and legs weeping blood, trails streaking to the floor and flooding from her mouth and nose.

And still she fought until she'd gone numb.

Senses dulled by the unbearable pain.

Weak.

Because she was losing this fight.

Her arms slipped and her stomach lurched when it was struck with another direct blow.

"No," she cried. Her body recoiled with the force, and she heaved, rolling onto her side in a silent wail, cheek pressed into the carpet, her insides curled, and she vomited on the floor.

"That's enough," he said, as if maybe he needed to convince himself.

The room continued to spin with her fear, with her hatred—with the glaring shock that seemed to have taken her whole.

She watched with the same unblinking eyes as the man who'd beaten her stepped over her as if she were a piece of trash discarded in the middle of the floor. Leaning down in front of the dresser, he took a few pieces of jewelry that had been littered across the floor, then he snagged her grandmother's ring and necklace and stuffed them into his pocket.

She wanted to cry out, to beg him not to take something else so precious to her, but her tongue was swollen and thick, the words stuck on a muted cry bottled in her throat.

The three of them hustled out, and the back door slammed.

An eerie silence stole over the house.

It echoed back her surrender. Drowsiness pulled at her consciousness, the pain too great. She had the greatest urge to close her eyes and never wake.

No.

Somehow she found the strength to roll to her stomach. An agonizing pain tore through every inch of her body as she fought to climb onto her feet, but they wouldn't hold, and she fell back to the ground.

Whimpered cries wept from her as she dragged herself on her elbows across the room, the flashing light of her cell phone like a beacon where it had been knocked from her hold and skidded across the floor.

Her bloodied fingers stretched toward it, inches away. They were shaking…shaking. Eyesight blurred. Yet somehow she managed to place the call.

"911…what's your emergency?"

She could do nothing more than weep.

twenty
Shea

I POUNDED DOWNSTAIRS WITH the address Austin had given me clutched in my hand. A frenzy had lit in my heart, a desperation seated so deeply I could feel myself moving without giving thought to any consequence.

I figured it'd been much the same for Sebastian yesterday. The innate need to protect and defend. To right wrongs that had occurred so long ago.

Those wrongs had started with me being set at the feet of a vile, vicious man. They'd trickled down, fed by the mistakes made over the years. Leaving all of us susceptible to Martin's evil manipulation and greed. Over-indulgences and self-hatred and the overwhelming longing to cover up pain, Mark, Austin, and Sebastian had been prisoners to their own pasts that had somehow merged with mine.

But this time.

This time I would set it right.

My feet hit the landing of the hushed living room. Windows that soared to the sky provided the perfect view of the gorgeous pool and gardens where my precious child hopped from foot to foot on the grass, blonde curls wild and free, innocent smile gracing that cherished face.

Cherished.

Zee had his hands stuffed in his pockets, the smallest of smiles hinting at the edge of his mouth as he stood protectively at her side.

Cherished.

This child who'd been the root of it all. An obstacle standing in Martin's way. One he'd sought to do away with when I'd refused to do his bidding.

When for the first time in my life, I'd refused to cave.

Cherished.

Emotion clotted in my chest. Too heavy. Too full.

I struggled to breathe because I didn't know how to do that anymore without Sebastian in my life.

He'd found everything I never thought I would have.

Simple, simple dreams.

I rushed toward the kitchen and slammed to a stop at the entryway, hands darting out to support myself. Lyrik and Ash stood inside, leaning back against the dark granite of the island, sipping at beers, stewing in a silent misery of what had come to pass.

"Car." The demand shot from my tongue with the velocity of a torpedo.

Lyrik straightened, frowned. He rubbed the back of his hand across his mouth as he tried to make sense of my outburst.

Ash shifted toward me and placed his bottle on the counter, eyeing me the same way he might eye a wild animal that'd been backed into a corner.

Honestly, that perception didn't feel too far off.

"What's going on, darlin'?" he asked with a resurrection of his cocky twang.

"I need a car. Now." I had no time for explanations, didn't want to feed any false hope, the same hope that seared like a fire raging inside me.

Ash slanted Lyrik a perplexed glance, before he turned back to me with a shrug and dug into his pocket, quick to toss me a set of keys.

Metal clanked as I snatched them out of the air.

"White BMW. Be careful with my baby," he shouted after me when I flew into action.

Without a parting word, I bolted from the kitchen and out the front door. My boots thudded against concrete as I ran down the walk to the cobblestone drive, gaze scanning the line of muscle and metal and flash, landing on the white M5 parked at the end.

I clicked the fob and jumped inside.

The deep roll of the powerful engine vibrated, and I shifted into gear, jerking in the drive, totally unaccustomed to manning a stick. I wouldn't be deterred. I ground the gears, finding traction. At the first stop sign, I punched at the navigation, fumbling as I entered the address.

Chaotic nerves jumbled through me as I made the forty-five minute trip in L.A. traffic, sickness roiling in my belly.

The last time I'd seen her I'd been in the hospital, bandages and braces holding together the broken pieces of my body.

I'd bled.

But somehow…somehow Kallie had been strong.

I'd made a statement to the police. I had claimed Martin had been responsible, that I thought I'd recognized Donny, sure in my heart it hadn't been a random burglary like the investigators had suspected because of the jewelry that had been stolen and the way the place had been ransacked.

"Stupid girl," my mother had seethed when she'd leaned over me.

Charlie had stepped from the shadows where he'd stood guard and physically removed his sister from the room. He'd warned her I was no longer her concern, and that he would be *taking care of her* if we ever heard from her again.

Maybe she'd wanted to insult me, but I was sure being that *stupid girl* had ultimately saved my life. Even though there'd been no proof Martin was involved, just like Austin had said, I'd still raised the question. There was now a permanent record in a file with his name on it. I was certain that's what had held Martin's vengeance back for all these years.

Unrestrained tears broke free when I pulled into the lot of the worn-down apartment building. Two stories of dreary, faded white brick walls faced out to the parking lot. Cheap black metal railing ran the length of the second floor and exterior steps.

Impoverished and destitute.

Easing Ash's car into a vacant spot, I cut the engine and frantically wiped the wetness from my cheeks, sniffled as I tried to compose myself to face a woman I both loved and hated.

I grasped the handle and slowly released the latch. Every cell in my body thundered with anger, resolve, and determination. My spirit was a floundering mess, ruminating with the echo of a little girl's dreams and a trusting heart that had so badly wanted to believe. That had so mutely trusted.

I lifted my chin and forced my feet forward. My hands shook as I clung to the railing for support, when I climbed the exterior steps. With every step I took, my heart felt like it might explode in my chest. Pressing. Pressing. Pressing.

Uneasily, I glanced once more at the rumpled piece of paper. *2706.*

Gulping over the knot in my throat, I raised my fist. My eyes squeezed in a moment's indecision, hand hovering in the air, before I pounded on the door.

There was rustling behind the thin wood, and I braced myself for what I would find. I knew the address was old and Austin had only been here a couple times, but I had to take the chance she still lived here.

Hinges creaked and wood scraped when the door cracked open an inch. A thin metal chain secured five inches from the top kept it from opening all the way. Through the gap, brown eyes narrowed on me.

That knot at the base of my throat throbbed.

She expelled a resigned breath, before the door closed and metal dragged as she completely freed the latch. It swung open to her back as she strutted away. It was as if my presence didn't affect her all that much.

She plopped down on the couch that faced where I stood aghast in the middle of her doorway.

Groping for the pack of cigarettes on the end table, she cocked her head to the side and lit a cigarette, brown gaze never wavering from me the entire time, lines around her thinned lips, legs and arms haggard and frail.

Sadness engulfed me. My mother appeared as worn down as the building surrounding her.

She inhaled deeply, held it, before she lifted her face toward the ceiling and slowly blew it out. A thick cloud of smoke lifted in a haze above her head.

"Been a long time," she finally said as she flicked ash in a tray.

"It's been a long time?" I couldn't keep the anger from trembling through my voice.

She laughed a hollow sound. "What did you expect, Shea? A welcome party? Balloons and confetti and a goddamn cake? You always did have your head in the clouds."

"You're right...I guess I should have expected the worst."

As if amused, she shook her head, words fueled by sarcasm. "Heard you went and snagged yourself a rock star. That's my girl. I always knew you had it in you."

The mention of Sebastian cut through me like a knife, and I grasped for the courage to speak.

"You don't get to do that." I took a step forward as my brow pinched. "You don't get to demean what's good in my life."

And God, everything surrounding him was so good and so very, very bad. My beautiful, beautiful man.

The thought of living without him was more than I could begin to bear. The fact this woman had set the events into motion years ago, held partial responsibility for Sebastian's downfall, made it that much worse.

My mouth quivered, and I fought a futile battle against the pain welling high and fast, a flash flood of hurt and rejection and devastation rising over my head. I pulled in a choked breath as realization crashed over me.

"That's what you've always done, isn't it?" I blinked as I tried to *see* her. "Had that always been your goal? To take whatever was good and pure and spoil it?"

She sneered at the insinuation, and I took another step propelled by years of simmering rage.

"Was it?" I demanded. I touched my chest as the words broke on my tongue. "I wanted to *sing*, and you took the gift I was given, something beautiful that brought me joy, and turned it into something ugly. I wanted to grow up and fall in love, and you manipulated that into something nasty and obscene."

She went hard in her expression, posture, and tone. "I took what was mine and turned it into what I wanted it to be."

I grabbed the cheap vase boasting a bouquet of dead flowers sitting on the table next to me and hurled it across the room.

Attention.

That's what I wanted.

For once, I wanted this woman to *look* at me. To see me as a person and not the ticket to her fucked-up dreams.

It busted on the wall behind her, shards of glass and water spilling to the couch and floor.

Tears blurred my vision as everything I'd kept bottled for all these years wept free. "You let them beat me, didn't you? You knew, and you let them hurt me. *Your own daughter.* Didn't you?"

Beneath all her roughened exterior, I saw her flinch.

"Those contracts you made me sign? I know you exploited me. Had them written up so you and Martin would be the ones to financially gain while I was forced to remain under your control."

"And look where it got *me*. After all I did for you," she spat, pure contempt.

Anguished, I swallowed and took a step back, the oldest pain clawing at my chest.

Momma.

Momma.

Momma.

My soul cried out for her, those little girl dreams confused with this sick reality. I'd tried so hard. I'd given her everything I had while she just took and took and took. I'd loved her so purely, trusted until that trust proved just how blind love can be.

"And you know what? When I look back, that's not even what hurts. What hurts was how you turned your back on me when I needed you most. I loved you." I shook my head, laying myself bare, the words a jumble of humorless laughter and sorrow, my feelings once again freely given. Again completely at my expense. "I guess it makes me a fool I still do."

She sucked in a breath.

With my fingertips, I wiped the tears from my face. More just fell in their place. "I know you know Martin's back and trying to destroy my life." My face twisted with the thought. "And I'm pretty sure he was coming for me before…that he was going to hurt me when I least expected it, and somehow…somehow this guy I didn't even know…"

Mark.

My spirit bled for him, praying he was finally at peace.

"...somehow he stopped whatever Martin was going to do."

The words came harsh with the implication. "And I know you know Sebastian, the man I love with everything I have...with *all* of me...is sitting behind bars right now because he was trying to protect me. Because he was trying to protect his family."

She'd proven before she cared about none of that.

Family.

Loyalty.

Sacrifice.

But my grandma, she'd taught me to see the best in people. To believe when nothing seemed worth believing in.

I lifted my quivering chin. "And I know you know enough to make this go away. If you've ever loved me...if you've ever cared at all...if you have one shred of decency left in you, you will *fix this*."

Kallie threw her head back as she propelled herself down the slide. Giggles floated on the gentle breeze, the trees surrounding us rustling in the cool air as my daughter played on the small playground down the hill from Sebastian's house.

"Look at me, Momma!"

I hugged myself across my chest and pasted a smile on my face, doing everything I could to stay upright.

"I see you, Butterfly. You're such a big girl."

She whooshed to the bottom. Little feet hit the ground and she was off running again, climbing right back up the steps to do it again.

What they say must be true.

Children are resilient.

It was proven in the unending smile that graced my daughter's face.

In the gentle way she hugged me in the moments when I was certain I couldn't withstand one second more.

In the sure and indisputable way she promised, "Everything's gonna be all right, Momma. Don't cry."

Even though we were so far from home.

Surrounded by so many people except for the one we'd come here for.

Buried in questions and agony and the dwindling hope Sebastian would find his way back to us.

Her tiny spirit exhibited the greatest show of strength.

I desperately tried to hang onto it.

Faith.

But it was difficult when the only thing we were met with were roadblocks and setbacks and disappointments.

Four days had passed since I'd gone to my mother. Four days since I'd walked away and not heard another word. Four days of Kenny scrambling and Anthony encouraging, and all the guys doing everything they could to stand up and stand in, trying to make me and Kallie feel at home when I'd never felt so alone.

Four days of going through the motions. Four days of *pretending* I could make it through this.

In that time, I'd not even been granted clearance to visit him.

God. I just wanted to see his face. To touch along the lines and the curves and the scars. To see that he was okay and then maybe I could be okay, too.

The absolute worst part? It had also been four days of worrying what Martin might be planning to do, constantly looking over my shoulder, scared I would find those fears were valid.

But still somehow sure he would bide his time. Unwilling to strike in the middle of this public battle.

Now we were doing everything we could to strike first.

"Be careful, Kallie Bug," I warned when she started climbing a metal ladder to the elevated bouncy bridge stretched between two play towers.

From the third step, she grinned back at me. "I'm bein' so, so careful, Momma. Did you know I have to learn to climb way up high in the sky 'cause that's were butterflies fly *and* I'm gonna be in big girl school? And I'm not scared at all, at all."

Okay.

I guess I shouldn't have been surprised that even with everything I was going through, my daughter still held the power to bring a smile to my face.

"She's beautiful." The hoarse voice coming from behind froze my blood, and I went rigid when I felt her approach, the instinct to safeguard and shield flipping to high alert.

But somehow I felt the resignation in her step.

The surrender.

My attention remained fixed on my daughter as my mother erased the space and came to stand directly beside me.

Locks of her stringy hair whipped in the wind.

Neither of us said anything for the longest time. The silence screamed back all the pain she had caused, my heart aching in a way it'd never ached before.

Her voice cracked in the December air. "They were *never* supposed to hurt you."

My body quaked with the intrusion of her words.

"I would never have given the okay for that. They were just supposed to shake you up. Scare you into making the decision you needed to make."

My eyes dropped closed as if it could shield me from this brutality.

She'd known.

But I already knew that, didn't I? Still, the confirmation struck me like the sting of a lash.

Something helpless seeped into her tone. "By then, I was in deep." Her mouth pinched as if the confession was sour. "Got myself mixed up in things I never anticipated, but by the time I realized what was happening, it was already too late."

My head shook, rejecting any justification.

She glanced at me as if she could read my thoughts. "I'm not sayin' any of that gives me an excuse, Shea. I'm standing here taking responsibility for what I've done."

"Why now? Why did he come after me now?"

She turned her attention away, back to my daughter, as if she couldn't stand to look at me while she spoke the words. "Martin Jennings has always viewed you as a threat. As a loose thread that needed to be snipped. With everything I've gone through with him all these years, my guess is when he found out you were with Sebastian Stone, he thought it was time to take action. Martin couldn't stand aside and wait to see what happened with the tie between Sebastian and Mark. He didn't know what Mark had revealed to him or anyone else. He didn't know if Sebastian had sought you out because of something Mark had said to him. He needed to end your relationship with Sebastian any way he could. And what better way to take you out than through your daughter?"

She shook her head. "He loves instilling fear, controlling people that way. He gets off on it in some sick way."

An incredulous snort shot from my nose. As if I didn't have front-row experience with that.

Her voice spread through me like ice as she continued, "But make no mistake. He would have dealt with you if it weren't for the fact he didn't know if or who you'd confided in. Or if you hadn't made that complaint to the police."

I shot her a glance full of old hatred.

She caught onto it immediately. "Yeah…told you it was stupid. What you did was *stupid*. Trying to leave when he didn't give a second thought to hurting you. But it gave you leverage he didn't anticipate. Still, there's no doubt in my mind it didn't stop him from planning…conniving and figuring out how to erase the threat he viewed you to be. Until that boy Mark stumbled upon it."

She huffed like it wasn't all that big a deal. "He would have taken me out a long time ago if he didn't believe I was just as dirty as him." Self-deprecating laughter rolled from her like a toll of death. "And I won't deny that I am."

I stood there reeling. Trying to wrap my head around what my mother had dragged me into, where all the greed and selfishness had led us both.

Kallie swooped down the slide and my mother choked over a sob, ushering in an entire shift of her demeanor.

"I've done *so* much bad." Bitterness made its way in. "Believe me, I've gotten everything I deserve. Don't have a damned thing. Nothing. Not a dime of that money I wanted so bad, and I sure as hell don't have the family I didn't realize I needed. But it's too late now, and now I'm going to be gettin' more."

I looked at her, wind stinging the tears wetting my face.

She met my gaze, chin raised.

"My own daughter stood in my shithole apartment and demanded to know if I ever loved her…if I ever cared at all. You demanded to know if I had any decency left inside me. Truth is, there was never a whole lot of that to begin with."

Her voice grew thin and wispy. "But I do love you, Shea. Always have. But that took a back seat to everything I thought I had to have, and then got completely forgotten when every day was spent just trying to survive my deplorable life."

"All I ever wanted was to make you proud."

She nodded slowly. "And you were right. I made that ugly, too. I'm finished with making things ugly.

Wistfully, she turned back to watch my daughter who laughed and played, before she looked back at me, expression going deathly sad. "You're the only truly beautiful thing I ever made."

I sucked in a lungful of air. Then why did every action she ever made have to be opposite? I wanted to scream, *why*? Why'd she have to be so vile when I would have happily given her everything?

She cleared her throat and straightened. "I'm leaving here and I'm going straight to the police station. I'm going to turn myself in. Tell them every last thing I know, every name and every detail. I'll be going to prison, Shea. That is if I make it there. I imagine Martin will be going away for much longer. I just wanted you to know."

I felt something inside me splintering, old hurt and resentment breaking free. As much relief as her statement brought me, there was no satisfaction.

Nothing to assuage the enormity of what she'd done. The danger she'd put her own daughter in, worst of all allowing it year after year.

She could have stopped this so long ago.

Kallie all of a sudden came skipping over to us, blonde curls a hurricane, her smile the most brilliant force. "Momma!"

She grabbed onto my hand, swaying in my hold as she peered up at the woman who'd done everything to stop her life.

"Hi," she exuded with all that childlike curiosity.

My mother smiled down at her.

Softly.

Flickers of a memory hit me, and I thought maybe...maybe she'd once looked at me that way.

"And what's your name?" my mother asked as she stooped down to bring them to eye level.

A hint of interested shyness injected into her tone when she answered, "I'm Kallie Marie."

"Well...it's an honor to meet you, Kallie Marie."

Chloe Lynn didn't introduce herself to Kallie as anyone, not as my mother or her grandmother or a long-lost friend.

Because both my mother and I knew Kallie would never see her again.

For the briefest flash, my mother touched my daughter's cheek, hesitating, before she stood.

Sorrow crowded every crease in her weathered face. "Goodbye, my shining star."

Then she turned and walked away.

Night echoed back from where I stood on the balcony off Sebastian's bedroom. City lights gleamed and glinted where they stretched across the valley, the pool below in a slow roll from one color to another, the high-pitched drone of bugs floating in the cool night air.

A chill blew across my skin. Thick strands of my hair and the silky material of my short nightgown billowed in the gentle breeze. The same as the billow of the shimmery drapes whipping out from where they hung just inside the room, the large French doors open and bleeding the darkness from within.

My spirit stirred and I grasped the cool railing as I lifted my face to the sky and sent up a silent prayer.

A thank you.

My daughter was safe and sleeping down the opposite hall.

Protected.

Permanently.

Thanks to my mother, the one who'd done so much damage and caused so much pain, Martin Jennings would no longer stand as a threat against my daughter.

Would no longer stand as a threat against me.

Yesterday, a warrant had been issued. DEA had swept in to

search every pretentious inch of his home.

Three hours later he'd been arrested.

Fraud and theft and trafficking.

It was all there, hidden in safes and files and computers.

Arrogant, stupid man.

Kallie and I were free.

But my heart…my heart was bound. Tied to the only future I could see.

Wind gusted—howled and thrashed.

Chills skated across the surface of my skin as a swell of that energy crested.

Pressing full.

Consuming.

My hands clamped down on the railing and my body swayed. My ear inclined to the muted click of a door, and my pulse spiked as footsteps moved across the bedroom floor.

Slow yet filled with severity.

And I could feel it. Everything he was. Everything I wanted us to be. Standing right behind me.

I gasped over a breath when I looked over my shoulder to catch sight of this magnificent man.

My magnificent man.

The weight of his stare was overpowering, those strange grey eyes trained on me.

Darkness clung to the defined curves of his face.

All harsh lines and broken beauty and mystery.

My eyes caressed, taking all of him in, the stunning bulk of his imposing body, gaze trailing across his full, full lips that were a little crooked on one side, on to the old scar that split through his right eyebrow, and the trace of another at the bottom of his chin. There was a new scar high up on his left cheekbone, a row of stitches standing as evidence of his stand for me.

No, this man was not perfect.

Just beautiful and dark and a little bit frightening.

The one who'd led the chain of events that had finally set us free.

"You see me, Shea?" The grating question slammed me like a full body blow.

Powerful.

Unyielding.

A force I could never resist.

I'd thought I'd had no time for distractions. No place for interference or disturbance in Kallie's and my secluded, lonely life.

But he was the one I didn't know I'd been waiting for.

Slowly I turned. My body was basked in moonlight while Sebastian remained obscured in the fluttering shadows that flitted like strobes across that gorgeous face.

"Yes," I whispered, swallowing around the emotion that rushed.

I'd never seen anyone so clearly.

The one who was willing to give it all.

"Won't apologize." His voice was a hard rasp, and his eyes flashed. "Did it for you. Would've died for you. Killed for you. Rotted in that cell if I had to. As long as it meant you and that little girl are safe."

He had been willing to give up everything for Kallie and me so we could live in peace.

Just like my mother had done.

After everything, she'd offered herself up and knowingly taken Sebastian's place. The state had dropped all charges against him late this afternoon when the evidence my mother provided had steadily mounted against Martin.

Kenny Lane had scrambled to find favor on our side and pushed the legal envelope, citing a convoluted trail of self-defense. To keep Kallie away from the media frenzy, Anthony had picked him up and taken him to his place to shower and change out of his bloodied clothes.

And now Sebastian was here.

Some would say it might be too little too late.

That the acts she'd committed were unforgiveable.

But I'd make a case there was no such thing.

Where there is repentance, there is always room for mercy.

No.

I wouldn't visit or forge bonds broken long ago.

But I would no longer cling to bitterness and sorrow.

I was giving thanks and letting it go.

Sebastian took one step from the shadows into the light.

God.

I'd thought there'd never been a more brutally beautiful man.

And it was true. But that savage beauty was so much greater than the surface. And I didn't just *see* it. I experienced it.

Selfless loyalty.

Flawless faithfulness.

This powerful man willingly becoming vulnerable for us.

My heart beat frantically. Wildly.

A stampede of desire and an onslaught of lust.

Devotion and passion.

Absolution.

"Come here," he commanded, voice low and seductive.

As if I could ever say no.

Slowly, I approached. Inhale. Exhale. Breathing him. Breathing me.

He cupped my face, thumb caressing the pulse point on my neck. "Shea."

I watched the thick bob of his throat as he stepped back and stared down at me, hands gathering the silky material of the nightgown at my hips. Slowly, he peeled it away. Cool air skimmed my naked flesh. My hair fell in waves around my shoulders and tumbled down to brush over my breasts.

Goosebumps scattered, the man managing to touch me everywhere when he wasn't touching me at all.

A sharp gasp fell from me when he picked me up, one arm around my bottom and the other sliding up my back to grasp onto my neck.

I wrapped my legs around his waist.

"Shea."

That pretty, pretty mouth slanted over mine.

Savage.

Raw.

Unrelenting.

Demanding tongue and nipping teeth.

He poured his desperation into me, relief and salvation and deliverance.

His kisses never ceased as he carried me across the room, careful when he laid me on the center of his bed.

My hands fisted in the blankets and I arched.

Slowly, Sebastian began to undress.

He toed off his shoes and pulled off his shirt. Muscle and strength bristled across all that glorious skin while he looked me up and down.

The words falling from his mouth dripped with sex. "Every fantasy I've ever had is right there. My wife naked and writhing on my bed. Wet for me. Dyin' for me."

I absolutely burned.

He unfastened his jeans, took his underwear with him when he shrugged them off. Need twisted through my belly at the sight of him.

Sebastian crawled on the bed and situated himself between my thighs. He gathered my hands and pressed them into the bed over my head.

He stared down at me.

Falling.

Falling.

Falling.

I'd been so scared of where I would land.

Little did I know I'd be falling forever into the safety of his arms.

Held and adored and never touching ground.

Swimming in a sea of darkness and light.

The bliss of eternity.

He gathered my wrists in one hand. With the other, fingertips trailed across my face, gliding down my neck and brushing my breasts that tightened and tingled with need.

That hand fluttered lower, pressing between my thighs, fingers sliding through my slick sex.

I trembled, and a tiny moan rumbled up my throat, the intensity of those knowing eyes searing me.

He gripped himself, aligning himself at my center, the nudge of the thick head of his cock filling me with fire.

Every nerve came alive.

Sebastian never looked away as he slowly pushed into me. So full he stole my breath.

My lips parted on the force of it.

Sebastian stilled, body rigid as he held himself in restraint.

Silently screaming the promise.

Forever.

Forever.

Forever.

And I felt it.

Sheer and utter completion.

"Shea," he said again, before he began to move.

Unbridled and impassioned.

Sweat slicked our skin. Pants and grunts fed the crackling air.

And I knew. And I knew. And I knew.

Sebastian had scarred me in the most beautiful ways.

Pinpricks of pleasure lit up my body and Sebastian tipped me into ecstasy.

I chanted his name while he chanted mine as we both fell into that blinding bliss.

Struggling for air, he dropped his forehead to mine.

My arms encircled his neck, hugging him tight. "We made it," I whispered.

Sebastian pulled back with the hint of a smile, shifting his weight off to the side.

His big hand spread across my belly. "We made it."

twenty-one
Sebastian

I PUSHED MYSELF UP the steep hill, wiping the sweat from my brow as I rounded into the drive of the house. All too eager to get back to my girls after my run.

Overhead, birds chirped in the still of the trees, branches outstretched and even though it was nearing winter, still shading everything in their spindly path, little darts of sunlight breaking through.

I inhaled the calm.

For once in my life, I finally felt at total peace.

Three days had passed since I'd been cut loose and we'd finally sent Martin straight to hell.

Exactly where he was always supposed to be.

Taking the walkway on long strides, I burst through the front door to the silence ringing back.

Afternoon light bled in through the windows, the large living space lit up like a torch, casting the corners and niches and halls in shadows.

I rounded the corner to hit the stairs.

I stumbled to a stop when I saw the lone figure sitting on the bottom step of the staircase.

Hoodie pulled up over his head, arms hugging his knees where they were tucked to his chest, feet planted on the floor as he slowly rocked.

Austin.

A huge duffle bag sat on the floor in front of him.

When he noticed me there, he jerked his head up.

His sorrow hit me head on.

Crazy that even in all that peace, with the purpose I now had in my life, the thought of my baby brother still provoked a feeling of devastation.

He slowly stood as I inched closer.

"Austin," I muttered quietly, feeling the question that came off with his name. Unease whittled its way through me. Stoked something fierce and protective in my gut.

He swallowed hard as those grey eyes met with mine.

Remorse.

Shame.

Sadness.

My heart stuttered and clenched. Uneasily, my gaze dropped to the tattered stuffed monkey he fisted in his hand at his side.

Shit.

This kid…this fucking awesome kid.

"Austin," I said again. This time with caution.

His mouth trembled as he choked through anguished laughter. "Knew you had this hidden somewhere."

A tear slipped free from the corner of his eye. In anger, he swiped it away. "My whole life I've lived in guilt. It's the only thing I've felt for so long, I hardly recognize anything else."

"Aust—"

"Let me finish, Baz. You need to hear this. Maybe as much as I do."

His mouth worked, hesitation thick, before he set the words free. "Losing Julian killed something inside me, Baz."

Steadily, he met my eye. "And I know you loved him. I'm not about to belittle that. I know you loved him the same way you love me. But I don't think you can understand the kind of bond I severed that day. The piece of me that died with him, because *he* was a living part of *me*. All these years I've searched for something… anything to fill the void he left. Then I moved on to doing anything to mask it when I realized that void was never gonna go away."

Fuck.

I wanted to go to him.

Wrap him up and take it away.

Same way I'd been attempting to do for years.

Watching the way his entire body heaved just about ruined me. But I kept silent, respecting what he asked.

"All it did was pile on more guilt. Every decision I made just hurt someone else. The lies I told. The secrets I kept."

Disgust lined his face. "Since I was eight years old, I've been reliant on you. You took that burden and wore it like it fit, and I just let you because I didn't think I had anything else."

He looked toward the ceiling. "Then Shea showed up and finally gave you something truly worth fighting for. Someone who would *appreciate* it. Someone who gives you just as much as she gains. It made me realize how much more is out there, Baz. Everything I'm missing and everything it costs you by me being here. Shea and Kallie…they deserve all of you."

His gaze dropped to the bag on the floor. "I have to go."

Grief fisted my throat. "No, Austin. You gotta know you mean everything. Just because my family has grown doesn't mean there's not room in it for you. I can't stand the thought of you leaving me."

A somber smile just touched his face. "I'm not leaving you, Baz. It's just time I found myself. Told you before, the way Shea looks at you? Someday…someday I want someone to look at me the same way. And when she does, I want to be strong. Someone who can stand up for her the way you stand up for Shea. And I'm not that guy, Baz. Not yet. I'm nothing but a broken little kid living inside this body, trying to pretend I'm a man."

The words cracked. "I've got to find a way to be him or *I'm not going to make it*. Can't continue to go on like this."

The expression on his face twisted through me like a dull, bitter blade, this kid showing so much innocent hope and so much seasoned fucking pain.

Longing desperation.

Scared the hell out of me to think of him out there on his own in this fucked-up world.

But I finally got it. What he'd been trying to tell me before.

My feet felt heavy when I took two steps forward and pulled my baby brother into my arms. He heaved out a breath and buried his face in my chest. I wrapped my arms around his head while he clung to my waist and just fucking sobbed.

For a second, it felt like I was holding that same eight-year-old boy who'd wept that day. That fucking devastating day when we'd lost everything. The day when everything had gone to shit and we knew things were never gonna be the same.

Just like we knew it now.

Things weren't ever gonna be the same.

Finally, he tore himself away, eyes red and bleary and blurred.

He sniffed and I gripped him by the sides of his neck, squeezing in emphasis. "No matter where this world takes you, no matter where you go, I'll always be your home."

He grasped my wrists. "I know."

Taking a step back, he bent over and grabbed his bag and slung the strap over his shoulder, still clutching the worn monkey to his chest.

His eyes were downcast when he edged around me.

"Just..." I called, this old piece of me breaking free, feeling like he was ripping it away. Like this kid needed to take a part of me with him.

And God, if that's what it took for him to finally *break free* of this past, then I'd let him.

"Keep in touch," I finally said. "I need to know you're okay. Where you are. For my own sanity."

For a moment, he paused with his hand on the knob of the door, before he turned to look back at me from over his shoulder.

The smile he projected was soft and thankful and somehow resolved.

Then he dipped his head in a nod and my baby brother walked out the door.

epilogue
Sebastian

I PULLED TO A stop at the curb and cut the engine. A smattering of stars hung in the darkened sky. They peeked through the spindly branches adorned with the few remaining leaves that had long since turned red and gold, those tall trees stretching out to brush the high eaves of the historic white house that rested in the heart of Savannah.

A feeling of ease and welcome swept through me. Like everything dialed to wrong had suddenly been set to right.

You'd think after years of traveling, out on the road living in a damned van trying to make it big, five days wouldn't make a man homesick.

You'd be wrong.

Lights glowed from within the windows of the old, majestic home. The sight of the porch swing where I'd spent so many nights rubbing Shea's feet and talking to her belly after we'd tucked Kallie into bed quickened my heart, that front door calling out for me like my marrow had become ingrained in the wood.

I stepped from the Suburban in the same second that front door swung wide open.

A streak of blonde flew down the sidewalk. All those wild, wild curls struck like white flames in the moonlight.

"Daddy!"

My quickened heart damned near burst.

I hustled around the front of the truck and scooped Kallie up just as she was hitting the end of the walkway. I swung her around in circles, lovin' the feel of making my Little Bug fly.

She squealed and clung to my neck. "Daddy, don't you dare drop me!"

I hugged her close. Squeezed her tight. "Never."

She settled and stilled, like she was washed in a wave of comfort as she tucked herself into my chest. I could feel her little heart going boom, boom, boom as she found her own ease.

"I missed you so much," I murmured into those untamed locks at the top of her head.

"Me, too," she whispered back.

She flashed me one of those brilliant smiles. Though now that smile was missing two front teeth. Considering Christmas was rolling up fast, I couldn't help but relentlessly tease her about it in song.

One-hundred percent not my fault.

Uncle Ash started it.

Go figure.

I hooked Kallie to my side and let my needy gaze travel to the doorway.

Shea leaned up against the jam.

She was wearing a tank top and some of those short, short sleep shorts she liked the wear, a cascade of blonde falling down her shoulders, those tempting strands a couple inches longer than they were when I'd married her just over a year ago.

Her adoring expression screamed so many things. *I missed you. I need you. Home—this is where you're supposed to be.*

Like her dial had also been shifted to *right*.

My wife was cradling our tiny son, rocking him in her arms as her head tilted to the side in the softest welcome.

That sweet, sexy mouth tipped up at the corners.

Shea.

Shea.

Shea.

My spirit never got tired of singing it.

With Kallie still tacked to my side, my feet were moving.

Drawn.

Had been since the second I'd seen her.

I'd just had no idea that being drawn to all that dark, into her light and heavy and soft, was drawing me right into *life*.

My boots thudded up the wooden steps, becoming a heavy echo as I crossed the porch.

Tenderly, I caressed across my son's head before I moved to settle my hand on Shea's neck. Her pulse thrummed like content and thunder beneath my touch.

She exhaled something that sounded like relief. Ease and comfort and perfect harmony.

"You have any clue how much I missed you, baby?" I asked, voice raw. Coarse with five days of pent-up need.

She peeked at me, driving me mad with that coy, playful grin. "Um…about half as much as I missed you?"

Chuckling, my thumb set to tracing her jaw, my famished eyes roaming her gorgeous face.

A familiar stir of devotion ran hot in my veins, words dropping even lower. "You think so, huh?"

"Mmhmm. Considering I didn't stop thinking about you for one second while you were away, I'd think giving you half would be generous."

The girl was teasing me with the soft, seductive lilt of that Southern drawl.

My entire body hardened, thinking just how fucking sublime it was gonna be to get lost in hers.

Sleek legs and hungry hands. Complete. Body and soul.

Couldn't wait.

"Have to say, think you're way off base, Mrs. Stone. Got to L.A., and there I was, missing my family for three extra hours. Torment."

I smirked. Time change and all.

The laughter that trekked up her throat was flirtatious, and she started to sway in my hold, while she kept our son in the protective cocoon of her arms.

"And we had to wait for you three extra hours to get here tonight. Torture," she fired back with another grin.

My insides fluttered like all those butterflies Kallie loved to talk about.

But this?

This was ripping wings.

A battering beat of loyalty and dedication and need.

I prodded my girl's chin, lifting her to me so I could dip down and kiss the *one* who'd seen *this* inside me.

Someone worth something more than sex, drugs, and rock 'n' roll. Someone better than one-night stands and an empty soul.

The one who'd trusted in it.

Believed in it.

She received me with plush lips, soft and sweet and tender, the briefest flash of her tongue fueled by desire. I lingered there, kissing her a little deeper than maybe was modest. But fuck, who could blame a man who had a girl like this?

Kallie giggled, little body wiggling in my hold, plucking me from the salacious direction my thoughts went strayin'.

"Daddy," she sang like she was givin' me a good scolding with that precious voice. "Too many kisses."

I cut her a guilty albeit unremorseful smile, before I dropped my forehead to my wife's.

Emotion grew thick, this feeling swamping me as I turned my gaze down to the child we'd created.

God.

He was incredible.

A miracle.

Connor Julian Stone.

I dropped a quick kiss to Kallie's temple. "Let me say hi to your brother, okay, Little Bug?"

Never wanted her to feel like she now came second. Like she were less when that was impossible.

Like she totally got it, she nodded in her sweet way. "'Kay."

I set her on the ground and turned back to my son.

Wide grey eyes locked on mine, and Connor gave me this gurgling sound and a lopsided, crooked smile.

God, felt 'em both right in the center of my chest.

"Hey there, little man," I said quietly as I lifted him from Shea's arms.

I held him out in front of me. Just needing to take him in.

Then I brought him near, softly kissed the corner of his mouth.

Tiny fingers dug into my face as he curled into me, one of those giggles he'd just figured out how to make bursting free and sinking right into me.

Joy.

So much joy.

"Were you a good boy for your momma?" I cooed.

Nope. Couldn't help that, either.

My kids had me all wrapped up, twisted and tied and tangled in baby blue ribbon and pink butterfly bows.

A ripple of gentle laughter floated from Shea. "He's always good…just as soon as we make it through the two a.m. feeding."

Hated knowing things got rough for my girl when I was gone.

I lifted a brow in question, rocking Connor slowly where he was all tucked up like a frog stuck to my chest. "April hung around while I was gone, yeah?"

After Shea and I'd gotten married and Austin had set out on his own, it didn't take us all that long to figure out L.A. wasn't going to be the place we raised our kids. The guys…they were always careful with my girls. Protecting them the way I trusted them to. Cooling shit off and acting like responsible adults while Shea and Kallie were around.

And there was no doubt about it. Shea and I would've made a home wherever the world took us. But these old walls called to us, echoing the sounds of Shea's childhood and shouting out the hope of our future.

Like somehow Shea was made up of Savannah and then Savannah had gone and sank right into me.

This was where we wanted to be.

April had found a place of her own a couple miles away. She was usually all too eager to stay with my family when I had to be out of town.

"Most of the time." Shea arched a brow, eyes going wide as if she was keeping back all the juicy details, and mouthed, "She met a boy."

"No?" I countered, incredulous.

"Yes." She uttered it like was the most scandalous thing trending on Facebook.

Kallie hopped around beside me, tugging at my arm to get my attention. "Yep! Yep! Yep! Auntie April stayed for two whole days and we had a sleepover in my room since Connor sleeps in her old room."

Her tone got serious. "But she said she didn't mind. Not at all. At all!" Her prattling shot right back to double time. "It was so super fun! Almost as fun as I had at Marley's sleepover on Friday.

Daddy, did you know I got to ride on Marley's bus all the way to her house?"

Those words flew from her tongue at warp speed, an adorable tumble of excitement and adventure and country flare. Now that she was in kindergarten, that chatter seemed to come nonstop, her days with her new friends supplying her all kinds of new stories to tell.

Some would ask if someone like me would bore of it.

Get impatient and antsy and irritated.

Hell no.

Every single word was precious.

Never minded getting caught up in the whirlwind that was Kallie Marie Stone.

Well.

Almost.

Stone that is.

Papers were well under way. Ones that would legally make her my child.

Two months ago, the court had finally severed that bastard's parental rights, finding him unfit to be a parent. As if he would have ever wanted to step up and assume that role, even if he wasn't going to have his pretty-boy ass locked behind bars for the rest of his miserable life.

Kallie didn't even slow down, just jumped along at my side when we all wandered inside. She grinned up at me the entire time. "And her mommy helped us make our own pizza and let us have ice cream and we stayed up almost the whole night. Marley says Tommy is her boyfriend, but Momma said I'm too little to have a boyfriend so I don't have one. Not until I'm thirteen, right Momma?"

I slanted Shea a look that I knew came with a warning. *Over my dead body.* Hell, I probably wouldn't even allow it then.

Shea laughed. "Don't worry, Daddy Bear. That's a long time

away."

"Not long enough," I mumbled.

Shea popped up on her toes and brushed a kiss to my mouth. "Why don't you get these two tucked in while I finish up the dishes?"

"Oh, man! Do I have to?" Kallie pouted.

Shea just shook her head. "I let you stay up an hour past your bedtime so you could be awake when your daddy got home, and you promised you'd go right to bed once you got to see him. Remember?" she drew out, the graze of her knuckles down Kallie's cheek a gentle encouragement. "You have to get up for school in the morning."

"I know," Kallie conceded.

Knew I'd be getting in late, past Kallie's bedtime, but I'd left the second I could get out of L.A., eager to get home. Desperate, really.

"Why don't we get your baby brother into bed? Then you can read me a story. How's that sound?" I offered.

Curls flew when Kallie nodded. "Okay, Daddy!"

Stepping forward, I dipped down and gave Shea another kiss and a quick squeeze to her hip. "Later," I whispered.

Shea hummed.

Yeah. I'd be showing my wife just how damned much I missed her. I'd put bets down she'd be amending any assertion about me missing her *half* as much as she missed me.

We climbed the stairs. I held my son, chest to chest, my arm secure across his tiny back and head, my other hand one with Kallie's.

At the top of the landing, my attention went right to the wall of photos I couldn't help but study the first morning I'd woken up in Shea's bed. The morning I'd had every intention of running.

Little did I know, I'd be running right back to Shea.

Find love and bring it here.

Those words were inscribed in black cursive letters along the top of the wall, like a vocal statement of what the stilled images hanging on the wall proclaimed.

All the original pictures were still there.

A wedding picture of Shea's grandparents graced the center, the frame surrounded by others that showcased the people Shea adored. People who'd helped to shape her into the magnificent, caring, gentle woman she was today.

I grinned at the young picture of Charlie sitting off to the side, back when he'd barely been a man and not the scruffy old guy now slinging drinks at his bar down the street.

Of course there was the one of Shea holding Kallie as an infant in profile. Seeing that picture the first time had unleashed some kind of fear in me, a fear I was dragging all my ugly onto sacred ground.

Tainting and marring and ruining.

But Shea had turned that vision around.

Wanting more, more, more.

Filling me with good. Or maybe she'd just discovered it.

I gently bounced my son as my gaze moved to the picture of Shea's mom still on display. Yeah, she'd been responsible for so much negative in Shea's life. But she'd ultimately been the one who'd set it in order. The one who'd put herself on the line and accepted responsibility. The one who'd provided enough information that the judge had issued a warrant to search Martin's house. The one who'd stood up at the sick bastard's trial and testified.

The one now serving ten years in a women's prison back in California.

Her testimony had helped convict Martin Jennings of drug trafficking and extortion. But that didn't even come close to grazing the tip of the iceberg. The rest of his vile practices had been lurking just under water.

He got life for the murder of Donny Alstinger.

The part I still couldn't stomach? What was always gonna haunt me?

They'd found evidence of plans to have Shea *extinguished*, the first time stopped by Mark's intervention.

The second had been in the making—first getting me out of the way so he could easily access her. With Lester running for governor, they couldn't risk the condemning evidence Shea had against them coming back to bite them.

Just the thought, the *possibility*, sent pangs of anger and fear spiraling through me.

Lester Ford was currently standing his own trial.

Added to that?

Martin Jennings's conviction in the murder of Mark Nathanial Kennedy.

Fucking agony.

Truth was, it'd always been agony. Didn't matter how he was stolen from the earth. He wasn't here and somehow we had to learn to live with that reality.

Martin had thought himself untouchable. Out of reach. Above the law.

Knew in my heart it was Mark who'd finally knocked him down.

Martin being responsible for Mark's death had compiled all that bitterness and hate. But somehow knowing Mark had stood up for Shea, that he'd dared to try and protect a girl he didn't even know—the one who'd ended up becoming my entire life—eased something inside of me.

It filled me with a mournful gratefulness I'd honor my best friend with for all my days. Even though he'd been so damned lost, he'd always had something brilliant inside him. A light he'd never let shine. A goodness he'd never set free. A peace he'd never found.

Not until he found something good worth fighting for.

Guess he and I had a whole lot in common after all.

Even with the score of evidence that'd come down on Jennings, there hadn't been enough of it to prosecute him for anything related to my brother.

But Austin was okay with that.

He just wanted to move on.

Grow.

Without a doubt, that's what he was doing, the kid out there on his own figuring out who he wanted to be.

Once a month or so I'd receive a letter from him. Every time I read his pained words, they just about broke my heart in two. Yet at the same time, they somehow healed a part of it, too. So many of his internal struggles and newfound joys were scrawled across the pages as he openly bared his soul to me, exposing all his thoughts and worries and hopes.

Sometimes facing our pasts was more painful than letting old wounds lie. It was easier just to leave them buried by years of callus and scars that never quite healed. Because ripping off those scabs? It exposed what was seated deep, everything festered and compressed and ready to erupt.

But churning under that decay was a spirit poised to flourish.

Crazy that even though I hadn't seen him since he walked out the door back in L.A., hadn't spoken to him in all that time other than through letters, I felt closer to him now than I ever had.

My eyes traveled to the newer pictures that had been added.

There was a huge canvas-style one of my family, taken on Shea's and my *second* wedding day. It'd taken place in the old church where Shea's grandma used to take her on Sunday mornings, in that special place where my girl had fallen in love with singing.

We were standing on the steps just outside the ornate wooden doors. I was wearing a dark suit and Kallie looked like a princess in her white, flowy dress with a ton of flowers woven in her curly hair.

And Shea…

Shea.

She was wearing a white silk strapless gown, hair twisted up on her head, pieces falling out and brushing her slender shoulders. Her belly was round with our boy and the happiness on her face was the most brilliant thing I'd ever seen.

So stunning it verged on devastating.

Didn't matter how many times I looked at it…how many times I looked at her…the reaction was always the same.

Overpowering.

Connor fussed, and I made a shushing sound and bounced him softly. "Think we need to get your baby brother into bed. What do you think, Little Bug?"

We moved on toward his room. Kallie skipped along, glued to my side, voice a whisper. "I think we better. He's gotta be so, so tired. Momma kept him up so long 'cause she knew you were gonna want kisses 'fore he went to sleep."

I cast her a smile and proceeded to press a bunch of soft kisses to Connor's face.

"Like that?"

"Yep, just like that."

A nightlight glowed from within, the walls painted a muted blue, musical notes and lines of lullabies painted on the walls.

Fitting, yeah?

I lay my son in the center of his crib. A small cry rattled from him, and I spread his blankie over him, the one he always had to have.

He fisted the satin edges in his tiny hands and pressed it to his face, drawing his legs up around it like he was giving it a welcoming hug.

So fucking cute.

I palmed the top of his head, and he leaned into it as he looked up at me with sleepy eyes. "Goodnight, little man."

Hand-in-hand, Kallie and I tiptoed out. The second we were out the door, I swept her up. The way she tried to hold in her squeal, this sweet, subdued laughter rolling from her, melted me a little more.

Kid always had me a puddle at her feet.

Always so thoughtful.

So good.

So much like her mom.

Still wondered every damned day how I got this lucky.

"Did you brush your teeth?" I asked.

Her eyes went wide, before she shook her head as if she'd committed some sort of horrible crime. I set her back on her feet. "Run in and get it done."

"I'll do it super fast."

"Not too fast," I warned as I paused at the bathroom doorway, arms crossed over my chest as I watched her climb up the step stool.

I nearly jumped out of my skin when she slipped.

There was a huge part of me that wanted to swoop in and make it better. Protect her from anything and anyone who could possibly harm her. Freak out and beg her to tell me she was okay.

But I didn't. I held it in and let her deal with the short fall that clearly hadn't injured her. Let her learn, because when she climbed up again, she did it more carefully.

Maybe that's something I learned from my baby brother. You can't grow wings if you're forbidden to fly. He'd been right when he said I'd protected and protected and protected until it was suffocating. That sometimes I inhibited rather than sustained.

And God. Only thing in this world I wanted?

For my family to grow. For them to experience life in the best ways possible. With me always standing at their sides rather than in front of them.

But when they needed me? In whatever capacity? I'd be there. Whether with a watching eye or a father's fury, I'd be there.

Kallie finished, rushed right back out and to her room, hopped into her bed.

I knelt down at her side and listened to this amazing kid sound out the words that she was just learning, the butterfly book little more than a picture book with a couple of small words for her to make out.

"The end!" she said emphatically, all kinds of proud when she close the last page.

"Whoa, you read the whole thing? When'd you get so big?"

"Daddy," she admonished, "I'm growing and growing. You know in only four months I'm gonna be six and I'll be in first grade and then I'll stay at school all, all day."

I chuckled.

My little hurricane.

I put her book aside and pulled her covers to her chin, dropped a kiss to her nose.

"Goodnight, Little Bug."

She beamed up at me. "Goodnight, Daddy Bug."

My heart skipped a wayward beat.

Apparently, I'd gotten a promotion.

"I'll see you in the morning, sweetheart."

She clutched the top of her covers, smiling up at me. "'Kay."

Flipping off her light switch, I left her door open a crack, the way we always did, and headed straight for the stairs. Itching to get to my wife.

I hit the ground floor. At the end of the little hall, I nudged open the swinging door leading to the kitchen.

And there she was, dancing around on bare feet as she wiped down the countertop, singing just below her breath with that amazing voice.

Quietly, I slipped in, edged up behind her and wrapped her in my arms. For a flash of a second, she startled, before she relaxed into my hold.

I leaned closer, my cheek embracing hers before my mouth made a pass down the slope of her neck and back up to her ear. "How many women are in this world? And somehow…somehow I found the one that was meant for me."

Shea might as well have purred as she leaned back, hair brushing at my chin, face upturned and capturing me in the warmth of those eyes. Words flowed with her undying, beautiful faith. "I never said I didn't believe in soulmates. Don't ever forget you're mine."

Her statement had pleasure rumbling through me like the roll of distant thunder, her body pressed closed to mine.

"Come here. I have something for you," I whispered, brushing a piece of hair from her face.

Slowly, she turned in my hold, lips full with that adoring smile.

She yelped when I suddenly lifted her against me, laughed as I spun her around and then propped her up on the edge of the island. I was quick to wedge myself between her knees.

Right where I always wanted to be.

I gathered her left hand in mine and brushed my lips over the intricate weave of diamonds and platinum she boasted on her ring finger.

It was no replica like she'd requested the morning after our wedding.

It was the real deal.

Her grandmother's wedding ring.

It was part of the evidence that had been found stowed away in Martin Jennings's safe. Proof he'd been responsible for the assault on her.

Yet another charge the scumbag had fallen to. He'd been so full of pride and pretention, so narcissistic, he'd kept it like a prize in the safe in his office.

Shea gazed down at it when I pulled back. "It's so beautiful."

I kissed it again. "Even more beautiful on you."

She just smiled, tilted her head, like her awe of me went as deep as mine went for her.

Still was hard to make sense of. Someone wanting me for me.

All bullshit and money and fame aside.

She didn't want it.

She wanted me.

"So what's this surprise?" Shea's eyes suddenly glimmered with mischief, a flash of excitement.

I fished my phone from my back pocket and thumbed into the file, keeping one hand on her side. I quirked a smile up at her as I turned the speaker as loud as it would go and set it on the counter at her side.

Then I pushed play.

The soft strum of my acoustic guitar.

She gasped when she recognized the song. Eyes that had been looking at my phone swung up to meet mine.

Adoration and grace.

"Sebastian."

Fingertips felt along my face, fire to my skin and comfort to my spirit.

She pressed her mouth to mine. Nothing obscene. Just the pressure of her lips as wonder poured free.

God, she was sweet.

So damned sweet.

The chords deepened a fraction, a shift of the music like static electricity scattering through dense air.

That pounding, pulsing energy.

It was the polished song that'd seeped from us on our wedding night. Like it'd always been hidden somewhere inside the two of us, waiting for the right moment to be cut free.

The one she and I had mastered then sat down with the rest of the guys and recorded it months ago, before we made the permanent move back here to Savannah.

You would be on our album releasing in two months.

Sunder featuring Shea Stone.

No.

Not Delaney Rhoads.

Just like she'd told Martin.

Delaney Rhoads had died a long time ago.

This song was nothing like what *Sunder* normally put out. There was no anger or hate. No screaming lyrics or smashing beat.

It was slow reverence.

Creeping awe.

Love.

Pure, unadulterated love.

From my phone, my voice wove with the chords. Deep. Naked. Exposed.

You.

Came like a storm.

In the distance.

Coming closer.

You.

Took me whole.

Broken pieces.

Mended perfectly.

Leaning in closer to my girl, I began to quietly sing along with the elevating chorus that played from my phone, my raspy voice a low, pleading rumble.

Our breaths mixed on ragged pants as we got lost in the promise of the words.

Don't want to look back.

Don't want to move forward.
Just want to stay.
Right here with you.
Forever.
Just want to stay.
Right here with you.
Forever.

My nerves pinged like lightning bolts, a zing of ecstasy striking me through when her siren's voice slowly lifted into the recording, low and sultry, Shea singing *With you forever* three times over. A layered, honeyed harmony, her voice braided through mine.

Redness rushed up Shea's neck when her melody infiltrated the space. Delicious color paintin' her cheeks in innocence and modesty dabbled with awe. Ever so subtly, she began to move her mouth, tipping her face up toward mine as I sang down to her and she sang up to me.

Didn't matter how many times I'd heard it. I still felt my axis shift when the chorus drifted out and into the delicate frame of her verse.

You
Like standing in quicksand.
Slowly sinking.
Deeper and deeper.
You.
All I was missing.
Lonely hollows.
Completed flawlessly.

I wound Shea's hair up in my fist, tugging her head back as I hovered over her, nose-to-nose, breath-to-breath. Intensity that would never dull blistered between us. Voices deepened in the same moment they gained power, twisting and twining as the momentum escalated, the roll of the drums and the beat of the bass, a pounding furor that trembled in the air and vibrated from our tongues.

Don't want to look back.
Don't want to move forward.
Just want to stay.
Right here with you.
Forever.
Just want to stay.
Right here with you.
Forever.

When the song hit the bridge, Shea's voice rose above mine. Her time to shine. Bold. Glorious. Gushing beauty. A river of serenity. A voice unlike anything any of us had ever heard.

Be still, right here with me, for eternity.
Be still, right here with me, for eternity.

A shining star always so content to hide.

But no.

Not today.

Not tomorrow.

Not when the world got a real taste of this amazing girl.

What would it bring?

I didn't know.

It was like I could feel the clock ticking down on my days with *Sunder*.

So much had changed in the last year. All of our lives were going down paths none of us had anticipated. Karl Fitzpatrick had warned me settling down with Shea would be the downfall of *Sunder*.

Maybe it had, because none of *Sunder* really knew were we stood, each of our lives taking paths none of us had anticipated.

Truth was?

I'd rather be *right here*.

Making beautiful music with my wife.

Reveling in the truth of our words.
Savoring in the tenor of our kisses.
Relishing in the crescendo of our bodies.
I'd rather be right here.
Writing the lyrics to an everlasting song.

The End

Thank you so much for reading *Drowning to Breathe*! If you enjoyed it, if you'd consider leaving a short review on Amazon, it would mean the world! Writing brings me more joy than I could ever describe, and a reader like you picking it up and falling in love with my stories the way I do is the most incredible feeling. From the bottom of my heart, thank you for taking giving my characters your time!

Keep loving and keep reading ~ Amy

<u>Watch for more *Bleeding Stars* novels, coming soon from A.L. Jackson</u>

Where Lightning Strikes ~ Lyrik West
Through The Storm ~ Austin Stone
Embers and Ash ~ Ash Evans
Whispers in Winter ~ Zee Kennedy

Want a sneak peek at *Where Lightning Strikes* before anyone else?
Text *jackson* to 96000 to subscribe!

You'll get all the latest updates, releases, sales, and freebies. This is my absolute favorite way to keep in touch with my readers, and I promise to only send important updates and not more than 2 texts per month, usually less!

Do you want to discuss DROWNING TO BREATHE and other A.L. Jackson Books? Come join us in the The A.L. Jackson Reader Hangout (http://bit.ly/AmysAngels)!

Subscribe to receive email updates with News from A.L. Jackson, including exclusive excerpts, giveaways, and news!

News from A.L. Jackson (http://bit.ly/ALJacksonNewsletter)

about the author

A.L. Jackson is the *New York Times* and *USA Today* bestselling author of contemporary and new adult romance.

She first found a love for writing during her days as a young mother and college student. She filled the journals she carried with short stories and poems used as an emotional outlet for the difficulties and joys she found in day-to-day life.

Years later, she shared a short story she'd been working on with her two closest friends and, with their encouragement, this story became her first full length novel. A.L. now spends her days writing in Southern Arizona where she lives with her husband and three children.

Connect with A.L. Jackson online:

www.aljacksonauthor.com
Facebook (www.facebook.com/aljacksonauthor)
Twitter: @aljacksonauthor
Instagram: @aljacksonauthor
Newsletter (http://bit.ly/ALJacksonNewsletter)
For quick mobile updates, text "jackson" to 96000

CPSIA information can be obtained
at www.ICGtesting.com
Printed in the USA
FSOW01n1617221217
42686FS